Edwina Preston is the author of *Not Just a Suburban Boy* (2002), a biography of artist Howard Arkley. Her writing and reviews have appeared in the *Age*, the *Australian*, the *Sydney Morning Herald*, *Heat* and the *Griffith Review*. She lives in Melbourne, where she teaches creative writing at the North Melbourne Institute of TAFE.

The Inheritance of Ivorie Hammer

Edwina Preston

First published 2012 by University of Queensland Press
PO Box 6042, St Lucia, Queensland 4067 Australia

www.uqp.com.au

Cover design by Design by Committee
Cover artwork by Josh Durham
Author photograph by Miles Standish
Typeset in Spectrum MT by Post Pre-press group, Brisbane
Printed in Australia by McPherson's Printing Group

This project has been assisted by the Commonwealth Government
through the Australia Council, its arts funding and advisory body.

National Library of Australia cataloguing-in-publication data
is available at http://catalogue.nla.gov.au/

The Inheritance of Ivorie Hammer / Edwina Preston
ISBN: 978 0 7022 4921 1 (pbk)
       978 0 7022 4865 8 (pdf)
       978 0 7022 4866 5 (epub)
       978 0 7022 4867 2 (kindle)

University of Queensland Press uses papers that are natural, renewable and recyclable products
made from wood grown in sustainable forests. The logging and manufacturing processes
conform to the environmental regulations of the country of origin.

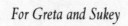

For Greta and Sukey

Contents

The knot family is a large one. According to the Standard Dictionary it has seventy-nine members, but to my certain knowledge that census is far from complete. The individual members are very much like those of any other family; some are true, some false; some hard and others easy. We have the Lark's head, the Sheepshank, and the Cat's paw knots; the True lover's and the Diamond knots; the Baby, the Granny, and the Shroud, and, as a finish, some have the Hangman's knot.

HARRY HOUDINI

The House of Jupon

It should not surprise the world when a young woman with neither friends, family nor livelihood turns to the age-old profession of prostitution. We may not like the idea, but it is a fact, and one might as well pronounce it baldly just as one might pronounce the fact of 'bridge builders' or 'grocers' or 'shipping clerks' and acknowledge their role in keeping the economy turning. Certainly, for the unskilled girl, it is a profession that offers better return for labour than match-selling or flower-selling or begging for alms on a dirty street corner.

But it is not without its attendant risks; some girls are blinked out in an instant by the perils of the profession: a knifing in a dark alleyway, a beating in a little frequented street, a throttling with piano wire in a hotel room. Others have long careers only to find themselves disfigured and diseased or old before their time. The luckiest, however, find themselves in a well-regulated house in which a form of sisterhood prevails and their interests are taken care of by a person more qualified and experienced than themselves. Here, a sum of money might be made without the requisite risk of body and soul.

So it was in the case of Miss Marianne Ward, who might have retired a rich woman at five-and-twenty had events not conspired otherwise.

Marianne Ward was an orphan and acquired her name via a peculiar condition of that situation. Placed in the care of Sister Jerusha Price of the Broad Brethren Orphanage, Pitch, when just a foundling, she was given the surname common to all Sister's charges, that being 'Ward', and, courtesy of a ticket tied to her elbow, christened 'Marianne'; thereafter, she was put in a crib and left largely alone.

Being a Ward was a distinct disadvantage in life; it did not equip one for much in the way of social mobility, for instance. But another drawback was the disproportionate representation of Wards in the profession mentioned above (so far as the profession was tolerated in the upstanding town of Pitch). The good Sister Jerusha had a long-term arrangement with the local brothel madam, by which certain of the Broad Brethren girls were transferred to the House of Jupon at the age of seventeen. It was no bad arrangement: these girls proved happier, better fed and cultivated than the unfortunately plain and misshapen, who were farmed out as domestic labour instead – and might well find themselves performing the same services only without the expectation of a fee.

The House of Jupon was a good house; its madam encouraged self-improvement: her girls must be deft conversationalists, able to speak appropriately on a variety of topics from local politics to cabbage growing and animal husbandry or whatever else excited the passions of their clientele. They must be able to sing or play an instrument; and they must certainly know how to read and write. The proprietor possessed, what's more, that heart for which women of her occupation are often famed. She prompted her girls to save, and invested their money, via circuitous avenues and lawyering, to ensure them an income when their whoring days were at an end. Yes, as well as she could, she loved them. And when Marianne Ward came into her house, she loved her especially dearly.

Marianne had grown up as happy as one might in an orphanage – that is, aware of her solitude amidst the pressing existence of company; rather rigidly bound to bells and the colour grey; and very competent at the handling of mass laundry and food preparation. Otherwise, she was sunny of temperament (to the point where some suspected she was stupid), pretty as a little yellow flower (not a rosebud, perhaps, but something smaller and wilder-growing), neat of body (and surprisingly nimble – she could somersault, cartwheel et cetera) and was capable of great love and loyalty, if not fully successful in exercising them. The only quandary she had encountered in her seventeen years of life had been choosing a most-perfect friend from flocks of admiring devotees.

Not much changed in her first years at the House of Jupon. The gentlemen adored her, though she did not take them much to heart; the other girls pampered her; and the brothel madam had for her a spot of tenderness so kind and forebearing it might almost be maternal, and which was returned in full by its grateful recipient.

Why did the brothel madam love her so? It was never clear, not even to that woman herself. Perhaps it was Marianne's trustingness – but they all started off trusting. Perhaps it was that Marianne ignored the brothel madam's brittle exterior and simply assumed a friendship was there to be had. She came to the brothel madam for advice on her hair, her diet, the best treatment for blemishes of the skin, how to soothe a corn on her toe. She propped herself nimbly on the edge of the kitchen table while the brothel madam measured out quantities of licorice root (for chest phlegm) and ginger powder (for nausea); or flitted down the stairs behind her when she went to bring up the beer crates; or helped to count the evening takings when the night was over, or feed the chickens or haul out the pigs. She became a little blonde presence at the brothel madam's side – winsome and silly and generous and curious. 'My, how the wheatgrass has grown on the windowsill!' she said, and, 'Is that a gardenia, madam, or a daphne tree?' The brothel madam did not encourage or engage the girl greatly, but she began to notice if she was not there, and to look out for her interests, and spare her from the more detestable of patrons, and see to it she got chicken broth when she was ill.

Marianne thought herself very well looked on by the world.

And then, on the eve of her twentieth birthday, two gentlemen arrived at the House of Jupon and her destiny took a new turn.

Here is a photograph of the two gentlemen in question: *The Brothers Cirque*, it says in ink on the photograph's back. One would not guess these men brothers: there is no likeness between them. The elder is broad-shouldered, with a great deal of waving black hair, and spirited eyes. The younger is the palest man imaginable, so blond as to appear to be on the point of vanishing, and with skin the colour of milk. The elder, what's more, has a beautiful liquid voice, while the younger has none at all – 'mute', it is explained, 'from birth'. Indeed, it is as though Nature has carefully distributed her gifts between these brothers to avoid any duplication, with the result that the elder has been endowed

3

with such purposeful things as *pigment* and *musculature* and *vocal cords*, and the younger, only a strange, persistent luminosity.

Arcadia Cirque has his hand on brother Otto's shoulder, to keep him inert or to steady him, or perhaps merely to ensure the symmetry of the pose. Otherwise there is no clue to these men's occupation or the quality of their relationship. Stuffed into their colourless suits, they could be bankers, or jewellers, or accountants.

They are no such things; they are founders of the Saturnalia, a travelling circus show that has made them rich and, in some quarters, famous. They do not look like itinerant showmen. They look like men accustomed to clean sheets and clean shoes and solid ground. And that is what they have recently become.

Having hitched their wagons in the neighbouring town of Canyon – a town with the geographical advantage of containing, in its very centre, a vast natural amphitheatre – they have decided to make it their home.

Their presence, that ill-fated night, in the soft-lit parlour of the House of Jupon, caused much excitement amongst the girls. The Pitch newspapers had been running for weeks a vociferous campaign against these very gentlemen. Their Saturnalia was roundly condemned as an affront to morality. 'They are worried,' said Arcadia Cirque, crossing his long legs and sipping at a liqueur, 'that we will corrupt their young.'

At this they all laughed.

'But the fact is, we have been too long on the road. It is time our audience travelled to see *us*! And they will, my friends. They are starved of entertainment.'

The brothel madam smiled and poured more drinks for her guests. It was a shame, she said, that the mountain range separating Pitch and Canyon made traffic between the towns so difficult. 'Most unfortunate,' she said, 'when there is obviously economic advantage to be had by you and I.'

'True, madam,' said Arcadia. 'But there is a mountain pass. Not a good road perhaps, but traversable. For the venturesome.' He eyed the ladies. 'For the feckless.'

'Oh, we are feckless,' the ladies assured him. 'We are the very *definition* of it.'

And so it was that, a fortnight later, twelve lovely young ladies, of varying refinements and skills, departed in covered wagons for the town of Canyon. Included amongst them was Miss Marianne Ward.

The land around Canyon was flat and barren and provided very little relief for the eye or heart. The town itself had been founded on a uniquely transient form of hope: a man had dug into the ground here ten years previous and unearthed a thousand-ounce nugget of gold. The vast canyon from which the town took its name still bore the marks of the prospector's pick. But Nature had put all her energies into that one-off production, it seemed: no other gold was ever found. When Marianne Ward and the girls of Jupon arrived, the canyon was being transformed into a circus arena. Rudimentary byways were being built up into proper streets, with connecting thoroughfares and little half-lit alleys where illicit trade might flourish after dark. Timber premises were everywhere under construction, and a hotel had even been built from bluestone drawn from a distant quarry: it was called the Grand Hotel, and it was here, on the second floor, that the girls were deposited under the care of the hotelier, Mrs Martha Glass.

Marianne Ward watched quietly from a corner of the room. The girls had kicked their shoes off and Martha Glass, a portly woman with a good face and a kindly manner, distributed beer and lemonade amongst them. She had just had a player piano delivered and this spooky wooden apparatus caused them all to shriek and laugh when it launched into its playerless runs.

'I know what – we shall have a séance!' said Martha Glass. 'Yes, yes, girls. They are all the rage. We shall summon this piano-playing ghost!'

The girls had played at séances before, but Mrs Glass took the game to a new level of seriousness. She covered the table with a cloth and replaced the lamps with candles. She wore fantastically large skirts and as the room became dark and quiet, all the girls could hear was the rustle of these skirts against the floor. There was no giggling. Mrs Glass seated herself soberly at the head of the table, and began a deep throaty burble that sounded conspicuously like an incantation. They held their breath; if they had started out excited, they were now apprehensive. The girls put their fingers to the top of the champagne glass, and everyone leaned inwards, and the glass slid with unearthly speed across the tabletop, spelling out all manner of dead people in their acquaintance. The hysteria built till they were all fluttery with fright and shaking and could not prevent small shrieks escaping their throats. Martha Glass, being a most convincing medium, rolled her eyes and droned on in her tone of unearthly possession. Suddenly she stopped, and a new high note of alarm entered her voice. 'But who is that?' she said. 'There is another. A dead man walking amongst us. Who is this presence? Come hither!'

It was at this moment, with the girls in a near state of apoplexy, that the door opened and a wan white figure appeared within its frame. Marianne screamed. The glass spun off the table and shattered. Marianne stood and screamed again, and then fell. She was caught by the ghost himself, who proved to be inexplicably solid and, saying nothing, comported her to the sofa.

'Dear, dear,' said Mrs Glass, standing and flapping at her face with her hands. She lit the lamps and the room resumed its regular comforting aspect. 'You quite scared us, sir. We are playing at séances and thought you a ghost risen from the dead. It is not a ghost, girls – it is Mr Otto Cirque, come back from the still with my bottles!'

Marianne looked up into the face of Otto Cirque and found it smiling steadfastly at her. She smiled back.

'Martha Glass,' wrote Marianne Ward to the brothel madam, 'is much the nicest married woman we have met, for she has no children and her husband is dead.' The brothel madam laughed. 'But she is not *you*,' the letter continued, 'who I miss beyond expression!'

Marianne Ward had become friends with the ghostly Otto Cirque. This also she confided to the brothel madam: 'I have never before had a friend who is a man, outside the expected conditions of my employ. Though he does not speak, I have elicited much information from him. He was a locksmith, once, before he joined business with his brother, and he can pick a lock faster than I might turn a key, which is convenient as I have three times now mislaid the key to my room. He has very rapid, beautiful hands, which are like musical instruments in their dextrousness. Now he operates the still and makes the liquor, which Mrs Glass says "keeps the wheels turning". I have no understanding of the manufacture of liquor and he does not take me to the still, naturally, but he has taken me to meet the circus actors, and they are fine and interesting characters to a one!'

There were large tracts of vacant time during the day, and in the hot afternoons when the sun bore down and the other girls lay limply on their beds, Marianne went with Otto to see the caravans arriving, and the strange exotic persons disembarking from them. Thus it was she met the Legless Lady, who drank tea with her little finger extended and kept her hems pinned so discreetly beneath her rump that Marianne thought her the picture of gentility; and stumbled upon Mademoiselle du Calotte, the Lady with the Iron Jaw, washing her removeable metal mandibles in alcohol; and brushed the golden flanks of Ingomar, the Horse with the Human Brain, who could point to France on a map of the world and puff smoke rings from a gentleman's pipe when prompted by the reward of sugarcubes; and most especially, became friends with Arabella Finch, the Venus Contortionist.

Miss Finch was, in Marianne's eyes, the epitome of beauty, with a face so large of eye and diminutive of feature that it resembled a doll's. She sat at her dressing table and combed her hair with a mother-of-pearl comb. She had a mirror studded around with small swatches of colourful glass, and a wardrobe packed tightly with bright dresses. 'How long have you worked as a *prostitute*, Miss Ward?' she said.

Marianne had never quite thought of her work in these terms, and it shocked her to hear it so brazenly pronounced. 'Two years, perhaps,' she said, changing her position on the small stool on which she was perched.

Arabella Finch gave her a piece of candy from a silver-coloured bowl, and leaned confidentially towards her. 'I too,' she said, 'once must work in that capacity.' She sucked a sweet into her mouth. 'But there is a better kind of money to be had. You are young, and quite lovely. Your occupation leaves you vulnerable.' She took up a handful of Marianne's long yellow hair and let it spill from her palm as though it were grain or honey. 'Disease, for instance,' she said.

Marianne wished Otto were beside her, for he would squeeze her hand or look at her in a way that gave her comfort. She had not thought of such things as disease. She remembered the powders and tinctures concocted by the brothel madam.

'But what can you *do*, Miss Marianne Ward?' said the sublime Miss Finch. 'Do you have any talents upon which you might base a routine?'

Marianne shook her head, and then spoke. 'There was once an instructor,' she said, 'at the orphanage. He said I was naturally gifted in the area of gymnastics.'

'Well, that is a start,' said Miss Finch, turning back to her mirror. 'That is something better than nothing.'

Arcadia Cirque did not pay for services required. Though the girls from the House of Jupon were all in love with him – how could they not be? He was handsome, charismatic, exciting – he was not susceptible to them. He visited and drank with them and introduced them to his associates, but he did not retire to their rooms. Then one evening – a quiet evening – he arrived alone. The piano, having lost its supernatural powers, punched through its holes as usual; the girls chatted to the few patrons in attendance, and Martha Glass loosened tongues and pockets with whisky-and-water.

'Mrs Glass,' Arcadia Cirque said. She produced a drink for him.

Arcadia had hair just above his shoulders, black, and a malleable face. Viewed disinterestedly, his face was monkeylike, but if his looks testified to primate origins, they were also testament to his alpha status in any grouping in which he might find himself. He was dashing and slim-hipped and his voice was eloquent without being affected. When he was in the room, no one could remain indifferent to his presence. Though the ladies gathered around him and pretended to be on an equal footing with him, it was so clear he was their superior that even the kindest and most measured of his courtesies could not counter the fact.

Marianne did not try to compete. She was not immune to his charms, but she did not seek him out. And so it surprised her when he extricated himself from her friends and engaged her instead. She could not help a feeling of pleasure at being marked out in this way. He sat beside her and didn't say anything for several minutes, drinking his whisky and observing, with amusement, the women and men about them.

'Marianne Ward?' he said finally, still looking out at the gathered party and sipping contemplatively.

'Mr Cirque?' said Marianne.

'I believe you have come to know my brother well.'

Marianne adjusted her position so she too looked out at the others and not at him. 'Otto Cirque has become my friend,' she said. She experienced an oddly conflicted sensation: at once, a desire to be loyal to her friend, and yet to clarify her availability to the brother. 'Otto Cirque,' she said again, as if to fortify herself, 'has become a most valuable friend.'

Arcadia was temperamentally incapable of scoffing, but some small derision crept into his tone. 'So then,' he said, 'you are not a *conversationalist*.'

'I am quite capable of conversation!' she said.

Martha Glass arrived at this point with refreshments and there was a brief pause while their glasses were refilled.

'Otto can communicate on any range of subjects,' Marianne said.

Arcadia remained unaffected. 'On love?' he said.

Marianne reddened.

'For I think,' said Arcadia, and now he looked at her properly and those amused eyes, falling on her, were bright and not unkind and seemed ready to indulge her, 'for I think he is falling in love with you!'

If Arcadia had known his target better, he could not have more perfectly taken his aim. For Marianne — perversely, like so many women — was not easily able to convert friendship into love; was, furthermore, made uneasy by the prospect.

'He is *not* in love with me!' she said.

Arcadia resumed his appraisal of the room. 'My dear innocent girl,' he said. 'He most certainly is.'

Arcadia then stolidly ignored her for a week, and Marianne spent that week vexed by his sudden indifference, and further vexed by her feelings for Otto. When she first saw the latter after Arcadia's intimations, she was both pleased and disappointed to find him nothing but his usual self — reassured by this, she picked a dandelion and stuck it in his buttonhole and he blushed. It did not mean anything; being a pale

9

man, he was prone to blushing. He had brought almond brittle in a slab he tried to break across his knee; they laughed and pounded at it but it would not give; finally, Marianne took her shoe off and knocked it clean in the middle so shatters of toffee flew out and they must scrabble in the grass to collect them. And there, in the grass, she found herself face to face with him, eye to eye. Up close, his eyes were such a pale grey they reminded her of oysters seen through glass or in a mirror or deep at the bottom of a stream. And then he reached over and kissed her. Marianne closed her eyes. She had been kissed by many men in the course of her work; it was an occupational hazard. But she had not been kissed like this. Her hand went up to Otto's hair, and then to his face. They kissed a long time and Marianne felt curiously at peace.

Had Arcadia Cirque continued to ignore her, had he set his sights instead on a woman more clearly his match or found something in Marianne to manifestly dislike, all might have proceeded smoothly between Otto and Marianne. But Arcadia could find no reason to dislike Marianne and plenty of reasons to seduce her.

He appeared again in the parlour and again sat close to Marianne. His mood was different this time. Perhaps he was drunker than before; he crossed his legs and smoked and slouched in his chair so his jacket rucked up above his shoulders. He resumed his habit of speaking to her as though addressing a lamp post up against which he had sidled.

'Do you like it here?' he said.

She was surprised to be asked; no one had previously canvassed her opinion on the matter. 'I like it well enough,' she said.

'Come now,' he said. 'All these bores.' He indicated, with his foot, the other men. 'Fat. Smelling of horses.'

'I have learned,' she said cautiously, 'to have very little in the way of a sense of smell.'

He laughed and was silent again, and then he leaned down and caught hold of the sleeve of her dress and yanked it slightly. 'And what of this?' he said.

She looked at him in some confusion.

'Cheap stuff,' he said, but he was smiling. He eyed her up and down.

His eyes were bright and transfixing, but she could not take his measure from them. 'From whom did you inherit this piece of cheap stuff?'

She glared and did not know if he teased or insulted her. 'I did not inherit it from anyone! It is my very own.'

'It is past its date, my dear,' he said, letting go of her sleeve and putting his drink back to his mouth, finishing it with one swallow. 'Come with me tomorrow. I will take you to the dressmaker's.' Then he smiled, bowed and left.

'He has installed me,' wrote Marianne to the brothel madam, 'in my own rooms in his apartment on the top floor of the Grand Hotel.' The brothel madam rubbed at her forehead and read on. 'I have a wardrobe of dresses and go with him every evening to the show. He has escorted me to dinners with his business associates at which there is such variety of cutlery I do not know how to manage it all.'

Marianne Ward looked out from her balcony and saw the lone figure of Otto Cirque below. She had not met with him in many days. He sent her pictures he had drawn; caricatures of the troupe members, mostly, and detailed drawings of fruit and flowers. She sent him pictures in return, but they were so poorly executed they did no justice to her feelings.

'He promises me an act of my own,' read the brothel madam. 'I will be trained for the stage by Miss Arabella Finch. And so, I will not be returning with the others at the end of the season. My dear friend, this causes me both happiness and sorrow.'

The brothel madam was surprised by the pain that assailed her. It was both sharp and dull and it would not relent. She had spent a lifetime buffering herself against such blows, but it seemed her efforts had been in vain.

Miss Finch proved a good teacher. Despite her apparent fragility, she was disciplined and tough and transmitted those qualities to her student. And Marianne, for her part, was a quick learner. Her body naturally inclined to the choreography of the contortionist, the knots and enfoldings that must be effortlessly contrived and seamlessly flow from one to the other; she must only learn a certain melting expression in her face to be completely convincing.

Their act was to be called 'The Eastern Mirror' and Marianne was to play the role of 'Other' to Miss Finch's primary role of 'Vanity'. It was an act of reversals, of opposites: when Miss Finch swung high, Miss Ward fell. Arabella painted Marianne's face in graduated tones of blue and black; her lips were pearly white, as were her eyebrows. She must wear a black wig, glued on, so it was peeled off painfully at the end of the night. She thought herself demon-like, but beautiful in a fierce way she had not been before. Miss Finch was done up in gold and white and red. The contrast was striking. They linked arms; they were the best of friends; their act was well received. Marianne was in love with everything. Miss Finch kissed her on her blue-black forehead and said, 'See, my dear! I have saved you!'

Otto left flowers in her dressing-room for her, and she put them in a vase. They had large flat petals, almost colourless, and they smelt of nothing. Arcadia later described them as 'breadflowers'. 'That,' he said, 'is their common name.' But Marianne thought they looked like windmills.

'Come here,' said Arcadia. 'I have something for you that will not wilt and die.' He thrust a hand out and made her work to uncover its booty. She prised open his knuckles, though he pretended resistance ('Like all women,' he said, 'you are too eager'), and found inside them a small trinket box. She thought for a moment it might be a ring, but it was not; it was a pair of very unusual earrings in the form of large waxy yellow stones.

Arcadia observed them over her shoulder. 'They were my mother's,' he said. 'But they are yours now.' She put her arms around his sinewy torso and kissed him, and he laughed. 'One day they will belong to my wife,' he said. He raised one eyebrow at her, the meaning of which she could not misconstrue, and broke off a petal of the breadflower.

And so things went on. Marianne rehearsed by day, performed in the evening, and at night sank into bed with Arcadia beside her; again, she thought herself very well looked after by the world. 'I send back to you a large portion of my earnings, for investment,' she wrote to the brothel madam, 'I trust only in you. Invest it however you think best. I miss you without exception. I am very happy.'

Then, the following year, a young person by the name of Jane Casey arrived in Canyon, and things changed.

Miss Casey was an equestrienne. She possessed a mane of chestnut-coloured hair and was tall beyond normal expectation for a woman. While the Eastern Mirror was popular, it could not compete with the spectacle of Miss Casey, blindfolded, driving six horses around the ring at lightning speed while smoking a cheroot. The men turned out to watch her ride and spoke of her prowess in awed tones.

The arrival of Miss Casey coincided with a cooling off of Arcadia's attentions to Marianne Ward. She found herself less visited than usual; he gave her fewer notes on her act; he did not comment on a new way she wore her hair. At night, sometimes, she found the bed empty beside her.

There was, one day, a rehearsal he had promised to attend, at which Miss Finch and Miss Ward were unveiling a new routine they had been preparing. They were keen for his opinion; his enthusiasm, when given, worked a kind of magic. But though they waited for him, he did not show. Marianne felt in her stomach that stone whose presence must always torment she who is no longer loved. For she loved Arcadia now – as drastically and injuriously as any girl might ever love a man, perhaps more so, as she had in her no shred of hard metal or streak of cunning with which to protect herself. 'How does such a thing happen?' she wrote to the brothel madam. 'That one day I did not care for him and then I should care for no one else?'

Somehow, in the process of loving him, the stakes had changed. If she had once amused Arcadia by the mere act of being, now she must exert herself to more deliberate measures. She must use a certain tone of voice when speaking; refrain from some topics of conversation; above all, not repeat herself nor wear particular items from her wardrobe that did not please him.

Marianne left her rehearsal and stopped a hostler on his way to watering the horses. 'Where is Mr Cirque?' she asked. The man pointed to the amphitheatre.

There were canvas tents at the mouth of the amphitheatre, and temporary stalls for the horses. She went from one to the other, flinging open their makeshift doors and calling. Finally she found him. Behind a flap of canvas, with sawdust underfoot and pale light casting in from above, she saw her beloved with his arm curled around the slender waist of Miss Casey and his mouth up close in her hair.

Marianne's horror was immediate: without knowing what she did, she threw herself at them. She clawed at Miss Casey's hair and dragged her nails down Arcadia's face; she swore and she screamed and kicked out with her boots. Such was her rage that it took two men to pull her off them. Once free, Arcadia strode away, flinging his hands out behind him. Miss Casey followed, attended by the men. Marianne sat alone on the sawdust ground and sobbed. She had never sobbed like this in all her happy, pretty life. She sobbed and sobbed, but her tears would not abate, given desperate poignancy by the small and awful fact that she had just discovered herself to be with child.

She was about four months along, far enough to make rehearsal uncomfortable and her costumes tight across the middle. She retched in the mornings and often, standing up, could not keep herself steady.

Arabella Finch had rooms, privately rented, with a kitchen and shared bathroom. It was here that Marianne relocated after Miss Casey was installed as Arcadia Cirque's mistress. She could not hide the fact of her pregnancy from Miss Finch for long.

Miss Finch pursed her little face up into a moue of pity. 'It is too late for you to do anything easily,' she said.

Long hot baths and gin proved insufficient; Marianne's colour was bad; she neglected herself. She lay in bed, could not rehearse, ate sparely. Arabella took it upon herself to accost Arcadia with the facts of Marianne's condition. But that man did not surprise here: 'It has nothing to do with me!' he said.

Nevertheless, he came to see Marianne in her sick room. He hitched his trousers up and sat by her bed; the mere shape of him beside her revived hope in Marianne's breast.

'You look unwell, Marianne Ward,' he said. 'Pregnancy does not suit you. You have lost your looks.'

Marianne tried to summon whatever prettiness she had left, but without success.

'I have no choice but to cancel your contract,' he continued after some moments, 'as you cannot rehearse any longer, and will be unable to perform in the coming season.'

She made a sound of astonishment.

'It is beyond my control,' he said. 'I am the manager of a large enterprise. I am not a charity.'

'But you are the father!' said Marianne.

'Come now, Marianne.' Arcadia laughed. 'You do not expect me to believe your attentions were exclusive?'

Marianne, pretty no longer, choked.

'Oh, do not *cry*,' said Arcadia. 'I thought better of you than that.' He gave her some money then, which she did not bother to retrieve from the counterpane where it fell, and he left.

The brothel madam received no more correspondence from her favourite charge. She wrote once, twice, and then she ceased to write and let the friendship grow into a historical fact, stowed away, not to be further interrogated.

She sent another contingent to Canyon; she did not forward her regards to Miss Ward. If she was hurt, she refused to know it. It was not long after the girls' arrival in Canyon that she received a letter from Miss Althea Hunt.

'We are all of us concerned,' wrote Miss Hunt, 'about the state of Marianne Ward. She has got herself pregnant, but is abandoned by the man. She staggers like a ghost about the township, quite wretched and desolate. We have encouraged that she returns home with us when we leave, but she says she will not.'

Soon after, the madam received another correspondence in the hand of Otto Cirque: 'I write as the friend of your friend, Marianne Ward. Miss Ward is in a state of depressed spirits. She is nearing her confinement but is physically and spiritually depleted and her friends fear for her.' The brothel madam sat, letter in hand, and did not know what to feel.

'Dear Madam,' wrote Arabella Finch. 'Marianne will surely die if you do not come immediately and help her.'

The brothel madam packed her things; she hired horses; she wrote for Otto Cirque to meet her; and she departed immediately for the town of Canyon.

Otto Cirque had made it his habit to sit with Marianne of an evening until she fell asleep. Then, when her breathing was even, he would unwind his hand from hers and return to the still, or the horses, or his dwelling, or wherever it was meaningful for him to be. One night he could not attend her; the next morning she had gone.

Arabella Finch rose to find her tenant's bed unslept in. There was a note on the dresser, in a shaky hand that did not fortify Miss Finch's confidence. 'I have gone home,' wrote Marianne, 'to Pitch. Where I hope my friend will tend me when I need her, which will be soon. I thank you, dear Arabella.'

Arabella made off immediately for Otto Cirque; and Otto Cirque saddled a horse and went after Marianne. But Marianne was never seen again, not in Pitch nor in Canyon.

A fortnight later, Arcadia Cirque was found dead in his apartment on the top floor of the Grand Hotel. A pistol lay across his lap; a scattering of letters across his desk.

Part 1

Canyon

Chapter 1

Archaeology and osteology

The wind had always made life difficult in Canyon. It was a saboteur of hair and hats. It could disturb the line of an ironed skirt, or disperse irresponsibly one's careful stack of newspapers. But there was nothing malicious about it. It did not rip off roofs. It did not demolish town monuments. Until one day, some forty years after the tragic death of Arcadia Cirque, the town's founder, when Julian Paratha unearthed, from outside a shed on his parents' property, a very odd, very auspicious-looking bone. Being keen to the scent of opportunity, he set off immediately to enquire into its archaeological value.

He always had *rashes*, Ivorie Hammer recalled, watching him come down Main Parade. Julian Paratha's face had always the appearance of having been scrubbed with a nailbrush. It was red and lumpy; you felt you might catch the condition if you went too close.

Ivorie was seated on a three-legged stool at her husband's shop window. She was pregnant with twins, and it was a strange choice, the three-legged stool, but she had insisted. The stool forced her to keep her back straight. She was a good-looking woman, and she found the additional weight of pregnancy hard, sometimes, to bear. The thought that she might maintain a good straight back by sitting on a three-legged stool was fortifying. She re-crossed her legs with some difficulty; she kept her eyes on Julian.

There did not at first seem to be anything exceptional in his progress towards them and yet she found herself observing him with more interest than usual. She peered close to the window glass, as though, by squinting the eye and leaning the head forwards, she might form a more accurate picture of his intent. Indeed, from this angle, it became clear that Julian *was* doing something he did not habitually do: he was *hurrying*.

Ivorie's husband, Mr Ernest Hammer, did not notice Julian Paratha hurrying. He was not easily distracted from his work. If spoken to, he was able to respond appropriately and then return to whatever he was doing as though the interruption had not occurred. Thus Ivorie was at liberty to perch where she might on her stool, in his shop, and comment as she might on whatever range of topics took her fancy. Which she now did.

'To think!' she said, half-turning towards her husband. 'How trying it must be for his mother . . .!' She paused, seeking greater accuracy. 'He's so *homely*, for instance.'

Her husband, Ernest, immersed in the mechanisms of a broken fob watch, had little to offer in response to this observation. 'My dear?' he merely said, fastening his pincers upon a minute gold spring.

'The thought is enough,' said Ivorie, 'to make me nervous! If I were a religious woman, Mr Hammer . . .' She shook her head and clasped her hands across her stomach.

'Are you, then, an irreligious woman, my dear?' her husband said, popping the spring into place. 'I had not thought it or I might not have married you.'

Ivorie ignored him. 'You remember his birth, do you not?' she said. 'The birth of Julian Paratha? Oh, of course you do not. Men do not recall even the births of their own sons, let alone their neighbours'.'

Ernest took this graciously, pressing the casing into the back of the fob.

'Well, *I* recall it,' Ivorie continued. 'It was horrible. The umbilical cord,' she said, 'the cord which attaches the baby to its mother – the umbilical cord was *wrapped* around his neck! Choking him, Mr Hammer!'

Ernest put down his pincers and the fob watch, and made his way towards where she sat, looking out the window.

'Don't fret, my darling,' he said. He leaned down to her and kissed the tip of her nose – a gesture scarcely noticed by its recipient except that she blinked, briefly, in irritation.

'It was lucky, I suppose,' Ivorie went on, 'that Morag Pappy resuscitated him quickly as she did.' She sighed deeply, unhappily, and gazed out the window at the object of her pity. 'Still, you know, you could see

20

the mark around the baby's neck a great many days. Like a hangman's rope . . .'

'Don't worry, my dear. *We* are not the Parathas,' said Mr Hammer. He might not say it at a different time – he was too good a man – but he said it now, for the sake of his wife.

Julian was upon them then, in the doorway. He closed the door with his shoulder, all the while holding his fist away from the rest of his body as if he had something dangerous captured inside it.

'Julian!' said Ernest. He liked Julian Paratha. He liked him for his awkwardness, his endeavouring nature. He adjusted his half-spectacles and rubbed the side of his nose. 'What have you got there?'

Julian presented his fist on the counter, looking all the while at Mrs Hammer, who was busily repositioning her stool, smiling meaningly (and, she wrongly believed, encouragingly) at Julian as she did so.

'I found this,' he said. And he opened his fist.

Ernest Hammer had already established something of a commercial relationship with Julian Paratha, supplying him with petty cash for the articles of questionable value he exhumed from the disused amphitheatre. An inventory of these items so far included: a chipped ivory key from a Bösendorfer pianoforte; a cut-glass stopper from an old flagon; half a brass nutcracker in the shape of a female leg; and a paperweight made of some kind of resinous material, inside which was a bright blue scarab beetle. All items remained unsold and undisplayed, rolled up in a small bag in Ernest Hammer's bottom drawer.

Ernest took the latest offering in his hand and looked it over. Despite knowing a thing or two about antique paraphernalia, he was by no means versed in the art of osteology, beyond recognising a chop bone when he saw it, and the ability to distinguish the frame of a chicken from that of a squab. Now, however, he turned over with unease the object supplied him by his young protégé, lifted it closer to his eye and then further away, removed the half-spectacles from the bridge of his nose and looked again, produced from his bench drawer a magnifying glass and, finally, his brow shining with the efforts of concentration, tapped the said object with his forefinger and said: 'I believe it is a bone you have found,' and, when this pronouncement failed to produce effect: 'A metatarsal, to be precise – a foot bone – a bone directly from the knuckle of a toe.'

Ivorie gasped and huddled closer in to her husband's side. 'A human toe...?' she whispered.

'But is it a *fossil*?' Julian said. 'And is it *worth* anything? Because,' he said, 'I have a whole sack of them if you think they're worth anything.'

Ernest suggested their retrieval would be worthwhile and, dusting the metatarsal off, he returned it to its finder – who seemed a little anxious lest the fossil be wrongly appropriated – as a token of trust between them.

Later in the afternoon, when Julian returned, Ernest and Ivorie had before them on the shop counter a stack of medical texts. They had gone methodically through these texts and, with the help of Ivorie's encyclopaedic dictionary, become quite comfortable with the basic terms relating to the human skeletal system.

In the absence of other samples against which some comparative study might have been made, they had not successfully ascertained whether *their* bone (for so they had come already to refer to it) was a proximal, middle or distal phalanx or whether indeed it was no such thing but the equivalent as occurring in the metacarpus, the hand.

This distinction seemed of less importance once Julian deposited the remainder of his collection with them. He upended his haversack on Ernest's shop counter, showering forth numerous fragments of bone, along with dirt and gravel and the dried heads of various flowering weeds. He leaned back and looked smugly up at them, as though he had just delivered to them a sack full of Spanish ducats. Ivorie, pressing her hands across her belly as if to shield the eyes of her unborn babies, suffered a small moment of indignation.

'A graveyard!' she exclaimed, 'Just what do you mean of this?' And to her husband: 'He has been pulling apart graves, Ernest, pulling up the poor, rested dead.' She turned and glared at Julian, who withstood her invective nobly. 'It is your job to *put them in*,' she said, 'not dig them up!'

But Ernest had already begun to sweep the bone particles into a pile before him, and had taken from his waistcoat pocket a pair of tweezers, with which he now extracted various fragments, holding them up to the light one at a time for proper investigation.

'They were not took up from a grave,' Julian said, shaking his head.

'Nor did I dig them up from any public place. It was on my own side of the fence line. It was ground that belonged to my family. I was not where I had no licence to be!'

Mr Hammer nodded and patted Julian's arm to show he in no way suspected him of trespass, or theft, or any other misdemeanour.

Having neither the appropriate tools nor the requisite training to reach easy conclusion on the origins of Julian's fossils, Mr Ernest Hammer put aside for the afternoon and all that evening the many erratic watches of Canyon, and applied his pincers instead to the consideration of *distal extremities* and *epiphyses*.

His dinner plate was brought to him at due six (according to the unerring precision of their own wall clock) where it languished at his elbow until cold, having no effect on his labours except to remind him, when it caught his eye, of the miracle of the marital institution, which supplied such provisions without them being in any way solicited.

In the meantime, Julian Paratha being loath to depart without his haversack and its contents, Mrs Ivorie Hammer found, much to her displeasure, that she must share her otherwise solitary meal with him.

She resented everything about her predicament. She resented the way Julian pushed half his potato to one side, as though it were not to his liking. She resented the way he, upon finishing his meal, put his plate on the table without even straightening knife against fork. She resented his oversized legs on the hearth, the after-dinner cushion behind his neck, the way his head made the doily on the armchair sit awry. She cleared her throat.

'Shouldn't your parents be notified?' she ventured, for she had calculated that Julian could hardly be much older than fourteen. He had the beginnings of an Adam's apple in his neck; it moved up and down like a baby mouse in a snake's gullet.

'They wouldn't matter,' he said, limply waving one hand, and allowing it to fall back on his chest. Ivorie Hammer was uncertain whether he meant by this that his parents' peace of mind was no matter to *him*, or that his personal livelihood was not a thing that warranted particular attention by *them*. Either way, it was unsettling.

Her husband did not retire to bed that whole night, leaving Ivorie to provide overnight attire and bedding for Julian Paratha, as well as dispatch a missive to his family notifying them of his whereabouts – be such warranted or not. She lay in bed with a strange hard knot of anxiety in her chest and could not sleep. And though her wakefulness was partly due to Mr Hammer's absence, and partly due to disquieting images at play behind her eyelids – of whole rib-cages, disconnected from their corresponding limbs and vertebrae – it also resulted from the fear that, through her sleep-suspended vigilance, some ornament from the mantelpiece or side cabinet might find its way into Julian's pockets.

She did not like herself for harbouring such suspicions, but she was a pragmatic woman and she did not wantonly expend her generosity.

In the morning, Ernest summoned his wife to him. Using delicate amounts of carpentry glue, he had configured, from the pile of bones, small portions of a skeleton, much as a jigsaw-puzzler might his component pieces, so here were parts of a pelvic bone, he explained – 'quite obvious, if you looked long at the thing' – here again, various carpal and metacarpal bones, in as close an approximation of their original order as Mr Hammer dared to make; a trochlea bone with its radial head as smooth and polished as a bed knob, via which, he explained to his wife, the lateral movement of the forearm is achieved; and finally a series of ribs, arranged in descent from an imaginary sternum, like a malformed tree missing several of its limbs and bereft of foliage.

The sleeping Julian slept on, with his head wedged tightly between sofa cushion and armrest, and his lower jaw drooping slightly so that one might investigate with considerable ease his execrable dental history.

Mrs Ivorie Hammer felt no such equanimity. Somewhere in her belly, a snake was uncurling. It was the same snake that had upset her stomach on her wedding day. It was two parts fear, and two parts excitement: a snake that had eaten a peculiarly rapacious butterfly. Mrs Hammer needed no prompting from her husband (who, after all, had never been known to prompt his wife in anything) before departing the house in search of Mr Borrel Sweetley, that exemplary man who (like him or not) possessed the intellectual and experiential equipment that rendered his advice (like it or not) quite indispensable in all matters of civic importance.

Chapter 2

The Parathas

In almost every pocket of the world, it seems, there is a family especially despised by circumstance. Though they might look, broadly speaking, much as we do – except perhaps, a little shabbier of dress, a little less pleasing of feature – there is something about them that is out of register. No matter how upstanding, good-natured, hard-working they are, we instinctively know they are *not like us*.

What is it that makes them so? Is it a character flaw of which they are unaware, let alone free to change? An excess of good humour, perhaps, or of generosity (they want to *give* one things all the time!). Perhaps they talk too loudly, or are too effusive, or defer to our opinions too easily. Certainly, it is not just their poverty that irks us; for, no matter how well dressed, they will never fit in at the party. We discharge our obligations to them as quickly as politeness allows: we excuse ourselves and leave them on their own, in the parlour, holding lonesome forks up to plates of cream sponge, trying desperately to appear as though such desserts merit extraordinary attention.

It is the tragedy of such persons to spend their lifetimes being avoided by those whose friendship they court. But the fact is, we cannot bear to be implicated in their cycle of misfortune.

Money, as we know, changes these things. If the members of such families had money, we would tolerate them. We would attend their parties and might even consider their daughters marriageable. However, I think it safe to say they generally occur at the lower end of the economic ladder, these families. They do not attend the good schools, they are not likely ever to win scholarships or bursaries. They do not become doctors or lawyers or teachers. Instead they find themselves being paid to perform those thankless tasks that are beneath the rest of us. They clean up after us, dispose of our rubbish, dig our sewers, bury our loved ones. No wonder we are repulsed by them: they remind us too starkly of our waste and our dead.

Such was the case with the Paratha family. Originally of the circus (in some capacity or other – no one could remember: surely it had to do with the maintenance of the animals), they now scratched out a living gravedigging in the locality of Canyon. It was a dwindling trade. It was a dwindling population – there were a dwindling number of deaths. What small income they made from gravedigging they supplemented with the digging of wells, the burying of dogs, the burning of rubbish and fumigation of vermin. On more than one occasion, coming into town and passing the wretched hovel in which the Parathas live, Mr Borrel Sweetley has thought to himself: 'By God, if they were Hindoos, they would be Untouchables, no doubt about it!'

Mr Borrel Sweetley hås lived in the broad brown lands of India, where such peoples as Hindoos live. Fortunately, though, there is no caste system in this country. Here, one might happily consign such families as the Parathas to the whims of our great meritocracy, and if the outcome is their increasing invisibility, so be it – it could just as easily be the opposite. Because even if they decline, they do not die out, these types of family. They are necessary. They persist. More than once, I hear, precisely such a family has won the lottery.

Mr Borrel Sweetley, black quasi-clerical coat rising about him so he resembled some kind of bloated raven, led the small party of volunteer excavators to the Paratha residence. Situated some way off the dusty, potholed coach road, this residence was a study in dereliction.

'A blot on the landscape,' Mr Borrel Sweetley said.

'A *blight*,' corrected Ivorie Hammer, who was amongst the party, despite the unsavoury nature of their mission.

The Parathas' house comprised several lean-tos of rotting timber and punctured tin, from which rough windows had been cut and sheathed with flapping waterproof canvas. Ropes and stakes reinforced the arrangement. The garden was overgrown and disorderly, dotted with piles of refuse, cast-off toys and broken tools. In its centre stood a single preposterous tree, a cross between a fig and a baobab, which had been struck by lightning so many times and in so many places that it bent and forked in a manner quite at odds with nature.

Florence Paratha stood dwarfed beside this tree, her hand against her forehead to shield the sun and enable a more precise picture of her visitors. When she saw her eldest son amongst them, she began to wave in a great frenzy, as though beset, all of a sudden, by a terrific onslaught of march flies.

'Juliaaaan!' she called out, hitching up her skirts and making her way towards them. '*Jooolian!*'

Ivorie rested against the Parathas' fence post and surveyed the small figure as she drew closer. She felt, for a moment, profound regret regarding Florence Paratha. Florence Paratha had once been Florence Bean, a girl of her acquaintance; a small, tidy, well-spoken girl. She had always worn very tight plaits. Florence Paratha was none of these things. Her hair was crisscrossed with bobby pins. Ivorie could see the dirty lace of her petticoat dangling below the hem of her dress. There was, in fact, very little about her that resembled the girl she had been. One *becomes*, Ivorie observed sadly, the person whom one chooses to *marry*. It was regrettable. One made mistakes so easily.

She turned her eyes away, and bent with great difficulty to knock a stone out of her shoe, leaning her bulk against the fencepost. When she returned to standing, the party had halted behind her, and Mr Sweetley now insinuated his way, with shuffling sidesteps, to the front. He cleared his throat and was on the point of commencing a short address to Mrs Paratha explaining their presence there (with shovels, picks, hessian bags, sieves and brushes) when Florence Paratha opened the gate expansively and ushered them in.

Such easy access was quite unexpected, and once the gate was shut behind them, no one knew quite what to do. The men smiled at Florence Paratha unhappily, and attempted to hide their excavating equipment behind their backs, until finally, apologetically, they began to make a slow circuit of the garden, paying particular attention to an odd and ramshackle outhouse at some fifty yards' remove from the main residence.

Though she did not like to admit it, Ivorie Hammer was suffering from ailments attributable to her condition. Her husband organised for a chair to be fetched, which he set beneath the shadiest bough of the lightning-struck tree. And there, in as close to companionable silence as might ever be possible between them, Ivorie Hammer and Florence Paratha sat and watched.

Julian led the men to the threshold of the dilapidated outhouse. Its door was locked with a large padlock, and a pile of firewood and kindling was stacked against it. Julian bent down, stood up again, and, with great theatricality, directed attention to a disturbed plot of earth before them. He prodded the ground with his toe. He stretched his neck. The performance made one want to avert one's eyes; if there was anything more painful to watch than Julian Paratha being awkward, thought Ivorie, it was the spectacle of Julian Paratha being cocky. Cockiness on a naturally cocky man was one thing, but on a person who was, by temperament, self-effacing . . . well, it became quite sinister.

Borrel Sweetley struck the first shovel into the earth. He ground it in with his foot proprietorially, as though staking a claim or planting a flagpole – one might imagine he applied the same moral fervour to the sowing of lettuce seeds in his garden. His chest puffed out, and his black coat-tails flew up behind him as he bent and straightened, bent and straightened, making all the outward signs of vigorous labour, but only managing to extract from the ground a little superfluous rubble, which he flung in a shower about himself.

Florence Paratha squatted beside Ivorie Hammer. Her elbows were propped on her knees and her skirt hung, trailing on the ground, between them. She did not seem discomposed, nor even particularly curious as to *why* the men were digging up her garden. The digging itself, however, was a source of interest to her, and she delivered several observations on the matter to Ivorie.

'They say,' she said, confidentially, turning her head, but not her eyes, towards her former schoolfellow, 'that if we kept digging downwards . . . down, down, down . . . if we were to dig ourselves clean through the earth, in a straight line, we would come out in China, Mrs Hammer. China!'

Above them, hanging from the lip of the Parathas' faltering roof line, windchimes – glass and bottletop, cowrie shell and teaspoon – set up a sharp clamour and then died down again. From a temporary cloud of dust at the bottom of the garden, Mr Borrel Sweetley stood up, holding aloft – much as another might a nugget of gold to the admiration of his fellows – a piece of bone. If Mrs Ivorie Hammer was not mistaken, she thought she heard him say: 'Eureka!'

It was mid afternoon and hot when Florence Paratha's husband arrived home with the couple's other children. In the interim, Mr Sweetley had inspired his volunteers to great heights with his exhortations to 'Bring to light all unconsecrated remains!' – with the result that much more of the yard had been dug up than had seemed originally necessary.

Thomas Paratha was taken aback by what confronted him. For several minutes, dropping his children's hands, he looked about him in bewilderment. Finally, he began to stroke his beard gently, as if it were brushed velvet or some other such commiserative material. He made his way slowly towards the men, who had suspended their work and stood leaning on their shovels. When he saw Julian, he applied a questioning look to his son that caused Julian to immediately drop several inches in height.

Indeed, all the men diminished somewhat. They made a thoroughfare for Thomas as he approached, and those who had not seemed previously possessed of a conscience now demonstrated all the signs of acute discomfort. Mr Sweetley, however, continued to smile down invincibly from his mount atop a pile of freshly dug earth.

'Bones, Mr Paratha!' he cried out, holding something up in his hand that was patently *not* a bone but which we might presume was meant symbolically to represent one for Mr Paratha's benefit. 'Bones!' cried Mr Borrel Sweetley. 'Brought to the light of authority!'

In fact, they had so far unearthed only the one bone, the same which had caused Mr Sweetley to exclaim 'Eureka!' some hours before, and which Ernest Hammer now studied with great unhappiness from behind a green baize-covered card table at some remove from the rest of the party. Borrel Sweetley descended and began to prowl slowly around the outhouse, knocking on its silvery wooden shingles, prising at smutty window edges, while Thomas peered into the large hole in his garden. Not looking up, addressing no one in particular, and certainly making no accusation, he said, 'Well, you have indeed made a hole . . .' And then, considering further, 'My gosh, what a hole you have made!'

He went on a little longer, rearranging grammatically this basic premise, until any authority he might have had over the situation was well and truly spent.

'They have found things other than bones, my dear!' exclaimed his wife from her perch at Ivorie's side beneath the baobab tree. She extricated herself from several of her children, and bounded over to her husband, righting herself deftly as her ankles splayed on rabbit holes and other grass-obscured obstacles. 'Just look!' she said. She took Thomas's arm and gestured towards a small pile of recovered objects the men had put to one side. 'Look!' She bent to retrieve the uppermost article. 'It is the Christmas angel . . . and here, it is what they call a Mary Ann doll and . . . Look, Thomas, look! It is an old plate of your mother's!' She picked up what she could of these long-lost items and hugged them to her chest. 'Oh, I am glad of it, Thomas, my darling. I am glad of neighbours who come to procure things from the ground, long hid!' Thus an end was put to any authority Thomas Paratha might have had as male landowner. He returned quietly with his wife to the baobab tree and resumed his usual tacit acceptance of the conditions larger, more important men had decided for him.

Ivorie put her arms up to resist, but Florence Paratha had clearly decided the Mary Ann doll belonged to her. She thrust it into Ivorie's lap. 'I remember,' she said, plopping to the ground in a puff of skirt and petticoats. It was like a crack in otherwise flawless glass, this memory of Florence Paratha's. Ivorie had not thought it possible that Florence Paratha would remember anything from her life as Florence Bean. 'I remember,' Florence continued, turning to her husband to enlist his support, 'Mrs Hammer had a doll just like this. At school. Her mother gave it her.' She turned again to Ivorie. She had become, momentarily, smart and tidy: Florence Bean. 'I remember,' she said. 'We were all jealous. She was better than the ones we had.'

'She was not given to me by my mother,' said Ivorie.

'Oh,' said Florence Paratha. 'You carried her to school, every day.'

Florence's fingers twitched. 'One of my children found her, discarded or something, I suspect, and brought her home. That must be how she came to be here!'

The Mary Ann doll was light on Ivorie's lap. The fabric body was creased and strung with cobwebbed dirt, and a seam was undoing about the neck, but otherwise she was intact. Her head was cool and fitted precisely in Ivorie's hand. A little spit on the finger, a circular motion on the cool surface, and a plume of clean white porcelain showed through. On the soft fabric of her leg, the ink-stained initials: M. W. Ivorie fell still and silent. She broke a leaf off a drooping plant and flapped it in front of her face.

On the other side of the tree, Mr Sweetley was preparing for a private interview with Thomas Paratha. He had removed his raven's wings coat and laid it out on the buffalo grass. Thomas Paratha, enjoined to do the same but having no jacket to remove, only a three-button waistcoat with torn lining, declined. Nor would he take a pinch of the tobacco Mr Sweetley held out to him. One could hardly blame Sweetley for being annoyed.

'Mr Paratha,' he said, 'what we have uncovered here today is the mere tip of the iceberg.' He smiled thinly. 'To use a cool phrase on a hot day, Mr Paratha.' He smiled again, before resuming with greater sternness. 'Any further evidence situated on your premises must be gathered and duly dispatched to the proper bodies of authority. Clarity is the objective here, Mr Paratha. There is something hidden on your property that must be brought to light.' He thumped his palm with his right fist. He had quite forgotten Mrs Hammer, all ears behind a large leaf. 'Your coopera-tion, Mr Paratha, will ultimately cast you in a good light. Do you see?' He nodded his head encouragingly. 'Your cooperation will be perceived as a *mitigating* factor.' He lowered his voice and shook his head, and had he been a thin man, his Adam's apple might have trembled. 'The thing is, Mr Paratha,' he said, getting to the heart of the matter, 'we must *get in to* this shed of yours.'

He indicated with his arm the outhouse at whose threshold their excavation had been carried out. As if on cue, a volunteer now prod-ded the door gently with his foot, illustrating how the wood might be caused to splinter under the very smallest force. The padlock lurched to a taut right angle against the hasp, and fell back again loudly.

'In some circumstances,' Mr Borrel Sweetley whispered, almost directly into Mr Paratha's ear, 'a padlock is a flimsy article indeed. It cannot protect a man from the law, when the law wants him.' He winked. 'We wouldn't like to occasion any violence you know. We shouldn't like to go ahead without your consent, willingly given.'

Ivorie Hammer, with her palms down flat on the leaf and the leaf down flat on her knees and her knees brought tightly together, smelled a nasty smell in the air. She saw the face of the Mary Ann doll and her own face and another face that was not quite a face yet had all the hallmarks one would expect of a face . . . All these faces, coming in and out of one another in great soft waves. She swung herself out of her chair and, refusing the helping hand of Florence Paratha, made her way to where her husband sat behind the card table.

'Ernest . . .' she said. And then a terrible weakness overcame her and, toppling the green card table, and the unsuspecting figure of her husband, she fell forwards into the dirt and buffalo grass.

When she came to, she found herself on a narrow day bed in Mrs Paratha's enclosed verandah. It was an L-shaped room with algae-coloured walls and windows that were hammered shut. The sun beat hard against a drawn blind. She rolled her head a little to one side.

'Mrs Hammer?' said Florence Paratha, groping for Ivorie's hand. She felt Ivorie's forehead; her hand was cool and chalky. She lowered her voice to a whisper. 'Mrs Hammer, are you all right?'

Ivorie shook her head and opened her mouth.

'No sharp pains? No odd sensations?' Florence Paratha brought her little ear close to Ivorie's mouth, as if to catch her dying words. Ivorie shook her head again.

A yellow light had fallen across the windows, and when Florence sat up, her silhouette was sharp and pointed against the canvas blinds. 'I had a cousin once,' she said, looking not at Ivorie, but at a spot on the wall above the bed head, 'whose baby got lodged in the tubes.' She turned back to Ivorie. 'In the tubes!' And shook her head in wonder.

Ivorie was not sure whether this brief reflection was intended to frighten or reassure her, or was merely a testimony to the wilfulness of unborn babies who might plant themselves anywhere.

'I'd like a drink . . .' she croaked.

The drink came. The glass, Ivorie noticed, was smeared about the lip with what looked like some sort of condiment, but she did not let it matter. She smiled tautly at Mrs Paratha – she would not let any of it matter – and returned the empty vessel to her.

'I think I had better . . .' Florence began, twisting and turning the drinking glass. 'I think I had better send for Morag Pappy.' She smiled. 'Don't you think?'

Ivorie Hammer lurched forwards and attempted to throw off the blankets.

'There is no need for Miss Pappy . . .' she said, 'not now, and at no time in the future –'

Florence Paratha placated her as best she could. 'Well, of course, we shall do no such thing!'

'It is my prerogative!'

'Indeed, Mrs Hammer. I only thought . . . she did so well with me, all my times . . .'

'There are reasons,' said Ivorie.

'Of course, and they are very good ones. We all of us place much stock in your reasons . . .'

'It is only a little rest I require, Mrs Paratha. A little rest. A little quiet.'

'Ssh, now. Put yourself well under.'

'A little quiet . . .'

And so saying, Ivorie Hammer dropped steadfastly into sleep, and Florence Paratha tiptoed out of the room. So steadfast was her sleep, in fact, that Ivorie remained oblivious to the sound, issuing from the rear of the Paratha yard, of an axe-head against wood. All she heard in her small, L-shaped room was the canvas blind, which banged at irregular intervals, and the flutter of windchimes, occasionally touching.

When she woke for the second time, it was dark. One of the blinds had twisted itself to the side and now pounded the window frame violently. Overhead the windchimes were maniacal. A little shower of maverick plant spores swept along the windowsill and a palm leaf flattened and recoiled on the outside of the glass. Ivorie Hammer did not know where she was, but there was a smell in the air: a dank, luscious smell like rotting flowers. She groped about her in the bed and found the Mary Ann doll. When she knocked its head with her knuckles it sounded hollow, and a little clod of earth-coloured sediment dropped out of its burst neck and onto the counterpane.

There was another figure beside her now, but it was not Florence Paratha — it was her husband. He was soft in the half-light: he appeared to be composed of grey snowflakes.

'You've had a good long sleep, my dear,' Mr Hammer said. He drew his chair in closer to her bedside. 'But you have not eaten all day. The whole day through, and not a morsel.' He patted his pockets, front and back, looking for something: a tin of peppermints, an old bag of licorice.

'Don't concern yourself, Mr Hammer,' Ivorie said, still croaky. She pushed herself up slowly on her elbows. 'I have absolutely no appetite. I fear I could not hold down a barley sugar.'

The blind bumped and made a small series of frenetic sideways clatters. Ernest Hammer stood up and straightened it, only for it to twist back as soon as he sat down again. 'There's a nasty storm sprung up outside, Ivorie. Nasty, nasty, whipping wind.' Next to the bed stood a sidetable; Ernest leaned over and lit a stump of candle that sat upon it. The flame danced like a dervish, and went immediately out. He re-lit the candle and made a small shelter for it out of two books.

Ivorie gripped her husband's arm. 'I do not like it!' she said.

She had meant the weather, but Mr Hammer misinterpreted her alarm.

'You are right,' he said in a low voice. He kept his eyes on her, but began absently to wind his watch — backwards-forwards, backwards-forwards, as if he were adjusting, in smaller and smaller increments, some delicate internal mechanism.

Ivorie put her hand on his wrist. 'What has happened?'

'It has all turned out tragically, Ivorie,' he said. 'They disposed of that shed all right. Did you hear them? They broke down the door. Thomas Paratha wouldn't give them the key.' He shook his head. His eyes looked very pale and tired. 'There was an old man in there, Ivorie — an old, *old* man.' Ernest held his hands above the candle flame as if to warm them.

'He was like a ghost. When the door came down, he was huddled in a corner. I did feel for him, Ivorie. We all felt for him, I think. It felt like a crime to take such a fellow and drag him into the light . . .' He stopped again and a thin line of black smoke rose from the candle where he accidentally touched the flame. 'But Mr Sweetley has got him in custody now.'

'They found something then?' Ivorie prompted quietly.

Ernest hesitated a moment. He moved his open palm slowly over the candle flame. 'There were more bones in there. Two *skulls*,' he said. 'Human skulls. It was the strangest thing, Ivorie. They were laid out like . . . well, on display, clean and polished. On a little table. With candles.'

Ivorie laughed then: a rude sound in the small room. 'Well, he is just an old, old man, then, digging up graves, looking for trinkets. Some sad old relative of the Parathas'.' She was sitting up now, with her back against the bedstead, and she felt annoyed and uncomfortable and impatient.

'Well, they seem to think he is is not just *some old man*, Ivorie.' Ernest was quiet for a moment. 'Mr Sweetley believes he is Otto Cirque, brother of Arcadia.'

Ivorie laughed again. 'Come now! He is long dead!'

'Perhaps not,' said Ernest. 'Perhaps not. And Ivorie . . .?'

'Yes, Mr Hammer?'

'They found something else.'

'And what was that?'

'They found a rifle, an old-fashioned one. They found it lying right next to the skulls. And now they have taken him away, Ivorie. He went quietly. It was very strange, my darling, as if he expected it.'

'We must get out,' Ivorie said. She had begun to sweat. She pulled the covers back and slung her legs over the bed frame, feeling around with her feet for her shoes. 'I do *not* like it!'

She found her shoes and wrestled them onto her white, swollen feet.

Ernest indicated the door that led to the rest of the Paratha residence. 'Shall we say goodbye?' he said. 'Shouldn't we? Wouldn't it be neighbourly of us . . .?'

'It would not,' said Ivorie, holding fast to his arm, 'be neighbourly.

We must just creep out. We must just ever so quietly take our leave.'
And so saying, she inched open the door of the L-shaped room and they
padded out into the adjoining corridor. But when they unlatched the
back door, the wind caught it and sent it cracking on its hinges so the
household could not fail to be alerted of their departure.

'Come *on*,' said Ivorie to her husband. She could already hear footsteps in some other part of the house, and a door open somewhere with
a voice behind it.

Outside the wind had risen. A hail of grit and dust and sand flew into
their eyes and against their legs. Ernest shielded them from the worst of
it with his jacket.

'It is tragedy, is it not,' Ernest cried, hopefully, into the wind, 'that
brings out the best in us? From deep within, the best?'

Ivorie did not know why her heart beat so in her chest. 'Adversity,'
she said distractedly, 'not tragedy, Mr Hammer. It is *adversity* that brings
out the best in us.' But Ernest Hammer did not hear her, the wind had
sucked her words away directly they were spoken.

In Ivorie's pocket, almost but not quite forgotten, the head of the
Mary Ann doll jumped and rattled, and its loose glass eyes rolled back
into its head.

Chapter 3

Mrs Ivorie Hammer carries some lunch to her husband

Meteorologically, Mr Sweetley had names for it. 'A temporary surfeit,' he said, 'of knots, and counter-knots, all vying for atmospheric precedence.'

Ivorie Hammer had observed Morag Pappy considering the air with unusual interest that morning. The two women did not, of course, exchange pleasantries. They had not exchanged pleasantries in some years. But each was aware of the other nonetheless. Morag Pappy had considered the air and Ivorie, taking her cue, had breathed with great deliberation all morning.

In all other things, Ivorie considered Morag Pappy a model of impropriety. She was broad and brown and she wielded such things as saws and hammers in a robust, competent way. She did not attach sufficient importance to personal grooming, and had the effrontery to show no interest in her neighbours' private lives beyond that which concerned the ladies' reproductive systems (an interest that was entirely professional).

She was also an example of the worst damage done unto the female form by the sun. Morag's lack of precaution (headgear, parasol shade, mid-afternoon curfew) had had a severely deleterious effect on her complexion. Her face, never pretty, was brown and leathery and, over time, had been sub-divided by four deep furrows. Looking at her front on, you could no longer conceive of her face as a whole; rather, it comprised a chin quarter, a forehead quarter, and two shining, buffed cheek quarters, her features having all but disappeared in the crevices between. The rest of her body had been similarly ravaged, but, hidden as it was behind quantities of clothing, remained less vulnerable to public scrutiny.

That Morag Pappy was quite ancient there was no doubt. When she had first come amongst them — with, improbably, a tiny baby in tow — her hair was already white and her face lined. She was not the slightest bit friendly. She did not chat, or gossip. She had sufficient wealth to build an excessively sturdy, over-engineered house (a project viewed unfavourably by her neighbours), and then proceeded to set up what she called her 'dispensary'. A rumour prevailed that she specialised in women's ailments, but no woman with an ailment had the courage to present herself and test the hypothesis.

So it was that Morag's first professional success — the containment of a threatened miscarriage in a thirteen-week pregnancy — was acci-dental. A young woman had come to grief in the road near Morag's house. The woman was quickly brought inside the house, deposited on the cushioned window seat in her parlour, and made to swallow a pint of raspberry leaf tea Morag brewed for her. Throughout that even-ing, under Morag's watchful eye, she drank three pints more of the tea, and at bedtime was persuaded to scull a bottle-cap of tincture of False Unicorn Root. By the morning, she was quite well, and Morag's white sheets, between which she had slept for eleven uninterrupted hours, remained pristine. The pregnancy had restored itself, the infant latched back on to the placenta, the uterus tightened protectively over him.

Thereafter, having won a first and voluble convert (the young woman told everybody), Morag quickly established a reputation amongst the women. With droplets of distilled water and bags of powdered meadow-sweet, she restored their vitality and regulated their cycles and brought their babies effortlessly into the world. She taught them other vital lessons too, including the various methods with which they might constrain their fertility — methods Morag discussed unflinchingly, and which they assured her, red-faced, they had no need of practising, but practised nevertheless, every one of them, with greater and lesser suc-cess. Over a period of years, Morag brought to term so many dubious pregnancies and saved so many jaundiced, undersized infants from post-natal perils that all enquiries about her background and credentials were put aside. Morag Pappy became — and remained — beyond censure.

Except, of course, in the opinion of Ivorie Hammer. Having once suf-fered a more proximate relationship with the good woman (yes, she had been the baby in tow), Ivorie felt no reserve in abusing Morag Pappy whenever she was provided with public occasion. This she did now to the small group of people gathered outside the courthouse, where some days before, a strange old man of dubious identity had been locked up to await the arrival of the Authorities.

'Miss Pappy,' announced Ivorie Hammer, 'did not seem to note the *gravity* of this whole affair. It seems to her —' and she looked around in mock-horror, '— that a matter of "a few bones" is no matter at all! She said as much herself to me this morning!' (She had not.) 'Her dire presentiment, she said, attended not to this discovery but to the *patterns of the weather.*'

This evidence of Morag Pappy's misdirected concern did not relieve the private fears of Ivorie's little audience: it was not intended to.

'Miss Pappy says,' proceeded Ivorie, configuring herself into an appropriately confidential posture, 'that she has never, in all her experience, witnessed conditions such as these. Not once! *Malevolent*, was the word she used to describe it. She says she has never known weather so *malevolent* — and she wonders what it signifies.'

'What *does* it signify, Mrs Hammer?' said one nervous man, leafing his coat collar up against his cheek and shivering, though it was not cold.

'Yes,' said another, 'what do *you* think it means?'

'Perhaps,' said Ivorie, looking them in the face, one by one, 'the wind has been sent to move us on.' She did not know she thought it until she said it. She was puzzled, for a moment. Then, recovering, she continued up the steps to the courtroom door without a glance behind her.

It never occurred to the people of Canyon that large words could conceal small meanings. They had not experienced firsthand the subterfuges of the politician. They were wont to believe the opinions of a person who expressed themselves well. They were wont to believe these opinions all the more if their speaker wore a well-cut suit. It did not occur to them that superior tailoring might be evidence of undemocratic impulses.

Canyon was a small town, and it was too remote from the places where history is made to be canny to the subtleties of politics. In Canyon, personality was trusted absolutely. Reputation was everything.

A shopkeeper was much more than the sum total of his wares: he was a rallying point for the whole way of life that depended upon him. A thin baker could not be trusted. A milkman must have strong forearms and a belly laugh. A fireman ought, reasonably, to have ginger hair and a case of sunburn. All in all, it was not a reliable state of affairs, for personality, once encouraged, is apt to grow, and the ferocity with which personality grows when there is space enough for its unencumbered development is nowhere so apparent as in the small town. In such places as Canyon, fallacious opinions gain too easily the ring of credibility.

Ivorie Hammer was not a consciously calculating woman, yet she had about her a remarkable quality of *purpose*. She gave the impression of being able to do things, and of knowing clearly, precisely, *why* she was doing them. This quality of hers, coupled with her aptitude for the English language (she was a collector of dictionaries), enabled her to cultivate a considerable reputation for herself as a woman of great example. Had she been a man, she would have made a memorable civic leader.

Under the circumstances (i.e. her not being a man) Mr Borrel Sweetley assumed this role. Mr Sweetley, as I think I have already suggested, was a man of vast life experience. In his private collection (portions of which he exhibited annually to his interested public), one might see evidence of his extensive intercontinental travels: ebony carvings from Africa; a garishly painted wooden Ganesh from India; whitest of white cowrie shells from blackest of black New Guinea. On his office wall, he attached a map of the world upon which was traced, in black ink, his strange and circuitous route – black hairlines crossing oceans and continents, backtracking and intersecting: the itinerary of an illogical, impetuous traveller. When asked about his travels, he was disappointingly short, and failed to supply nourishment to the local imagination: 'Oh countries!' he said, and opened his arms wide as if to indicate an immensity beyond comprehension. 'Oceans! Vast, *vast* things!'

No one quite knew how it was that Mr Sweetley had come amongst them. He had simply arrived one day with the mail coach, rising above the brown paper packages like a clergyman from a flock of sinners. In a matter of hours he had leased the ground floor of the old courthouse in Main Parade, pasting up his big black-lettered sign, which did not bother with particulars, but boldly announced his presence amongst them: MR

BORREL SWEETLEY: CONSULTATION BY APPOINTMENT ONLY. It was considered a triumph for Canyon that a man of his calibre had come to settle there, and share with them his appreciable knowledge. In fact, they wondered how they had ever got along without him.

In truth, no one was quite sure of Mr Sweetley's professional status, but certainly he wore all the accoutrements a man of standing ought, and possessed, too, a brilliant command of Latin dicta, which he put to frequent though not always appropriate use.

His legal expertise (in his youth he had worked in a clerical capacity on the Crown Lands Law Reports) qualified him abundantly for any official role he might undertake in Canyon, be it of bailiff, sheriff or constable. He presided over the reading of wills; he resolved conflicts between disputing parties; he was consulted on the drafting of contracts, the appropriate punishment for truancy, the erection of fences around the disused amphitheatre. He was the voice of officialdom when it came to shop closing hours, marital dissension, issues of charity and water catchment and taxation. He was also on hand to offer spiritual aid. In this respect, the gentleman was something of a radical – a polytheist ('not', he pointed out, 'an agnostic'), he had put together an impressive collection of scraps from numerous sources (religious and otherwise) to create what counted as a Philosophy for General Living. He expounded this with great generosity.

In the present case, having made the official arrest of the man believed to be Otto Cirque and appointed himself custodian of the prisoner, he had taken unto himself the combined activities of the three functionaries above (bailiff, sheriff and constable), as well as the lesser ones of turnkey and general warden. An onerous burden, and it surprised nobody when, two mornings earlier, he had turned his administrative energies to the borrowing of one of Mr Archibald Sherry's most reliable horses. He was soon after seen harnessing Sherry's best mare, and dispatching himself to Pitch, several days' hard ride west, where authority was a much vaunted, highly visible presence, as were the institutions set up to serve it.

It was enough to cause a communal intaking of breath. The ride to Pitch was hazardous and no one had undertaken it for many years. They prayed for Mr Sweetley's safe path and the sure-footedness of his horse.

In his absence, a substitute custodian for the prisoner had to be found.

In previous days, Mrs Hammer might have been considered equal to the task (such was the measure of her competence). Now, however, the duty had been conferred elsewhere; upon, in fact, none other than that woman's husband.

Harbouring a suspicion that he was quite the wrong man for the job, Ernest Hammer resigned himself to it nevertheless, taking with him to the courthouse the small leather briefcase that contained his tools of trade. He had much to do. He had been besieged, in recent days, by pocket watches that had ceased to tick. 'It must be all the grit in the air,' he observed to his wife, 'all the sand and dust and sediment. It has clogged the mechanisms.'

It was true: the grit had got into everything. It was bad enough that one could no longer take a pleasant walk outside but even in the sanctity of one's home one was not safe from windborne residue. It sabotaged the most basic comforts of domestic life: it collected between piano keys and in the perforations of saltcellars. One could not have music. One could not have salt. One could not even have a fire in one's grate: on the contrary, chimneys had to be blocked off completely.

However, it was the watches that worried Ernest Hammer, and he conveyed this worry to his wife when she arrived at the courthouse with his cold luncheon at noon.

Ivorie listened attentively to her husband, nodding in encouragement and disposing of the ham, pickles and cheese she had brought. When he seemed to have exhausted his feelings on the subject, she popped the last onion in her mouth, and wiped her hands on a sheet of Mr Sweetley's copy paper. 'I shall go now,' she said, meaningly, hoping her husband would ask her to stay. He did not. So she pleased herself, and while Ernest held up watches to his ear and made his diagnoses, she took a small peek behind the heavy brocaded curtain that separated Mr Borrel Sweetley's office from the cell containing the prisoner.

She was familiar with Mr Borrel Sweetley's inner sanctum, as he called this portion of his commercial premises, having once conducted business of her own therein (regarding the investment of a small sum of money she had inherited). It did not merely contain a cell, but a small reading library and an enviable leather lounge suite, studded with round brass buttons, in which she had then gratefully reclined.

Now, seeing an actual prisoner contained inside the cell, the true purpose of Sweetley's inner sanctum revealed itself. A wave of pity passed over Ivorie Hammer – that a structure might be built like this to house a human, precisely as it did now, and for no other reason! It vexed her, too, as she moved closer, to see the prisoner provided for so parsimoniously: a tankard (of water, presumably), a camp mattress, a flat pillow, and a grey blanket. She did not mind so much for the prisoner's sake – he was asleep on the camp mattress and did not appear uncomfortable – but in the larger course of things . . . ! Something liberal and passionate stirred in her breast. She came further in and dropped the heavy curtain to the floor behind her.

Like the rest of her townsfolk, Ivorie had not known of this old man's existence. Now, seeing him in the flesh, he remained strangely unconvincing. His body seemed made up of large amounts of air and water, so that he reminded her of a particularly unnerving species of fish Morag had once kept, pink and liquid, in an aquarium. A see-through fish, its bones apparent from the outside. Morag had gone to great lengths to acquire this fish – its transport had taken months of preparation and correspondence – but Ivorie had considered the final product an insult to all normal taxonomical distinctions: it seemed, for instance, to possess *legs*. She bent lower, to look at the old man more closely. She turned her head to the side, and to the side again. No; the old man, like the fish, was not solid in the normal way. And yet, was there something . . . She peered and peered again. Yes, there was something familiar about him, as though perhaps she'd once dreamed him, or read a book in which he'd been a character, or seen him in an old black-and-white engraving. She rested her forehead against the cell bars and placed her hands on top of her stomach, watching him sleep.

The wind had dropped and the room was very quiet and with her eyes closed she could hear the breath going in and out of the old man's chest. She could also hear birds, and a break of laughter, and a heavy box being dropped with a thud. Sunlight came down from the single aperture in Mr Sweetley's cell and fell on the small form of the prisoner. She could see his pulse beating in his temple: how thin is the barrier of skin, she thought. He was so small. And so old. And so utterly unprotected.

She was astonished to find her face damp. 'Mrs Hammer!' she said to herself, putting her fingers to her eyes. 'Come now!' She wiped her eyes again and as she did so, something jangled faintly at her feet – a hairpin dropping onto the stone.

It was only the tiniest sound, but the old man woke.

She patted the front of her hair, whence the hairpin had been dislodged. 'Oh . . .' she said.

She looked down. There was the hairpin on the flagging. It was a nice hairpin, with a little metal bee attached at its bend.

'Oh . . .' she said again, and looked at the prisoner. His eyes caught hers in a gaze she could not decipher. She did not like to put her hand between the bars and get the hairpin. It had fallen a little beyond her reach. She smiled, less confidently than she meant to.

The old man stood and bent and picked up the hairpin. He held it out to her, at arm's length, on the palm of his hand. His hand trembled, but only slightly, and the flesh of his palm was pink and white. The hairpin lay in its crease like a little brown fishhook.

She could not take the hairpin and she could not look him in the eye. She left it there, in his palm, held out, and stepped back through the curtain to resume her role as Ernest Hammer's luncheon-bearing wife. But she did not quite feel like a wife any more. She did not feel hard and brusque with the world. Part of her had become soft and small and a little frightened.

On her husband's side of the curtain, those papers that were not held down by one of Mr Borrel Sweetley's novel paperweights leaped and fluttered about the room. Ernest had tried to render the courthouse impenetrable – draught-stops at the doorway, cardboard panels to reinforce the window glass, three cushions crammed up the chimney flue – but to no avail.

'My dear,' said Ivorie, moving to the door and readying her palm on its handle. 'You should not have bothered with your receipts today!' She opened the door wide, letting in further gusts of wind, and left her husband thus, trying hopelessly to collect from about him the disintegrated blossoms of a vase of everlastings.

Chapter 4

Flying aspirations

There were some things in her life about which Ivorie Hammer was convinced, despite the absence of authenticating facts. One such was: that she did not belong in Canyon, she came from *elsewhere*.

It was not just Morag's infuriating silence on the question of her origins – a silence that, without apparent limits or reasons or conditions, had so soured relations between the two women that their estrangement, at first temporary, had long been an intractable proposition. Nor was it the lack of memorabilia. There was, in Ivorie's possession, a single tin box containing a large curiously shaped earring that Morag told her had belonged to her mother, a copper token stamped with the profile of a woman, and a lock of brittle yellow hair, which had apparently once been connected to her mother's head. The Mary Ann doll, recently repatriated, was a happy addition to this meagre collection. But this woman, her mother, whose actuality was never proven beyond the mementoes described, was the hovering ideal against which Ivorie pitted herself. A presence so elusive that she might make it into anything, but never satisfactorily weight it with flesh and blood. Her mother was sometimes small and frail, sometimes Amazonian in her largeness; sometimes impassive and long-suffering and gentle; sometimes fiery. Morag would tell Ivorie nothing about her, but that she had died – a fact that was not helpful. Even her name was withheld; Ivorie had only the initials on the Mary Ann doll to go by: M.W. As a child, she allowed herself to invent whimsical variations on these letters (her favourite being *Marguerite Willow*) but there was a point at which whimsical names were not enough and actual names were required. 'There is a point,' she told

45

Morag, 'at which I have a right to know!' But Morag was unforthcoming. Still, as painful as this was, Ivorie's sense of difference did not rely solely on the mystery of her mother for its certainty. Nor had it much to do with physical attributes, despite the wealth of evidence on this head: the obvious superiority of Ivorie's figure, for instance, her finer, paler skin. She did not need proof of this kind. She knew she belonged elsewhere like arthritis sufferers feel the weather in their joints, or artists feel the arrival of the muse, or water diviners the telltale tremble of the rod.

She held similar irrational convictions about her pregnancy. On the question of her dual progeny, however, she *had* sought physical proof, though not at the hands of a practitioner of midwifery or obstetrics. If taxed, she would lay her evidence out on the table like playing cards, turning each one up triumphantly: *Ta-da!* First, she would say, no single baby could produce so much incessant activity. (It never stopped! It had four legs, six arms, thirteen fingers on each hand.) Second, there were (incontestably) *two* heads – a very round one, and a slightly round one. (She refused to consider that the slightly round one might in fact be the reverse end of the same child.) Thirdly, she had cravings for the most absurd things: dirt, turnip, whipped cream. And finally (her trump), she had ugly red stretchmarks all over her stomach. She herself knew, from her brief and preferably forgotten apprenticeship with Morag Pappy, that women bearing twins were considerably more likely to develop such wretched marks. Sometimes, when faced with an especially sceptical audience, she would produce the stomach itself to prove her case. It was the sort of demonstration she would never have imagined performing prior to her pregnancy, but such was pregnancy, she sighed, that one inflicts one's body upon whomsoever shows an interest.

She did think the stretchmarks wretched. It looked as though a cart had driven back and forth across her stomach. The merest activity beneath her dress, and when she pulled it up, another faultline had appeared. Sometimes it filled her with panic, this accumulation of ugly red stripes. On better days, it merely reminded her of the little shifts and compromises one made to accommodate one's own life as it unfolded.

Being built of timber, like every other dwelling in Canyon, the house in which Ivorie Hammer and her husband lived had a lopsided, weather-beaten appearance. There was by no means any shame in this. All houses in Canyon boasted an identical quality of downtrodden-ness. Even if inhabitants were the proud owners of damask table linen and silver cutlery, the exteriors of their houses gave no indication that such luxuries existed within.

No one knew how the convention had come about, but nevertheless, it remained inviolable: in Canyon, one did not make improvements to one's abode, unless by unanimous agreement with one's neighbours. The essence of this idea was socially democratic – for what did an unnecessary coat of paint do but render neighbouring houses conspicuously *unpainted*? In practice, however, it merely resulted in the houses of Canyon being uniformly shabby, rundown, barely weatherproof.

Now, as the wind rose, the people of Canyon began to wish they had attended more closely to their window frames and roofs, their shingles and verandah posts and loose weatherboards. Ivorie Hammer had the distinct impression they were about to topple one against the other, these flimsy neglected houses – *flip-flap, flip-flap, flip-flap* – like dominoes, or a city of cards.

Ivorie was returning from the courthouse, her tenth visit in as many days, though she had not visited the prisoner again. She pressed a handkerchief to her face. Her dress blew and flattened against her middle and thighs, and hair whipped across her cheeks. There was a slapping sound above and behind her: the sign from Rosa Minim's schoolhouse, torn off and caught on the hands of the courthouse clock. She made her way across the road, towards the disused amphitheatre. A fence had recently been built around its perimeter to stop children from falling in. The fence was already broken in some places, but being new, it was sufficiently solid, and Ivorie edged herself along it like an ice-skater on a first nervous round of the rink.

She did not like to cast her eyes down over the edge and into the amphitheatre itself. It was not that she feared heights; quite the opposite, in fact: it was *descents* that unnerved her. She could not help looking today though, as she measured her progress along the fence line, and she saw how the wind swirled about the canyon's sides, thick and fast, as if trapped there. You could not see the canyon floor at all.

She believed there was a distinct term for the phenomenon now prevailing in Canyon – something more precise than 'duststorm' – but she could not think of it with her handkerchief flapping in her eyes and her left hand grappling for the wood and wire of the perimeter fence. It occurred to her that perhaps, when the wind ceased, the canyon would have filled in altogether with dust and sand and sediment. Perhaps it would no longer exist and there would only be rolling flat space, as far as the eye could see. The more she thought about it, edging towards home, the more the idea pleased her. She was sure she had read of instances where whole towns were swallowed up completely. 'A *simoon*,' she thought. 'Yes, yes, a lovely big *simoon*.'

She could not sustain this disinterested curiosity when it came to damage inflicted on her own home, however. Arriving at that dwelling, she discovered the back door had been left slightly open, with the result that the floor and tabletops, the grate and windowsills, the bedspreads and twin cots were all covered in quantities of silt and sand. The lamps, when Ivorie lit them, gave out a feeble mauve light. Her pillowcases streaked with dust when she brushed them down with the palm of her hand. She coughed intermittently and blew black stuff into her handkerchief.

She was not, however (and she thought on this gratefully now), incapable of enduring a little dust and dirt. Nor was she one of those overly adapted beings who must do a thing when they see it needs doing. Mrs Ivorie Hammer was not duped by the inexhaustible demands of housewifery. And so, while resenting the state of disarray in which she found her house, she suffered no compunction in putting herself directly to bed for the necessary afternoon nap of the very pregnant.

The babies, however, were resistant to this idea: they kicked and squirmed. Ivorie sat up in bed awhile, listening to the wind and wondering about the durability of her house. Everything creaked and splintered and flapped. She made a few notes in her lady's journal. She pressed her fountain pen to her underlip and thought. On the sidetable, her ointment jars chimed in the vibrations of the wind and the Mary Ann doll made a sound like porcelain teeth on a necklace.

And then the babies stopped. The wind roared outside, but inside

Mrs Ivorie Hammer all became calm. She observed, in passing, the smooth pale skin on the back of her knuckles and fingers, pressed against the open pages of her journal. She held one hand up to her face and turned it this way and that. The skin, when she pinched it between forefinger and thumb, retracted immediately. You could see the blue veins below the surface. 'I was right,' Ivorie said softly, stroking the sleeping babies in her belly. 'The wind has been sent to move us on.' She repeated this curious certainty into the semi-dark and it gave her comfort. The babies were quiet. She had become immensely tired. For the first time in her life, she did not wish to be responsible for anything.

Whatever its intention, the wind now grew impatient. By six o'clock that evening, Mrs Ivorie Hammer was perhaps the only person oblivious to it. She did not hear when part of someone's tin roof blew off and caught against the side of her house, where it shrieked and pounded in the wind; she did not hear the tree in her front yard lurch and heave and split down the middle. A piece of mortar collapsed with a grunt into her fireplace, but she did not notice.

When Ernest returned from the courthouse he found her in a state of slumber from which she could not be roused.

'Ivorie!' he shouted, prising open the violent apparatus that had once been his front door. There was no answer. The door shut on him, blew briefly open; the hall mat lifted from the floor as if possessed of flying aspirations.

'My dear!' shouted Ernest, making his way to their bedroom. 'We must leave at once. We must repair to the hotel.' But Ivorie only turned heavily in her sleep and sighed, leaving Ernest alone with the urgent task of her transportation. Wrapping her in her more weatherproof of overcoats, he half carried, half pushed her into the tempest, and towards the Grand Hotel across the way, well lit and defiantly solid amongst the dust.

Chapter 5

A good woman and a bad-luck charm

Inside the Grand Hotel, papered walls rise to great, vaulted ceilings; and the combination of bluestone underfoot and exposed hard-wood beams above creates an impression of great solidity.

'A reinforced establishment,' says Mr Archibald Sherry, proprietor, supplying large quantities of his namesake liquor, gratis, to the bedraggled persons queuing in his hallway. 'We always trusted in stone.'

His wife says nothing, but fishes for the piece of cord around her neck – upon which, below her collar, hangs an African gris-gris. Once grasped, she holds onto this item as if the circumstances render its wearing more propitious than usual.

The doorway continues to admit small spells of evacuating people, all of whom are met by Mrs Sherry, unburdened of bulky luggage (which would seem presumptuous in the circumstances), supplied with basic victuals (tea, soup, bread) and directed to the expansive dining room, cleared of previous furnishings and kitted out with makeshift trestle beds and sundry items pertaining to human comfort.

'Beds upstairs – all gone,' Mrs Sherry explains, with a general swipe of her hands up and outwards. 'Sheets supplied . . . More soup . . . See Mr Sherry . . .'

But while Mrs Sherry conjures miraculous economies from the linen closet, Mr Sherry perches on a chair arm and dispenses various liquors from various decanters on his sideboard, making his guests comfortable with the pronouncement of irreverencies at the expense of the weather and his wife, and does not so much as fold a blanket or retrieve a butterknife for a slice of bread. Now and again there is a brief explosion against the window glass, signalling the collision of some object there-with, and the fortified, sherry-pink company ceases temporarily its banter. Then: 'Glaziers!' someone says. 'There will be a fine job after all this for the glaziers!' And Mr Sherry proposes a toast to those fine men who commit their labours to the manufacture of sheeted glass; and another again, to the miracle of glass itself, that fabulous compound of sand and soda, without which draught-free living would be well-nigh impossible. (Mrs Sherry, throughout, climbing up and over couches and people and cushions and luggage to adhere yet more waxed tape in criss-cross formation to the window panes.)

Amidst all this revelry, one person remains unusually still and silent. Mrs Ivorie Hammer has recovered her senses after being push-pulled through the night, has eaten a little something from a chipped bowl, watched her husband construct a sleeping apparatus out of a miner's couch and three wooden beer crates, and now composes herself for thought.

Here we must leave her, for her thoughts are of an uncharacteristi-cally abstract bent this night and she will not for some time be roused from them. Perhaps the only detail worthy of remark is that, despite her apparent composure, Mrs Ivorie Hammer's left hand clutches the Mary Ann doll like a small child's would.

Midnight brought the return of Mr Borrel Sweetley, much windswept, from Pitch.

'The authorities,' he announced to the dining room, flinging his raven's wings behind him and placing one knee atop a bar stool, 'have been notified.'

The people of Canyon were all half drunk and half asleep. He wiped his large shining forehead, and resented their lack of enquiry. 'It was a harsh trip, and some of you will wonder that I made it back in such time?'

Silence. He continued in spite of it.

'Nevertheless, the authorities were most interested in our situation and will follow immediately to take charge of the prisoner.' He raised his voice and made his hand into a fist. '*In interim*, be assured that the cell currently holding the prisoner is one hundred per cent secure. The weather cannot touch it. It is unassailable. Indeed, Mr Cirque has no more chance of escaping than the boys from the Tower.' (Which analogy had, unfortunately, little or no meaning to most of his audience.)

He would have gone on in this manner for some time, but what the publican could manage with sherry this evening, Mr Sweetley could not equally inspire with words. In the discovery that no room was available in the hotel (Mrs Sherry twisting her gris-gris anxiously and apologising) he quit the establishment altogether, pulling open the front door with great gusto, and thrusting himself outwards and back to the comforts of his own premises.

The bodies now resumed their interest in sleep. The wind beat an unsteady tattoo against the windows and the walls; a high-pitched whine rose and fell as if the air were strung taut like wire. But here, in the dining room, the comforting warmth of sleeping bodies prevailed.

Mrs Sherry went about the room extinguishing candles and lamps and testing her reinforced windows with a flat palm against the glass. Here and there she secured a blanket about a child's chin, shifted a head more squarely onto its pillow, returned covers to a person whose spouse had usurped their share, and, in short, allowed herself a tenderness denied her in her daily dealings. When all was done, she left her husband where he had fallen, curled about the legs of an armchair, and sat a moment on the bar stool recently vacated by Mr Sweetley, surveying the scene before her.

In this moment of quiet wakefulness, when all others are asleep, Mrs Sherry is suddenly overcome by an entirely new feeling. It flows into her, warm as honey or milk. It is a feeling of goodness, of unconditional empathy for her fellow beings. She clasps her hands together and can feel the tight region around her heart expand and thaw and the warmth spread to her limbs and extremities, like the sap (she thinks) of an ancient living tree. Holding fast to her gris-gris, she believes it has finally imparted its secret to her soul.

And then the feeling is gone. And she is an unloved woman in a room again. She blows out the last candle and retreats.

Chapter 6

In explication of the character of Mr Ernest Hammer

We hope the reader will forgive us if, at this juncture – with Ivorie Hammer safely asleep in secure lodgings – we spend a few moments in analysis of this good woman's husband. For gentle, discreet as he is, Ernest Hammer is also, though one would never guess it, invincible.

Consider his small, innocuous form: there is no bluster or pretension about it. It wears a hat. It wears a shirt. Occasionally it smokes a pipe, but when it does you can be sure it is very clean about it. There is a solidity about this form, however. Looking closely, you might suspect its arms and legs capable of much vigour. The interesting thing about Mr Ernest Hammer is his ability, over time, to cause intractable objects to give way. All that he must do is plant his feet on the ground, and wait.

It was via this method that Ernest Hammer sought, and acquired, his wife. Ivorie proved, however, to be the most recalcitrant of types, and the softening of her heart was only achieved via truly great endeavours.

A slightly-older-than-young woman with a very grave face and fine skin, Ivorie resembled her former guardian, Miss Morag Pappy, in no manner whatsoever. In fact, ever since her release from that woman's guardianship, she had been at great pains to erase all evidence that might connect them. Certainly, there was nothing in Ivorie's elegant stride that reminded one of the dull, insistent walk of Miss Pappy. There remained not a single expression or turn of phrase that marked them as having ever belonged to one another. And yet there was one thing they had in common, and this was their ostentatious commitment to spinsterhood.

Morag Pappy's state of spinsterhood did not seem to have come about by choice. It seemed far more probable that circumstance had imposed it upon her. But the way she maintained her independence singled her out from other lone females. She ruffled it up about her throat as though it were an expensive collar. She pronounced the word 'Miss' between her teeth as though it were an aristocratic title. Even when she sat with her feet in a bucket, soothing her corns, and enquiring into the state of a particularly worrisome placenta previa, she retained still her essential quality of 'Missness'.

On Ivorie's part, the state of spinsterhood was inextricably tied up with her vanity. There were philosophical underpinnings to it certainly – any interlocuter hazarding a question would find himself instantly demolished by the force of her philosophical underpinnings. She had read certain books, ordered from subversive book clubs to which she subscribed. And unlike other girls, she suffered no suspension of her rational faculties upon spying a white lace bridal display in a dressmaker's window. Indeed, she picked confetti derisively from her hair and collar if it had the audacity to land there in the course of other people's marital proceedings.

Ivorie's objection to the marital state, however, was somewhat less convincing than that supplied by emancipatory rhetoric. It was this: that marriage did harm – great harm! – to one's face and figure. Everywhere about her she saw the evidence: once women married, they inevitably coarsened, their pores enlarged, their hipbones broadened, their bosoms and their behinds swelled to alarming proportions. They gave in, it seemed to Ivorie, to the pull of gravity.

And so Ivorie courted her spinsterhood like another woman might a well-situated gentleman – without respite, and with much attention to personal grooming. So fetching was she in her bodiced, dark-coloured spinster dresses; so mindful was she of the turn of her ankle in her narrow maiden-aunt shoes; and so milky and fresh was her complexion that she gave the impression of being scarcely mortal.

'I shall never marry,' she pronounced upon quitting the home of her guardian. We must be lenient with her. She was only seventeen years old. She was wearing a pair of her guardian's stockings and they wrinkled about her kneecaps. 'I shall remain alone now, forever,' she said.

Hearts went out to her. Really – and everyone understood this – Ivorie had brought herself up.

Upon quitting Morag Pappy, her former guardian had given Ivorie a large sum of money in a flat grey wallet – 'Your inheritance,' Morag said, declining to explain further. Ivorie knew better than to enquire. She transferred the contents of the wallet into a receptacle of her own choosing and decided that everything she put on herself from now on would be fresh and new and previously unworn. Everything would smell like herself. Everything would be compelled upwards: suspenders would hold stockings alert; waists would properly retract; undergarments would cling neatly to hips and legs. She purchased these items, fresh and flat and undarned, along with a mail-order dictionary, two inches deep and leather bound; the remainder of her inheritance she wisely put aside.

Thereafter, Ivorie acquitted herself exceptionally upon the stage of her own drama. Hers was not quite a tragedy, yet it had at its base a hard kernel of sadness, upon which she expended much time and energy, till it was a lovely smooth polished thing, whose origin she could no longer properly recall. As time went on she began to see her sad, melancholy solitude as a vehicle for something, but was unable to remember precisely what. She patted her inheritance, but did not spend it.

In the meantime, keeping her head alert and her vertebrae in correct alignment, she accepted a position as a seamstress under Mrs Ava Haricot, a highly strung local woman given to threatening her underlings with a large darning needle in moments of high tension. Ivorie endured the minor hardships of her work environment – steam, bad ventilation, inadequate lighting – and became a permanent lodger at the Grand Hotel, where she spent her leisure time quietly tending to her complexion and turning the pages of her dictionary. She did not mend the rift with her guardian.

As the years progressed she earned a substantial reputation for her moral rectitude and expansive vocabulary. It was unanimously agreed that Ivorie could *put a thing* like no one else. You could count on her, in fact, to put a thing *just* the way it ought to be put. Her opinion was regularly canvassed, and though often unable to provide any real succour, she gave a very good impression of wisdom. She was able to pitch old things from new angles and crystallise otherwise vague sentiments; to articulate, in more economical form, great and complex dissatisfactions. In this way, she made herself necessary to them. Yet the more necessary she became, the more aloof also. She was hard and glassy and unreachable: a sheer cliff face one might peer up at respectfully, but never actually climb.

What could possibly have occurred then to soften such an altitude? Who might be qualified to scale so painfully sheer a height? Mr Ernest Hammer was of the mountain-goat species, but even then, with a good head for heights and the ability to survive on meagre rations, it took him nearly a decade to win Ivorie over. Still, it was to his credit that he persisted in the face of her much-publicised stance on the subjects of love and marriage.

He himself was no expert on those subjects, but he had reason at least to believe himself a novice in the arts of the former. Ivorie, as he saw her, was an inventory of perfect details:

- a miniature waist, which gathered inwards in a mayhem of darts and hooks and invisible binding;
- an aquiline nose, with the tendency to dilate vigorously upon the pronouncement of an opinion;
- wrists that extended elegantly from beneath the confines of neatly turned cuffs;
- sumptuous hair, which escaped in small black loops from its pins;
- a pale white ring finger, which clutched on a purse, an armrest, a pair of flesh-coloured gloves . . .

These attributes, when assembled, formed such a complete picture of his beloved that Ernest did not require extensive recourse to the original. When summoned to her, for a game of cards or a glass of dessert wine, the thought of all her attributes in fluid, integrated motion was almost too much to bear.

And then, suddenly, with no pre-emptive signs, after refusing so long to even entertain the notion, Ivorie accepted Ernest Hammer, married him (quietly) and became almost immediately pregnant.

She was thirty-nine years old.

She had a little premature down on her chin, and her youthful wisdom was hardening into what might in time be called an authoritative manner.

What had Ernest Hammer known? How had he persuaded her?

Quite simply, Ernest Hammer had patience. He was prepared to wait and watch. He loved Ivorie, but he also recognised her foibles. And above all, he knew about clocks.

Tick-tick-tick went Ivorie's clock. It came from deep down inside her abdomen. It chimed in moments of unguardedness: when Mrs Grosvenor's pretty niece requested her, 'Please thread me this needle, Miss Ivorie . . .'; when one of the Fancy girls fell from a fence and required her assistance in the application of sticking plaster; when Will Tooth brought her a painted wooden footstool 'too small for any other lady's foot'. Her clock chimed. It gleamed gold and white inside her and sometimes made her clumsy.

Truth was, the maiden aunt role did not become her as before. She could not help but recognise that the life of the spinster was a cold and lonely prospect not satisfactorily ameliorated by public admiration for one's skin and moral rectitude. The precise contour of Ivorie's youthful ambitions had blurred some time ago, and she had begun to grow frightened. Her head ached at odd intervals, and something in her spine cracked when she reached for objects on high shelves. She had alarming dreams in which she was pressed, pastry-like, upon the flat, hard earth of the amphitheatre floor and could not move.

Ernest Hammer intuited these feelings. He did not openly exploit them, but they did inform the method of his seduction. He sent Ivorie seemingly innocuous gifts: small papier-mâché boxes in which to keep hat pins; postcards mounted in brass frames; imported china figurines. Each bore some reference to maternity: a cherub depicted on the glazed lid of the hat pin box; a Madonna and Child gazing listlessly from the brass picture frame; a bone-china peasant woman attempting to transport a small child across a sty.

In the dispatch of these gifts, Ernest was neither too forthcoming nor too reticent. The gifts arrived. They were duly opened, admired, and assigned a position in Ivorie's hierarchy of things. She speculated a moment on the identity of her gift-giving admirer. She opened a window and looked down into Main Parade. The dying palm trees snuffled like parched elephants in the breeze. The dust rose briskly and fell again. And there was Mr Hammer, loitering below her window, but in such an undemanding, non-threatening way that she felt her personal freedoms in no way impinged upon. In time she began to seek his form with nothing short of anticipation. If she experienced aggravation in any capacity of her life, his quiet regularity allayed it. If the day was hard and made her frown, his presence soothed and softened that portion of her brow thus afflicted. Still, it took the expiration of five whole years before she would invite him to her room for a glass of the aforementioned wine. And it was another five before she assented to offers of marriage which, though present in Ernest's every gesture and expression, never found their way onto his tongue – allowing Ivorie to believe in the end that it was *she* who had initiated the idea, which in turn enabled her to carry it through to its natural conclusion without feeling her principles in any way compromised.

'A woman's prerogative . . .' she said if quizzed on her about-turn. Or, more evasively, 'Wisdom is not gained by wisdom alone, you know.'

Chapter 7

Two fellows consider their civic duties

There was a difference in the air the next morning. The sun, when it rose swollen and misshapen on the horizon, had a strange dusty heat in it, and the wind had changed direction.

Overnight Mr Sweetley had left his prisoner under the vigilant watch of Lawrence, his some-time clerk and errands boy. He himself had spent the night comfortably in his upstairs apartment, where the weather might clamour at his windows, but could not dent his peace of mind. Next morning, he emerged well rested from beneath the covers. His chickens were squawking in the adjoining bedroom, where they had been sequestered the previous afternoon upon the collapse of the hen house; and when Sweetley went to check, he found two brown eggs deposited in the curtain hem.

He placed the eggs in a bowl on his dressing table, and took a long hard look in the mirror. He pared his lips back in a grimace; then, holding the lax skin on his chin in place with one hand, patted it firmly, briskly with the other, counting as he did so. He was well into his second round of hundreds when he heard a commotion on the stairs, a crash of feet and a kind of choking sob. Before he could enquire, his door was swung open so violently it cracked the glass housing a print on the adjacent wall. Lawrence did not pause, as he might usually, to apologise and retrieve the glass, but threw himself on his employer, and shook him with such gusto that Mr Sweetley's vulnerable jawline shucked its slack skin to and fro like a turkey's neck.

'He's gotten out! He's got away,' shrieked Lawrence.

Sweetley, detaching Lawrence from his pyjama collar, proceeded immediately to the stairwell.

'I swear I didn't fall asleep for long, sir,' cried Lawrence, right behind him, 'just two minutes, or three. I trained my eyes on him all night just like you said. Here's the key, and it has not left my hand. The bars have not been broken, sir. There ain't no hole in the floor. Indeed, there's no escape unless he were a conjurer that could conjure himself through solid walls . . .'

Sweetley did not hear this last utterance; he was down stairs, heart pounding, at the scene of the prisoner's escape. Needless to say, the cell was empty.

The padlock did not appear to have been in any way tampered with — and Lawrence was right, there was no obvious point of egress to be found. Sweetley could not make it out. He prowled the cell for a good quarter-hour, tapping his foot in search of unwarranted echoes, investigating methodically the three enclosing walls, slipping one shoulder between the bars to test the possibilities available to more slippery human forms than himself. In other circumstances he would have congratulated himself on the cell's evident impregnability; as it was, having exhausted his faculties of reason, he could only drop now onto the cold hard flagging, with his elbows about his head, and await the arrival of the authorities.

It was a quarter to seven in the morning when the publican awoke to find himself concertinaed between two chairlegs and an ornamental footstool. He had kicked off his small share of blankets in the preceding hours but was by no means cold: on the contrary, the room sweated and steamed.

He stretched his neck and disentangled his limbs. His head felt compressed as never before. He rose partially, and then dropped back onto his knees.

There existed no easy pathway between the assortment of bodies on the floor. Sherry made his way groggily through them and headed for the front door, peering first through the rose-coloured glass panels in case they might provide an edifying glimpse of the outside world (which they did not, being of frosted glass), then attempting to look through the letter-slot (which provided only a disappointing view of the front doorstep), and finally, applying himself to the door handle, which, when released, brought the door suddenly open in an onslaught of hot, dry wind. Once outside, he managed to make purchase on the side-whiskers of one of the stone lions on the hotel portico. He held fast, and surveyed his countrymen's prospects.

Archibald Sherry was a man who found opportunity in the most meagre of circumstances, the tiniest pockets, the darkest nooks. But even he could see no way to turn this immediately to advantage. All around him, timber dwellings gaped with holes. Thatched roofs had lifted free and dessicated across the district. Wooden pins had not held down rafters, and revolving pivots in doorways had proved unequal to iron hinges – doors and shutters swung miserably from single points of attachment, or had been thrown off altogether and clattered dejectedly down steps or had become lodged in fence rails. The accumulated wealth of bird and possum nests in ceilings, vaults and eaves had been exposed to the weather, and the debris thereof – along with feathers from sacks burst open, inadequately secured bags of meal, soot and ash from fireplaces, lime and soda and flour, chicken feed and straw and sand – all flew in a tremendous combined agitation (like failed lottery tickets, thought Mr Sherry obtusely, in a blast of furnace heat).

Mr Sherry was mortified to discover that even the bank, which he'd long admired as an exemplary piece of stonework, was not actually stone at all, but constructed of weatherboards cut and painted to *resemble* stone. Several portions of this facade had broken loose and Sherry hoped fervently that the bank vault was indeed fashioned of genuine steel and not, in similar manner, of some inferior material *conniving* at being steel.

The only buildings that remained intact were his hotel, Borrel Sweetley's courthouse and the abode of Morag Pappy, which, while several decades old, had been built according to construction principles not shared by the rest of Canyon, and now proved its superiority by remaining almost entirely unscathed.

The whole region was dark with dust and silt and sand.

Sherry really did have to work hard to find a good slant on all this but ultimately he realised his hospitality might be imposed upon for longer than originally indicated. It then occurred to him that he could hardly be expected to provide indefinite periods of hospitality to indefinite multitudes of persons without some hope of remuneration. He then took to calculating (for, slow at other things, he had a quick mind for numbers) what pecuniary advantages might accrue to him. The resultant figure was not disappointing.

The publican began now to experience a strange sense of satisfaction at the turn of events. He felt light and ebullient. He clung to the stone lion in a kind of elemental fellowship. If he should let go, he thought, he might be carried off like a balloon.

In this pose, he was not at leisure to notice a black-suited figure advancing down the road, and so was unaware of Borrel Sweetley until that man was actually upon him, coat-tails billowing so it seemed to be the apparel and not the man therein that accosted him.

'Open up!' Sweetley demanded, pounding on Sherry's back. 'Open up! No time to lose! Must act quickly!'

Bald Sherry gave a start, let go of the lion, and did what he was instructed as well as he could with Sweetley's appreciable volume bearing down upon him. The door was brought open and the two men tumbled in onto the hall runner. Mr Sherry jammed the door shut with his free foot, and Sweetley, untangling his coat-tails, brought them into submission about his torso.

Borrel Sweetley was swift in assuming an office-bearing demeanour, but upon entering the dining room (where the majority of evacuees were now, if not dressed, in a state very near it) he was unable to activate his usual qualities of leadership. He lifted his hands, opened his mouth as if to impart something of great moment (they all waited), and promptly shut it again, with an involuntary clink of his very large, very white teeth. A thin hiss of air escaped from between them, and he sank into a nearby armchair.

'Well?' said Archibald Sherry, after an extended pause in which Sweetley only sighed once or twice and looked with profound regret at his trouser knees. 'Well, Mr Sweetley? What of it outside then? We have *weather* – do we have houses left?'

Mr Sweetley relinquished his gaze upon his knees, but though drawing air in again as if to speak, found he could not. The best he could do was utter 'The authorities . . .' and return his attention to his pants' knees.

'Devastation!' said Mr Sherry all of a sudden, interposing himself between Sweetley and the room. He said it gleefully, like an excited child in a sandbox. He made a shearing motion with the edge of one hand against the flat of the other, and whistled a toppling, demolition-inflected whistle. 'Devastation,' he said again, and shook his head. 'Not – much – left – standing.'

There ensued much excitement throughout the room at this: recriminations between husbands and wives; frettings over animals and possessions; and many fitful starts towards the door – which Bald Sherry managed to avert, uncapping yet another decanter of whisky-coloured liquor.

It was wholly negligent, Sherry thought, that in this crisis, the two individuals whose guidance they most relied on – Mr Sweetley and Mrs Hammer – had sunk independently into states of unresponse. So he called on Nelly, the maid, who had been sometime occupied in the dismantling of beds, and sent her to wake his wife, who, as he added, 'has no call to be keeping in and leaving *me* to all *this*!'

Nelly dispatched, the people of Canyon drank. Mr Sweetley and Mrs Ivorie Hammer stayed still, and the clamour rose about them.

Bald Sherry had just given himself over to thoughts of his horses when a piercing cry, ringing from the back quarters of the hotel, cut through the lesser sounds of communal chaos and entered his whisky-sodden heart. Like a skewer in butter, it slid in deep and without obstruction; he did not properly register it even when it made its exit out the other side.

Chapter 8

Pecking orders come undone, and other articles are fatally fastened

Oh, most vicious of fates! Most pernicious of narratives – to heap misery upon misery and murder upon murder! For, on entering the bedchamber of Mrs Sherry, Nelly had been met not with that slightly wet, percussive snore to which she was accustomed, nor to the spectacle of Mrs Sherry in some difficulty with her tight lacings (to which she was also accustomed), but with an absence of sound altogether, and, at eye level, a pair of cold white feet.

Hence, the cry expelled from her lungs, for above the feet swung the body of Mrs Sherry, face turned sideways, mouth half open, and neck – Mrs Sherry's sure white neck, which had nodded at Nelly, and strung itself into hard knots to help Nelly lift tubs of water, empty a boiler, carry in firewood – Mrs Sherry's neck was pulled taut by the cord of her gris-gris, strung up and over the curtain rod.

With an effort of almost super-human proportions, Nelly manoeuvred Mrs Sherry down from the curtain rod and onto the bed. She rolled her to the side and back again, till the sheets covered her.

'Let me in!' shouted Mr Sherry from the other side of the door. 'Confound you, miss! I shall break down this door.'

'I'm coming, sir,' said Nelly, sobbing audibly once more. She coaxed Mrs Sherry's eyelids shut and smoothed her brow. 'Only allow me a moment, sir, to compose myself.' The final impression was convincing: Mrs Sherry to all outward appearances had not hanged herself; she had died in her sleep.

Now Nelly took from her apron pocket a small pair of nail scissors and, inching the blade gently between Mrs Sherry's skin and the taut double-knotted gris-gris, she snipped the latter free, bundled it into her apron pocket, and stroked Mrs Sherry's cool ruined neck with the back of her hand. When she let Mr Sherry in, there was no sign of self-disgrace.

It is an oft-observed phenomenon that the accumulation of tragedies does not always meet with a corresponding accumulation of despair. Or rather, that despair, when added to despair, has sometimes the effect of nullifying itself.

It was in this way, dry-eyed and utterly still, that the population of Canyon responded to the latest tragedy. But where pity faltered, fear stepped in. People looked shiftily at their neighbour, and at their neighbour's neighbour, and put uncertain hands to their hearts. Mrs Sherry was dead, and it would seem possible she had been murdered.

Only Racine Pfeffersalz, the octogenarian amongst them, was unaffected. She arranged for Morag Pappy to be fetched and retreated to the kitchen for boiled water and shredded linen, correctly supposing that, for the ceremony of death, materials similar to those employed at a birth might be required.

Borrel Sweetley had long ago triumphed over any personal queasiness on the subject of death. He had, in his time, presided over so many funerals, made out so many death certificates and levied so many death duties that he could afford to be businesslike about the matter. He had even found himself acting, by default, the role of mortician several times in his career, and had once, many years ago, been forced by circumstance to cut a dead man from the wheels of a buggy that had driven over him. So what now perturbed him about the body of Mrs Sherry was not the unsightly ring of evidence about its neck, but the absence of the gris-gris, which would seem to have been responsible for it.

Mr Sweetley was more likely than any to recall Mrs Sherry's fretful attachment to that item of jewellery. It was he who had sold it to her. He remembered the transaction quite clearly: Mrs Sherry had seen the oddly shaped ornament in his collection and had admired it. He had invented a little story about its origins and symbolic purpose. It was an African curio, he told her, believed to impart good fortune and happiness to its wearer.

How old was it? Mrs Sherry wanted to know.

Oh, *centuries* old, Mr Sweetley had said.

Money was exchanged. Mrs Sherry held the African good luck charm gently between her fingers. He offered to put it on a silver chain for her, but, Oh no, she said. She liked it as it was. She only wanted a bit of leather with which she might do it up round her neck. That would be more in keeping, she said, with its African origins.

Of course, it did not have African origins at all. The strange object had been brought to Mr Sweetley's attention by Julian Paratha one cold September morning. He had shown Sweetley the artefact and Mr Sweetley had agreed that it might be a souvenir from the days of Arcadia's Saturnalia. But he did not really mind about its provenance. He was taken with the thing in and of itself. It had a lovely shape and polish to it, and he guessed it was made of amber. He shook Julian Paratha's hand and told him he would forward the appropriate commission upon sale.

He had not, of course, but that was the least of his worries right now. For the second time that morning, Borrel Sweetley felt the failure of his authority rise like an alien beast in his throat.

He was struggling with this beast when Nelly re-entered Mrs Sherry's bedchamber with a large tureen of hot water. She started to find him there, sitting quietly beside the body, and put the water down less gently than she intended, so a little splashed on Mr Sweetley's shoe.

'Nelly,' said Sweetley softly, and crooked his finger towards her.

She wiped her hands on her apron. 'Yes, Mr Sweetley?' She knelt down, as he seemed to be suggesting, so her ear was near his mouth. His breath smelt of pineapple.

'The gris-gris,' he whispered. 'When you found her . . . was she wearing it?'

Nelly was not a good liar. On account of this failing, she had never made the most of the perquisites of her profession – small keepsakes, confidences, good-quality stockings. Thus it was fortunate that, at the precise moment when an answer was required of her, Mr Sweetley's pocket watch suddenly set up an ear-splitting trill. It continued to ring for a full half-minute before Mr Sweetley managed to activate its off lever. Nelly, meanwhile, ducked out of the room.

But the resumption of activity in Mr Sweetley's trouser pocket did more than provide Nelly with an opportune escape route. In recent days, Sweetley's pocket watch had, like so many other timepieces in Canyon, ceased altogether to function. It had become ominously silent. It no longer even ticked. Now, its sudden, sparkling revival, echoing through the hotel's nervous system, had the effect that a bump on the head or an electric shock can sometimes have on a severely despondent patient. It reactivated normal instincts. It reminded everyone that the minutes continued to anticipate the passing of hours, that the hours continued to constitute days, and that the days themselves could not help but form together into weeks. That such phenomena could persist, uninfluenced by bones, wind or inexplicable deaths seemed entirely miraculous! Hands dropped from necks and hearts; chatter started up again in the various rooms and passages of the hotel; suspicion sizzled out like an ant beneath a magnifying glass.

Borrel Sweetley stood up. He felt his natural facility for leadership return. He marched into the hall, flung his coat-tails out behind him, cleared his throat, and tapped three times on the wooden dado.

'My friends,' he began, when attention was satisfactorily fixed upon him. 'My friends . . .'

But he succeeded only in prefacing his speech thus, for a sudden beating at the door caused the sea of heads to turn, dumbly, to witness the arrival of Morag Pappy.

Miss Pappy had always a disquieting effect upon Mr Sweetley. He could not reconcile the opposing ideas that Miss Pappy represented: her unblemished professionalism, on the one hand, and her acute personal neglect on the other. It seemed wrong to him somehow. It *was* wrong! It did not follow that someone could show so little attention to their articles of trade as to carry them about, unpolished, uncared for, and still elicit respect from all quarters.

Morag did not say anything upon her arrival, but surveyed them all with an inordinately bland expression. 'Mr Sweetley,' she said, and looked at him briefly. She took off a large wind-blown coat and continued down the hallway, disappearing into the small nether passageways that led to Mrs Sherry's bedchamber.

It was a disappointment to everyone that Morag might arrive, offer not a single word of warmth or encouragement, and immediately sequester herself in the dead woman's room. It was a disappointment, but it was hardly a surprise. Morag had been known to attend three-day labours without uttering a single word of warmth or encouragement. If warmth or encouragement were required, one would not turn to that large brown woman for it. Her absolute competence in the practical world precluded her from being any use in the subtler realms of the heart and psyche. No, if warmth or encouragement were required, one would turn to Ivorie Hammer – and though she laced her warmth and encouragement with copious amounts of sternness, plenty of precautionary lingo, and much hearty admonition, she was always reassuring, one could always rely on her. One could always arrive home afterwards, take one's bonnet off, rest one's feet at the hearth and say: 'Well, now, I have *seen Mrs Hammer* . . .'

But Ivorie Hammer was lost to them today. She sat in the dining room with her back straight, and her face turned away. Something had blown into her hair, and she had not bothered to disentangle it. Her husband sat beside her, reading to her from a book.

In fact, Morag's arrival had introduced a fresh cause for concern. Flurries of dust and sand had accompanied her through the doorway, along with bits of twig and dried yellow grass. But another element had also been introduced; a bitter noxious element. There was a strange velvety dust on Morag's coat, hanging in the hallway. What looked like a soft grey butterfly wing floated gently onto Borrel Sweetley's shoulder and when he went to brush it off, it disintegrated like talcum powder.

Mr Sweetley's brain perversely refused to register the significance of this strange grey substance. His forehead, however, had begun to sweat profusely, and he was just in the process of removing his coat and fortifying himself yet again to make his speech when a second pounding commenced on the front door, accompanied by a loud 'Open UP!' uttered in tones of unquestionable authority. This instruction being immediately fulfilled, the dust and smoke and ash (yes, smoke; of course, ash!) received temporary readmission, and then cleared to reveal the latest addition to the party. In charcoal-coloured greatcoats, much singed about the hems and cuffs, it was none other than the authorities (who could mistake them?) wearing dark expressions and brutal moustaches.

Wasting no time, these men clambered in over the doorstep, stamped their boots, brushed down their coats, and announced themselves 'in the service of the Municipality of Greater Pitch'.

Chapter 9

The Municipal Authority of Greater Pitch

They were impressive men, those representing the Municipal Authority of Greater Pitch. When they looked at the people of Canyon gathered in the hotel hallway, their eyes grazed the tops of heads. The man who was their superior was particularly impressive. He took a step forwards and dropped his gaze to the common eye level, stooping a little to do so.

'We have fought your fires!' he said, meaningly. His voice was gravelly and not entirely unpleasing. He looked into their faces, searchingly, as if discovering the arsonist amongst them. 'We did not come here to be *firefighters*.' He shifted his weight a little, leaning towards them as though resting his upper body on a walking stick or up-ended musket. 'It was not part of our instruction.' Several of the women observed an interesting ripple animate the side of his jaw. 'Nevertheless,' he continued, 'we have put your fires out. They have abated, most of them. For how long, is not for us to say. However –' He stopped and, meaning to remove it, smudged a flake of ash across his forehead. 'We did not come here to ruminate on such things. We have come here . . .' He sustained a pause, '. . . to take custody of a dangerous criminal.'

He now withdrew from his pocket a very official-looking cream-coloured document with a broken wax seal and fancy script. 'We have it on the authority of Mr Borrel Sweetley, Justice of the Peace, that a suspected murderer is held here, in temporary confinement, and must be transported, under guard, to the Greater Pitch Penitentiary.'

There was a pause and then Mr Borrel Sweetley stepped forwards to present himself, bowing deeply.

The face of the superior officer relaxed. 'Aha, Mr Sweetley – Conduct us, if you may, to your lockup. We do not waste time, Mr Sweetley. We have snuffed already time and fires enough!'

Sweetley looked unhappily down to the floor, back to the Senior Sergeant (for this was his rightful title, and we might as well call him by it) and fastened on that man's greatcoat, upon which a vertical row of brass buttons shone, more brilliantly than they would seem to have a right to, having just borne their wearer through a heroic campaign of firefighting.

Mr Sweetley sought now to usher the Senior Sergeant into more private quarters. But when he attempted to guide him thus, the Senior Sergeant moved his elbow conspicuously out of reach.

'There has been –' began Mr Sweetley, and he smiled stupidly, 'something of a mishap.' Sweetley hated to apply the term 'sir' when it was not reciprocated, but nevertheless: 'Indeed, sir, there has been *another* tragic occurrence since my notification – another death, a suspicious death. They are in there now, preparing the body for interment.'

Morag Pappy opened the bedchamber door at the Senior Sergeant's first authoritative knock. She acknowledged him without a hint of surprise, and moved her chair out from the bed so as to accommodate his inspection of the victim.

The Senior Sergeant leaned delicately over Mrs Sherry's body, his hands clasped behind his back. He indicated for Morag to draw the sheet back, which she did, very cleanly and swiftly, down to the dead woman's waist. He noted the bruising about the neck. He paid special attention to a mark about the dead woman's collarbone that remained much lighter in colour than the skin which surrounded it. He measured it and sketched its peculiar shape in his notebook.

'Have articles been removed from the body?' he asked, seemingly to the world at large, but mainly to Morag Pappy, who did not answer. He repeated his question loudly to those gathered in the narrow passage beyond, who did not respond except to look baffled. The Senior Sergeant spied the widower and beckoned him closer.

'Did you, Mr Sherry, remove any trinket from about your wife's neck?'

Mr Sherry put his hands up, as well as his shoulders, and then dropped them again.

'Come now,' said the Senior Sergeant, smiling a not disingenuous smile. 'A man understands another man's need for mementoes. A gift given, perhaps?' He put a hand on Bald Sherry's shoulder. 'Naturally, any items will be returned once investigations are complete . . .'

Bald Sherry wracked his brain but could not summon into being any trinkets, any gifts. He had been so long in the habit of looking at his wife and not seeing her that the presence, or absence, of ornaments upon her person was moot.

The Senior Sergeant contained his frustration. He returned to the bed-chamber and shut the door behind him. Inside, Morag was rolling small portions of cotton wool into balls and lining them up on the dressing table.

'My dear lady,' he said, arranging himself at the end of the bed. 'I understand your discretion.'

Morag Pappy smiled her indefatigable smile, which gave up nothing.

'But it is not in your interests to hinder us. We are only here to assist.'

Morag ripped a strip of white cloth and dipped it into a bucket of steaming water. She did not appear to have heard him.

'Will you tell me, madam,' he continued, 'if there was anything upon the person of the deceased that, now removed, might contribute to our understanding of her death? Anything that might have produced that mark on her chest?'

Morag looked up, a strip of wet white cloth dripping from her hand. 'Sunspot,' she said.

She did not rush. She squeezed the water out of the dripping cloth and laid it on the edge of the dressing table. She then rolled back the sleeve on her right arm till excess flesh inhibited its further progress, and turned her elbow to the perpendicular. The skin on her arm, the Senior Sergeant saw, was brown all over, but not so on her elbow, which had the appearance of having been dipped, accidentally, in whitewash. 'Ah . . .' said the Senior Sergeant. He pulled his head back from the elbow (Morag kept it hovering there, in line with his eyes) and noticed she had another similar blemish, smaller in size, on the side of her neck.

'Sunspot,' she said, and, nodding slowly, pulled the offending elbow away.

Out in the hallway, Borrel Sweetley had broken into a sweat. His breath was coming in bursts. He wanted desperately to avail himself of the Senior Sergeant's attention, but the Senior Sergeant was busy getting down details: dates and times and names. With a pencil, he drew diagrams in his notebook. He solicited information from Bald Sherry with short sharp jabs of his pointer finger. But nowhere did he provide a point of purchase for Mr Sweetley. Finally he shut the notebook and returned it to the inside pocket of his coat.

'Now,' he said, turning to face Borrel Sweetley. 'I trust everything is resolved to your satisfaction? To the perpetrator! To your lockup, Mr Sweetley!'

Mr Borrel Sweetley sank heavily, miserably, into his midriff. He shook his left leg to worry the trouser cuff back over his boot heel. He twisted and counter-twisted and said finally, 'I do not know what to say! I have the key . . .' He produced this item and passed it to the Senior Sergeant. 'It was on account of the laxity of my clerk . . .' He turned now to his fellow townspeople and implored them with slightly upraised palms. 'He did not mind the prisoner. He let him through his hands somehow. It's confounding, entirely confounding. I have no explanation.'

'What exactly are you saying?' said the Senior Sergeant, suddenly overcome with fatigue.

Mr Sweetley put his arms out, limp at the wrists, as if the shackles brought for Otto Cirque might rightfully, legitimately, be secured thereabouts. 'The prisoner has escaped.'

Chapter 10

The aftermath of battle

Upon what, all this time, has the good Mrs Ivorie Hammer been cogitating? Though we might attempt to plot with words the general geography of her reverie, it is doubtful we could adequately describe the battle playing out in Mrs Ivorie Hammer's conscience. As with most matters of the psyche, potency falls away as soon as words are attached.

But make no mistake, hers has been no idle rumination. Mrs Ivorie Hammer has not retreated into the soft, warm nesting-world of the very pregnant. Hers has been a delirium of epic proportions, a battleground, upon which swords crashed and horses reared. There have been thrusts and counter-thrusts; retreats and advances as intelligent conclusions vied with less-intelligent ones for supremacy. Now, as she comes to, Mrs Hammer finds that certain facts are much clearer in the aftermath of battle. Certain obstacles, which last night seemed insurmountable, are no longer any such thing. Patriotic banners have fallen limply in the dust and dirt. Upon the disposal of some rubble, the ground might be comfortably traversed. She can see a golden-haired woman with an enigmatic smile coming through the dust carrying a child in her arms.

Mrs Ivorie Hammer comes to and is oddly surprised to find herself in her undershirt. Not only that, but the undershirt is sticking unpleasantly to her belly and upper arms. It is hot. She is sticky. She does not need to see smoke to register the presence of fire.

All about them, there was the smell of spent fire now: in the air; seeping between floorboards and roof tiles and door cracks; trickling in diamond formation through taped-up glass.

By the time Mrs Ivorie Hammer returned the smell of fire and ash was paramount.

Left to themselves, and replenished by a large evening meal of salted mutton, the people of Canyon had become expressive again. They began to talk excitedly of 'recovery missions'. Lists were consigned to husbands detailing articles that might be rescued from the wreckage of domestic premises. But when the men made for the front door, they found their progress impeded by the presence of a large and intransigent lesser constable.

Lesser he might have been, this bulwark-shaped constable, but he was no less inclined to follow his instructions than his more senior colleague. Indeed, the Pitchian constabulary took their offices very seriously. In light of this, the bulwark-shaped constable was maintaining the peace with every pore of his being.

The menfolk of Canyon had no alternative but to sit quietly and watch their watcher for signs that his vigilance might relax.

Ivorie Hammer, in the dining room, in a gentle, post-cogitational swoon. It was their luck to have her back.

'It is our luck,' they said, wetting her brow with a damp sponge and popping peppermints into her mouth, 'to have you back.'

They groomed her silently, carrying her back to them through the gentle motions of brush and comb.

Finally Ivorie Hammer was fresh and clean again, and they turned their attention to her vital signs. Her ankles and feet, they discovered, were noticeably swollen. It was vaguely remembered – from pregnancies of their own – that this could be a worrying symptom – of what, they were not sure – and recommended that Morag Pappy be called on for a 'professional examination'. Morag had returned home some time ago, accompanied by Nelly the parlourmaid, but they felt sure she would return immediately for Ivorie's sake.

Ivorie had said little so far beyond 'tea' and 'yes, please' and 'thank you, thank you', but now she unleashed a sequence of protestations which featured among them very determined repetition of the word 'No'. Even in her weakened state, she was not a woman to be crossed.

Her friends quickly withdrew their suggestion, and made efforts to repair what damage they had inadvertently done, declaring that large quantities of weak tea would relieve any undue swelling. The kettle was boiled and the dregs from her last cup disposed of.

They fell silent. Mrs Hammer sipped. The wind bullied the windows and sent hot gasps through unplugged crevices.

Chapter 11

The Senior Sergeant

When the Senior Sergeant returned, not long after sunset, it was to the women that he applied himself. He left his men in the hallway, along with a deflated Mr Borrel Sweetley, and entered the dining room alone.

Before we venture further and reveal the grave nature of the Senior Sergeant's intimations, let us hover a few moments in the dining room with this man, and consider freshly his qualifications and approach. Certain impressions may have been formed regarding Senior Sergeant Robert Starlight – impressions applicable perhaps to the genre of man to which he belongs, but wrongly ascribed to him as an individual.

Watch him now remove his jacket before the ladies and lightly fold it over his arm. In the absence of his jacket he is an altogether different man, a man with a belly (soft, perhaps, after a large meal), a man with sisters and a mother, a man with a medical history. On his left shoulder, unbeknown to his audience, is a strawberry-coloured birthmark. He has, on his chest, an area of brown curled hair about the size and shape of a lady's foot. Up close, there are fine white hairs in his ears, though the start of his beard (a chisel-shaped wedge on either side of the jaw) is black, almost maroon. His face is full of tortured handsome lines.

It might also be observed that as this man sheds the outer skin of his uniform, certain traits of office also fall away from him. His face, previously wooden, appears elastic after all. When he smiles, as he does now, he reveals physical peculiarities that were not remarkable before. The lid of one eye, for instance, closes almost inscrutably more than the other, giving his face an interesting asymmetry. Such things the women notice, and it profoundly influences their feelings about him.

In truth, the Senior Sergeant belongs to that quite large, though little confessed, order of men who *prefer the company of women*. Senior Sergeant Starlight is a strong believer in the intelligence of women. Although by no means prepared to canvass such possibilities as a woman's right of enfranchisement, participation in civic or political affairs, or capacity to join the higher professions, he attributes to the fairer sex more refined powers of understanding. Women, it seems to him, are more inclined to *weigh* an opinion before deeming it worthy of expression. Nor does their intercourse seek so tirelessly to establish the primacy of one set of persuasive powers over another. Amongst women, it seems to Sergeant Robert Starlight, loss of face is not entailed in every exchange, mockery not implied in every slip, humiliation not present in every rebuff.

He is wrong, of course – women are capable of every social slipperiness. But some of them, the better ones, are made of more virtuous stuff – his sisters, for instance.

You knew merely by looking at the sisters of Robert Starlight that these were women of extraordinary quality, the product of generations of careful breeding.

Mary and Ann Starlight did nothing with hurry or alarm: when they rose from bed of a morning, their ascent from the pillow was carried out in one smooth effortless movement. At breakfast they ate and conversed without seeming to move their teeth or lips, applied their condiments expediently, and always left a little something on their plates. After breakfast, they embarked religiously on their morning walk to the springs. In the afternoons, they read quietly, wrote in their day books, or studied, with elegant turns of the neck, the many black-inked limbs of their family tree.

Their minds were by no means rendered inactive by the quiet regularity of their lifestyle – at night, by the reading lamp, they tackled larger, more difficult volumes than any their younger brother attempted. They were natural diplomats, Mary and Ann, morally unassailable, too thoughtful to appear self-interested; apparently beyond reproach.

And though they were several years older than Robert, there was not a line on either face to suggest it had smiled too much, thought too

78

much, worried too much, or generally commiserated unwisely with the world. They were like roses, which, having reached the point of maximum perfection, had been dipped in wax.

It was torture for a discomposed young man like Robert Starlight to have the example of such sisters always before him. He could never follow their example; his nature precluded constancy. 'He is excitable,' said his sister Mary, without excitement. 'He will grow out of it,' said his sister Ann, rather imposing than predicting that outcome. But he had not grown out of it. As his character formed, it became clearer and clearer that it was not a character to be relied upon.

It was not that Robert Starlight had no plans; he conceived, every day, new and great ideas. His problem was that once conceived, he could not carry any of his plans through to completion.

He would begin recklessly, with abandon, often without the necessary tools. He would decide, for instance, to build an ornamental garden for his mother and his sisters. It would be paved and would boast wooden boxes for herbs and flowers. He would install a birdbath at the garden's centre, espaliered lemon trees, a rotunda, a garden setting in wrought iron. While his enthusiasm prevailed, it was self-sustaining; he would work with frantic energy. But little by little, his fervour would leave him. Little by little, doubts would occur. His spade would hit a dense bed of rock; an exorbitant quotation from a builder would arrive; an area of exposed wall would prove rotten beneath the age-old ivy. It would occur to him that certain practical compromises must be considered. He would decide to rest for a while, think it over, drink some tea. But after the tea had been drunk, his predicament was only ever worse. The simple act of picking up after his labours, putting away gloves, shovel, sweeping up dirt and leaves, was unmitigated drudgery. He could not bear to do it.

And so his life (and his sisters' and his mother's) was littered with the detritus of unfinished projects – half-plotted garden patches, a partially built fence to keep in the sow and her piglets, a parlour papered only three walls around.

Yet when a task was imposed upon Robert Starlight – when the small matter of free will was removed from the equation – he completed the task, whatever it might be, and he completed it well. He was efficient.

When he sat the entrance examination for the Pitch Constabulary, he extracted great relief from the strictness of the whole procedure. Here there were questions and there were answers, and there was a specified time in which the latter might be affixed to the former. An examinee was permitted to have a pencil, an eraser and a wristwatch beside him on the table. He must spend fifteen minutes reading the examination paper, in which such items might not be applied to, and then he was at his leisure to employ them as necessity dictated. At the end of two hours and forty-five minutes, he must stop writing, fold his paper into three sections, stand up, push his chair into the desk, and wait behind it until his paper was removed by the examination authorities.

Within such boundaries, Robert Starlight saw the potential for immense freedom. A calm overcame him when he marked the last of his answers (*d. all of the above*) onto the examination paper. This sense of calm remained with him throughout his preliminary training period; and he came to rely on it as he rose through the ranks to the office of Senior Sergeant. He became hardworking, disciplined. When he put on his uniform, his direction became clear, and he could not be distracted. It was generally remarked that he was an 'excellent officer, unremitting in his attentions to duty'. Only his mother and his sisters – loving him nonetheless – found the description difficult to fathom. For when Senior Sergeant Robert Starlight came home and took off his uniform, things were as they always had been. The parlour remained three walls speckled, one striped; the pigs escaped through broken wooden palings into the neighbour's yard; the courtyard collapsed into its unfilled holes and mud.

You might now have sufficient understanding of this man's character and background to appreciate in what manner the removal of his jacket imperilled him, both personally and occupationally. Nevertheless, for the sake of the women in the dining room of the Grand Hotel, he did it: Senior Sergeant Robert Starlight took off his jacket and hung it neatly over his bent arm. He looked into the eyes of the women about him, and saw reflected in them, in every pair, miniature fires, licking at doorsteps, consuming family photographs.

He coughed, looking for a neat way forwards. There was none. 'Evacuation,' he said in the way a dentist might utter the word *extraction*. 'You have a felon on the loose – we have not found him. You have fires – they have so far been held successfully in check, but for how long I do not know. You must wait for the next lull.' He had been speaking quietly, ticking the reasons off on his fingers and now he looked up. 'And you must evacuate.'

Ivorie Hammer stood up slowly; she was already rolling her things into neat little bundles.

Chapter 12

A parlour in need of
a parlourmaid

What a front parlour might represent to any other self-respecting housewife, it did not to Miss Morag Pappy. Where it might seem the natural place to entertain a guest, or play a hand of whist, it was to Morag Pappy merely another room, albeit one that afforded superior natural light and a northern aspect, thus making it the preferable spot for morning activities.

Arriving the previous evening, Nelly had been too tired to take much stock of her new environment. Waking this morning, however, she was struck by the peculiarities of Morag's parlour. It contained, for one thing, wall-to-floor bookshelves that housed no books but instead displayed an array of petrified flora, dried sea creatures (and some live ones, in plankton-green aquariums), and numerous artefacts made of wood and clay whose original function was largely unclear, but which were, nevertheless, intriguing. For another thing, the room contained barely a stick of furniture, only a circular rug so congealed with wax and sand and dirt that its original pattern was no longer distinguishable; a wicker chair, whose bottom was on the point of falling out; and a window seat, upon which were stacked an excess of cushions and bolsters. It was on this window seat, stiff from sleep, that Nelly now found herself.

Morag was already awake, rocking on the wicker chair and knitting, with oversized wooden needles, a length of coarse brown wool. Nelly wondered, mildly, what she might be knitting – the wool had a crimped second-hand look, as though it came from an unravelled garment. But she asked nothing about it, having long ago learned that a serving girl is rarely rewarded for unsolicited curiosity regarding her mistress's private endeavours.

For that was the relation now embarked upon: unspoken, but mutually understood – a maid-sized gap that Nelly neatly filled. There was no sentimentality in it. Morag was simply impressed by an organised mind and Nelly the possessor of such. Packing Morag's medical bag at the hotel the previous day, Nelly had stacked the glass phials between swabs of cotton wool so they would not break. She had positioned heavy bottles at the bottom of the bag in such a way that they would not fall over. Morag recognised her innate sense of method: Nelly did things with the perfect economy of the born to serve.

And Nelly, adjusting to the piquant strangeness of another person's home, felt grateful. At every crisis in her life – every termination of employment, every change in circumstance – an abyss had opened terrifyingly before her. She had stood on the edge of this abyss, with fog all around, and infinite space beyond. But always, just when the earth began most dangerously to crumble and she began most alarmingly to teeter, there had been a mistress in need of her. In fact, it amazed her how quickly and completely she was able to transfer her loyalties. The fog would retreat. The abyss would close swiftly up, a mere wrinkle in the earth. Nelly's hands would latch onto something (a broom, a waffle iron, a butter-churn) and the future would come into clear and detailed focus again.

There was only one small rupture in the future she now envisaged. Not quite buckling nor warping it: the effect was more like a problematic tree root, corrugating and cracking, very slightly, the ground. This rupture originated with the Senior Sergeant, who had escorted Nelly and Morag home the previous evening. No man had ever escorted Nelly anywhere. She had held to his arm tighter than was strictly necessary as they crossed Main Parade in the dust and wind and she noticed, when she turned to him, the crepey skin around his eyes and the narrowness of his neck. For a second or two, she felt part of herself attach to him without condition, like the press of a body in a crowd. It did not matter that he noticed, or reciprocated; only that she felt it, however briefly. Then she relinquished his arm, as she must, and accepted the maid-sized bargain that awaited her (a good bargain). She did not let herself look again, and only imagined his return to the big gloomy hotel, with its dolorous stone lions and taped-up windows.

Now, as the sun rose, and the hotel loomed into view, she hoped for a further glimpse of him. But he was not there. No one was there. She squatted on the window seat, looking out. Nor could she see any fires; the sky was a smoky pink and the wind had largely subsided. Small waves of dust rose and fell, along with large black ashes.

She had been watching vaguely like this for some time when, all of a sudden, she rose up on her knees. 'Miss Pappy!' she said, turning to Morag, 'They are coming out!' She hitched her skirt free of cushions and returned her face to the window. 'Yes, yes, the door has opened and they are coming down the steps . . .'

Morag did not look, but her knitting slowed, and a few stitches slipped off the right-hand needle.

Mr Sherry soon appeared with the horses. He came around the side of the hotel, accompanied by several other men, and one could tell he was swearing and sweating even if one could not hear the oaths or detect the moisture. 'He has harnessed up three wagons, and the dray cart,' said Nelly, perplexed, peering even closer to the glass. '*And* the barouche, with the roof up . . . though it looks to fall down again . . . oh – there it goes, it has collapsed!'

Morag kept knitting, kept nodding, as Nelly described the scenes unfolding beyond the window glass: women salvaging possessions from their ruined houses; the valiant attempts of husbands to pack belongings into ever-smaller bundles; the endeavours of Mr Sherry and his men to load already overladen carts and horses; the straining and strapping and stuffing and securing of buckles and saddlebags and stained canvas tarpaulins . . . Nelly reported on all, only occasionally indulging in small philosophical asides, the tone of which wholly agreed with Morag. To wit:

'I have always thought, Miss Pappy, not to get too attached to things in any way, so as to spare myself pains on being separated from them.'

And:

'To have a change of dress and a wholesome dinner is all a person needs in this world.'

Then, after a moment's contemplation:

'And, of course, a roof over one's head – that goes without saying!'

And, having no way of congratulating the roof for its constancy, she tapped firmly on the wall instead.

Nelly did not quite apprehend the gravity of what was unfolding before her. Though it was natural to her to observe details (dust in a dining room, a lopsided carpet in a hallway, dead rosebuds in a vase), it had never been her job to consider the larger implications of such details – the grander purpose of a dining room, for instance, and the machinations that go on inside it; the significance of a dead rosebud on a lady's bedside table. Now, watching intently the activity outside Morag's window, she did not draw from it any particular conclusion.

In her apron pocket, she felt something against her thigh. It was Mrs Sherry's gris-gris. Suddenly she understood. She turned. 'They are leaving!' she said.

Morag nodded.

Nelly sat there on the window seat, in her pale yellow parlourmaid's dress, completely still. 'Could it come to that then,' she said, 'that they will just pack up their things and leave?'

Morag said nothing.

Nelly felt a stone travel down her windpipe and into her chest. 'Oh, Miss Pappy – you must *stop* them.'

'Stop them?' said Morag. 'What makes you think –' she held a knitting needle out at a distance to check her progress, '– I have any power to stop them?'

There was about Morag a terrible quality of solitude, and it frightened Nelly, who might not belong, but did not want to be cut adrift. 'They cannot just *leave*.'

'You may join them if you wish,' Morag said. She said it without censure. She looked back to her knitting needles. 'I believe they will head for Pitch.'

'Well, then, they will never come back.' Nelly sank into the window seat. She saw, again, her Senior Sergeant: his straight back and oddly beautiful eyes . . . she had fitted directly beneath his arm, as though made for it.

'But,' she said. A new thought had occurred to her. It was a startling thought. It made her address Morag in a way she would not otherwise. 'But we are *not safe*, Miss Pappy. We have a felon on the loose.'

Morag rose at this point, and Nelly, rightly imagining herself beckoned, also rose. She followed Morag from the parlour into the kitchen. In a cupboard there was a loaf, from which Morag carved three pieces with a knife. Upon these pieces, she laid cheese, and dried meat. She poured milk from a pitcher, and separated the fare onto three plates.

'Eat this,' she said, indicating one portion, 'and then take this,' she indicated another, 'down the hall. You will find a door, on your left, at the end. Beyond it there are stairs – take care – the stairs are steep. Take a candle.'

Nelly did as instructed, ate her own bread and cheese and then set out to deliver the remaining serve.

The hall was dark and the ceiling low, with a slant and a smell that was not damp or dust, but medicinal in origin. She came to the end, went up the stairs, and could not at first see a door. There was a wall upon which hung the skin of some kind of red-brown animal. She put her hand on the skin; the fur was soft, and the skin fine, and she could feel the distinctive shape of a door beneath it. She knocked gently, and pushed the skin aside to undo the latch.

She had not known Morag entertained a guest. Indeed, she was not sure any such person inhabited the darkened bedroom in which she found herself. It appeared to be entirely empty and it was not till her eyes became accustomed to the dark that she perceived a bed and upon that bed, a form. She looked again: there was certainly a head on a pillow, turned towards her and, below the head, the suggestion of a body. She cleared her throat. The sleeping form did not move. Beside the bed was a small dressing table, devoid of ornaments, upon which she laid the plate and glass. There was a candle too and she lit it so she might see the face.

It was an old man's face, very smooth. Not a gentleman's face, nor that of a labourer – the face of an invalid. The bones rose cleanly against the skin, and the skin provided, at best, a mere coating for the skull. There were veins that could be seen, faintly pulsing. The face was very pale, as though the pigment had been sucked from it, leaving only a memory of colour. The hair, too, was more transparent than white. When the invalid breathed, there was only the smallest movement in his chest. She felt suddenly a terrible pity, like one might feel for a deer, or a kid, or a baby lamb that was hurt. It was a most unusual sensation. It alarmed her.

She must simply observe the details. She must not wonder at their meanings. She moved the milk glass a little further from the edge of the dressing table, so it might not be knocked accidentally, and adjusted the position of the plate accordingly. Then she blew out the candle and returned to the parlour.

Outside, the first wheels were creaking into action. She saw Mrs Hammer being handed up into the barouche. Around her wrist was a drawstring bag, the type of article known as a hanging pocket. It was heavy; it did not so much swing as bang and lurch against her. Nelly watched her lose her footing momentarily, then disappear, in a crush of skirts, behind the carriage door. She leaned in closer to the window and followed the dust thrown up by departing wheels.

Part 2

Outer Pitch

Chapter 13

The vacant lot of Outer Pitch

The path to Pitch proved true to its reputation. It was perilous. Its curves and straights took the people of Canyon through one of the most unaccommodating geographies known to civilised travellers. Indeed, a proper account of their journey could fill an entire volume in itself, so teeming was it with hazards and difficulties, treacherous moments and near misses.

Unfortunately, however, we are not at leisure to fill volumes, so let us move swiftly onwards, noting only a few brief and important details from those monumental fourteen days on the road.

Firstly, that after tearful remonstrations, many unnecessary items of furniture (as well as other sundries, including – accidentally, due to its enclosure in a locked desk drawer – Ivorie Hammer's three-thousand-page dictionary) were dispensed with (there was a horrible clattering, splitting sound as objects catapulted, rock to rock, down the mountain face).

Secondly, that the body of Mrs Sherry, having not endured beyond the first thirty-six hours, was buried with very little ceremony beneath a strange spiky tree with bark like elephant hide.

Thirdly, that the further the party's progress from Canyon, the cooler the weather became, the sweeter the air, the gentler the breeze.

And fourthly, that the hearts of the people of Canyon, heavy at first to be leaving their homes, proved to have a surprising resilience. They expanded; they caused their owners to exclaim joyously over small clumps of wild heath and unusual flowering grasses. One could almost say that – in spite of the authorities – an air of festivity prevailed.

By the time they rounded the last of the mountain's treacherous hairpin bends, the people of Canyon had become positively goat-legged.

At the bottom of the mountain range they met with a landscape unlike any in their previous experience. Fields of lucerne-fed cows; trees occurred with satisfying regularity in lines or *copses* or little confidential rectangles. The earth itself contained interesting diversions: gentle rises and falls, dips and glades. Even the sky seemed to bend more compassionately over the earth.

In the covered carriage, Ivorie Hammer was relieved to be lurching and bumping no longer. She had watched the wooden carriage wheels skirt dangerously close to the edges of mountain paths. She had held her breath as wooden furniture – yes! And her dictionary! – plummeted to their certain ends. She had nursed grave fears for her treadle sewing machine. Little girls had passed posies through the window to her, and they were scattered now on the floor of the carriage, dried and dead. Her babies had pushed her stomach up to just below her ribcage, causing much discomfort.

She asked Mr Sherry to stop and let her out.

Unlike her compatriots', Ivorie Hammer's heart had not been invigorated by a fortnight's exercise – it remained a little sour with old blood, a little stagnant. She tried nevertheless to marvel at the beautiful green scenery around her.

Ann Starlight saw them, from more than a mile away, through her binoculars.

'Robert has brought them back with him,' she said, turning to her sister. 'And they are just as you would expect . . .'

'A motley party?'

'*Exactly* so.'

Mary dabbed cottonwool on the front of her dress where a drop of rosewater had spilled, then came to join her sister on the balcony.

'And how many?'

'I couldn't say . . . I would estimate . . . in the vicinity of two hundred . . .'

'Two hundred!'

'... and fifty ... perhaps.'

'Well, where shall they be put? They're not to be housed amongst us, surely?'

'No. They couldn't possibly ...'

'We haven't enough rooms!'

'They will have to stay out there somewhere ...' Ann waved her hand vaguely outwards and returned to her binoculars.

'Oh my dear, how our mother would be imposed on ...!'

'Their founder, you know, he *took his own life*! Shocking!'

Ann did not respond. She had been perturbed a moment ago, but now a small smile appeared on her face. 'Oh relief, my dear, relief! They have come to a halt! They have not even *stepped* onto the Ring Road.'

'They have, then, no intention ...?'

'No intention, my dear, no intention.'

'We will take them tea and cake then, when they're settled.'

'Yes.'

'Yes. Robert will take it.'

'Yes. With a card, of course.'

'Of welcome.'

'*Such* a long way ...'

'... for us to travel.'

'All the way out along the Ring Road.'

'We are not vigorous, like them.'

'Not vigorous, no. Not able to go over *mountain tops*.'

'After all,' Mary pressed her lips together, and took, finally, the binoculars from her sister so she might look for herself, '*we* are not descended from the circus.'

Indeed, things had not seemed so circus-like in decades. Bright carpets were being pulled out of boxes and laid across the damp grass on the outskirts of Pitch; bits of furniture – chairs and stools and writing desks – stood serenely in the open air as though quite at home there; someone had set up a toy piano and children took turns bashing at its wooden keys. Several children had secured ribbons and bits of string to sticks, and were running around swiping figure-eights in the air. One of the Fancy girls had made a drum from an upturned wash bowl and Rosa Minim had initiated a series of wheelbarrow races.

This was the site, the authorities had informed them, gruffly, without much cheer: it was here on this large square of ground (rather like a playing field) that they might camp. For the time being. Until better arrangements were made. Senior Sergeant Starlight had given them matches and several kerosene lamps. A stream ran down from the mountains, providing their needs in respect of water, and there was plenty of damp kindling and logs.

Otherwise, it was not a bad plot of ground at all – a little marshy in places, but flat enough for camping. What's more, it contained three spare grey structures – they could not be called buildings, for two of them had no walls as such, just roofs, supported on poles, and the third looked more tumbledown than intact.

'Shelter is shelter!' Borrel Sweetley said, sounding bright, but looking glum as he watched the first tarpaulin being stripped back and boxes and crates being shunted from cart to person to ground.

With the assurance that they'd be back soon with 'victuals', the authorities left them to their own devices, and the population of Canyon unfurled itself and its possessions upon the abandoned lumber yard of Outer Pitch.

The Senior Sergeant did not, on that first night, return with victuals as promised. It became dark and cold, and Mr Sherry got the men drunk too quickly on empty stomachs. Fires were built – dangerous, drunken fires, Ivorie thought – but there was nothing to *cook* on the fires except bread. No one seemed to mind, apart from Ivorie and Racine Pfeffersalz and, at several telling moments, Borrel Sweetley, who had spent much of the time since their arrival making covetous little reparations to his luggage.

'I did not think it would be like this, Mrs Hammer,' said Racine to Ivorie Hammer. 'I am old. I thought we would be *put up* somewhere.'

Ivorie sat on a case of linen. She felt the same as Racine. Nothing about this situation impressed her. She liked the countryside, of course – it was green, and pretty, and fragrant, and she had spied all sorts of unfamiliar birds in the trees. But apart from these few rustic compensations, she was disappointed. She had not, as it was earlier remarked, experienced the gruelling, cheek-ruddying grind of the journey. She had sat in a covered vehicle and played cards. Ivorie did not, therefore, adequately appreciate the sheer relief that a large piece of flat ground represented to her fellows.

The slight dampness of the earth bothered her. Her shoes would be ruined. The linen case upon which she sat impressed itself nearly an inch into the ground. Inside one of the half-built sheds, Ernest was busy constructing 'private quarters' for them. Ivorie could see him from a distance, a small blue-shirted figure moving back and forth, hanging makeshift curtains, layering the ground with paper and sticks against the cold. She shivered.

'It's not what I expected either, Racine,' she said. 'I can only hope it's temporary. I hope soon to be housed closer to town.' She lowered her voice to a fraction of its normal volume. 'I hope also, Racine, to begin making enquiries *about my origins*!'

'My dear!' said Racine, intuiting, from her confidential tones, the significance.

Now Sweetley drew up a chair beside the two women. He had procured a walking-stick on the journey. Though the journey was over, he had become much attached to the stick, and now he punched its pointed end into the ground before him. Racine moved her foot out of the way.

'Well, Mrs Hammer, Mrs Pfeffersalz,' Sweetley said. 'What do you *make* of all this then? It's a lovely place, isn't it. Lovely. Green.' He tried to smile and sigh at the same time, but could not. 'We'll make a *fist* of it here, all right,' he said, clenching his own and looking tortured. 'Mark my words.'

He had not, it seemed to Ivorie, fully recovered his composure since the escape of his prisoner. He suffered, it was obvious. She felt sorry for him, but any attempt at comfort was plainly out of the question. One could not say such things as 'there, there' to a man like Sweetley: it would ruin him.

'But the authorities,' went on Mr Sweetley, shaking his head, 'have been detained, it seems.' He picked his stick up again and thrust it into the earth like a spear. 'I have a mind,' he said, 'to seek them out. And not just on the question of provisions. We still have, for instance, unsolved murders.' He picked up his bag, which had the appearance of having been packed and unpacked several times in a hurry; a corner of white paper stuck out from its opening. He leaned in a little closer to the two women, and holding it up at ear level, shook it gently with two hands. It made a rattling, fragmented sound, as though it might be full of jigsaw pieces, or doll's furniture. 'Yes, Mrs Hammer.' He tapped his forehead. 'I have still the evidence.' There was a short silence. His eyes were a little glazed. 'I do not give up on a thing, Mrs Hammer, Mrs Pfeffersalz. Once I get going, I go all the way to the end.'

'Oh, must we bring it all back up, Mr Sweetley? We are here now. Can't we let it rest?' Racine clutched Ivorie's hand.

'No no no no no,' said Mr Sweetley. His eyes continued to shine strangely.

'Are you all right, Mr Sweetley?' Ivorie said.

He hugged the bag to his chest. Ivorie noticed he was no longer wearing his raven's wing coat. 'Tell them, will you, Mrs Hammer,' he said. 'Tell them I have gone to find the authorities. I know where to find them. Tell them I'll be back before sunset tomorrow. That I have their interests at heart.'

He stood up and Racine and Ivorie watched him, with some concern, proceed along the track in the dark, in the opposite direction from which they'd come, swinging his bag and jabbing at the ground with his walking-stick. Just before he disappeared around a bend, he stopped and turned back to them. 'Mocsa!' he yelled out, hands around his mouth. (Or that's what they thought he said.) 'A release from the cycle of existence. That's what it is.' He shook his finger at them savagely. 'Nose to the earth. Eyes to heaven.' Then he picked up his things again and disappeared into the darkness. It was an exit of surprising ease and no one, witnessing it, would have guessed at its finality.

Chapter 14

Mrs Po

Mr Borrel Sweetley did not return before sunset the next day. And he did not return *after* sunset. The following morning – another just like the one preceding it, clear, fresh, green – Ivorie told Ernest she was going for a stroll, and set off to look for him.

Ivorie did not have a walking-stick, nor a leather briefcase, but she did have a hanging pocket. The hanging pocket was full and at certain moments – a stumble, a trot – its contents clinked. She stilled it with the palm of her hand; she was not sure if it was wise – or dignified – for a lady to have a big full bag of money, slapping at her thigh as she went.

She followed the track that Sweetley had taken, and pretty soon, it became less a track, and more a road, properly graded for a carriage and boasting a surface of lime. The lime blew up in small puffs about Ivorie's ankles as she walked. It was peaceful. The babies in her stomach slept. Small twittering sounds could be heard from the trees, and the occasional hush of seedpods and leaves brushing against each other. Around her, with quiet stealth, the scenery was changing, the pretty low-lying wilderness of Outer Pitch replaced by market gardens and cottages.

She came soon to a stone pew, set beneath the shade of some kind of oak tree. Her spirits had greatly improved as she walked and now, spying the stone pew – put there, it would seem, expressly for the purpose of resting – she felt almost optimistic. How considerate a neighbourhood, she thought, to provide like this for the public! She was in need of such provision – there was a pain in her back, dull, intermittent, with a similarly dull, intermittent nausea attached. She eased herself into a sitting position and turned her thoughts to the small fortune she carried in her hanging pocket.

It was a small fortune indeed, equivalent perhaps to an average man's income in an average year. Over time, Ivorie had added to it and taken from it in small increments, with the result that it remained largely unchanged in volume. It represented the potential for *betterment* – she did not know how exactly, but felt sure she would know the opportunity when she saw it. The hanging pocket rested in her lap and she put her hand over it protectively. The sun made buttery patches on her skirt. She closed her eyes and the sunlight turned red and green behind her eyelids, and when she opened them again she thought she saw a figure coming towards her along the road.

It *was* a figure on the road. A very small figure with a basket. It made uncommonly swift progress, though the steps it took to achieve such progress were tiny. In fact, it wasn't until the figure was almost upon Ivorie that she could confidently say it was a woman and not a child: a very small woman in boots. 'Oh!' the woman said, seeing Ivorie, and put her basket down on the road.

She was about sixty: a well-groomed, well-preserved sixty, with steel-grey hair pulled back so tight that her eyes were catlike at the corners. She brushed away a leaf or two, and some acorns, and took a seat beside Ivorie on the stone pew. Though there was ample room, she sat so close that Ivorie could see an eyelash caught wetly on her lower lid.

'I am Mrs Po,' she said, after some moments' examination of Ivorie. 'And you?' Her eyes shone. 'You are *expecting*?'

Ivorie nodded and made the sign for 'two' with her fingers. Mrs Po's eyes widened. 'Aah!' she said, and cocked her head. She considered Ivorie's stomach like this, from the side, then put the back of her hand against Ivorie's forehead and, removing it, shook it as though it were a thermometer. 'I think,' she said, standing up, 'you had better come home with me and take a refreshment. Something cool. With salt in it, or sugar.'

She took Ivorie firmly by the hand – she was surprisingly strong – and assisted her to stand.

Mrs Po did not alter her walking pace to accommodate her new friend. Ivorie detected no meanness in this, but nevertheless, it was difficult to keep up, particularly when they veered off the Ring Road and onto a narrow lane that curled and twisted unpredictably between houses and hedges, and regularly degenerated into puddles. Ivorie stumbled and avoided the worst of the puddles and occasionally Mrs Po waited for her to catch up. Finally they came to a narrow street flanked on either side with berry bushes, and, stopping at the prettiest in a stretch of pretty brick houses, Mrs Po put her basket down and pulled open the front gate. In a matter of minutes, Ivorie found herself installed in a soft chair in a lavender-coloured sitting room, sipping cordial and resting her feet on a footstool.

Mrs Po observed her intently from a chair opposite. Ivorie's stomach made three uncomfortable shifting motions to the left. The pain in her sitting bone expanded into her lower back and then shrank again.

'Hospital!' said Mrs Po suddenly. It was the first thing she'd said since their arrival and it took Ivorie by surprise. 'Hospital is the place for you. There is *no* other way. *Twins!*' She shook her head and relaxed into her chair as if relieved of a great burden.

Ivorie leaned a little forwards. 'I have always,' she said, 'been a *staunch* believer in hospitals, Mrs Po.'

'They are clean,' said Mrs Po, nodding. 'They have modern equipment. We are lucky, here in Pitch, to have a hospital. One of the best.' She stopped a moment, and her brow puckered again. 'But you are not *from* Pitch, Mrs . . .?'

'Hammer,' Ivorie supplied.

'You are not from Pitch, Mrs Hammer, are you? You are certainly not, or I would have known you. I would have seen you. Oh dear . . . You will not get an appointment.' Mrs Po bit her lip and looked deep into the carpet. Then a smile crept onto her thin mouth, and she tapped the air smartly with her finger. 'You shall have my card!' she said. She got up and began to rifle through a roll-top desk in the far corner of the room. Her face had become pink and pleased. 'Oh, it is such a marvellous solution!' She found the card (which was actually several, attached at one corner with a piece of coloured string) and held it up for Ivorie to see. 'It has my very own number, see, on the top there,' she said. 'We do things correctly here in Pitch, you will find, Mrs Hammer. To the letter.' She brought the card over and pressed it into Ivorie's hand. There was a large ring wedged onto Mrs Po's very large wedding finger. It was unfortunate, thought Ivorie, that Mrs Po's hands seemed to have been erroneously bestowed on her, like spare parts from a much larger machine. Mrs Po whipped them out of the way as soon as Ivorie had accepted the card.

Ivorie smiled gratefully. 'Oh Mrs Po, I cannot,' she said. 'I could not take advantage of such generosity . . .'

'Don't *think* of it, Mrs Hammer,' said Mrs Po sternly. 'You must have every modern facility. You must have everything. Goodness knows . . .' She broke off a moment, and looked away. When she turned back to Ivorie, her face was very serious. 'A woman does not have a baby every day, Mrs Hammer. Think *if something went wrong . . .*'

It had never occurred to Ivorie to think of such an eventuality. Her years as Morag's apprentice had produced in her a conviction that giving birth was the most natural undertaking in the world. Now the spectre of 'what if' was born, a bright mischievous glimmer, capable of untold damage. 'Then thank you, Mrs Po,' Ivorie said. 'Of course I will accept your card. It provides me with immense peace of mind . . .' She stroked the card gently, to show Mrs Po how well she would treasure it. Then she smiled warmly at her benefactress and pressed herself up and out of the armchair. 'But I feel much improved,' she said. 'And I am so taken with your house! Would you honour me with a tour?' She took Mrs Po's arm in her own, snugly, as though they were old school chums. 'You have obviously some decorative talent . . .'

As they descended the stairwell – having minutely inspected the many clean square rooms and matching clean square furniture of Mrs Po's house – Ivorie felt a strange sensation in her lower abdomen. She gripped the banister with both her hands. '*Mrs Po?*' she said. She felt the sensation once more, then, looking down, saw what she would later describe as a 'torrent' of water cascading from between her thighs and onto Mrs Po's lovely lilac carpet runner.

She could not have asked for more perfect timing.

Chapter 15

The Ferris wheel of opportunity

There was a room in Mrs Po's house that was perfect for a nursery. Pale blue walls and white wainscotting. A small sash window through which the afternoon sun softly filtered. A painting of a vase of flowers and a pomegranate.

It was nothing like the room in which Ivorie now found herself. Here everything smelled new, metallic. There were lots of sharp creases and starch. High walls. Silence. Buzzing. Silence again.

On a clipboard somewhere, her medical card had been stamped and authorised. Her levels of this and that had been noted. They had laid her out on a trolley and wheeled her away, Mrs Po becoming smaller and smaller at the other end of the corridor. They had transferred her to a bed and her ankles had been briskly, unceremoniously, buckled into stirrups. When each pain came on, only a small square of her back was free to move. She wailed. No one smiled or comforted her. The nurses wore masks and hairnets and she could not see their mouths. She wailed again. It felt like someone was cleaning out her insides with a broomstick. They gave her gas and she swooned for a moment or two and then the pain came back. 'Shush, shush, Mrs Po,' they said, crossly. 'A million others have done this before you, you know — and not half such a fuss was made then.' She bellowed again. One of the nurses glared at her, and then a soft, sweet-smelling wad was pressed firmly over her nostrils.

Floating above her, Morag's face had split into quarters. She wrung the Mary Ann doll in her fingers and brown brackish water came out of it.

'Mama,' said the Mary Ann doll, 'Mama, Mama.' Only now the Mary Ann was made of wool, and Morag was rocking in a large rocker, knitting her, stitch by stitch, only backwards, so each stitch unravelled the one that preceded it, taking away its eyes and nose and mouth until it no longer had any face at all. And then the Mary Ann was a weeping child and its tears were bright beads of blood that splashed and spread into the shape of a flower, a large mushrooming flower. Larger and larger the flower became, larger and larger and larger, and then suddenly it condensed and became hard and small and it was no longer a flower at all but a gold coin, spinning, spinning, cracking against the sides of a chute along which it travelled, splitting and multiplying and refracting into a great shower of money.

When she woke up, Ivorie had a baby. Or rather, a nurse on the other side of the room had a baby, which she was rocking back and forth too vigorously to be of any conceivable comfort to it. Ivorie half sat up. She could see her own face in a steel basin at the end of her bed. There was a squatness about her features that recalled to her a bull frog. 'Where's the other one?' she croaked. A lump of pond-weed was caught behind her tongue. Something stoppered up her throat.

'What other one?' said the nurse. 'Just the one, Mrs Po. Lovely little girl.' The nurse had pale blonde hair, so neatly parted and smoothly combed that it looked like a sheath of tight-fitting silk.

'No, no,' Ivorie continued. 'You don't understand. There were two...' She felt colossal. There were towels banked up between her legs and under her buttocks. Everything was slow and heavy.

The nurse smiled and showed Ivorie the baby – quickly, tipping it down, blankets and all, so Ivorie could just make out a small face, rather orange in colour.

'A little jaundiced, but she's a pet. Have you a name for her?'

'Pet...' said Ivorie. She was falling off to sleep again, wondering about the other one. 'Pet.'

Bald Sherry could hardly contain himself at the news. He took lids off bottles and put them back on again. He slapped Ernest Hammer's back.

He opened a packet of biscuits from the hamper the authorities had brought that morning. He told Ernest Hammer to 'Go! Go!', and then said, 'Come back – I know I have a cigar somewhere!'

It had lasted for some time after Ernest departed, this ecstatic, electrifying warmth. The grass was dry from the afternoon sun. Mr Sherry and some of the other men had built a latrine that afternoon and he felt hot and elated in the aftermath. He had seen small wild animals in the shrubs around the camp site – he would set traps for them. He had noticed soft juicy berries on a certain ubiquitous low-lying bush. He had ideas – they multiplied like rabbits; he had to get drunk to slow them down.

The next morning, he decided to make his way into town. He took the path Borrel Sweetley had taken, and then followed the signs.

In town, he noticed everything with an unusual clarity. He noticed how close set the buildings were, how narrow. How every extra space was taken up with balconies and dormer windows, miniature bell towers and watchtowers, attics and garrets and overpasses. He could hear the *drip drip drip* of green lichenous water from gutterings overhead.

He noticed how well-dressed and sullen the people were, as though the enthusiasm that went into their clothes somehow leached that quality from their personalities. They appeared to have too much liquid in their bodies and not enough air. The girls especially. He had never seen such overly hydrated girls. They looked as though they had been kept in jars of salted water. He must have been looking too intently as he thought all this, for someone threw a cabbage head at him from a window and he only just ducked in time. The cabbage burst against a wall opposite and fell to pieces. Bald Sherry removed his hat and bowed to his anonymous assailant.

None of it bothered him – the strange looks, the cabbage, the girls. He made his observations. He walked his jaunty walk. He wore his purple jacket. He bought a small posy of flowers to hold beneath his nose in those areas where the drains were insufficiently closed. The cuffs of his suit trousers became damp; they sloshed dully around his ankles.

He did not miss his hotel. He did not miss his wife (though he regretted his *failure* to miss her). He did not miss Borrel Sweetley. Nothing could perturb him because, in his mind, he had an image.

He was not sure he could quite call it a *vision*, for it still existed in the realm of metaphor: a basic shape that might be imposed upon the future. And it was certainly not well-thought-out enough to be considered an *idea*. But whatever it was, it towered above all else. It was red and yellow and blue and hung with hundreds of coloured flags. Great whelps of joy came from its swinging cars. Lines of people queued at its ticket box. It went round and round in a clockwise direction, jutting and retreating, jutting and retreating, like a series of mechanical nodding chins. Privately, Bald Sherry called it 'the Ferris wheel of opportunity'.

'Pette Po,' it said on the Municipality of Pitch birth certificate. It was a thin piece of paper, with a gold-embossed letterhead. Mrs Po showed it to Ernest Hammer, then slipped it into a secret compartment in her desk.

It was the Po part, naturally, that bothered Ernest most. His daughter's Christian name was a manageable accident. With the addition of 'te', it had become pretty, French-sounding.

Ivorie was strangely unconcerned. 'It's just a formality,' she said. She was still tranquil from all the effort and drugs. 'It ensures she will get the best of everything.'

Mrs Po was in the kitchen, doing something: her heels clacked purposefully on the floor and cupboards opened and closed. Ernest lowered his voice.

'It is against the law!' he said.

'Oh, Mr Hammer!' said Ivorie. The baby had broken off feeding and was sleeping now with its mouth slightly open. Ernest, refusing to subscribe to the convention of paternal absence, had remained for the feeding ritual; Mr Po, however – a silent, moribund creature who seemed to exist mostly in the shed at the back of the garden – had been banished there until further notice.

'I won't go back to the campsite, Ernest,' Ivorie said. 'It's cold and damp. And I'm not interested in being *stoic*.' The baby made a little spastic motion with its hands and then settled back into her elbow. It was not a particularly pretty baby, yet, and Ivorie was still trying to get used to the fact that there was only one of it. She regarded it with some distance while she talked. 'I don't see why we should cast our lot in with everyone else. If Mr and Mrs Po will have us . . .'

Ernest took a deep breath. He was about to be implacable, Ivorie knew it. He would say nothing, he would just look at her, and it would be unbearable. She felt cross and defensive.

'They have enough rooms. It will be a help to *me*. I don't see why we should give up an opportunity to be comfortable!'

Mrs Po had arranged the convalescent in an excess of pink ruffled eiderdowns, and Ivorie rose up now from this sea of bedding like the figure-head on the prow of a ship. Her cheeks were very red and her breasts were positively enormous. If you met her on the high seas, carved of wood, you would swiftly turn tail for home.

Ernest had no wish to cross her. But he did not have a small fortune in a hanging pocket. He had a case full of watchmaker's instruments. He put his fingertip on the crown of his head where the hair was becoming thin. It was a little smoother, a little oilier, than when he'd last checked.

Of course he'd do what Ivorie wanted. He was not being implacable at all. He opened his mouth to tell her so, but Ivorie beat him to it.

'Besides,' she said, 'they have already offered and I have already said yes.'

This was not strictly true. In order to attain their mutually desired outcome, the two women had performed a small monetary transaction across the Po kitchen table not long after Ivorie's return from the hospital. It was by no means an honest transaction, if only because both women pretended fiercely that it had not occurred, but nevertheless there was what might legally stand as *consideration*. Something was exchanged for something else. Spring-cleaning soon commenced in the upstairs rooms.

Mrs Po had taken responsibility for the nursery – she had in her possession a seemingly endless collection of bunny rugs and booties and white crocheted shawls. In the adjacent room, Ivorie opened the crates her husband had retrieved from the campsite. She lined her books up on the mantelpiece, regretting for a painful, lingering moment, the absence of her dictionary. She took the tin box that contained the facts of her mother's existence – the dry, bleached lock of hair, the single preposterous earring, the copper coin with the imprint of a lady's profile – and placed it next to her books so it acted as a bookend. Next she took the Mary Ann doll, shook out the folds of her dress, looked again at those strange sad inky initials on her leg, M.W., and propped her on top of the box. The doll's head promptly fell chin-down onto the chest.

She turned then to consideration of her wardrobe.

The oval mirror in the Pos' guest room did not reflect Ivorie Hammer at her best. It was stuck at an unfortunate foreshortening angle, which made her look larger and squatter than she actually was. One by one, Ivorie took pale white garments from the linen chest and held them up to her no-longer-slender form. She could not pretend she was not disappointed. She had expected the delivery of *two* infants, not one, and the immediate resumption of her former shape. Instead she was slovenly and large, like a stretched boot. She thought of horrible words to use against herself. A hot burst of hatred and hopelessness formed behind her eyes.

Had they missed something?

She hitched up her nightgown and scanned her stomach for the tell-tale shape of a head, a shoulder, the projection of a knee. But she detected nothing: the stomach hung a little lower than before, but its surface conveyed no signs of life, apart from the faint grumbling of her own digestive system.

She remembered a woman Morag had once treated: a very old woman – or so she had seemed to Ivorie at the time. She had already had ten children. 'It is like *that* with me,' she said, snapping her fingers, and swinging nimbly onto the examination table, talking to Ivorie, not to Morag, who did not invite conversation. She went on like this, brightly proclaiming her remarkable fecundity, while Morag felt all over the small drum-tight bulge that was its latest manifestation.

'There is nothing there,' Morag told Ivorie when the woman went away. 'It is all imaginary. All in her head.'

Ivorie had not believed Morag. Surely imagination could not so convincingly deceive one's body. 'Put your hands on her yourself then,' said Morag, 'you won't feel anything.'

The woman had come back, two times, three. Her stomach grew in keeping with her dates, but there was no milk in her breasts. Ivorie did as Morag said, and felt her stomach, seeking out the head, the spine. There was only the pressure of water or air.

'There is no baby,' Morag told the woman finally. The woman smiled sadly and went away. Two weeks later Ivorie saw her at market: picking through apples, dress flapping loosely at her empty stomach. 'As though she had been pricked with a pin,' she reported to Morag. 'As though she were an egg pudding with the oven door slammed. As though all the air had been let out.'

Morag had said nothing. Morag did not explain.

Chapter 16

In the name of Bodicea Sweetley

What, you might wonder, has become of Mr Borrel Sweetley? Or perhaps you wonder no such thing at all, trusting that this gentleman can take care of himself. But when we left him, he was in a strange and confusing state, much attached to his bag of bones and his pointed stick.

Yes, they were bones, those rattling articles in his bag: the selfsame bones that started all the fuss. Mr Borrel Sweetley had the bones, and he *had* had the felon, and he was not going to rest until he had connected the latter to the former once and for all. It was a matter of principle.

In the interim, he could no longer remain amongst the people of Canyon. He could not bear their civility and solicitude, knowing, as he did, that it was all an attempt to show him that his error did not matter. His error *did* matter. He had *lost* the prisoner. He had had him and then he had *lost* him. His error mattered unbearably. Reparation was crucial to his sense of self-regard: despite his bombast, he was a man demolished by the ill opinion of others.

But Mr Sweetley was also, like many in public office, incapable of admitting his faults. He could not own the truth, and so move forwards in the peculiar human journey to personal enlightenment and self-knowledge. He was, to put it crudely, wrenched back on his own chain. If he could not resume, with equanimity, his former place amongst his townspeople, he would absent himself entirely.

He had made this decision during the treacherous mountain crossing; thereafter, all participation on his part was for the sake of form only. At night, under the stars, he had counted silently the shards of bone in his leather briefcase. Every time, the number was different. Perhaps this numerical inconstancy was due to imperfect light, or perhaps the artefacts were breaking up, crumbling away. There was a thin powder, a residue, caught in the hard leather seams of his bag. On the point of his index finger, holding it up to the light of his candle, it looked like gold dust.

Ex post facto, he thought: by subsequent action would he redeem himself.

It had not occurred to Sweetley that Senior Sergeant Robert Starlight might continue to be ill-disposed towards him. In his official capacity, the Senior Sergeant was careful to conceal his personal likes and dislikes. But in his unofficial capacity – as a brother, a son – he was not so dependable. He found it difficult (I have already mentioned this) to remain constant. When Borrel Sweetley turned up on his doorstep at luncheon, he was so surprised that he opened the door and let the man in.

The Starlight family were at their dining table. It was cold and damp in their dining room and no one had lit the fire. They were not a prosperous family, though they once had been. Papa had been a magistrate and lifelong member of the Inner Pitch council. He was now deceased, but, having died with large debts to ignominious establishments and people, his surviving relations were not what you could describe as well off. Nevertheless, the Senior Sergeant's twin sisters were excellently dressed. Today, Mary was in pale blue and Ann wore pink. The colours suited them, the cuts were fashionable. The two women turned their faces to their unexpected visitor and Borrel Sweetley thought he had never seen two more beautiful women in such close proximity to one another.

A plate was set for him. He took a chair. Mrs Starlight, having no maid to perform the duty, ladled stew into a bowl for him. Sweetley observed that it contained little meat and much potato. Ann smiled at him. Mary made the observation that Mr Sweetley did not seem to resemble his townspeople.

'From the little I have seen of them, anyway,' she finished, dipping her chin towards her stew spoon. In fact, she had seen nothing of Mr Sweetley's townspeople, and based her observation entirely on what she had *heard*: a not-very-judicious appraisal, in which the coarseness of the women's complexions was made much of, and the manners of the men deplored.

'Correct, madam!' said Borrel Sweetley, and though he no longer wore his raven's wings, his chest became birdlike and rose with pleasure. 'I was born,' he said, 'in the hot and sandy regions of *India*.'

There was a widening of eyes at this admission.

'Yes, in the desert state of Rajputana, where I also spent my childhood.' He identified a large lump of meat in his stew, rolled it around in his bowl till evenly coated in gravy, and continued. 'My father was in the diplomatic services. Long, long hours. Hot, hot days. I was in the care of an ayah, but otherwise much left to my own devices . . .'

Their eyes were absolutely upon him, and they had stopped eating.

'I had a strong constitution and fortunately became immune to all types of disease that are endemic there.'

The point was not, it seemed, immediately clear. Mr Sweetley elaborated. 'The people are very poor, you know. Living on rice and *aloo ghobi*. Not enough clean *panni*. I did what I could, from my position, to ease their hunger pangs.'

The sisters were very gallant in their attentions to Mr Sweetley now. Ann noted the pleasing way he paused between sentences and struck his two narrow index fingers in the air as though touching his next thought with careful precision before articulating it.

Mary Starlight picked up a gravy-soaked potato with her fork prong and held it, quivering, at chest level. 'What a predicament . . .' she said, 'to be . . . well-off . . . amongst the poor and destitute!'

Borrel Sweetley shook his head, confirming, rather than contradicting, her observation. 'Indeed it was. It was precisely that. Everywhere, you know, such desperate need. It has ingrained in me, I believe, a desire always to help those less materially comfortable than myself.'

This gave rise to a general philanthropic consensus about the table. Mary's eyes positively brimmed with charitable intentions, and Ann got up from her chair and very forcibly served their visitor a second helping.

'And what *happened*, Mr Sweetley?' Ann said, returning to her place with the clean-scraped stew-pot. 'Did you continue to grow up amongst them, the Indians? How did you come from *there* to *here*?'

'I'm afraid . . . I hate to tell.' Sweetley borrowed Robert Starlight's napkin and wiped his chin. He sighed and looked for a moment as if he might not go on. Nobody but Robert was eating now. 'There was a terrible tragedy. Terrible. In my adult life, I have given myself much grief wondering . . .' he crumpled the napkin into a ball in his fist '. . . if I could have done something to avert what transpired. But then, tragedy is a day-to-day occurrence amongst those unlucky people.'

'Oh, Mr Sweetley,' said Mary. Her lovely curved lips parted a little, and she looked at him with great sympathy and interest.

'And what was the tragedy?' said Ann (more practical than her sister, less pretty around the mouth).

Sweetley sighed. 'One can hardly blame them – such poor people, you understand, such destitution.' He chewed on some meat, swallowed laboriously. 'There was a theft, you see, of my mother's jewellery.' Sweetley was contemplative. 'She had only a small box of jewellery. Just a neckpiece or two, a few gems set into brooches, a bracelet. And one evening, she went to retrieve an ornament for an official function and found the jewellery box empty. Completely empty!'

Silence reigned at table. Mary's mouth was still slightly open and one could see the small white teeth in her lower gum, and the pink oval of her tongue.

'If left to my mother,' said Sweetley, 'it would not have mattered. She did not care, she was more attached to the people than she was to her jewels. But the servants there . . .' He shook his head. 'They are loyal to a fault. Before a week was out, they had discovered the thief – an Untouchable boy, who had come to the house once to clean the gully trap. My father refused to believe it was so: he spoke up for the boy.'

The Starlight women were captivated; how dignified, how selfless seemed Mr Sweetley's mother! How benevolent his father! And how the jewels sparkled and gleamed in the paw of the brash little monkey – (here they faltered for, try as they might, they could not quite imagine the thief as human, but only as a small swift-footed animal).

'Go on, Mr Sweetley,' prompted Ann.

'There was nothing to be done,' Sweetley said quietly. 'The boy was subjected to their traditional system of justice – a thief is dealt with summarily there.' He stopped. He did not have to say more, because they knew what he meant. Ann was looking down at her place setting. Mary could not tear her eyes from Sweetley's face, and was wringing in her frail white hands the tough white dinner napkin.

Mrs Starlight silently gathered dishes and dispersed pudding bowls. 'After that,' said Sweetley, 'things rather fell away for us.' He blew on his spoon, and unthinkingly shovelled the first hot mouthful of pudding in, so he had to speak and blow all at once. 'It became quite awful. My mother never recovered.'

'Oh, it must have weighed on her conscience,' said Mary.

'Indeed,' said Sweetley. 'Indeed, it did.' He pushed the bowl away. (It was bread pudding; the custard was thin.) 'For they were wrong, you see.' He looked up at them and his blue eyes watered. 'The boy had nothing to do with it.'

'*Nothing*?' echoed Mary.

'*Nothing at all*?' said Ann.

'The jewels were found, finally, in possession of my father's manservant. He was injured in an accident one morning, hit by a rickshaw, and the jewels were found on his person. It was too late, of course, for the young Indian boy. He had been . . . well, *immolated* . . . months previously by the locals.' He rather hoped the pretty sisters did not know immediately what he meant by this. They did, however, and were both horrified and excited by the notion. Ann felt a not-unpleasant movement in her loins. Sweetley went on. 'For myself, I had never trusted the manservant. I had always thought him suspect. He had those particularly long, surreptitious limbs of the Indian criminal classes. But my mother never recovered. It was all her fault, she felt . . . and of course, the manservant being never properly brought to justice . . .' He sighed, and tried again the thin yellow custard.

'What became of him?' continued Ann. 'What became of the manservant?'

'He escaped from custody. Escaped from the teeth of the law, as it were. We saw neither hide nor hair of him again.' He shook his head; he pushed away, once and for all, the pudding. 'Needless to say, my mother could not wear those jewels again. Thereafter she could bear nothing about the country. She could no longer tolerate the climate; the food made her ill; she suffered the strangest maladies . . .'

'Oh, we know *all about* maladies,' said Mrs Starlight, having at last a point of reference. Ann coughed slightly into her fist and Mary fidgeted with the tight collar of her dress. 'Your poor mother, to suffer them!'

'Yes, she suffered terribly. And so it was recommended my father take her elsewhere, and subsequently, when a post came up, in this country, my father took it.'

'Indeed, yes, how fortunate.' Mrs Starlight was smiling at him now; she had one hand on each of her daughter's shoulders. 'Will you have madeira now, Mr Sweetley? And tell us,' she said, 'what is your view to the future?'

But the future evaded Mr Sweetley; his hands made a useless gesture and fastened instead around the madeira glass. 'I have travelled in my life,' he said quietly. 'I have not put down the roots a man of my age ought. When I settled in Canyon, I thought my talents, my knowledge, might be beneficially implemented. But it has all turned out otherwise.' He made circular motions with his glass on the tablecloth. 'I have disappointed them.'

The three women had never encountered a man of Mr Sweetley's temperament: it was intriguing. They listened closely to his account of Otto Cirque's escape from the Canyon courthouse, and found their low opinion of his townspeople absolutely confirmed in it.

'Your error,' said Ann, 'was only to *delegate*, Mr Sweetley.'

'A man must sleep, after all!' said Mary.

'If they think to abandon so good a man as yourself,' said Mrs Starlight, indignantly, 'well — if one turns the thing around, sir, you have the better cause to abandon *them*, after such treatment . . .'

'But I do not abandon them, Mrs Starlight.' He looked up, and Ann thought she could see herself reflected in his pale aqua eyes. 'The people of Canyon may no longer require my services, but I will put things right with them. Having once suffered the terrible repercussions of failed justice, I do not allow it to happen again. And that is my commitment. My commitment is to justice. In my mother's name, if nothing else, Mrs Starlight. In the name of my mother, Bodicea Sweetley.' He lifted his glass here, and the others all followed suit.

'Bodicea Sweetley,' they chimed.

It was an inferior wine, sugary and with scarcely any alcohol content – in fact, he was not sure it contained alcohol at all – but Mr Sweetley drank it to the bottom of the glass. Thereafter he felt himself subside into the sweetest state of sleepiness, and when the family retired for their post-prandial naps, found himself borne off to a little room on the top floor, where the softest, downiest pillows awaited, and, from below, the pretty muffled sounds of women talking could be faintly heard.

Chapter 17

Hospitality

Before the week was out, Borrel Sweetley was securely installed in the aforementioned garret bedroom, a tenancy further bolstered by the Starlight women's efforts on his professional behalf.

'We must find you an appointment,' Mary said. 'A man cannot otherwise hold high his head.'

It was not a difficult project to accomplish, the employment of Mr Borrel Sweetley. 'Anyone,' said Ann, 'can tell you have the right credentials.'

'You are equipped . . .'

'. . . with the right set of attributes.'

'Only don't mention you're —'

'We shall say you are from out of town.'

'A cousin.' Mary hooked her arm into Mr Sweetley's. 'A *distant* cousin!'

The Starlight sisters had advantageous friendships with their brother's superiors, and the appointment they found Mr Sweetley was that of Acting Bailiff of the Court. It had recently come up. There was a paucity, so the women told him, of qualified candidates for the job. They did not mention that the duties entailed by the position were notoriously taxing.

The Senior Sergeant accompanied Sweetley to his new office.

It was more than satisfactory. His appointment provided Mr Borrel Sweetley with all sorts of access. It would get him into the heart of the machinery. He bowed to the Senior Sergeant when he left, and shut the door of his new office. Then, taking from the pocket of his dark grey suit a white handkerchief (both articles supplied by the Senior Sergeant) he wiped a leather blotter clean of dust, and placed his briefcase upon it. He got up to check the door lock, then returned and began to lay out his booty, bone by bone, on the leather blotter. From the folio pocket of his briefcase he took a piece of flat white paper, set a small sequence of bones upon it, and began, with minute attention, to trace their outlines.

Sometimes, watching the baby feeding, Mrs Po felt so jealous she must strike her heels together on the floor to contain herself. Her love for this tiny creature was unexpected; she knew not where it came from but it was intense and heated and made her weep with joy, sometimes, and sometimes in despair.

It was in this state that she sat with Ivorie Hammer – quiet, roaming for things to talk of – when, one morning, perhaps a week after the baby's birth, a loud knock set up on Mrs Po's front door. Mrs Po feared it was her husband, who habitually locked himself out. If it was her husband, she would ask him to go around the back.

It was not her husband. It was a guest: a guest of her houseguest. Mrs Po ushered the guest into the sitting room, where she looked large and weather-beaten against Mrs Po's pale colour scheme.

'Racine!' said Ivorie warmly.

From her large features and angular physique, one might expect Racine to be the owner of a correspondingly mannish voice: useful perhaps for bringing dogs to heel. It was no such thing. Her voice was high and thin like a bird's. When she spoke she immediately woke the sleeping infant. 'Oh, Ivorie!' she said, putting a hand to her mouth. 'I'm so sorry!'

Mrs Po pushed forwards a chair for the old lady and stood vigilantly beside it. Racine sat gratefully and smiled at Mrs Po, who didn't smile back. She took her hat off, and her jacket, and lay them on the chair arm. Keeping her hands in her lap, she looked admiringly at the baby in Ivorie's arms. 'And the other?' she said, brightly. 'Of the pair?'

Inside Ivorie, something cracked drily. She took a deep breath. 'There was only one. In the end. Racine, I was wrong.' She tried to sound like it didn't matter, but her voice went a little shrill on 'wrong'.

'Oh?' Racine's smile remained on her lips, but her eyes looked around and blinked very quickly. 'Well, he's *lovely*.'

'She!' squeaked Mrs Po.

'Oh, *she*?'

Racine's presence, all of a sudden, in Mrs Po's lavender sitting room, produced a vestigial pang of loyalty in Ivorie: a kind of shadow-loyalty, sad but reconciled. 'Mrs Po,' she said, 'would you be so kind as to get us a refreshment? Miss Pfeffersalz has walked such a long way. And your cordials are so revitalising.' Ivorie smiled at Mrs Po, and Mrs Po trotted out to do her bidding; anyone who didn't know better might have thought her quite the lap dog.

'How are they *enduring*, out there, Racine? How are *you* enduring?' Ivorie used her softest voice. 'You do understand the reasons for my departure?'

'Oh, Ivorie, I am all understanding,' said Racine. 'You have been absolutely right to go. And *look* what you have found!' She presented her hands to the living room like big flat serving dishes, and then dropped them again. 'Out there, we are forced to submit to charity.' She leaned in closer. 'They bring down baskets, Ivorie – we are like beggars.'

There was an uncomfortable pause, then Racine got up suddenly, walked to the fireplace, and began examining the knick-knacks on Mrs Po's mantelpiece. It was an unexceptional collection, and did not warrant close attention; nevertheless, Racine studied intently, for some moments, a bow-lipped and bonneted china shepherdess. 'I have never before . . .' she said. Her large brown fingers turned Bo Peep upside down and studied the blue maker's mark on her base. '. . . Faced the future with such uncertainty.'

Having expressed herself thus, Racine returned to the chair by Ivorie's side, and sat down on it. She sat very close to Ivorie and thrust out her chin. It was a large square chin, like a doorstop, and it jammed its way into Ivorie's consciousness. 'You don't think I'm too old?'

'Absolutely not!' said Ivorie. She did not ask, 'Too old for what?' The baby had a large white curd spilling from its mouth. She shuffled it into a different position on her arm and wiped the curd away.

'A new situation,' said Racine, 'is what I need. A new situation. Perhaps Ivorie, you might help me . . .' she struggled for the right word. '. . . apply?'

It was not quite clear what sort of situation Racine was after, unless, thought Ivorie, there was a family in need of a maiden aunt. She put aside this thought, which seemed unnecessarily churlish.

'I have also heard,' Racine continued, 'that you were afforded great attentions in that *hospital*.'

'That is true . . .' said Ivorie, 'strictly speaking.'

'I wonder,' said Racine, 'if they could not do something for my various ailments –'

Mrs Po took this moment to return to the room, and she snapped up the word 'ailments' like a little starving crocodile. 'Ailments! You poor dear lady – what ailments do you suffer?' She distributed the glasses – barberry cordial, mildly alcoholic, deliriously sweet – and a warmth grew in the cold space between herself and the unexpected visitor. Ivorie was pleased.

But a spell of living-room warmth, though it might ameliorate the pangs of awkwardness, does not necessarily open two women up to the prospect of bosom friendship. And Mrs Po is not as pliable as she seems. She is, however, much softened by the nerves and reserves of her new friendship with Mrs Hammer. And though she has not yet felt sufficiently confident to foist upon her friend the whole dead carcass of her life, the presence of this second woman – this strange old lady, brown as a strip of town-hall carpet – creates a little space for Mrs Po and her story.

Mrs Po's was not a long story, and it was not markedly different from many others, but it was tragic in the way of most narratives of domestic estrangement.

'I,' said Mrs Po, 'could not have children of my own.' She blinked quickly several times. 'It is a terrible affliction, to be barren. But the fault, as it turned out, was not mine. The doctors assured me of that. It was the fault of my husband, Mr Po.' She stopped. It was an unseemly topic of conversation; she did not know that such questions were the stock-in-trade of Ivorie's childhood instruction under Morag Pappy. When she saw she was the only party discomfited by the intimation, she went on more boldly. 'One does not know these things when one marries. How could one know? It is a terrible unfairness. There should be a way, I have always thought, of finding out.'

'Alas, there is not!' said Ivorie. It occurred to her as an unfairness too, though not one that she need contemplate except distantly.

Mrs Po plucked at a cushion cover. 'Oh, he was a good enough man, James Po. He worked all his life at the penitentiary. He was very popular amongst the other employees. But those were different days in Pitch. If a man did not choose to come home to his wife, there were gambling houses and coffee houses — none of the prohibitions that operate now operated then. Oh, life was easy for a man if he was disappointed by circumstance.'

'It is so,' said Racine. 'It always has been.'

'We were very happy at first,' Mrs Po continued, 'but then . . . we were not. And Mr Po seemed as desperately to regret his choice to marry as I did. And so he did not come home very often.'

Racine cluck-clucked.

'See, when a woman misses that vital chance in her life, merely through a bad choice, a mistake that was not her own — well, how could I forgive . . . ?'

'Forgiveness,' Ivorie said sternly, 'cannot be forced where pain remains, Mrs Po.'

'When they closed the gaming houses and stopped the sale of liquor, Mr Po became as wretched as I. He retired from his work, but we no longer had a word to say to each other.'

'Such is the way between men and women,' said Racine, and put her hand on Mrs Po's.

'And like this we have existed year after year; it is a terrible way to spend one's life. And yet when we were young, I thought there was no other man I would rather spend my life with than James Po. I suppose I am a silly old woman.'

'How strangely life turns out sometimes,' said Racine. 'I myself have never married.' She pondered this as though it were a regret, though it was nothing of the kind.

'I thought no other man but James Po might make me happy. And yet he has made me miserable, and I have made him miserable, too.' Mrs Po looked down at her knees, and then up again. 'How does such a thing happen?'

Racine Pfeffersalz said she did not know.

Ivorie said, 'Poor, poor Mrs Po!' and at once gave her the baby to nurse. 'But now we are here and we are your friends. Take heart, Mrs

Po, take heart!' And then, in an impulse of kindness: 'Little Pette will provide all the opportunity you have missed. Look how she loves you already!' Pette had gone to sleep in Mrs Po's arms. Ivorie laughed. 'See! I am already entirely redundant.'

The three women laughed at this and Mrs Po felt, for the first time in many years, blessed.

Chapter 18

Two gentlemen procure employment

It had become apparent to Ernest Hammer very soon after arriving that Pitch was a town that did not require the services of another watchmaker.

The people of Pitch took time seriously, and cared for it accordingly. In only an hour of walking the Inner Pitch streets, Ernest had seen four men, strangers apparently, stop and adjust their pocket watches one with the other. He had seen three different groups of well-dressed children diligently remove watches before commencing to play marbles. This was a population of the oiling, winding, polishing type: in his prior experience, Mr Po had found this type to be very rare. And now here he was, surrounded by them – and they had no use for him whatsoever. Everywhere he looked he saw members of his professional fraternity going out of business: dusty shop windows with the word 'watchmaker' half scratched out and doors bogged up with unread newspapers; pleading, wheedling chalkboards advertising discount repairs. He clutched the bag in which his tools lay, undisturbed, unrequired.

After some minutes' aimless walking, Mr Hammer found himself at the Pitch Springs. He stood on a bridge and looked down to where a trickle of tea-coloured water flowed over some rocks. To his finely tuned olfactory nerves, the smell of the water seemed a distillation of the unpleasant odours of the Inner Pitch streets: odd and vegetable, a smell of drains mingling and slops collecting. Somehow, in the primordial backwaters of his mind, he recognised it as the smell of failure.

So strong was this recognition, and so primordial, that for a moment, Ernest felt inclined to throw the bag containing his watchmaking tools over the side of the bridge. He did not give in to the inclination, but it was strong nevertheless. He saw the bag with curious mental clarity, sinking into the puddles and mud and wet grass till only the handle protruded. He was surprised to find it still there, beneath his arm, when he looked.

His bag persisted in the face of failure, and so he decided to heed it. He made his way back over the bridge the way he had come. He did not think about his predicament again, until he arrived in a street called Pardoner's Way and met a gentleman pushing a barrow.

The barrow was full to the brim with paraphernalia, and precariously balanced. What's more, the gentleman was attempting to propel the barrow while simultaneously propelling himself on a pair of crutches. It was a ludicrous proposition. The man lurched, so did the barrow. Ernest Hammer stopped to help. He nodded at the gentleman, and relieved him of the barrow.

In this way, Ernest Hammer escorted George Duke, dealer in antiques and paraphernalia, to his small dwelling in the heart of Inner Pitch. 'It is rare,' said Duke, when finally they reached their destination, 'to find a person willing to sacrifice their time. For a stranger.'

To which Ernest responded that, having currently no other employment to occupy him, it was no sacrifice at all.

In private, George Duke liked to call himself an 'antiquarian'. His shop had an unpromising frontage, but its window was crammed with curiosities. And if the window was dusty, the curiosities were not.

The two men sat inside, well below street level, where the little light that penetrated was curiously dappled as if leafy tree-branches brushed against windows (though in fact there was only a grate looking directly onto cobblestones and pedestrians' ankles). The antiquarian put on a pair of pince-nez, much fortified with wire. 'In my youth,' he said, 'objects meant much more to me than things to be bought and sold, Mr Hammer. I always thought of them as *repositories* of the past. I was interested in their history. They tell stories, you see, even the most homely object has a story to tell.' He lifted his teacup towards Ernest. 'Even something simple like this cup, for instance. See the chip on its rim – what, I wonder, put that there? A clumsy scullery maid? Or perhaps it was *flung* at someone in anger, or broke on a lady's tooth, or on her ring. The possibilities are endless. Many times, Mr Hammer, an object has turned up to tell the true story behind a crime. Such simple things as misplaced hair ribbons, snuffboxes, handkerchiefs, have sent men to the gallows!' Mr Duke removed his glasses and rubbed his eyes. 'But that is all for the book writers and the lawmen. I am old and tired now, Mr Hammer. Objects have become merely *a means to an end*, and I am afraid, as the main beneficiary of that end, I am not much chop at pursuing vigorously the means. All these . . .' he gestured to the many cartons that lay about the room. '. . . For which I no longer have the energy. And all the other things for which I can't seem to . . . *manage* . . . the footwork any more.' He looked at his feet dismally, then picked up a small black trinket box from the table next to him, and considered it while speaking. 'All of it. So tiring. The auction houses. The deceased estates. The markets. Even for the fit and healthy.' He prised the trinket box open, and fished out a small cheap ring. 'You say you think you can tell the value of a thing, Mr Hammer?' He proffered the trinket box. 'Just the box, not the ring. Give me your opinion.' He folded his hands limply over his chest and waited.

Ernest took the box. It was of a dark European wood, and the tiny dovetail joins were painstakingly executed. The lid was inlaid with a lighter wood – birch perhaps – finely worked in the shape of a tulip. Inside, the box was lined with red silk, and the silk was in almost-perfect condition. He made a cautious estimate of its worth. It was worth something. It was not worth much. The antiquarian nodded, observed him for a moment, fetched something else.

'And this?'

It went on for half an hour or so: an examination of sorts. Ernest was shown nutcrackers and bottle-openers and heart-shaped mirrors; he was asked to pass judgement on a bone-handled gentleman's manicure set, a cameo brooch, a poor replica of a Byzantine urn.

Through it all, the antiquarian observed him patiently. Ernest could not tell if he was satisfied until the end, when he removed the pince-nez and put out his long thin hand. 'Tomorrow,' he said, 'you can start. You can help me. I can't pay you much.' He shook Ernest's hand: it was not a robust handshake by any means, but it was sufficiently substantial for Ernest to rely on.

Then the antiquarian picked up an old manuscript from the table beside him, and began leafing through it; Ernest, assuming himself dismissed, left quietly.

In another part of town, with an office entirely to himself, complete with bookshelves and filing cabinets and dark, academic paintings, Mr Borrel Sweetley was feeling overstretched. The legal bureaucracy that propped up the Municipality of Pitch was a labyrinthine affair. There was a backlog. There was a 'pending' file like Mount Everest. Sweetley was having to read vast legal tracts, with the aid of vast legal dictionaries, to get on top of it all. There were original writs to formulate, summons and subpoenas to issue; there were search warrants to make out, and injunctions to impose, as well as other, more unpleasant, obligations: goods to seize and impound, landowners to dispossess, husbands to bear away from wives. It was onerous: aside from Mr Sweetley's first diagram-making day, he had not once been at leisure to consider his own personal interests. The bones languished in his office safe, along with the drawings he had made, and he felt sure, looking in on them, that every day they disintegrated a little more.

Then, just as he was foundering under the weight of it all, something low and ashamed slunk into his office. He hardly registered the knock that preceded this creature's arrival, but he must have said, 'Come in,' because when he looked up, there it was, quivering and wringing its hat. He narrowed his eyes.

'Well, well,' he said. He put down his pen. 'Well, well, well, well, well.'

Lawrence didn't falter. He raised his neck a few notches, as if mustering the courage, and then scurried forwards to float something on to Mr Sweetley's desk.

It was a letter. Cheap stock. It had been opened previously and its contents perused – there was a gravy stain and several thumbprints. Borrel Sweetley slid the contents from the envelope, keeping his eye all the time on Lawrence, who pretended to look up and about at the academic paintings. Sweetley unfolded the letter from its three-way concertina, and read. Re-read. Re-folded. Returned it to its envelope. He held the envelope between index and thumb, letting it swing slightly. He did not mean to imply that Lawrence should take it back, but Lawrence shot forwards, snatched it, and tucked it into his trousers.

'Thought you might be inter-rested,' he said, rolling his tongue in the bowl of his cheek.

'I *am* interested,' Borrel Sweetley said, with great measure. He cocked his head, as though Lawrence were a small wayward child. 'But can I trust you, Lawrence? You have already once let me down.'

'It's up to you,' said Lawrence. 'I'm just deliverin' information.'

'Well,' said Mr Sweetley. 'Let me put it to you like this, sir.' He came around to Lawrence's side of the desk. 'There was a time, you see, and a place, when such information was of crucial importance to me. And you did not *deliver* it then.' He eyed Lawrence with a calm curiosity, as though considering, from a great philosophical distance, how many strokes of the cane to apply. 'I was left to *squirm*, sir, for your error.' He shook his head. 'You were mad at me,' was all Lawrence said. 'Couldn't come near you with information or not.'

This was partly true; however, there was another reason Lawrence had not come forwards earlier with this information: he had not actually known it *was* information.

He had known, of course, that it was not *procedurally correct* to allow Otto Cirque to receive letters in his cell. He knew it like he knew you didn't allow a prisoner access to cakes, or baskets of fruit, or anything that might contain a file or a pair of scissors or a gardening implement. But he had reasoned his way through the conundrum. He had reasoned that, as the letter was from Morag Pappy, he had better deliver it, as one did not idly obstruct that lady's missives from reaching their intended destinations.

Nor, however, did he consider lightly his obligations to Mr Sweetley. So, although he did indeed deliver the letter to the prisoner, he studied it minutely first. He removed the single sheet from its envelope and unfolded it and smoothed it out. He held it up to the light, in case it contained a message in invisible ink. He scrutinised the triangular corners of the envelope for embedded evidence. He concluded that it was safe. He gave it to the prisoner, and, when the prisoner had read it, he took it back again. Unfortunately, there was one thing lacking in Lawrence, which made his assiduous study of Morag's letter utterly superfluous: he couldn't read.

This was why he had not come forwards earlier. In fact, it had taken him several weeks' detective work – scanning newspapers, asking seemingly innocuous questions, drawing the alphabet in the dirt – to determine what the content of the letter actually amounted to.

'Didn't reckonise the significance,' he said, trying to be offhand.

'That,' said Borrel Sweetley, 'is because you are a fool.'

Lawrence nodded, and stooped a little in recognition, as though a brick had just been placed on his spine.

'And you can't read.'

Another brick: misshapen with old mortar.

'I have a question for you.' Borrel Sweetley turned his back on Lawrence, and began tending to his things. 'The question is: Do you want to make up for the time you have wasted, Lawrence?' A paper skidded onto the floor from a pile of documents Borrel Sweetley was making. He passed the pile to Lawrence, whose arms came up automatically to receive it. 'Do you want your actions in life to be worthwhile, or do you want to go on being a fool?'

Lawrence, to be honest, was like one of those tragic old dogs you sometimes see, cankerous, half starved: its master proffers a bone and snatches it away again, time after time, and the dog never gets wise to the trick.

'No . . . don't want to be no fool,' he said.

'Good, Lawrence. Now give me the letter, and we shall check its authenticity, shall we?'

Borrel Sweetley resumed laying bricks, and Lawrence collapsed entirely.

Chapter 19

The sleeping genie

Whereas some of our company – the Hammers, Mr Sweetley, and now Lawrence – have found it entirely reasonable to abandon their fellow townspeople, you and I, dear reader, are not so heartless. We observe certain loyalties. We have certain narrative commitments. Let us return now to the outskirts of Pitch where the people of Canyon have set up camp – let us walk there alongside that good-hearted octogenarian, Racine Pfeffersalz.

It is twilight. Racine hums a little as she walks. She shakes her head affectionately, thinking about Ivorie Hammer and the poor little Po woman. She carries with her a bottle of Mrs Po's barberry cordial. By the time she arrives at the campsite, she is ready for a nip or two. Bald Sherry consents to join her.

Bald Sherry peers at the bottle of barberry cordial, and peers again. Next to him, on a wooden plank mounted on two tin drums, lie a couple of bush fowl whose necks he has recently wrung. Racine is absently fingering one of the bird's feathers. A louse wriggles out and she withdraws her hand abruptly.

'Oh, she just gathers them herself,' she goes on, 'from bushes round about . . .' She takes a small glass and holds it out towards Bald Sherry. 'She's a very nice lady, Mr Sherry. And life has dealt her a terrible hand.'

Bald Sherry picks at the wax plug in the top of the bottle neck. He pokes a nail in, wriggles it about, dislodges the plug, beaded with crystallised sugar. A smell oozes out (a 'bouquet', one should probably call it), contaminated by caramels, but promising nevertheless, more than promising.

'It reminds me of something . . .' Racine says, sniffing investigatively, '. . . from my first taste this afternoon, it had me thinking of my youth. What was it?' She has her finger up in the air, as if waiting for the lost fragment of memory to land upon it. 'It had a sing-song name,' she goes on, 'but was not at all sweet like this.' Bald Sherry fills the glass for her; a rather larger one for himself. 'Eau de vie . . . de-something . . .' Racine is thinking hard, batting her eyelids. 'Eau de vie . . . de-baie-de-houx . . . That's it!' She smiles, raises her glass. 'My grandfather made it. In Hohenlinden, Mr Sherry! He mixed it with honey, to help me sleep. Brandy made from the holly berries!'

Bald Sherry has a mouthful of Mrs Po's cordial, is rolling it around, letting it pool in his mouth. He swallows, and a smile passes over his face. He clinks his tumbler against Racine's sherry glass.

'To Hohenlinden!' he says. He takes a second mouthful, and looks around to ensure they are not overheard. 'It's my birthday,' he confides.

'Congratulations!' says Racine, dipping her tongue into her glass to get the last drop. 'Are you roasting chickens?'

Tonight is indeed the eve of Bald Sherry's forty-seventh birthday. But though the chickens lie there, expectantly, on his crude chef's table, he is not assessing their potential as savoury meats. For in the world he inhabits, and has long inhabited, food is merely an adjunct to beverages; and in the absence of said beverages, roast chicken is an obtuse and illogical proposition: he can see no application for it. It is his birthday and he is desperate.

Upon arriving in Pitch and opening his most precious article of luggage, he had found the liquor bottles inside the crate shattered, every one. There had been some irreplaceable specimens in that collection: a Très Vieille Grande Réserve cognac from the house of Augier; a single malt whisky from the Orkney Islands; a bottle of re-distilled Dutch gin, flavoured with coriander, cassia and orris root . . . Now it all sloshed together in an unbearable motley blend, soaking into the wood.

Perversely, inexplicably, his second unopened crate – the crate containing sweet cheap sherry and rough white spirits – remained perfectly intact.

There was not a single tavern to be found in Pitch. Not a wine shop, not a brewery, not even a solitary delinquent liquor merchant operating from a ground-floor window. Even the range of medicines on display in the chemist's window lacked anything with an appreciable alcohol content. Sherry had understood then the grim, lined faces of the gentlemen, the chilly aloofness of the young ladies. They were cold and self-denying, these people; they were *teetotallers.*

Bald Sherry swallowed the remainder of his cordial thoughtfully and, leaving Racine to pluck the chickens, picked his way through the overgrown grass. The light was dying, but thoughts had occurred to him, requiring answers, and he had three stops to make.

He stopped first at the nearest patch of berry bushes. There was no shortage of this plant. It ran wild, like blackberry, and like blackberry, these berries were no easy picking with their thorny stems and tough serrated leaves. He took a bunch, wrestling it from the branch. The berries were the size of sultana grapes, hard but moist: they left juice on his hand when he squeezed tightly. He brought his hand up to his nose and breathed deeply. The scent was not disappointing. It was slightly cherry, slightly plum, and slightly something else, unusual, elusive. It was also – no doubt about it – the stuff from which Racine's cordial had been made.

With a clutch of berries in his pocket, Bald Sherry proceeded to his next stop. Alongside the campsite, stutteringly, as though only just shaping a bed for itself, ran a creek. Further along, it ran more freely. Bald Sherry made his hand into a boat and scooped up a mouthful. It was just the way water should be: cold, fresh, and tasteless.

He stood up and wiped his hands on his trousers, leaving a dark berry stain, and proceeded to his third and final stop.

He arrived at the door of the single enclosed structure on the camp site. Leaning uneasily against the west-facing wall of the building stood a small disused water tank, overgrown with vines, and harbouring something slightly rotten in its shallows – an animal; several, perhaps. Sherry pulled his belt out of its loops and used it to measure the water tank's diameter and height; he performed a short equation in his notebook in which these measurements were transformed into gallons. Then he flicked the notebook shut, marking his place, and considered the building itself.

It was more like an outhouse or an engine room than anything else:

it was very small in dimension, and derelict. Its door sagged; its bricks were, in places, either punched in or tumbling out; and the spaces left for windows sported boards so rotten a child might put a hand through them. The back wall, facing out and away from the campsite, had succumbed to dereliction entirely: it constituted a wall no longer, but was merely a low and tumbledown ledge upon which a handful of bricks precariously balanced.

The interior of this decrepit structure was hung with strings of dust, and smelled damp and mouldy. Finding in his pocket the stump of a candle, Bald Sherry lit it and propped it on a window sill.

In the light thus produced – a spattering, guttering light that tended to the unreal – his imagination, to use a hackneyed phrase, *took flight*. It flew with both wings into the dark and broken ceiling of the little outhouse, and there it roosted, casting a small beady eye about it. Beneath its gaze, the future gathered into new shapes; it coiled and concertinaed into long copper pipes, and suspended itself between shining great urns; it hunkered down and became a huge brick-enclosed boiler; overhead, it shimmied and caught the light and multiplied into a series of copper-mesh sieves and glass chambers.

Bald Sherry could see the bright surfaces and the steam; he could feel the heat in the furnace and hear the infinitesimal drip-drip of condensation high above. He envisaged the little camp bed in which he would sleep, so he might tend the distillation processes at close hand. He saw himself, not far into the future, uncapping his first bottle, pouring fine-grade brandy into a small *ballon*, raising it to his lips. A buxom young woman poured similar glassfuls for a room of rowdy drinkers; coins slapped down on wood; glasses were drained and more glasses ordered. Someone, somewhere, played a fiddle.

Chapter 20

Breakfast

There was no doubt about it, the child born to Ivorie Hammer was peculiar. It went through the motions of early infancy – wet, dry, croupe, rash, most of which were competently taken care of by Mrs Po – but it failed to entrap its mother's sympathies. Its mother was not hooked. She tried, but was not in love.

The failure vexed Mr Hammer, who did love the child, instantly and fiercely; a love that was near to pain.

'Look at her, my darling,' he said to his wife. 'She has your ears – just the same!'

'A shame,' said Ivorie, going on with something or other she was folding, 'Not my best feature.' She looked sideways at the Baby Pette, who was inspecting her father's face so minutely that she had become cross-eyed, and folded several garments in quick succession. Her failure hung low and heavy and shameful with her, and she could not throw it off. Mrs Po was helpful in this regard, for whenever the cloud most overwhelmed Ivorie, she was able to pass on the troublesome, unusual creature to the superior ministrations of her landlady. In this manner, she slid away from feelings another might have investigated, or even resolved, and into the ease of practicality, which, though temporarily relieving, could not indefinitely sustain itself.

In the middle of the night, Ernest Hammer was woken by his wife. It was not that she shook him or kicked him or spoke out in her sleep; she did none of those things. She simply opened her eyes.

'Ivorie?' said Ernest. He hauled himself up onto his elbow and peered at her. She did not blink.

'Are you awake, Ivorie?'

In fact, she was not, but she gave such a good impression of it and was so forthright in her confirmation of the fact, that her husband did not contradict her.

'Are you having trouble sleeping, my dear?'

'I have been thinking,' she said.

'What about?'

Ivorie turned her eyes to her husband, and Ernest saw they were her sleep eyes, much rounder and fuller than the wakeful version. 'I have been thinking and thinking,' she said, 'and I cannot remember the name of our other baby.'

'My darling,' said Ernest, 'Which other baby do you mean?'

Ivorie's eyes returned to the ceiling. 'Well, I took one of them with me and left the other like a shopping bag on the seat, Ernest, would you believe? I suspect Morag has looked after it . . .'

'My darling, there is no other baby.'

'Well, of course there is . . . But what is its name? Oh, Mr Hammer! Why can I not remember its name?'

Ernest felt for her hand. 'It's all right, Ivorie,' he said, 'everything is perfectly all right. You have one baby girl named Pette. One lovely little baby girl. She's asleep in the next room. There is no other one.'

'But of course there is. The other one, Mr Hammer, the pretty one. And I am a terrible, terrible woman, for I have forgotten her name! Oh, where is my mother – she would be able to tell me!'

Ernest took Ivorie's hand. 'Our baby's name is Pette, Ivorie. Listen – she's in the room next door. If you put your ear up against the wall, you might even hear her breathing.'

Ivorie Hammer knelt on the bed beside her husband, pressed her ear flat to the wall and could not, of course, hear her baby daughter breathing. But the effort this required brought her back to consciousness, and she fell to sobbing very quietly with her husband's arms about her.

'Oh, Mr Hammer . . . I have not made a fool of myself, have I?'

'No, my dear,' he said. 'You have been many things, but never a fool.'

Nevertheless, when Ivorie returned to sleep, she dreamt of bookended girls, a dark one and a light, in matching dresses. They were quite grown up and elegant; one of them carried a tennis racquet, and the other a book of sheet music.

'I would like to make the purchase of a good dictionary,' Ivorie announced to Mrs Po next morning. She moved about the kitchen meaningfully, putting away a glass here, a tea towel there. 'You must recommend me a good bookshop.'

'A bookshop?' said Mrs Po. She said it up and down and up again, in wonder, as though Mrs Hammer had just asked her where she might purchase a clutch of poisonous insects, or a piece of ancient vellum. 'Goodness.' Mrs Po wrenched her ring back and forth across her large wedding finger. 'Well now, I really must think.'

There were no books in the Po house. Ivorie had noticed this some time ago. It was perhaps unkind of her to force Mrs Po's attention to the question of their procurement. 'Forgive me, Mrs Po,' she said. 'I know you're not a reader.'

The tea Mrs Po had brewed was a very strong, black variety. Ivorie could not help grimacing at the first mouthful; she felt it immediately stain her teeth. 'I shall go out myself and investigate,' she said, running her finger round the rim of the teacup, then pushing it away decisively. 'Yes. I shall take the baby, and I shall visit my husband at his new place of employ. And perhaps,' she said, '*perhaps* I will begin making enquiries about my mother.' A feeling of wellbeing overcame her. The curtains in Mrs Po's kitchen fluttered in the breeze, and the morning sun, where it hit her face, felt warm and benign. She became, suddenly, impulsive: 'Here I am, Mrs Po, here together, securely ensconced, with *you*,' she said, reaching across and squeezing her landlady's hand, 'who have been my guardian angel . . .' (Mrs Po could not help smiling) 'and now . . .' Ivorie withdrew her hand, 'I must get my bearings. It's disgraceful. I have not once been into town!'

She smiled at Mrs Po again. Mrs Po looked down at her hand and found something had been pressed into it. It was the second instalment. It was slightly sweaty, but otherwise unwrinkled. She smoothed it out and placed it under the butter dish.

'And we must speak,' Ivorie said, 'about *Miss Pfeffersalz*.'

'Miss Pfeffersalz?' Mrs Po's face was mottled and bright. *She* was not enjoying the sun: it was too warm; she was overdressed. She shook some crumbs from a linen napkin, and gathered them towards her in a little pile.

'Miss Pfeffersalz is a very old lady.'

Mrs Po nodded.

'I feel,' Ivorie placed her hand over her heart, 'a certain duty of care.'

Mrs Po nodded again. She neatened her pile of crumbs into a pyramid.

'It is almost a – oh, I cannot think of the word!' Ivorie concentrated on her memory lapse, then laughed, and shook her head. 'I am *useless* without my dictionary, Mrs Po, useless . . .'

'We cannot have her here,' Mrs Po said abruptly, not looking at her friend.

Ivorie continued to smile, but there was a small pout hovering at its corners. She waited a moment before going on. 'I had thought your acquaintance was flourishing, Mrs Po. Miss Pfeffersalz has been four times to visit, and you appear to get along famously, the two of you? Do you not?' Ivorie inclined her head. 'Was I mistaken?'

'It is all very well,' continued Mrs Po, not looking at Ivorie, 'to *get along*. I am happy to get along with anyone. But I am not –' she glared at the table-top, '– running a hotel.'

So there it was: Mrs Po's objection. She was a solid object after all. She had a will of her own. This fact caught Ivorie completely off guard. She made a neatening motion with her mouth as though there was lipstick on it.

'Oh, Mrs Po,' she said, a touch sadly. 'I had not intended to insinuate such a thing. Oh dear,' she said, 'I see I have been quite tactless.'

Mrs Po was wrestling with all kinds of conflicting emotions. She did not want to lose her tenant, who had already brightened, immeasurably, her lacklustre life. Part of her would indulge Ivorie's every whim. But another part of her resisted, firmly, despite herself, like a mother committed to a method of infant discipline.

Ivorie sighed deeply. 'It's so vexing . . .'

Mrs Po studiously didn't ask.

'There must be something we can do for her.' Ivorie put her knuckles to her mouth and contemplated. 'I suppose I will keep a look out, in town,' she continued. She eyed Mrs Po the whole time for signs of softening, but Mrs Po had become a squat grey object, made of ironbark or concrete or lead.

'I believe,' said Mrs Po, 'that there are several very good rooming houses. In Pitch.' She got up from the table, and disposed of her handful of detritus. A very slight cry from upstairs caught her attention, and instantly the Mrs Po of old returned. 'I shall bring the baby down, shall I?' she said, and was gone.

Ivorie sat at the kitchen table. It was certainly curious, it was certainly new, this objection of Mrs Po's. She took a mouthful of cold black tea and wondered how enduring the objection might prove to be. Then her left breast leaked a thimbleful of milk, and she remembered: there were some things, after all, that Mrs Po could not do herself.

Another exchange had occurred in that same kitchen some two or three hours earlier. Could one call it an exchange? There was no incident in it, no conversation. Mr Po and Mr Hammer had simply eaten breakfast together.

The kitchen of Mr and Mrs Po was a large room with slightly uneven floorboards. Mats cropped up where you least expected them, but otherwise, there was no cluttering of objects or superfluous receptacles. By the door stood an ice box. On the wall above the stove – the only sign of mishap – a burn that resembled a splat of meat juice.

Mrs Po had so far paid Mr Hammer only the most cursory attention. She had ascertained, for instance, her tenant's preference from her repertoire of cooked eggs, but beyond this she had not enquired. Her husband, however, took incuriosity a step or two further: *Mr* Po did not seem to mark the presence of his new tenants at all. Here were the two of them, at table, and Ernest felt no more acknowledged than the blowfly caught to a streamer of sticking tape above their heads. The silence was broken only by the leaves of newspaper shifting beneath Mr Po's hand and the clink of a knife handle against the rim of a plate.

Ernest had tried once or twice to initiate conversation with his host, but had not received an answer. There was nothing in Mr Po's expression that suggested antipathy: it was a bland expression, vacant, dull-eyed, but it was not hostile. On the contrary, it seemed entirely without opinion.

Nevertheless, in this quiet kitchen, on a quiet morning, Mr Po possessed a certain abject power. It was his lack of power, Ernest thought, that made him powerful. Because he did not care, he did not suffer.

Ernest watched him rise slowly from his chair and take his dishes to the sink. He bent at the waist, he soaped and rinsed. He proceeded from table to sink, from sink to doorway as though no decision were involved in his movements.

The door, which, taut on its spring, habitually banged shut in such a way as to cause people to jump, did no such thing when Mr Po left the room: it seeped into its catch with a wheezing sound. Mr Po made no noise going down the pathway to his shed. The newspaper, where he'd left it on the kitchen table, lay open at the death notices.

Chapter 21

Mackaby Lane

Stepping from the Ring Road onto the cobbled lanes of Inner Pitch, Ivorie Hammer did not feel immediately at home. The sensation was rather more gradual and it had to do with the streets themselves: their narrowness, the height of the houses that lined them on either side. There were first floors here, and cellars, but there were also second floors, and third; there were attics and garrets and rooftops. Way up above, the sky was a narrow blue rectangle, neatly cropped at the corners.

She had not, in the end, brought Baby Pette with her. Though Mrs Po had procured for her a large blue, well-sprung perambulator, the cobblestones, it was decided, would agitate the occupant excessively. Nor would Ivorie be able to manoeuvre the apparatus over shop stoops. Ivorie agreed readily. The baby had been cranky that morning. She would be better able to love her if she went without her. Something finely tuned quivered beneath her ribs at this reasoning; she did not quite know what to do with the reverberation.

Mrs Po had drawn a map, even though Ivorie had assured her it was not necessary. 'I have a natural sense of direction,' she said. But Mrs Po was right to insist; the density of buildings in Inner Pitch made it hard to gauge east and west, north and south; landmarks were not visible until you were on top of them. 'If you take the first cobbled street off the Ring Road, you will come out eventually at the town square,' Mrs Po said. 'There, on your right, is the hospital; on your left, the town hall. Now, the street running through the *middle* of the square *looks* like nothing much, but if you proceed down it, it will widen and you will see it is quite a thoroughfare. It is called Mackaby Lane, and there, Mrs Hammer, you will find the best shops.' She paused. '*Your* husband,' she went on, pointing to her map, 'is in the antique dealer's district. You can get there by taking any of the left turns off Mackaby Lane. But make sure you keep the law courts *to the east of you* at all times. If you cross them, you will be in the Fine Linen district, and although there is much to look at there, you will not find a dictionary, nor your husband.' She trailed off. Ivorie was trimming a hat and hardly listening. Later, she would wish she had taken more notice.

The town square was small and you would not know it was a focal point or meeting place if it were not for a slightly raised stone in its centre, decorated with a brass plaque. Ivorie registered, on her right, the hospital. She did not wish to revisit her time there – she felt a strange plummeting sensation in her stomach just thinking about it – so she went on, down the lane Mrs Po had recommended.

It did widen, but it remained nevertheless *compressed*. Mackaby Lane was a small, compressed glut of shops, and it was prohibitively busy. But it was busy with the best kind of trade. Everything seemed to glisten: from the sweets arranged in crystallised slabs in shop windows to the pendants in the jeweller's window and the glass buttons on a pale pink crepe de chine blouse in a dressmaker's shop. Even the eyes of the well-dressed women shoppers glistened. Silvery, mercurial, they darted carelessly over Ivorie Hammer without taking her in, certainly without assuming any interest in her beyond her status as an obstruction in the pathway.

Another less susceptible intelligence might have described these shining eyes differently: as 'glassy' perhaps, or 'cold'. It would not have made a difference to Ivorie, however, who stood on the pavement turning her head to left and right rapturously.

How had Pitch managed such sophistication? Ladies from fashionable cities, so far as she knew, did not scribble the town of 'Pitch' onto their holiday itineraries. It must have to do with singularity of purpose, Ivorie decided: everyone desiring the same result, and pursuing it relentlessly.

Although in other things Ivorie Hammer would prove to be quite wrong, in this, she was correct. She discovered it was so as soon as she entered a covered avenue called Mackaby Book Arcade and took off her gloves.

Mackaby Book Arcade, though narrow, had high ceilings fitted with white opaque glass. Small utterances rang out sharply. Heels striking the floor resounded like cracking whips. It was not a snug place, not a place in which one could bury one's head in a book without the pressure of purchase. And there was, in fact, only one wall of publications here that could properly be described as 'books'. The arcade consisted mainly of tables and magazine racks and long upright reading lecterns. Presented casually thereon were magazines and catalogues and picture books; large, hardbacked publications secured to the lecterns with chains. These publications had names like *City Leisure* and *The Boddington and Press Fine Fabric company presents . . .*' Ivorie picked up and glanced at a mail-order catalogue with the headline 'Latest Shapes in Blue Wolf' and another promising 'Frocks of True Artistry!' There were magazines given over entirely to buttons, and others that concentrated on shoe leather. Several magazines were in languages Ivorie did not immediately recognise; she was amazed to discover, looking closer at their dates of publication, that they were recent editions.

She might have spent several hours, pleasantly occupied, recapping *Mr Henry Clutterbuck's Year in Pictures*, but she was strict with herself: she allowed herself half an hour only. Then, eschewing entirely the joys of 'Men's Trouser-legs', she proceeded to the far end of the arcade where a long low counter stood and, behind it, a thin man with a wide mouth.

'Madam?' he said, seeing Ivorie approach empty-handed. His hair was sleek as paint. He smiled.

When Ivorie explained what she was looking for, his wide mouth narrowed and Ivorie thought he might put his hands on his hips. He did not. But he did close his eyes very patiently, as if recalling invisible boxes and bundles; he then disappeared, returning several moments later with a single black book.

It was small and its pages were edged with a chalky red dye that rubbed off on Ivorie's fingertips. The cover was thin, insubstantial. Worst of all, the type had been carelessly set so it sloped into the left-hand gutter and occasionally the beginnings of a word disappeared into the binding.

'I'm sorry,' said Ivorie Hammer. 'Don't you have anything else?'

The man shook his head, and slid the dictionary back onto his own side of the counter. He did not ask if he could be of further assistance.

Out on the street, Ivorie wished she had been more forthright. '*That* is not a dictionary!' she ought to have exclaimed. And: 'Do you call yourself a *bookseller*?' But she had not the requisite bravado. Her footing was all wrong. And though a part of her still thrilled to the prospect of millinery and button boots, she could not enjoy the elation properly now. She thought of her three-thousand-page dictionary crashing down the side of a mountain. She thought of miniature cauliflower holes bitten into proper nouns, verbs disappearing behind damp swells and pale green fur: earth composting language effortlessly.

She looked vaguely into shop windows, wondering if there were another bookshop somewhere nearby. She searched for Mrs Po's map. She had started out with it in her hand, but she seemed no longer to have it. Without this she could not remember how to proceed in order to find her husband. Was she to keep the law courts *to the east* or *to the west*? And what law courts were those? She could not see anything that looked like law courts, only a long, low, red-brick building that reminded her of a toy train station.

Ahead of her walked a slim woman and a child. Ivorie took several steps forwards and tapped the woman's shoulder.

The woman wheeled around. They were on the dwindling edges of Mackaby Lane now; the shops were thinning out, and one could smell vegetables from far away. The woman's face was white and the skin around her nose and chin was unnaturally smooth. Ivorie thought of leeks and hard white onions. 'Yes?' said the woman, pulling her daughter in towards her.

'Excuse me,' said Ivorie. 'I wonder if you would give me some directions if it wouldn't trouble you.' The little girl observed her with a degree of interest and admiration; the mother did not.

'It won't trouble me,' she said, swiftly and cleanly, in the manner perhaps of a well-handled scythe, 'if you get on with it.'

Ivorie was taken aback. 'Well, I did have a map but I've mislaid it . . .' she said, losing her place in the exchange. 'I'm looking for my husband's place of work. He is employed by the antique dealer, Mr George Duke . . .'

Now the woman did look at her properly, with grey eyes like highly polished river stones. 'Are you one of those circus people?' she asked.

It was a lightly executed question, but Ivorie could tell the curiosity behind it was savage. Something bristled in her: it was not loyalty. It had more to do with knowing her coat was the wrong cut, and wanting *others* to know that she knew it.

'No, I am not one of those *circus people*,' she said. 'But I *am* from out of town, and I'm completely disoriented.' The child smiled very earnestly up at her, trying to compensate for her mother's rudeness.

The woman shrugged one shoulder forwards as though slamming a drawer shut with it. 'Well,' she said, and waved broadly with her hand to the right. 'If it's George Duke you want, I seem to recall he's that way. About a five-minute walk that way.' She rubbed her top teeth with her tongue. 'Do not go too far, or you will fall into less charitable parts of town.' So saying, she took her daughter by the hand, and continued on her way.

Ivorie no longer felt like looking at the shops. She turned to the right as directed, and was horrified to feel a hot stinging sensation behind her eyelids. She knew that tears, once spilled, would be irretrievable. She would become someone else entirely. She clenched her eyes dry and plunged deep into the narrow right-hand streets of Pitch.

If she hadn't been concentrating so furiously on subjugating her tears, she might have noticed many things, of more and less importance, as she went. She might have noticed the gutters growing ranker. She might have seen melted wax on door stoops, and dogs sniffing hopefully at newspapers. A two-horse cart jogged past her silently through an area of the road laid deep with straw: she kept walking and her shoes no longer echoed. The rectangle of blue sky above narrowed, and shadows grew longer. There were certainly no shops here in which fine linen was sold, or husbands worked alongside antique dealers, polishing brass and silver.

She had stumbled into a dull, dead quarter: the potato peel quarter, the slop pail quarter. She had no idea where she was, or how to find her way back. All around her the last bits of sunshine were disappearing. Women were drawing curtains. She smelt smoke. She decided to try to work her way back the way she had come, turning left where she had previously turned right. Against all logic, however, her left turns seemed to drive her deeper into the fug and grime of the bad part of Inner Pitch.

She walked and walked and recognised nothing, until finally she became giddy and had to sit down. Somebody had left an empty pail and scrubbing brush on a door step. The door step looked welcoming. It looked recently scrubbed. Ivorie sat and tried to collect herself. The small lozenge of panic that had worked its way up from her stomach and into her chest left no room for extraneous observations. Hence Ivorie did not notice the peculiarities of the building upon whose stoop she now sat. She did not notice the ornate braziers on either side of its entrance way, the half-bent ironwork sign above the door with the word 'belles' still discernible. She failed to register the pale rose-coloured light burning somewhere deep within the house, like a heart.

She noticed only that the scrubbing brush was worn down almost to the stub, and that the bucket handle had come loose on one side. She noticed a piece of grey wool stuck in the dried candle wax and a small hole that required darning on her coat. Soon she began to feel calm enough to assess her situation again. But, as it turned out, she did not need to assess her situation at all, for someone was coming to her rescue. Her saviour appeared, at first, as a small charcoal smudge at the bottom of the adjacent street, walking hurriedly, with a kind of trip-trap officiousness and large hips. It was a gait Ivorie recognised, and as it grew closer she felt a great deal of love and affection for it. She stood up. 'Hello,' she called out, and waved.

Borrel Sweetley saw her and peered and could not make her out at first. When he finally recognised who it was, he felt emotions similar to Ivorie's own. He pulled himself up straight and performed a sort of half walk, half skip towards her.

'Madam,' he said, sternly but affectionately, upon arriving at her door stoop, 'that is *no* place for you to sit.' He took her hand, put his other behind her waist, and helped her down the steps. 'Come,' he said, looking around hurriedly, 'let me take you, Mrs Hammer, to a *much* nicer part of town.'

Ivorie was so relieved she did not care where he took her.

Chapter 22

The Starlight sisters

The Starlight sisters had not been impressed by the presence, at Mr Sweetley's side, of the thin dark boy with sloping shoulders. Mr Sweetley had introduced him to them as 'Lawrence, my manservant', but this did not put their minds at rest. They did not like the way Lawrence the manservant loitered, waiting for Mr Sweetley when he was not home. They especially disliked his expression when they spoke to him, as if he were entertaining unsavoury thoughts.

They were quite relieved, now, to be introduced to this *other friend* of Mr Sweetley's. Mrs Ivorie Hammer was in every way acceptable. Mary would comment later on her creamy complexion, and Ann would admire a certain dimpling Mrs Hammer's cheeks had when smiling. Neither were ill-natured enough to mention the cut of her coat. Lawrence was dispatched immediately to retrieve *Mr* Hammer from his place of employ, and bring him hither.

Inside the Starlight house it was cold; Ivorie's coat was removed from her nevertheless and hung behind the door on a hook. She rubbed her arms and proceeded up a long thin flight of stairs, and entered a somewhat roomier, somewhat warmer parlour. Here Ivorie gave herself up to admiration; she made all the appropriate cooings regarding draperies, furniture, and the excellent height of the ceilings. Ann accepted her praise with grace; Mary, however, was tut-tutting, because Mr Sweetley had just revealed where it was he had found Mrs Hammer.

'On the steps!' he was saying. '*Sitting* on the steps. Completely lost!'

Ivorie smiled tightly. It seemed that, without knowing it, when Mr

Sweetley had found her, she had been taking refuge on the steps of a House of Ill Repute.

'Oh, Mr Sweetley. We don't like to acknowledge that establishment,' said Mary, smiling back at her guest.

'You need not worry, Mary. Its heyday is well over. It will be boarded up in a year or two. Mark my words,' said Ann. She was busy now with the tea tray and if a faint shortness could be detected in her voice, it was in no way evident in the smooth, efficient way she slid the tray onto the table and began arranging cups.

Mary looked apologetically at Ivorie and filled her teacup, keeping her hand beneath the spout in case it leaked. 'Certain types of men,' she whispered, making sure Mr Sweetley could not hear, 'will *always* require such places.'

Mr Sweetley returned, biting a green apple he had taken from the sideboard. It did not make the crisp sound one would expect. He looked at it sadly. Then, turning his attention to Ivorie, he brightened.

'If I'd known that all this time you were residing so close by, I should have visited you, Mrs Hammer. I certainly should have. But I have taken on an exceptionally demanding position here. With exceptionally demanding responsibilities.' He leaned towards her. 'I am Acting Bailiff, Mrs Hammer.' He paused so she could make the requisite sounds of admiration and then lowered his voice. 'Though I am not – not for a minute – forgetting my obligations.'

'Already he is extremely dedicated.' Mary smiled. 'We feel quite guilty *poaching* him from you.'

'Oh, poach away!' said Ivorie. 'We can hardly deny the world his skills. Mr Sweetley can turn his hand to anything.'

Mr Sweetley's mouth plugged up, for a moment, with satisfaction. He launched then into a long speech in which Mrs Hammer's praise was reciprocated, and doubled, and which Ivorie must simply endure till it came to its natural conclusion.

The two sisters, however, were intrigued to learn of Ivorie's various gifts. They asked her how she had enjoyed her visit to Mackaby Lane. Ivorie had many positive things to say on the subject, but when she outlined to them, in brief, the fate of her dictionary and her failure to procure another, they were sympathetic in the extreme.

'We would lend you one ourselves,' said Mary, regretfully, 'but I don't believe we own one, do we, Ann?'

Ann shook her head. 'No. That is one volume we do without. If we stumble on a word, Mrs Hammer — if we are reading and come across an unusual term . . .'

'We try to put it in context.'

'Or use it in conversation.'

'It's very helpful.'

Ann smiled at her. Mary stood up, took Ivorie's hand and led her across the room to a dark-stained bookcase.

'We are great readers,' said Ann.

'Yes, we have read everything here . . .' said Mary, bending down towards the lower shelves, '. . . oh, at least twice over. Ann?'

'Thrice, some of them,' said Ann.

'They're too clever for me,' said Borrel Sweetley cheerfully, persevering with his less-than-perfect apple. Ivorie could not help wondering at his easy way in this house with these sisters. He even had his feet up on a stool. 'They stay up so late with the oil lamp. I tell them they will ruin their eyes.'

Ivorie smiled dutifully and returned her attention to the bookshelves. They were big, well-preserved books — none of them as large as her dictionary, but some of them very thick indeed. The titles were esoteric: St Theresa's *Way of Perfection*; *The Book of Spiritual Poverty* by Johannes Tauler; Sir Thomas More's *Utopia*. 'May I?' she said, and Mary nodded. She pulled out the tome nearest her. The paper was unexpectedly thick and the print was gothic. She found publication details in a little note at the back.

'Why Miss Starlight! This is a first edition! It must surely be an antique!' she said.

Mary Starlight looked scattered for a moment, like a bird at whom a handful of seeds had been too abruptly thrown. 'I suppose it is,' she said. 'I suppose many of our books are. Would you say so, Ann?'

'Antiques?' Ann said. 'Well, yes, one might say that. I had never thought about it much. I have always been very happy with our little library.'

Ivorie picked out another volume. 'Do you like novels?'

Mary looked curiously at Ivorie. 'I can't say,' she said slowly, 'that I have ever read one. Ann? Have you ever read one? A novel?'

'No, not once,' said Ann. 'I don't believe it's ever occurred to me. Though I have heard . . .' She put her cup down. There was a stray tea leaf on her lip, and she tapped it off with her fingertip. 'There's a *British* gentleman who writes them very well. And is very popular everywhere.'

'Novels?' said Mr Sweetley all of a sudden, crinkling up his chin. 'Not my thing. Unless there's something legal in it. There was one I read once that I did like very much. About a very long, interminable court case. I believe it was by that gentleman you mentioned, Miss Ann.'

'No. No,' said Mary, shaking her head as if, having pondered it very thoroughly, she had come to an unimpeachable conclusion that covered the whole party, 'none of us here read novels.'

'Well, that is simply untrue, Mary,' said a voice from the doorway. '*I* read them.' The party stopped suddenly at this unexpected contribution from the Senior Sergeant.

The sisters had not heard their brother arrive. They had not heard the front door pull shut behind him, nor the sound of his boots on the stair. He stood in the doorway now, taking up much of its rectangular space with his large shoulders. 'I enjoy a good novel very much,' he said. He cleared his throat, sat down on the settee and poured himself tea. 'I have read the British gentleman,' he continued, sipping, looking at Ivorie. 'He is the best.'

Despite the Senior Sergeant's having entered the room in a vaguely gallant way, defending the novel, Ivorie was not impressed. She was not to be won over by a man just because he *read and defended novels*. She herself was not even sure, right now, that novels were a good thing to read or defend.

Robert strode across the room towards Ivorie, taking his tea with him. 'Mrs Hammer,' he said. He congratulated her on her baby. 'It is very nice to meet you again,' he said. If he had entered the room with a degree of self-possession, the presence of Ivorie Hammer in his parlour now set in motion a whole swag of unhappy questions.

'How are things progressing *with your countrymen?*'

Ivorie faltered. She held an esoteric book in her hand; it seemed he might have asked her an esoteric question. 'Oh, I am not *with* them,' she said finally. 'We have found other accommodation.' She paused. She felt a little vindictive towards him. 'But I think it's hard, Senior Sergeant. I don't think it's comfortable. I don't believe it's as satisfactory as they had been led to believe.'

It did not look like they would be having any nice chat about novels.

'I am concerned about the *temperature dropping*,' Ivorie continued. Actually, this was the first time such a thing had occurred to her, and it only occurred to her now because the Starlight house was so icy. As if reading her thoughts, Robert made his way to the coalscuttle. 'Yes,' he said, bending down. 'It is becoming increasingly cold.' He stared very hard into the black bucket.

Mary and Ann Starlight looked uncomfortable. Ann coughed quietly into her fist.

'Is not the municipality providing blankets?' asked Mary.

'Oh, all sorts of things are being organised!' said Mr Sweetley. 'No one will freeze to death! Donations have been highly generous, more than could be expected, quite superlative.'

Robert Starlight left the coalscuttle – it seemed worse, now, to light a fire than not – and returned to his cup of tea.

The room fell silent. Mary and Ann Starlight couldn't help glaring a little at their brother, who had somehow – they weren't sure how, exactly – soured the nice mood they had established in the parlour. Not even Borrel Sweetley, racking his brains, could come up with a comment that might restore harmony.

So everyone was well disposed towards Lawrence the manservant when he returned with Ivorie Hammer's husband. There ensued a general ushering of people and things and coats. Hands were shaken, backs patted. Mrs Starlight was dragged up from the kitchen, where she'd been happily dicing potato, to be introduced and pick up the tea things. Everything was friendly and promising again. Only Robert Starlight remained ill at ease.

Finally, the Hammers took their leave, proceeding, with Mr Sweetley's accompaniment, to the front doorstep. Ivorie held a small, plain-covered book in her hands, pressed there by Mary. Ann had loaned her a pale green wool scarf for the journey home; it sat snugly about her upper body and concealed her outmoded coat collar. The three of them were destined to become great friends.

Outside, the air was cold and formed Borrel Sweetley's words into small bursts of condensation. 'Mrs Hammer. Ernest. Great things are about to happen.' The front door was half closed behind him. He closed it further still, so there was just a crack. 'There have been new developments, new evidence.'

Ivorie and Ernest looked blankly at Sweetley.

'We *know* where the felon resides, *has resided* all along.' Sweetley was nodding frantically. 'In my position as Acting Bailiff,' he said, 'I have been privileged to get *into the ears* of certain persons. Including,' his eyes flicked to the door, 'the Senior Sergeant. And others, high up in the council.' His voice had a taut strained quality to it, like a man who has just swallowed a tuning fork. 'You were right, Mrs Hammer. All along, your intuition was right.'

Ivorie's stomach began to cramp.

'Yes,' Sweetley was nodding again. '*Miss Pappy*,' he said. '*That* is who has been harbouring the criminal. I have documentary evidence of it. A letter, in her own hand!' He gave Ivorie another admiring look. 'She does a very good job, doesn't she? Only *you*, Mrs Hammer, saw through her. Hats off, Mrs Hammer. Steps ahead. Leaps and bounds. You were not taken in at all, were you?'

Ivorie Hammer no longer knew what to say, but a cold line of sweat had formed on her forehead.

'We set out,' Sweetley continued, 'in two days' time. Yes, we return to Canyon. To bring him in.' He walloped his palm with his fist. The fist made a dull sound, like a padded head against a curb-stone.

Ernest took Ivorie's arm in his, more tightly than he normally might. If he had not been thus constrained, Ivorie knew he would be winding his wristwatch, back and forth, back and forth. Winding and winding. Springs and cogs and pinions taut. All the machinery poised, awaiting action.

Part 3

Middle Pitch

Chapter 23

Near misses and fortuitous hits

At the same time that Mr Borrel Sweetley and the Senior Sergeant were saddling up hefty horses and loading nefarious-looking rifles with which to pursue their escaped felon, Otto Cirque was himself saddling a pony and taking his leave of Morag Pappy, his harbourer. The two parties crossed each other in the night – Borrel Sweetley and his party travelling east on the main path; Otto and his pony stumbling through bracken and dirt and bush and not lighting the lamp.

Further synchronicities ensued. At precisely the moment that Otto lowered his left foot onto the soft ground of Outer Pitch, Borrel Sweetley braced his right, warningly, against Morag Pappy's front door. Hereafter, however, their fortunes diverged.

Let us follow a short way with the felon.

It was nearly forty years since Otto Cirque had staggered down that long steep mountain towards Pitch. He was an invalid; one might expect the journey to have been beyond him, and yet he made it, and grew hardy in the process. The memory of paths proved strong; he arrived at the other side of the mountain range, unharmed and alive. Once there, he set the pony free, and made his way by foot, gliding through the wet grass as softly as a deer, occasionally startled by signs of life around him. He came to the camp site where the people of Canyon now resided. The end-of-daylight rituals had begun: children were eking the last moments out of ropes and hoops and balls; men were chopping wood; saucepans banged; people yelled to each other across the cold air. In this post-afternoon light, the smallest hint of colour dazzled: a red pocket on a girl's skirt; a blonde plait at the back of a woman's head; a bright purple flower.

Otto cut a strange figure. He had not seen the sun for a very long time. His eyes were glassy and pale, and his hair formed a ring of white around his scalp. Added to this was a very odd suit of pale clothes. At this time of night, in this light, you might think him conspicuous, making his way across the grass. But no one noticed him. Otto came closer and closer until he was right in the midst of them, and still no one noticed him. And so he was able to continue to the centre of their campsite, where a causeway had been built: a platform of crosshatching, ill-matched planks, sprawling unevenly above the mud.

Rising only about two feet off the ground, you could not quite call this platform a *stage*; nor could you properly describe it as a *road* or *path*, it being much too broad and purposeless. It certainly didn't have the elevation to qualify as a *bridge*. Really, one could only describe it as a *floor*. A vast wooden *floor*, constructed from an assortment of materials. The timber boards that comprised it were held in place with pins and nails, wedges and cork, and sometimes rag. As he made his way across, Otto observed holes plugged with wooden counters, or stones or, in one case, old boots. An occasional stumbling block or protruding corner was marked out with lime. In the very centre, a flagpole with, as yet, no flag. It was an odd and unwieldy construction, albeit solid. People clattered happily across it, carrying their buckets and their chickens and their children. For a fraction of a moment the hard stone-shaped pain Otto carried in his chest transformed into something almost tolerable. And then he stepped down again, onto the muddy earth, and the pain reassumed the form of a lead pellet.

Later that evening, when fires flared up, and stews cooked, and voices rose and fell, Otto sat on the outskirts of the campsite. The murmur of conversation rose and fell. Occasionally, and then more frequently, there was laughter. He lay on the ground with grass against his face, indifferent to the cold. Sleep came, and would have continued had Bald Sherry not stumbled over him on his way to bed. But Sherry did stumble, stumbled badly and hurt his foot. He kicked the sleeping form of Otto Cirque, thinking it a rock or a log of wood, and clutched his foot. Only then, at close quarters, did he recognise the rock or log of wood as a human creature.

'Sir?' he said, peering into the dark. Then, 'Sir,' again, hopping closer.

Otto did not flinch or resist, but had gone still as a rock. 'My dear sir,' Bald Sherry said, applying to Otto's shoulder the very gentle almost-touch he employed with his most nervous horses. 'It's Mr Cirque, isn't it? Mr *Otto Cirque*,' he said, 'It's all right, my dear sir. You can come with me.'

Things were not progressing well for Borrel Sweetley and his company. There had been no need for a forced entry to Morag Pappy's house; she had opened her door wide and let them in. No need either, so far, for the rifles, which hung stupidly over the men's shoulders and made Robert Starlight ashamed. Morag greeted them and provided for them as if she'd known they were coming with a pot of tea and a cake. When Borrel Sweetley showed her the letter, written in her own hand to the felon during his incarceration, she registered nothing. 'See here, it is proof that you harboured the fugitive!' Sweetley exclaimed, but Morag was indifferent. She stood up to latch the windows against the wind.

'I'm afraid, madam,' said the Senior Sergeant, 'that we must ask you to submit to a search of your home.'

Sweetley was beside him at once with the necessary warrants. Morag gave them only the most cursory glance. She pushed a draught stop against the door with her foot and hooked a poker up the chimney, wiggling it violently till something clanged shut up there like a trapdoor. Finally, turning to them, she made the slightest gesture with the corner of her hand to indicate that they might go ahead. It was not an acceptance of their will, as such; rather, a temporary removal, to some great and elevated height, of her own.

While his colleagues threw themselves into the task with great gusto – flinging open doors and rifling through wardrobes – the Senior Sergeant proceeded with a certain delicacy. He scrutinised, very respectfully, the items on Morag's parlour shelves: a twisted black shark's egg; the mandarin-shaped husk of a sea anemone; a pale blue octopus in an old fig jar, tendrils trailing like gauze on a felt hat. He turned these artefacts gently upside down and sometimes sand trickled out. The octopus made a silent glob-glob motion from one end of its jar to the other.

Morag threw uneaten clumps of cake into the fireplace, and blew crumbs off the plates. 'You will need this,' she said, finally, straightening and proffering a large key to the Senior Sergeant. She spoke in flat syllables. 'I would prefer if my dispensary were not reduced to rubble.' She turned away again, and the Senior Sergeant, repairing to the back of the house, found the door that fit the key.

The dispensary was more a passageway than a room, and it was lined on one side with neat, clean galley tables. With the utmost delicacy, the Senior Sergeant examined the strange powders, leaves and liquids arranged in jars thereon. None of them afforded him any clue. He knew nothing about poisons, natural or chemical, was not capable of distinguishing between a bay leaf and a leaf from the hemlock plant, a headache powder and a sachet of arsenic. After a short interval, of which you will hear more in a moment, he returned to the parlour.

In the end, much to Sweetley's disgruntlement, there was no sign in Morag's house of any felon — not even a stray white hair on a dark-coloured pillowcase. The men flagged in the parlour, listening to the wind, eating what they could find in the cupboards. In another room, Borrel Sweetley subjected Morag to a battery of questions, which she mostly refused to answer, and then locked her in. She must be held, he explained to the Senior Sergeant, *ad testificandum*.

But Robert Starlight could not attend properly to Borrel Sweetley's conversation, for the Senior Sergeant's chest was adapting to a new and unsettling occupant. A tiny white grub was burrowing into his heart. If the Senior Sergeant is lucky, if his blood nourishes it well enough, it will turn into a butterfly.

But he does not know that yet. All he knows is that, though the others searched all afternoon and found nothing in Morag's house, his own search was not fruitless. He did discover something. Something that would prove to be of great significance. But he did not find it on the shelves of Morag's dispensary. It was behind a door, a door that had seemed at first to lead to the yard outside, but did not. It was behind a door that led to a very small, very private bathroom.

He felt the heat through the door. When he opened it, all the air in the little room was charged by steam, and through the steam, stepping into a bath, was the smallest, most well-made woman he had ever seen. She had one foot in the water and was lowering a second over the lip of the tub. Registering a disturbance in the room, she looked up.

Upon seeing the Senior Sergeant, the woman's hands flew immediately to cover her chest, and she dropped the bottom half of herself abruptly into the hot water. Her eyes, which were large in a very small face, had a curiously vivid effect (later described by his sisters as 'perpetual astonishment') that made Robert Starlight feel as though he were really being looked at, and really being seen. It was she who was naked, but Robert Starlight suddenly felt he wore neither coat nor constabulary-order shirt. This sudden relinquishment of his uniform did not, however, prevent him, in that short baffling interval, from sending the young woman the strong precautionary signal to *stay where she was.*

Thus our narrative, once again, provided an escape route for Nelly the parlourmaid. She would remain that afternoon and all that night quiet as a mouse in the servants' bathroom. She would not come out till Mr Sweetley's party was safely gone, having taken her mistress with them.

No such escape route was available to the Senior Sergeant: in fact, one might say that the Senior Sergeant was now utterly trapped. Upon closing the bathroom door, he spent some minutes on its other side considering his entrapment. He wished the steam had made it impossible. He wished the steam had so obscured the girl that no detail of face or figure could be made out. But the steam had not provided such cover. Despite his embarrassment, despite the dematerialisation of his articles of office, one detail had immediately caught his eye.

Around the girl's neck, swinging near her breastbone when she plunged back into the water, hung a very odd pendant. He knew it because he'd sketched its distinctive shape into his notebook some three months previously: the shape of a small human ear.

Poor Senior Sergeant Robert Starlight: he had just stumbled upon the love of his life, and she happened to be wearing the missing murder weapon.

Chapter 24

Stagefright

Ivorie Hammer complained about everything on her way down to the camp site. Her feet hurt. Her shawl was too tight. There was a small insect in her eye she could not blink out. Ernest carried the baby under his coat and Ivorie said it made them look like gypsies. It didn't help, she said, that he had grown, of late, a thin moustache. He looked, she went on, as though he were a gypsy thief carrying a shameful object under his coat. Ernest reorganised himself, with some difficulty, until he was wearing the baby on the outside of his coat instead. Ivorie sniffed, and immediately fussed over the baby's swaddling.

She had been ambushed into this arrangement. Racine had proposed it with such ingenuity that Ivorie had had no choice but submisson. And Mr Hammer had dismissed entirely the headache she had engineered in the interim.

To make things worse, an invitation had arrived in the post that morning: luncheon with the Starlight sisters. 'We have made a reservation at the tea house,' wrote Ann, 'on Mackaby Lane. If you come to us, we could walk together.'

Mr Hammer had made her acceptance of the invitation impossible. He had not said much – indeed, he had not said anything – but his disapproval weighed heavily. Every time she went to re-read the letter, there was the disapproval: preventing her from even probing the corner of the envelope with a fingernail. She was thus imposed upon to send a reply 'sadly regretting a previous engagement'. And now here she was, plodding the three-mile walk, with a baby and a husband and a small flagon of water.

At the camp site, Racine had organised a party to welcome them. Chairs were arranged in a circle on the causeway, with tea tables in the middle. Rosa Minim buttered a scone for Ivorie. She was excited and slapdash: the butter was not applied evenly, and some of it remained on her thumb afterwards. 'We are like busy bees,' she told Ivorie. 'Ants getting ready for winter. Building, constructing!' She gave the scone to Ivorie and took, in exchange, the baby, over which she proceeded to coo and gurgle. Ivorie looked at the baby's plain little face and watched Rosa for signs of playacting. She could detect none.

'You will be grown up before you know it,' Rosa said, rocking the child and playing with her fingers. 'You will be grown up before you know it, my lamb, and coming to my schoolhouse for your lessons!' She sighed and smoothly transferred the baby to the next hovering matron (something of a queue was forming). 'Yes, I have plans for a schoolhouse, Mrs Hammer.' She took Ivorie's arm and steered her fiercely down the causeway.

Rosa was a middle-aged woman, but she gave a great impression of youth. She had a pink face and very black eyebrows. One could imagine her chortling over a joke with her third graders, or rolling a hoop down the hill with the preparatory class. It was only up close that you realised she was not youthful at all: that her rosiness had nothing to do with girlish blushing and everything to do with broken capillaries. When she *promenaded*, as she did now, she became even pinker. A forceful, unseemly pink, full of ideas.

'I am full of ideas,' confided Rosa Minim, 'which I have been dying to share with you.'

Ivorie kept her gaze on the causeway, which she did not trust at all. 'Ideas?' she said.

'Ideas, Mrs Hammer, for a *different* kind of school. A *progressive* style of education.' Rosa's eyes looked out beyond them, as though trying to take in more than they ought of the world and its possibilities. 'With nature walks, and painting classes, Mrs Hammer. With poetry writing and games. Physical exercise.' Her ideas had the quality of well-shapen little mud pats. 'It came to me one night, Mrs Hammer; it was a revelation. I thought: Nothing is the same as it was, and it never will be again! What tremendous freedom! What liberation! There is no *reason* to

157

continue doing things the same way as before. That's what I thought, Mrs Hammer. And it seemed to me the perfect opportunity for an experiment. Don't you agree?'

Ivorie would once have had misgivings; she would have told Rosa of her misgivings without reservation. 'Children,' she would have said, 'are not *guinea pigs*, Miss Minim.' She would have demolished her, in fact. She did not bother to do anything of the kind now. It was a relief not to bother. She smiled and nodded.

But there was no need to further humour Rosa Minim and her educational experiments, for Ivorie was now pounced upon by Racine. 'You must come and sit down now, Ivorie. We have things to show you. Talk later. Think later.' She herded Ivorie to a chair, looking up and around her, unable, it seemed to Ivorie, to fix her eyes on anything for more than a fraction of a second. Such skittishness was unnerving in an old woman – particularly in an old woman one wished to help. Ivorie caught Racine's wrist. 'Racine?' Ivorie said. Racine looked at her, with something strange and foreign in her eyes.

'Ivorie,' she said. 'Something astonishing has happened. You won't believe it.' Her voice was even higher-pitched than usual. 'I've got back on a horse!' she hissed.

Ivorie could scarcely imagine what she meant by this. 'A horse?'

But there was no time to enquire further. Racine skittered off across the causeway; Pette started crying, and was swiftly returned to Ivorie's lap; the tea things were pushed to one side; and a group of women began spreading something large and colourful at Mrs Hammer's feet.

At first, the article laid out before her made no sense at all: it was an incoherent assemblage of colours, shapes, and fabrics, sewn together into a rectangle; too large for a bed, much too large for a table; the size, in fact, of several beds and tables pushed together. Ivorie looked at it a good long while and made vague marvelling sounds – 'mmms' and 'hahs'. Then, hitching the baby up to her chest, she made a short perambulation around the patchwork – for that's what it was, she could see that now. A patchwork. There were odd pieces of felt and diamonds cut from working shirts and cord jackets. There were bits of floral skirt and boys' pyjamas. She was sure she spied a piece of her old best dress.

Ivorie appreciated the basic premise of patchwork and looked for the pattern in it: the radiating laterals of a sun or a windmill. There was nothing. For the first time, she was stumped. She had not a clue what she was supposed to be looking at, nor what she might judiciously say on its account.

'It's a flag,' Racine prompted.

'Well, a banner really,' someone interjected.

'Could we describe it as a coat of arms?' another suggested.

'It's a *flag*,' Racine repeated. She came alongside Ivorie. 'It's the *face* – can't you see – of Arcadia Cirque.' Ivorie's smile remained bland, horrified. 'Look, there – his moustache, see? And there – his ringmaster's epaulette. There –' Racine shifted Ivorie to one side, 'is his left eye, and there –' she shifted her to the other, 'his right. We thought him too long uncelebrated, Ivorie. We thought it high time he was commemorised.'

'Commemorated,' Ivorie said automatically.

Oh yes, she saw it now. It was crude but, once you understood what you were looking at, unmistakable. There were shiny seal-like pieces of black satin for his hair and navy blue serge for his jacket. They had made altogether too much of his moustache and his eyes were not quite identical in shape. But otherwise, you could not say it *didn't* resemble him – from what Ivorie remembered from the one photograph of him she had seen. She registered her amazement that they'd got such a likeness, and pointed out a small portion of his sideburns, which seemed to be falling off.

Fortunately, just as her stock of pleasantries began to dry up again, a sudden blaring sound relieved her from further conversation. It was a trumpet in the early throes of warming up, and it arrived on stage, still cold, sounding more like a farmyard animal than a member of the brass family. Ivorie clapped a little too enthusiastically.

A flute joined the trumpet, and then a cornet. A trombone dispatched a series of notes that sounded like old potatoes. And then the four instruments were playing in something approaching unison. Now, a party of twelve or so children marched up onto the stage. They bowed to the audience and formed into a loose circle. Someone had made them costumes: unflattering puffs of cheesecloth, already speckled with mud. The music died down. Rosa Minim, to one side, clapped her hands, and mouthed something at them with her black eyebrows raised.

I wish I could say that what ensued was a performance of unparalleled skill and inventiveness. That Ducrow himself would have been impressed by the somersaults and tumbles, the human pyramids and hoop-dancing that were demonstrated that day before the withering eye of Mrs Ivorie Hammer. But no such thing was to occur. There was a final, poorly executed blast from the trumpet, and Ivorie Hammer settled back to pay witness to the saddest, most pitiful public entertainment she had yet been privy to.

Most performers have experienced, at some time in their careers, that terrible malady known as stagefright. While waiting backstage for the curtain to rise – or worse, onstage itself, in the middle of a scene – it attacks like white light, erasing all images, all thoughts. Whole tracts of verse that were embedded, only moments ago, in one's memory, sink into a no-man's-land of mud and quicksand; a sensation of teeth-chattering commences, not just in one's mouth, but in one's whole body. Stage fright, so long as it persists, renders one useless.

'Go on!' said Rosa Minim, after several strained moments of inactivity. 'Your *tap* sequence, Miriam. Remember how you start . . .'

Miriam raised her left foot, cocked it to the side slightly, and gently scratched her opposite ankle with it. She did a one-two, and then another, but it was all she could manage, and she stopped and hung her head, and everyone could see the hives coming up under her white stockings.

Rosa turned to a large boy standing opposite Miriam and nodded. 'Your backflips, Will . . . He is a wonderful acrobat, Mrs Hammer!'

Will entered the circle, and attempted to fulfil this instruction. But his attempt was so lacking in momentum and confidence – he was so listless, so halfhearted – that he hit his head on the floor with a dull crack that made Ivorie Hammer wince.

In the face of these two failures, the children lost courage altogether.

'Go on,' called the mother of one child. 'Do that thing you do on the backs of chairs!'

'Yes, and your somersault, with the twist!'

'Your juggling, you know, with the spoons . . .'

'Oh, you should see them swing on the bars, Mrs Hammer!'

'You should see them walk the plank!'

'. . . vault the pole . . .'

'. . . leap the frog . . .'

'. . . skip the rope . . .'

'. . . pummel the bag . . .'

None of which the children were able to do now, neither at the exhortation of their desperate mothers nor under the expectant gaze of Mrs Ivorie Hammer. Finally, Rosa Minim shooed them off stage, patting them like small robust dogs, and whispering assurances in their ears.

Part of Ivorie felt for her old friends in their moment of failure – but another part of her was relieved. She feared that, had the performance been even vaguely competent, she would have been required to deliver, with precision and tact and even a little poetry, all sorts of opinions and congratulations.

As it turned out, she did not have to utter a thing. And in a few minutes' time, the performance would be forgotten altogether. Something much more momentous was about to transpire.

The women had been talking despondently for a short time, analysing the inadequacies of their children, when one of the women stood suddenly from her chair and pointed eastwards. 'What's that?' she said. The flesh on her arm trembled. 'There's people coming. There's a white thing, see? There's several of them. Up there. On the mountain range. They're coming down!'

Chapter 25

The art of the distiller

'Let me make one thing clear,' Bald Sherry said. 'I do not hold you responsible, Mr Cirque, for the death of my wife.'

He and Otto Cirque sat before the still's fire; it was a cold evening; they drank brandy they had distilled themselves – it was not bad; it was not as good as it yet might be, but it was not bad. They had consumed it scientifically at first, though now, onto their second and third rounds, science had given way to a more leisurely approach.

'I don't know about these other murders,' said Mr Sherry, 'if that is what they were. But no, sir, I do not hold you responsible for my wife's.' He imagined this might be a great relief to his companion, but Otto Cirque did not respond in any way, only emanating that strange dumb luminosity of his that might, by some people, be taken for *grace*, and by others, for *imbecility*.

He was no imbecile, that was for sure – and his muteness made him the perfect confidant. Bald Sherry found himself plumbing depths in himself he had not thought existed. And in the weeks Otto had worked alongside Sherry at the still, their methodology had radically changed. From something crackpot and experimental, erratically managed and inexpertly executed, it was now informed by refined and calculated process. Otto Cirque *knew* what he was doing; Bald Sherry did not.

The art of the distiller, Otto had shown him, was to expel the undesirable flavours and concentrate the desirable ones. What Mrs Po had made, what Racine Pfeffersalz had brought back in that first wax-sealed bottle, was a barberry-*flavoured* alcohol, so overladen with sweeteners, so infused with perfumes, that it could be more rightly understood as a confection. What Bald Sherry aspired to, under the direction of Otto Cirque, was something quite different: a vigorous, vital, *transporting* liquor. A liquor that allowed a man to see his own potential with clarity and purpose.

In these last months, Sherry had been secretive. Although everyone knew he was up to something, he had not risked exposure, disappointment, public failure — that whole string of eventualities that, once set in motion, led one to another as inevitably as stones down a hillside. He had his *pickers*, sworn to secrecy: a small party of boys, who, early in the morning, stole out and stripped the barberry branches clean. He had his *pick-throughers*: a small party of girls who, with nimble fingers and sharp little eyes, picked through the harvest, discarding any berry that bore mould or was underripe. They scrubbed their hands with Sherry's lye soap to get the stain out. There was no point in giving them money for their endeavours, so he gave them chocolate. He had a large store of chocolate and did not care for it himself. Mrs Sherry had enjoyed it. It had been one of the very few things that Mrs Sherry had enjoyed. He thought about her, with a strange sharp pang, while doling her chocolate out.

But he was too impatient to tend closely to the distilling process — Otto Cirque had the temperament for it; he did not. While Otto remained installed by the fire, Bald Sherry fluttered and buzzed from task to task. He consulted on the construction of permanent fireplaces. He gave his opinion on the distribution of charitable donations from the Pitch Municipal Council. He encouraged domestication of the sinewy bush fowl, and offered a simple but effective design for a rabbit trap. He knew an expedient way of building charcoal coolers from galvanised steel sheeting and wire netting. He advised which trees to fell and how the timber should be stacked for drying.

He was as surprised as anyone by his abilities. It was as if part of his brain, long clogged with yeast and hops and inactivity, was stretching and re-activating. He cleaned the constituent parts of the still they had built (with a used flat-topped milk can, copper piping and rubber) till even the boiler shone. He swept the floors of the distillery and climbed up high to disentangle cobwebs from the rafters. He acquired hard round muscles. He talked long into the night to his strange, silent, unjudging companion.

The evening was dark and he had just got started. 'I do not hold you responsible, Otto Cirque, for my wife's death,' he repeated. He sat and looked down at the floor between his knees, and what he was feeling, though not immense, not incapacitating, was real. 'I hold myself responsible,' he said. 'I do, Mr Cirque. I broke her spirit. I used it up.' He did not know where this had come from. He was surprised that it brought him, not pain, but relief. He reached for a bottle from a new stack and uncapped it.

Thoughts of Mrs Sherry were then swiftly supplanted for, if the first bottles had not been bad, the second were *excellent*.

Ernest Hammer might have proven to be a more forgiving spectator of the first public performance of Rosa Minim's acrobatic troupe than was his wife. But upon arrival at the campsite he had been immediately ushered into Bald Sherry's distillery, there to partake of a specially prepared luncheon. He did not know it, but he too was guest of honour at a significant event.

Bald Sherry whipped the cork out of the bottle and his eyes gleamed. He poured two small glasses, hand trembling. 'Go on. Try it.' His eyes reminded Ernest, very briefly, of two small inflamed creatures scuttling about on a mantelpiece, having just ingested fatal amounts of poison. Ernest tasted the brandy, firstly with his tongue in case it was bad, and then, realising it was no such thing, with his whole mouth.

'I have done all the right things,' Sherry said, counting them off on his fingers. 'I have passed it through the still twice, draining off the heads and the tails.' He was nervous. Though they were certainly more than acquaintances, you could not describe Bald Sherry and Ernest Hammer as friends. For several years now, the two men had come together periodically for the sole purpose of sampling Bald Sherry's now expired fine liquor collection. Bald Sherry, on account of his occupation, could handle these meetings better than Ernest Hammer, but over time, it was Ernest's nose that proved to be the more intelligent of the two, able to isolate aromas to which Sherry's shop-worn nasal passages were inert.

'The beauty,' said Sherry, watching his companion closely, 'is that it does not require aging for years at a time, like a cognac or whisky.'

Ernest was letting his opinions form.

'And it does not require to be stored in wood. I do not need barrels.' Bald Sherry swirled the half-inch of liquid in his cup. He swirled and swirled again, and then looked deep into the vessel and sighed. 'Which is lucky, because I do not *have* any barrels.'

Ernest Hammer was still silent.

'I did the gunpowder test,' said Sherry finally, worn out. 'It burnt clear and blue.'

Ernest was not listening. A small diamond-shaped glow was setting up behind his forehead, precisely halfway between the eyebrows, in that place described by Mr Sweetley's old friends the Hindoos as the 'third eye'. He swallowed and put his glass down.

'Mr Sherry,' he said. 'This,' he said, 'is very good.'

Bald Sherry became emotional; his head dropped into his shirt, so all that could be seen was his abundant hair, quivering slightly. 'I had hoped so,' he said. 'I had hoped – that's what I thought.' He was embarrassed for a moment about what he was next to say, but he said it nonetheless, looking up from beneath his hair. 'I will call it "Mrs Sherry's Ardent Spirits",' he said.

If their appreciation of fine liquor had not been so contemplative in nature – if their relationship had originated in the public bar, for instance – they might have been more exuberant at this moment. They might have danced a jig around the room, or shouted and whooped at the tops of their voices like men who've struck oil or found treasure buried deep in a sandbar. They did none of these things, however. They clinked glasses, and shook hands, and sat for some minutes – deep in independent reveries – savouring Mr Sherry's successful work of alchemy.

They would have gone on sitting quietly like this, too, if something in the air outside hadn't changed and this change hadn't infiltrated the room and with it, their reflections. But little by little Ernest Hammer and Bald Sherry became aware that the sounds of human activity from outside – the hammering and wailing and clattering of tools and children and feet – had all but ceased. It was as though a large parachute had descended on the camp site.

Outside, the sun hit them brilliantly: a cold bright light coming in shafts through tree leaves. It lit the figures descending the mountain range, and then returned them to shadow, so their progress was striped, undulating. But there was no doubt what it was, this little caravan progressing towards them: it was Borrel Sweetley's arrest party, on its homewards journey. Messrs Hammer and Sherry separated now, one to retrieve his wife and child; the other to jostle his way to the front of the crowd that had gathered on the causeway.

Archibald Sherry, of course, had superior knowledge regarding the outcome of Borrel Sweetley's felon-finding mission. The rest of the population of Canyon were not, however, apprised of this knowledge. They presumed that the indistinct figure on horseback was none other than Otto Cirque, successfully retrieved and being brought to justice. As they watched, however – and accustomed themselves to the striping effect of the afternoon sun – certain inconsistencies appeared.

'It's not Cirque!' someone yelled out. 'It couldn't be. It's too *big*.'

Quiet reigned for a moment, while this detail was absorbed.

'You can't tell from this far,' sang out someone else. 'Perhaps it's blankets and saddle bags. Makes him look bigger.'

'Yes, it's got to be saddlebags.'

'No, it's not saddlebags,' said a certain gentleman, who happened to be in possession of an old pair of opera glasses. 'It's skirts!'

It was true. Once the possibility was suggested, the skirts became clearly evident: crescent-shaped against the horse's flanks.

'Well, why,' said someone, a little horrified at the prospect, 'would Otto Cirque be wearing *skirts*?'

And now the fact of it became plain, once and for all. The riders rounded the last bend and forged straight into a clean pool of sunlight.

The people of Canyon pulled in a single giant hush of air.

As you know, dear reader, it was not Otto Cirque on the back of a medium-sized chestnut horse with his hands tied behind his back and his skirts hanging down: it was Morag Pappy.

Chapter 26

An appointment with the law

At the sight of Morag Pappy, Ivorie Hammer must sit down, immediately, and drink three cups of cold black tea and wait for her heart to stop banging. It shocked her to find that the memory of her connection to Morag persisted. She repudiated it with all her might; she recited alphabetical lists and Latin conjugations to ward it off. But it remained a nagging pain, in her chest at first, and then in her stomach, and lastly in her head. She did not find it possible to speak on the way home. She arrived at Mrs Po's and put herself promptly to bed. She dreamt of giant butterfly wings draped over the flanks of a horse, and woollen-wrapped ankles stuck hard in rabbit traps.

Ernest Hammer was also affected by what had transpired. So affected was he that when he put his daughter to bed that night he did not notice anything peculiar; he did not wonder at the odd position in which she had curled herself up: arms crooked under her knees like a little crab. Or, if he did notice, did not think there was anything strange about it. He kissed her and tucked her blankets in.

It was Pette's first trick but he did not properly register it because he was too busy rehearsing a conversation he meant to have, the next morning, with Mr Borrel Sweetley.

At 9 o'clock Borrel Sweetley was at his desk, arranging papers that Lawrence brought to him steadily: papers that required perusal, papers that required signatures, papers that had been pulled out of files and fastened together at the corners with similar papers. He was, as he repeatedly explained to Lawrence, 'shoring up his case'. 'Papers,' Sweetley declared, looking at them hopelessly, wishing he could love them more, 'are the key' – though the papers he now contemplated had nothing to do with the Cirque murders and dealt only with the labyrinthine bureaucracy of the Pitch Municipal Authority.

At the doorway, having already removed his hat: Mr Hammer.

'Sweetley,' said Mr Hammer.

'Hammer,' said Mr Sweetley. He smiled briskly. 'Are you here for an appointment? Lawrence, was there an appointment of which you did not notify me?'

'No appointment,' said Ernest, passing his hat from hand to hand. 'Just an informal visit, Mr Sweetley.'

'Aah! Welcoming me back, no doubt?' Sweetley relinquished his papers – they dropped, with a happy swish, onto the desk – and leaned back in his chair with his hands behind his head. 'No appointment required for that! Take a seat, Mr Hammer.'

Mr Hammer did so: a much larger seat than he was comfortable occupying; he felt himself disappear into its buttoned, bolstered contours.

'You have heard, and seen, I hazard?' said Sweetley. 'Of the latest developments?'

When Ernest did not immediately answer, Sweetley leaned forwards, frowning very slightly. 'I believe we have acted correctly,' he said.

Ernest tried to remember some of the better sentences he had constructed the previous evening. They had once existed – fleetingly perfect in the dark of night – but now they had evaporated. He kept his eyes on Borrel Sweetley's mouth as a point of focus.

'It was not arbitrary, Mr Hammer,' Sweetley continued. 'You know me better than that, surely.'

Ernest said nothing and continued to endure the psychological afflictions of his seating arrangement, which, he felt, was every minute depriving him of his stature.

His discomfort was not, however, evident to Mr Sweetley. On the contrary, Ernest appeared to Mr Sweetley to inhabit the large chair like a wise little gnome, taking up hardly any space and apparently impervious to its patrician comforts. The thought recalled him to his own love of comfort and made him defensive.

'You might sit there all you like and second-guess me, Mr Hammer,' he said, 'but I do not act without just cause.'

'I do not second-guess you,' said Ernest. 'Quite honestly, Mr Sweetley.'

Sweetley came around to the front of the desk, and settled himself against it, so he was very close to his visitor and consequently more imposing. 'We have evidence!' he said, throwing up his arms and letting them clap down again on his thighs. 'We have evidence, Mr Hammer. We have a letter, *in Miss Pappy's hand*, showing that she orchestrated the escape of Otto Cirque from the courthouse.' He became friendly again. 'Yes, yes, Ernest. It is indeed the case. She provided him asylum, and no doubt has helped him abscond yet again. To think: that Miss Pappy would harbour a fugitive! From the authorities! A murderer, Mr Hammer! A proven murderer!'

'I understand,' said Ernest carefully, 'that Otto Cirque's guilt has not yet been established?'

But Borrel Sweetley was not for a moment taken in by a question mark at the end of what was, decidedly, a statement, an assertion, a wedge of very plainly put opposition. 'Not established? Indeed,' he said. '*Not yet established*. And perhaps we should offer Miss Pappy the benefit of the doubt, too? Wrote the letter in her sleep, perhaps?' He slapped his hands on his thighs again. 'But you know, and I know – and above everyone, *your wife* knows – that Morag Pappy is not like the rest of us.' He shook his head in such a way that his jowls, looser than ever, seemed almost separate appurtenances. 'She never has been. Never will be. All is a fog with her. She hopes you will lose your way. She hopes the fog will obscure the details.' He reared alarmingly towards Mr Hammer, wielding his index finger. 'But I have the lamps, Mr Hammer. I have the torches of justice on my side.'

Lawrence, seated on a miniature stool before a miniature table in a very far corner of the office, giggled inappropriately.

'My wife,' said Ernest, 'feels very uneasy about this turn of events, Mr Sweetley. She has a connection with Miss Pappy that I recognise, even if she does not fully recognise it herself. She does not want to see Miss Pappy hurt, or ill-treated, or denied her rights.'

Sweetley proffered his body to Mr Hammer at a more companionable thirty-degree angle. 'I am only trying to get to the truth, Ernest,' he said. 'I am not holding Miss Pappy vindictively. I question myself eternally. You have no idea. The demands of my new position . . . they do things absolutely *correctly* here.' He ran his hands through his hair, and seemed to find a point of resolution. 'There have been women like Morag Pappy all through history, Ernest, and they *cannot* be allowed to prevail.'

Ernest had lost Sweetley's thread now. 'Where is she, Mr Sweetley?' he asked, quite simply.

'Where is she?' he said. 'Where do you *think* she is?' He looked resentfully at Ernest, demure against his backdrop of claret-coloured leather. 'She is an accessory after the fact, Mr Hammer. She may yet turn out to be an accessory *before the fact*. Subsequently, she has taken up residence at the Pitch Penitentiary, where she will be sure to receive what comforts are due to those held at the Crown's pleasure.'

'I think I should go now, Mr Sweetley,' Ernest said, getting up. 'Thank you for your information.' He put his hat on brusquely, as though it were a helmet, or some other protective device that needed to be firmly and swiftly secured.

Sweetley looked suddenly regretful, and stood up to take Ernest's hand. 'You must excuse me, Ernest,' he said. 'It has all been extremely hard. Extremely challenging.'

'I understand,' said Ernest, removing his hand in a manner that should have made it plain to Mr Sweetley that he did not understand at all.

But Mr Sweetley was not responding to signals, plain or otherwise; he found only relief in the fact of their parting.

And then Ernest Hammer found himself in the corridor outside the Acting Bailiff's office. It was a gloomy grey corridor, and the people who walked down it wore gloomy grey expressions. He picked up his briefcase; it made a pleasant clinking sound and he remembered, inside it, the bottle given him by Bald Sherry. It seemed to have been put there precisely for this moment and indeed, after a small nip or two, he felt very much revived.

Chapter 27

The upwards creep of expectations

It had become more urgent than ever that Ivorie expedite her relationship with the Starlight sisters. A fear had set in since Morag's appearance on the mountainside. It was like an undertow, threatening to draw her back, and down, and stifle the upwards creep of her expectations. She would not look at it, nor register the sharp pain at its centre; she only knew that its weight was intolerable, and could not be separated out into manageable components. Even Mrs Po – whom Ivorie had really loved and appreciated on her return from the campsite – had at present the quality of a boot clamped down on the back of one's skirts. Whereas the Starlight sisters were perfectly weightless: starlings on the breeze, balloons with the sandbags thrown away.

To effect the sealing of her friendship with Ann and Mary, Ivorie had brought with her her most treasured articles of faith. She did not do so lightly; nor were her motives merely opportune; but the time had come for her enquiries to begin, and she rightly intuited the sisters' interest.

'It has been my dearest desire,' she said, 'to discover who my mother was.' She lay them out on the table: the Mary Ann doll with its blue initialled leg; the yellow lock of hair; the item of jewellery she had always referred to as 'the topaz earring', though it was not topaz at all and could never be mistaken for such; and the copper token, stamped on one side with the profile of a woman. Ann Starlight turned this last round and round in her thin fingers, and pressed her lips together.

'I have seen something like it before,' she said. 'I am sure . . .'

'In a shop window, perhaps?' Mary, lepidopteran in a pale yellow dress with large hanging sleeves, turned and smiled at Ivorie, as though they were already the best of friends.

'Perhaps,' said Ann. 'Somewhere . . . In Papa's study, perhaps . . .'

Ivorie poked a little stuffing back into the Mary Ann doll's torso. 'They are all I have,' she said, quietly, 'of my mother.' For a moment, she felt this fact as she had always experienced it: at once large and minuscule, as though it expanded and reduced her simultaneously.

One could almost see compassion swell Mary Starlight's flat yellow bosom. 'Oh my dear,' she said, moving to Ivorie's side of the table, where she drew up a chair and laid her sleeves over Ivorie's arm.

'Do not suffer on my part!' Ivorie said. 'I am perfectly reconciled.' She laughed: a high-pitched laugh that instantly betrayed itself as false. 'I didn't know my mother. She passed away before I was born . . .' Her little finger wound its way through the ornate workings of her teacup handle. 'Or as near to –' She blushed. 'You understand.'

'Oh my dear, an orphan!' Mary looked at her new friend with grave admiration. 'I can hardly credit it, Mrs Hammer,' she said, shaking her head. 'You have nothing in your demeanour – nothing! – to suggest you are an orphan. How well you have overcome your trials and tribulations! Has she not, Ann?'

'Oh, they have not been so many,' said Ivorie, still blushing.

Ann, too, regarded Ivorie the orphan with new interest. She put down the copper token, and picked up instead the yellow lock of hair. She considered it carefully, pinched it in a strange manner – as though by so doing, she might cause it to divulge new information – and then gestured with it towards the Mary Ann doll.

'Now the contrast between yourself and your countrymen is explained to us, Mrs Hammer,' she said. She rose and went to a cabinet on the other side of the room, opening, with a key, its bottom-most drawer. She returned to the table with two boxes, set them down, one beside the other, and put the flat of her hands over their lids. 'Indeed, Mrs Hammer. The fact that you are an orphan . . . well, it is the missing piece in our puzzle!' She removed the lids of the two boxes, and pushed back the tissue paper, lifting from the first box a china doll that, though cleaner and better preserved and wearing a white organza wedding dress, was the exact replica of Ivorie's: so, too, albeit brunette and in peach-coloured garb, was the second. Ann passed them delicately to Ivorie and allowed her to examine them.

'But this is astonishing!' said Ivorie, turning over each doll and comparing them to her own. 'Where do they come from?'

'They are not to be found any more,' said Ann, 'but when we were young . . .'

'. . . every little girl in Pitch owned one. They were very popular in their time. We were given ours for our sixth birthday. Is that right, Ann?'

Ann nodded.

'And then every year,' continued Mary, 'we received another. Until we turned twelve – and then Mother,' Mary suppressed a cross snort, 'caused us to give them to charity!'

'She allowed us to keep only one each.'

'*We* chose to keep the wedding dolls!'

A buzzing had set up in Ivorie's forehead. Mary came close and squeezed her hand. 'As we said, you do not at all resemble your townspeople . . .'

'No more than does Mr Sweetley.'

'And you do not share the same – how shall I put it, Ann?'

Ann had a narrow face, and she held it with birdlike intensity. 'I believe that, once there is, in the blood, that peripatetic impulse . . .'

'It cannot be overcome.'

'Whereas *you*, Mrs Hammer . . .'

'You are *refined* . . .'

Ann's nose, though upwards-tilted, left nevertheless the impression of being slightly beaked. She lifted it an inch or two as though preparing to attack a seed tray. 'Now everything Mary and I have wondered about you makes perfect sense.' She nodded decisively several times and tapped the Mary Ann doll. 'If she belonged to your poor dead mother . . .'

Mary enveloped Ivorie's hands in her own. They were cool and smooth, like garment leather. 'Upon first meeting you, I was sure, from everything about you, that you were *one of us*, Mrs Hammer.'

The heavy weight that yesterday bore down on Ivorie lifted. 'That is what I have always thought,' she said. 'That is precisely what I have always thought and believed!' But even as she said it, an image flickered behind her eyelids of Morag on horseback, her mount attached by rope to its neighbour.

'Oh, Mrs Hammer. Let us welcome you home!' said Mary, pressing a kiss on Ivorie's cheek.

And with that Ivorie was swept up and held, cocoon-like, in the promise of future intimacies. A golden light, spreading through the parlour from the world outside, sealed the confidence.

The Starlight sisters, having eliminated their one and only objection to a friendship with Ivorie Hammer, were able hereafter to properly galvanise the relationship: with nothing less, indeed, than bricks and mortar – or, at least, the promise of such.

'We must,' said Ann – the excitement had subsided and they stood now, the three of them, at the window, looking out – 'secure you a tenancy.' She folded Ivorie's arm into her own. 'You must live in the *centre of town*, near to us. We shall find you a respectable residence. I will speak to the various agents.'

'You certainly ought not continue to reside in Middle Pitch with that landlady of yours,' said Mary, shaking her head.

'Indeed, no,' said Ann. 'It is vulgar, combining business and friendship in the way you describe. Friendship must be pure!'

The thing had not seemed quite clear before, but now, in the conspiratorial warmth of the Starlight sisters' parlour, Ivorie Hammer could not help but agree.

Chapter 28

Two small but significant incidents

Mrs Po could see very well how Ivorie Hammer would fit in with the wasp-waisted Starlight sisters of Inner Pitch. 'Oh yes,' she said out loud, 'I can see!' She could not eat her luncheon. When the baby cried, she lifted her out of the cot and lavished upon her all the love her hurt little torso could manage. 'My baby!' she said. 'My dear little baby!'

Pette rolled on the blanket Mrs Po laid out for her on the floor. She rolled left and right. She stretched up her head so that she resembled a turtle. When Mrs Po knelt down to play, her little face beamed a sudden heart-quickening joy, and Mrs Po had the strange feeling that the infant (of course, such things are impossible) was possessed of a sense of gratitude; and that it would, if it could, express this gratitude in the form of a gift, a behaviour, a first word or step or tooth.

The kettle boiled in the kitchen, and Mrs Po got up off her knees and went to fetch tea. It was Saturday afternoon. She stacked the tea things in readiness on the table, and put out plenty of cake.

When she returned to the sitting room, however, a great surge of alarm rose in Mrs Po's chest. There was a blanket on the floor, as there had been before she'd left the room, but there was no longer any baby upon it. Nor was there a baby in any other part of the room, not in any of its well-defined four corners, nor beneath the table or behind the curtains. There was no baby beneath the settee, and none was hiding behind the plant stand. She dashed to the hallway, but it was long and neat and entirely babyless. Mrs Po's hands made rapid tearing motions at her chest. She returned to the sitting room and looked again; her legs had begun to shake.

And now she heard a sound: a *peet-peet-peet*ing sound. It seemed to originate at the fireplace, though there was no baby to be seen on the hearth and the grate was empty of everything except a few stray lumps of coal. But the coalscuttle . . .! Yes, it was coming from the coalscuttle! *Peet-peet, peet-peet*: a little baby bird eating seeds.

How the child had climbed into the coalscuttle, she did not know. And how she had then folded herself so small as to be entirely hidden — that was a puzzle beyond the capacity of Mrs Po of Slabhill Road, Middle Pitch. The coalscuttle was a small brass box — but there inside it was Pette, rump up, huddled into an impossible ball. Mrs Po took a desperate hold of the exposed bottom, and pulled furiously. 'It's all right, little one!' she said. 'We'll have you out in a moment!' But when finally she came free — Mrs Po had the strange sensation of parting a periwinkle from its shell — Pette was quite unrecognisable. Her head seemed to have got lodged beneath her legs somehow, and her little arms had come out of their shoulder girdles and were pinned in between, so that when Mrs Po put her down on the floor, it was not at all clear how she might be returned to normal without being hurt in the process. And then suddenly, with all the coiled force of a spring: *pop, pop, pop* — Pette's limbs flew free and she was lying on her back again, kicking her legs and gurgling.

This was the first of two small but significant occurrences that day. But before we dispatch Mrs Po to the scene of the second significant occurrence — the kitchen, where the two men of the house are, amongst other things, currently taking tea — let us allow her first to hug and kiss the child, check all its vital signs, and put it back to bed. She does all this, and her heart-rate returns slowly to normal behind its wire and upholstery. She suddenly knows, and it makes her feel strangely bereft, that she will not say a word about it to the child's mother.

Ernest Hammer had become accustomed to his host's indifference, and had acquired the habit of bringing with him to tea time an article of diversion related to his current trade. An old leatherbound book of hand-coloured botanical specimens; a wooden puzzle box with six secret compartments; a pair of binoculars. Mr Po never showed a hint of curiosity; he sat and looked into his cup of tea, and sometimes sipped it.

Today, however, Ernest was surprised to notice him watching. Ernest had brought from his bag a packet of gilt-edged playing cards: he was going through them to ensure the deck was complete. Mr Po watched dully; but his eyelids flickered and transmitted a similar flickering quality to his fingertips.

Then Ernest did something else. He did not do it on purpose; it just occurred to him because, looking down into the neat black bag that had once contained the tools of trade of a watchmaker, he saw again the small bottle of spirits Mr Sherry had given him. It was a Saturday afternoon, and they were two men in a kitchen. He got up; he fetched from the cabinet two glasses, and poured into each of them a sup of brandy. Mr Po's eyes never left him.

When Mrs Po returned from upstairs, still pondering the strange contortions of her charge, she took in the sight with some astonishment. There sat her husband opposite Mr Hammer and, in his great knubby hand, he held a fan of playing cards. He picked one out and placed it face up on the deck. He poured himself a drink from a small bottle on the table, and, trumping the play, made a short guttural sound in the back of his throat that Mrs Po recognised as laughter.

One could not say that Mrs Po was horrified – this would be too strong a term to describe the contradictory feelings that now overwhelmed her. But her joy, upon witnessing her husband in a state of animation, was not unequivocal. She stood there in the doorway, and her hands went limp, as though they had held enormously heavy objects very tightly for an indefinite number of years, only to discover they could be let go of quite easily and without any repercussions.

Her eyes filled up with tears, but they were not helpful tears; they were hard: they hurt. She became brusque. She removed from the table the teacups and crumbs. She forbore from acknowledging her husband's transformation.

In fact, she forbore from speaking all together. In the kitchen, a taut silence prevailed: between the men, on account of the adversarial conventions of card-playing; on Mrs Po's account, because her emotions were like bilge water; they came in every which way, through holes she had not known she should plug up.

She crept into the infant's room and carefully – silently – slipped under the covers: she was a small woman; the cot supported them both quite easily. Pette's breath smelled of biscuit and milk. She shifted and the fingers of one hand wove briefly over Mrs Po's face, as though to check it were truly her: tiny tremulous movements that caught at every catch and hook of Mrs Po's ravaged little heart. It was truly wondrous, thought Mrs Po, that so tiny a creature might offer such comfort.

Chapter 29

John Thaddeus, Palaeoanthropologist

In another part of town, in a musty back room of the Pitch Municipal Museum, Senior Sergeant Robert Starlight awaited the arrival of John Thaddeus, Palaeoanthropologist. Borrel Sweetley sat beside him.

In response to Mr Sweetley's lobbying, the coroner's office had nominated the Senior Sergeant to head an inquiry into suspicious deaths in Canyon. It was bad enough that the Senior Sergeant shared his street and mail addresses with Mr Sweetley. But now the names of Starlight and Sweetley were twinned on a multitude of documents: on the documents committing Morag Pappy to jail; on those requesting funds from the public coffers; on the documents authorising removal, from the station house, of relevant osteological evidence – the two skulls the Senior Sergeant had originally confiscated from Mr Sweetley in Canyon. It was on account of these remains – as well as those smaller residual fragments Mr Sweetley had hoarded in his black briefcase for many months – that the men now awaited John Thaddeus.

The rooms of John Thaddeus constituted a small mausoleum: skulls and bones were everywhere displayed, ranged about the place like bric-a-brac. Anonymous eye sockets gazed down from high shelves. To the left of Thaddeus's desk, a skeletal hand draped elegantly over a porcelain ball, every delicate metacarpus intact. On the right side of the same desk, someone (presumably the incumbent officeholder) had placed a baby rat skeleton inside the sprung jaw of a large cat. A joke. Hah.

It was dusty and lightless and the Senior Sergeant's throat was dry. He could not help but imagine himself, with every breath, inhaling the fine dust of things long dead.

John Thaddeus, when he arrived, was much oilier than seemed appropriate for a man who spent his life surrounded by bones and fossils and the dried-out fragments thereof. He slid, with great suppleness, into the chair behind his desk, observing his two interlocuters with mole-like eyes and realigning a cord of hair that had fallen foul of its parting. Then, with one smooth, noiseless movement, he unlocked a drawer and brought forth a neat pile of papers. Borrel Sweetley, in thrall to the power of documents and the men whose erudition gave life to them, was unusually quiet.

Thaddeus turned a page with a licked finger. He turned another page and looked at his two guests with a mixture of boredom and contempt. 'Mmm,' he said, and licked, and looked down again. 'The specimens,' he said finally, 'were interesting.'

Borrel Sweetley chewed hard on his lip.

'Yes, the specimens were interesting. The skulls –' John Thaddeus looked at them meaningly, '– belonged to two individuals.'

A snort came out of Borrel Sweetley's nose. He flapped his hand apologetically.

Thaddeus, looking briefly up, ignored him. 'A man's and a woman's,' he continued. 'The wear on the teeth,' he ground his own illustratively, 'led me to hypothesise an age at death of the middle forties. And the latter teens. Respectively.' He took a deep breath; an oil patch gleamed on his forehead. 'If I were a practitioner of the science of phrenology,' he continued, 'I might assert certain conclusions on the basis of the *skull shapes*. But I am not a practitioner of phrenology.'

'Phrenology, phrenology,' said Borrel Sweetley, in such a way that it was unclear if he were *for* or *against*.

'As a scientist, however, of *anthropology*, I can draw other pertinent conclusions. Evaluating the shape of the bones, certain interesting features become apparent. The bones are those of two people, not one – male and female. And although the female's age at death, in my estimation, was no more than twenty or so years, the bones are smaller than they should be. They are less dense –' He stopped. If Mr Sweetley and Senior Sergeant Starlight had paid closer attention they would have noticed him becoming fractionally excited. 'They show, too, evidence of other, more interesting irregularities. Some of the bone fragments you provided,

Mr Sweetley, Senior Sergeant Starlight, retained *ligament residue*. Ligaments, you understand, are the bands of tissue binding the bones and cartilage together; elastic, more and less flexible. From this residue, and from the indications of wear on the vertebrae and joints, I was able to ascertain preliminary evidence of *generalised articular hypermobility*.' He looked at the men with bright wet eyes; they did not respond. 'In short, there appeared to be a *shallow* interlocking of the joint in combination with *long* ligaments.' The men continued to look at him blankly. 'Do you see? A very interesting anatomical detail.'

Neither of the two men knew what Thaddeus meant, and neither wanted to ask for elaboration: Starlight, because he did not want to be here in the first place; and Sweetley, because his personality did not allow for failures of comprehension. Thaddeus was disappointed and resumed his slightly contemptuous tone.

'You indicated, Mr Sweetley,' he said, 'some expectation that evidence of fatal assault would be found. There is nothing on the female skull to indicate assault: no fracture, no fissure. The cranio-facial bones are intact. However, I have isolated violent cause of death of the other of your friends.' He took a breath. 'You observed, Mr Sweetley, that the male cranium contained an area of shattered bone above the brow. It is not indicative of a wound made by a pistol. Such a wound would be less explosive, more distinct: it would leave evidence of a bullet hole. The gentleman did indeed die of a gunshot wound to the head. But it was an old-fashioned gun did the job, a gun that employed a thing known as a percussion cap. Brains scattered everywhere!' He giggled faintly and the Senior Sergeant saw the man who had put the rat skeleton inside the cat's jaws.

'And the woman?' ventured the Senior Sergeant.

'No such conclusions evident from her remains. Bones from the female pelvic girdle seem to indicate an android pelvis. Perhaps this caused complications.'

Borrel Sweetley had become suddenly agitated. He did not care about the complications of an android pelvis. 'So, while the male remains almost certainly prove a violent death, there is nothing in the woman's remains,' he said, 'to suggest foul play?'

John Thaddeus considered. 'Well, one would not detect a stab wound, or a bullet wound, if it merely punctured the vital organ and failed to penetrate the bone. One would not see death by loss of blood. Some poisons, some maladies, leave residue that might be detected in the bones. And certainly, the remains are not complete, and the bones, overall, are too broken up to say. My conjecture would be that the woman died of natural causes, disease, malnutrition –' He giggled again. 'Perhaps of a broken heart.'

Sweetley looked anxious. Then he brightened. 'But you cannot say for certain. There *could* have been poison. There *could* have been a knife?'

'That could be so,' Thaddeus said.

Sweetley lounged in his chair, satisfied.

'One final question,' said the Senior Sergeant, 'if I may. Have you any estimate, Mr Thaddeus, of how long ago these deaths occurred?'

'I cannot be specific, Mr Starlight, but I would hazard a guess of half a century.'

'Half a century!' said Sweetley. On his face, Starlight could see the processes at work, the reconfiguration of his theories: disappointment, and then a sudden burst of optimism. 'Ah, just as I thought . . . An old crime, covered up!'

John Thaddeus stood, bringing their interview to a close. 'A copy of my findings await you in the foyer,' he said. 'And the artefacts themselves – the osteological specimens – will be returned to the police station posthaste. Under guard. I'm glad I could be of service.' He bowed at the hip, a bow that was by no means intended as deferential, or even, really, respectful – a purely dismissive bow. He did not wait for them to return it, but closed the door and disappeared silkenly into his chambers.

Chapter 30

Dewlaps

The morning after his meeting with the palaeoanthropologist, Borrel Sweetley looked in the mirror and, with some horror, saw them. *Dewlaps.* One could not describe them otherwise. What had been nominal before – the slightest trim of skin, like the flounce on a curtain rod – now provided distinct drapery to either side of his jaw. A dismal feeling crept over him. He imagined it was how a fallen log might feel, having lichen grow upon it.

Yesterday he had not known himself as a man with dewlaps. In fact, so buoyant had Sweetley felt upon his return from the rooms of John Thaddeus that the laws of gravity had seemed to drop away entirely. His body, with its complaints and demands and objections, ceased to exist; there was only his mind: unshackled, infinitely creative, and hopefully capable of wresting the truth from an uncooperative array of evidence.

From the beginning he had had no doubt about Otto Cirque's guilt. The fact that Cirque had escaped from custody and made a mockery of him had caused his belief to harden into something much more personal than high-minded legal principle. It had become a solid thing with a nucleus of impossible density. It would not shrink, and he could not shrink from it. But how to make a story from the disparate elements he had at hand?

The coincidence of Otto's escape and the death of Mrs Sherry was circumstantially strong: this was in his favour when it came to proving that portion of his case. He had only to find the murder weapon, the bogus gris-gris he had sold Mrs Sherry on its bit of leather cord, to prove without doubt that she had been strangled. He suspected Morag Pappy knew of its whereabouts, but his experimental attempts at coercion had wrought nothing. Nothing could be brokered with her. He could hardly *starve* it out of her, could he?

He suspected, too, that she knew more than a little of what he now called the 'original murders'. Again, circumstantial evidence here was strong: the location in which the bones were found, the macabre display of skulls in Otto Cirque's dwelling, the presence there of the old-fashioned rifle. How could any interpretation but guilt be arrived at? *Motive* was what he sought. And *relationships*. These must be proved.

He had put his head down on his desk to think better; now he lifted it, and came face to face with a mountain of paperwork. Fifty years of archives, recently retrieved from the vaults of the Canyon courthouse and the even deeper vaults of the Canyon Historical Society. The mere sight of it had exhausted him previously. But now he viewed it differently — not with exhilaration exactly, but with something more solid and reliable: with fortitude.

It was a good number, fifty: it fit perfectly around the shoulders of Otto Cirque. He felt no doubt that circumstances could be lulled into doing likewise.

Sweetley felt his spirits lift and, under the influence of this sensation, an idea that had occurred and reoccurred to him over recent weeks began to gather renewed force. It grew and grew over the course of the afternoon, interrupting the flow of Mr Sweetley's important work, and reactivating certain of his conceits.

The archives would be there tomorrow; the courage might not. Mr Sweetley rose. He was pleased with his figure as it appeared to him in the surface of a polished table top. He had plenty of hair. In profile in the glass-fronted bookcase, he was able to reassure himself that the front and back sides of him were very nearly aligned. He was independent thinking, gainfully employed. If *she* was the perfect candidate, *he* was by no means undesirable.

And so, that evening, as the light in the parlour faded and Ann Starlight packed up her sewing, Borrel Sweetley made his case.

He approached his love object quietly, and, disburdening her of her sewing box, dropped to one knee, took her hand, and commenced to speak.

I will not tax you with the details of his speech, which was perhaps somewhat longer than it should have been, but I will, if I may, just suggest that it was not all self-congratulation and bombast: it had in it a moment or two of real emotion. There was a point at which he compared Ann to a perfect rosebud dipped in wax; another point at which he used the example of the grey butcherbird and its young to edify his thoughts on family life. Finally, he spoke of 'the twin firmaments of the marriage stronghold' with such conviction that any woman, should she momentarily close her eyes, might imagine herself a character in a Regency novel.

I am sorry – but only mildly so – to say that his proposal was rejected.

Ann, sliding her hand out of her suitor's, did not display discomposure at this unexpected turn of events. She bade Mr Sweetley return to his feet, and smoothly resumed possession of her sewing box, holding it in front of her as a small but effective physical buffer. Thereafter she acquitted her rejection very well, her counter-speech containing much repetition of the words 'flattered' and 'regret'; and a great emphasis on something she called her 'ill-equipped constitution'. For all the world, Ann's could not have been a more accomplished rejection.

However, seeing from his face that Borrel Sweetley was not easily assimilating the information, she employed that device that is her sex's prerogative. She squeezed her eyes tightly, and produced moisture; the moisture begot, of its own accord, more moisture; finally, there really was a visible wetness about the lovely woman's eyes and cheeks. She quit the room in a sashay of skirts, clinging fast to her sewing box.

Sweetley was crestfallen. He had to draw out a chair and sit down on it for several long minutes. Something had gone out in his legs and back; they had buckled on him completely. He proceeded blankly to his room, from where he could hear the murmur of feminine voices – discussing, no doubt, his failure. He ate a little cheese, and drank a little water, and finally went to sleep.

The next morning he looked at himself, dismally, in the mirror, and saw dewlaps.

Chapter 31

Items at the end of a list

Mr Ernest Hammer, assistant to the increasingly invalid antiquarian, George Duke, understands lists. He is more and more in the habit of list making. He compiles them painstakingly, assigning as he does so prices and stock numbers, dates of purchase and dates of sale. A man who has recently purchased a pair of carved rosewood bookends at 2/7 could easily find evidence in Mr Hammer's inventories that he had paid substantially more than he ought.

But the purchase of bookends is of no significance to us here. What is of significance is an item known as Lot 74B, a small brown portmanteau with a leather belt securing it across the middle. It is a fairly run-of-the-mill prospect, Lot 74B; Mr Hammer bid on it yesterday at auction on account of its containing a gentleman's effects, and those effects appearing, so far as he could tell from his preliminary inspection, in generally good condition.

He undoes the belt, and lifts from the top of the portmanteau the following:

- four starched and folded shirts;
- three neatly-stacked dress-collars;
- a hatbox, containing a black felt boxer;
- a tennis shirt, and a pair of striped winceyette pyjamas;
- three pairs of trousers: flannel, tweed and Canton flannel;
- a dinner suit with silk-faced lapels;
- several articles of underwear (lambswool and cotton); and
- a pair of black patent leather boots with hardly a scuff mark (no laces).

All these items he studies with great respect. He then stacks the items of apparel neatly on the table beside him, makes a series of shorthand notes on his notepad, and a new heading.

Items sundry:

- a Kerr Bros tennis racquet, unstrung;
- sheet music for piano: 'Études' by Liszt; Dvořák's 'Humoresque', and 'Apple Blossoms' by Leona Lacoste;
- a packet of photographs, featuring a heavy-set, well-dressed woman and a small dog;
- a scrap album with dark-coloured pages (largely empty);
- an Onoto Valveless fountain pen;
- a Rotable lightning calculator, stuffed with old pennies;
- a slightly dented tin canister (empty); and
- a flat bamboo and blackwood box containing a packet of bile beans, a sachet of headache powder, and a handful of odd and apparently obsolete currency: larger and less round than that currently in circulation, and featuring, in relief, the profile of a coiffed and possibly aristocratic woman.

So arrested by these coins is Mr Hammer that he fails to notice the false bottom in the blackwood and bamboo box (it will not be till the morrow that he uncovers the engagement ring hidden therein). He is completely oblivious to false bottoms, and absolutely taken with the coins. He is interested in the coins because, as we know, his wife has in her possession an identical item.

Later, he took the coins to George Duke, reclining on the box couch with a book on sixteenth-century marblework.

'Mr Duke,' he said. 'Do you know where these come from?'

Duke, barely awake, took the coins in the palm of his hand and seemed to weigh them. 'Seen' he said, struggling to sit up, 'something like them.' His eyelids appeared unusually heavy: when he blinked, they remained too long closed. 'Rings a bell. Somewhere.' He smiled, returned the coins to Ernest and looked as if he was going back to sleep; then, suddenly, his eyes snapped open again. '*Oh*,' he said. He stretched his hand a few inches towards Ernest to resume possession of the coins. 'I know exactly what these are. These are *brothel tokens*, Mr Hammer.' He looked at them and laughed and shucked them up and down in his hand. 'I have not seen these in years. But I do remember the establishment . . . a nose like a duck's bill, if I recall, and very small eyes, but possessed the most heavenly – What was the *name* of the place? Oh yes – the *House of Jupon*. That was it! I had forgot its existence completely! Goat Lane, if I remember. Atrocious part of town. I wonder –' But at this point, Mr Duke fell into a coughing fit that not only lost him his page in *Sixteenth-Century Marblework*, but upturned onto the box couch a glassful of water. Ernest fetched a towel and Duke, wriggling free, left his employee to dab at the wet upholstery.

'Anything else,' Duke said, 'in this gentleman's effects?'

'Clothes, mostly. In good condition. No moth. A few knick-knacks. Tennis racquet. I shall see what we can get for them.'

Duke nodded and, re-establishing himself on the couch, pulled his robes up over his chest and closed his eyes. 'House of Jupon,' he said, shaking his head, 'The House of Jupon.'

Ernest wrapped the tokens in a handkerchief and stowed them in his pocket. It was the end of the working day and already growing dark. George Duke was asleep, his arms curled into the upholstery and his bare ankles showing. Ernest found him a blanket, and then, reminded by a maverick clinking in his briefcase, a half-full bottle of Bald Sherry's spirits. Sherry had had them delivered: a dozen, decanted into a various assortment of bottles, left on the doorstep over night. Each one, Ernest had to say, was as good as the last.

Chapter 32

Madam Slipper

When Ernest emerged at street level, the lamps were being lit. In his pocket he had a map of Pitch, and he brought the map out and studied it under the light. It took some time to locate Goat Lane, strangled between two wider thoroughfares and indicated in tiny letters, in an area known as the Bread Basin, where all the streets grew so close that even on the map it looked dark. He estimated the distance at about a mile.

Ernest walked and the lamps were lit as he went, as if some invisible creature ran at all times just ahead, ensuring his safe passage – until he entered that part of town where lamps failed to penetrate. Here, twilight gave over to darkness and a certain dull silence, largely accountable to straw. There were buildings, looming and deceptively solid, and numbers that were difficult to make out. If the district had once been given over to the production of bread, such industry had long ceased to exist; cruciferous vegetables now provided the predominant aroma.

Goat Lane was wider than Ernest's map gave it credit for, but the House of Jupon had no number and no sign. Ernest found it via a process part elimination, part intuition. The building was larger than others, for one thing; for another, it had all the subtle signs of commerce without the advertisement: windows lit strategically, shades half-drawn, the distant sound of a piano. A red candle burnt behind lantern glass high up on the wall. Ernest rang the bell, and the door was quickly opened by a girl with sharp, irregular teeth and skin the colour of rocksalt. She did not smile, but nor did she show surprise.

Madam Slipper, brothel owner, wore a Chinese pyjama suit, and poured her guest hot bright tea from a square pot with a cane handle. She was an excellent-looking woman: fine-boned, with an almost-bridgeless nose and round nostrils. At seventy years of age, her skin had stretched rather than wrinkled, giving it a delicate translucent appearance. Her body, beneath the flat Chinese silk, was not vastly different to the one she had inhabited as a thirteen-year-old: devoid of curve or contour. Tonight, in the peachy glow of the saloon bar, she resembled nothing so much as a perfectly preserved rose, dipped not in wax, but in something more porous: yak oil or copha or even ghee. Ernest Hammer thought her quite magnificent.

She took time and care with her guest; he was not, as she soon established, a regular paying client. Indeed, she would not extract a penny from him in the normal course of business. But he possessed an intangible quality that made Madam Slipper – shrewd to a fault – trust him. 'In two hours, Mr Hammer,' she said, sipping her tea, 'in two hours, in this room, there will be music and dancing.' She leaned forwards cleanly from the middle like a hinge. 'Until then, you are custodian of my attention. So let us look at this curio you bring.'

The tea was not potent: it contained no opiates, no sleeping powders, no mysterious oriental ingredients. It was just tea, but something about it – something about his circumstance, perhaps – made Ernest feel unusually tranquil. He discovered that he trusted Madam Slipper in the same way that, unknown to him, she trusted him. He sipped tea and passed her the token he had retrieved that afternoon from a deceased gentleman's effects.

Madam Slipper held the token between forefinger and thumb, equidistant between herself and her guest. 'The *profile*, it is said, shows a human face at its noblest and yet, I think, not always its kindest.' She paused; she turned the thing over. 'Roman emperors could withstand the profile. Young ladies are sensitive, of course, about the nose.' She tapped her own rhinologically minimal specimen. 'Fashions change. You bring me currency from days long gone. Much better days, Mr Hammer. I was not here then, but I know. We do not use these tokens any more in our business. We have different forms of credit.' She smiled again at Ernest: her little teeth were worn down almost to the gums.

'You are here to find someone?' she prompted. 'She is your mother, perhaps. Or an old *acquaintance*?'

Ernest explained.

'Aah,' said Madam Slipper and, directing Ernest to remain seated, got up and left the room.

When she returned, she carried with her a large black ledger and placed it on a low table in front of Mr Hammer. She then sat beside him, perfectly still in her dark-blue suit, and turned the pages.

'Here,' she said, 'we will find the names of every girl in the House of Jupon in the years you seek. What was the name of the woman in question – or perhaps she went by pseudonym?'

'I don't know,' said Ernest, a little embarrassed. 'I have only her initials: M.W.'

And so, over the next hour, Madam Slipper and Mr Hammer compiled a list of all the names in the ledger that bore the initials M.W. One by one, they were ruled out, some because they did not correspond datewise with Mr Hammer's token. Others because their bearers died before the date of Ivorie Hammer's birth. Ernest watched Madam Slipper draw a neat black line through name after name till finally they were left with three: Martha White, Marigold Wiseman, and Marianne Ward.

The tea was cold. Ernest Hammer sat back in his chair. Madam Slipper continued to examine the records book. They sat in silence some time, until Madam Slipper, squinting, struck the page before her conclusively. 'It is not Marigold Wiseman,' she said. 'You may tell your wife that, Mr Hammer. Her mother is not Miss Wiseman.'

'How?' said Ernest.

'See here. It is medical information. It is all written here. Miss Wiseman had the clap, Mr Hammer. Miss Wiseman took the sweating cure and was relieved, but was barren thereafter, in the year 18—, two years before your wife's birth.'

'Astounding,' said Ernest, meaning not Miss Wiseman's unfortunate contraction of gonorrhoea, but the meticulousness of her employer, who kept account of such information.

'Miss White, then, or Miss Ward?' he said.

'There seems nothing,' Madam Slipper answered, 'in the medical records to preclude either woman. Let us see . . .'

But it was then discovered that Miss White had been so much in demand in the month in question that a birth, had it occurred, must have been a miracle of scheduling. Marianne Ward, however, appeared intermittently in the records of the preceding year, and then disappeared for good.

'It is possibly Miss Ward, then,' said Ernest quietly.

'If this were all the evidence . . .' said Madam Slipper. 'But perhaps you would like to study the records further? Our doors will open soon, and I must attend to our visitors, but you are welcome to sit in my office. The light is good. I will tell them to bring you more tea.'

Ernest Hammer accepted the offer, and relocated to the comfortable confines of Madam Slipper's office, where three large filing boxes were swiftly retrieved from the darkness of a cupboard and removed of their dust. And there, several hours later, Ernest happened finally upon further documents that corresponded with his reckonings.

But he had also found another name, a name with which he was alarmingly familiar, repeated again and again, on correspondence and bills and receipts – and that name, of course, was *Morag Pappy*.

Chapter 33

Two variations on happiness

Ernest understood his wife well enough to know that certain details need be omitted from his account of the evening. Thus it was that he described the House of Jupon as a respectable boarding house for young ladies. He had found out little about Ivorie's mother herself, he said, only that she was in some way connected with the establishment. He did not mention Morag.

'It does not seem very convincing, Mr Hammer,' Ivorie said, narrowing her eyes. 'It must be convincing, you see . . . I must be *convinced*.'

Ernest Hammer rubbed at his eyebrows.

Sometime later in the evening, his wife resumed the subject.

'What was it, Mr Hammer,' she said, 'that led you to this place, to this particular woman?' Ivorie was sewing; she bent her head over her work and did not look at her husband.

Ernest cleared his throat. 'This establishment,' he said, 'this particular boarding house, had an uncommon system whereby its young female boarders were allocated tokens. As a form of credit.'

Ivorie appeared satisfied with this explanation. She sewed three stitches. 'And how did you come across the place?'

'George Duke,' said Ernest. 'He knew about it.'

'And did they match?'

'Match, my dear?'

'The tokens. Did the tokens from the boarding house match that which has been so long in my possession?'

'Identical,' said Ernest.

Ivorie sighed and smiled at the same time. 'And there was no other woman in residence at the time who bore my mother's initials?'

'I believe not.'

'Well, temporarily, then,' said Ivorie, 'provisionally, in the lack of other evidence, I believe I must allow that this woman was – or might have been – my mother. At the very least . . . Are there no other such boarding houses that operate this system?'

'None other, I believe.'

Ivorie dropped her sewing. 'I had thought it likely that my mother belonged to a good family, Mr Hammer! I have always believed that . . . Was this a house for poor girls, Mr Hammer, was it? Tell me the truth?'

'For poor girls? Why no, no! For respectable girls, Ivorie, of – independent means.'

'Ah!' said Ivorie. '*Independent means!* So perhaps that is where my small fortune came from . . .' Ivorie's eyes glazed over; her mother briefly materialised as a well-heeled young woman with a parasol and a carpetbag. 'Oh, Mr Hammer! But who was she really? If I just had a photograph . . .'

'Would that make a difference? Perhaps it would disappoint you, my dear.'

Ivorie shook her head. 'It would enable me to believe in my mother *really* having existed, Ernest.'

'But of course she existed!'

'Oh, I know she did, as such, that she must have –' She took his hand. 'But not having known her, not having had a mother . . . it has scarred me, Mr Hammer.'

Mr Hammer, though he knew to go carefully, thought now the time to raise an issue close to his heart. 'Ivorie,' he said, 'if it is so, you must not allow your own scars to disfigure the present.'

Ivorie stared at him. 'What do you mean?'

'I mean Pette,' said her husband.

Ivorie's face changed, and she looked very much a child herself. 'Oh, Mr Hammer! You think me a bad mother. That I do not exist for my child!'

'No, my dear, that is not what I meant.'

'But it is true! I am a bad mother. I have not the right feelings. Look how Mrs Po can coddle the child and love it, whereas I –'

'My dear, you will grow to the role of motherhood. But you must *allow* it.'

'It is because I had no mother of my own, Ernest, that is why!'

'I have no doubt,' said Ernest, 'that Morag did her best for you in that capacity, as best she could at least.' He was silent for a moment while Ivorie digested this possibility. 'She is in jail, my dear. She must suffer. Why don't you visit her?'

Ivorie looked momentarily crestfallen. 'Perhaps I shall,' she said. 'But no, no, it will be too painful for me, Ernest . . . I cannot do it!'

He looked at her, and she looked down at the table.

'I cannot do it,' she said.

The next morning, Ivorie had an appointment with the Starlight sisters to visit several properties currently for lease in Inner Pitch.

Though they had to stop several times and rest – Mary on account of a mysterious condition of the skeleton, and Ann on account of 'compressed lungs' – she and the Starlight sisters looked at three dark, damp houses. Ivorie said she could put up with almost anything so long as it enabled her family good, self-sufficient living in a respectable quarter. The two sisters, however, looked at each other, shook their heads and led Ivorie off to their favourite tea house: a green-and-gold-papered establishment, where a dozen or so tables were laid with all the instruments of civilised tea taking.

Conversation had been energetic all morning – property was such an interesting topic! So, too, was the topic of Ivorie's mother, though all were careful to remember the *provisionality* of the evidence pertaining to her identity. But no sooner had the tea been delivered than the discussion took an unhappy turn.

'We have known some time now,' said Ann, looking confidentially at Mary and then at Ivorie, 'about your unfortunate countrywoman, whom Mr Sweetley has in custody.' There was silence for a moment while this intimation hung above the table.

'Mr Sweetley has several times been accosted.'

'Verbally harangued.'

'*Harassed* about that old woman.'

Ann looked at Ivorie over a piece of buttered white bread. 'Do you know her, Mrs Hammer?'

'No!' Ivorie said, scalding her tongue on her tea. She took a breath and corrected herself. 'I did once know her,' she said finally. In this room, with its tiny teacup clinks and delicate pastries, Ivorie's sentence had the effect, it seemed to her, of a large hunk of unleavened bread. She tried again: 'I had some acquaintance with her.'

The Starlight sisters watched, encouragingly. Ann cocked her head. Everything about their new friend was interesting and fresh. Soon they would help her acquire a really good-quality coat — it was a project to which they looked forward.

But for Ivorie, everything was wrong. Her cake, that a minute before had been light and easy to digest, now sat in her stomach like a rock.

'It is immensely generous of the Inner Pitch Council,' said Mary, 'to provide so well for the people of Canyon.' She wrinkled her brow with such force that, were she a less intrinsically good-looking woman, her face might eventually suffer for the expression.

Ann concurred. 'To provide what is, essentially, a leasehold.'

'And waive completely all expectation of rent!' Mary shook her head. 'But the plight of that old lady in the jail . . .' She looked to her sister for help.

'It seems, Mrs Hammer, that Mr Sweetley cannot bring the necessary *pressure* to bear on her.' Ann crunched down on a biscuit. 'She will not confess!'

'It's all very difficult,' said Mary. 'And if, of course, they *hang her* . . .'

For one moment, the floor fell completely away from Ivorie.

'Mrs Hammer!' she heard, as if from a great distance. Still she kept falling, down, down, down. She put her hand to her throat and found she could not swallow.

'Waiter!' cried out Mary, jumping to her friend's aid. 'I think she has choked on something!'

Water was brought and pressed to Ivorie's lips. Little by little she began to breathe again. She found she was gripping the table edge with her fingers and had knocked over her tea.

'A sudden . . . headache,' she said. 'A terrible sharp headache, I'm so sorry.'

Headache powders were produced and dissolved and Ivorie soon recovered though she found she could not muster enthusiasm for further conversation. The Starlight sisters put her change of mood down to discomfort: no one knew like they the terrible travails of headache.

In a coincidence of absolutely no importance to our narrative, beyond supplying a neat point of connection, Mrs Po and Baby Pette happened to be passing Mackaby Superior Tea Rooms at just the moment Ivorie was struck down with headache. They continued down Mackaby Lane, stopping once to look at a pretty bolt of poplin.

Mrs Po was feeling, for the first time in weeks, happy. She was happy because in her reticule was her medical card, attached to which was another medical card, in the name of 'Pette Po'. And on this second medical card, previously blank, there were now all sorts of tiny cryptic ink marks, several incidences of the exclamation point, and the word 'phenomenal', much underlined. Let us regress a few hours, and accompany Mrs Po on her trip to the Inner Pitch hospital.

An unhappy design feature of the Inner Pitch Municipal Hospital was that, in order to gain access to the rooms of one's practitioner, one must sit for some time in the public waiting area. The waiting area was not itself uncomfortable. But in the course of one's wait, one must encounter so many depressing human specimens!

Mrs Po was not a woman of prejudice. She did not mind if a man were a fireman or a barrister or a streetsweeper, so long as he was clean and upstanding and tolerably neat in dress. But the men whom one here encountered: they were of a different species altogether. They slouched in the chairs and took advantage of the free beverages. They did not care that a small woman with a large pram could not navigate her wheels about them. Mrs Po did not prevent, when it naturally tended that way, her pram wheel from jabbing a recalcitrant, unstockinged ankle. The bearer of such did not even wince.

Fortunately, her discomfort was short lived; the door opened and Pette's name was called.

The doctor's office smelled pleasingly neutral and his face was so clean-shaven as to be almost girlish. Mrs Po explained to him the child's peculiarity, and was pleased to find he took her quite seriously.

He was all business, in fact. He turned Baby Pette over, and straightened out her limbs to measure her. He pronounced his satisfaction with her weight. 'She is small, your little girl,' he said, 'but in perfect proportion.' Mrs Po glowed. He bent Pette's elbows and knees backwards and forwards, rotated her hip and shoulder joints, pulled sharply at her right hand. Mrs Po was startled to see the corresponding shoulder girdle dislocate, like a chicken leg tugged off the frame, and then, just as swiftly, pop back into place. Pette blinked in the light. The doctor proceeded then to palpate each disc, every vertebra, in the infant's spine; as he worked his way down from the cervical vertebra to the coccyx, Pette turned to watch, with such acute rotation of the neck that her head appeared wrongly attached. Mrs Po made an involuntary sound in the base of her throat and sat up in her chair.

'You need not worry, madam,' said the doctor. 'The spine of the infant is a marvel of elasticity.' He continued to prod and tap at Pette's back. 'In the case of this child, the marvel is just rather accentuated.' He dislocated the right hip briefly, and the knee socket. Then he returned Pette to Mrs Po and, after writing for some minutes on the medical card, sat down opposite her with a look on his face that Mrs Po could not decipher. She held her breath in case the news was bad.

'Try to imagine the spinal column, madam, as a pile of black and white checkers,' he said, 'placed alternately, one atop the other . . . Imagine the blacks, then, to represent pieces of bone, called the vertebrae, and the whites to be discs of very strong, tough, elastic gristle by which they are held together. Such a column would be at once very strong and very flexible, would it not?'

Mrs Po nodded.

'It could bend backwards, forwards and to each side. It could be swung around so that its upper end would describe a circle, and it could be twisted to some extent on its axis.'

Mrs Po was struggling.

'You would perceive now, madam, would you not, that the amount of motion would vary correspondingly with a change in proportion of bone to gristle.'

Mrs Po looked blank. The doctor demonstrated with his hands.

'The more bone, you see, the more stability. The more gristle, the more motion.' He leaned forwards and spoke very clearly. 'Now, the issue is quite simple, Mrs Po: the proportion of gristle in the infant spine is always much greater than that in the adult.'

'Ah,' said Mrs Po, a trifle sadly, 'so she will grow out of it.'

'The average child, yes. There is also the question of the proportion of muscle to tendon. An infant has a much greater proportion of muscle, you see, and this also reduces over time, if not cultivated. All in all, the infantile condition – the extraordinary flexibility you see now – is in most persons merely transient.'

'So, then, as I said, she will grow out of it.' Mrs Po dared not look at him, she felt so disappointed.

Here the doctor stood up and began to walk about the room. 'The range of individual variation in the human structure is wonderfully great,' he said. 'I have seen human shoulder blades so different that if they were sent for examination to an inhabitant of Mars he would ascribe them to completely different species!'

Mrs Po's mental terrain could not quite accommodate such vast imaginative propositions.

The doctor looked intently at Mrs Po now. It was almost uncomfortable, but she would not look away. 'Your child exhibits an *uncommon* freedom of movement in the joints. In such loose-jointed persons,' he said, 'it is probable that either the shape of the joints or an unusual laxness of the ligaments allows the bones, when in certain positions, to become displaced. When this occurs, the pull of the muscles is sufficient to retain stability, aided by a peculiar shortness of the ligaments.' Mrs Po looked lost. 'Quite simply,' the doctor went on, 'if such a person has the power of completely relaxing the muscles, and providing the peculiarity is cultivated, persons with this condition might achieve extraordinary effects.'

He handed her Pette's medical card. 'It is very interesting to me, Mrs Po, and I would like to see your daughter again in a year's time to monitor her progress.' Mrs Po stood up. 'Madam,' said the doctor, giving her his hand to shake, 'I must tell you, I have never before seen an infant with this degree of natural hypermobility. It is really . . .' he searched for the word, '. . . exceptional.'

Mrs Po did not mind any decrepitude on her way out. She did not mind dirty grey men with blank faces. The word *exceptional* rang in her ears: it made her chattier than usual with the fishmonger, and even persuaded her to buy two pounds of frenched cutlets. She wanted to tell them both, the fishmonger, the butcher, about Pette Po's 'exceptionality'. Pette blinked and smiled and pressed the packet of lamb chops with her finger.

When they arrived home, someone was waiting for them on the front porch. It was Racine; she had been sunning herself, she said, quite happily for an hour, waiting for them.

'Oh Miss Pfeffersalz,' said Mrs Po, exhaling with relief. She took Racine's hands. 'I have the most exciting news.'

Chapter 34

Enchantment

Otto Cirque had spent the winter in enviably warm conditions. Having transformed Mr Sherry's amateurish distilling operation into something viable, he spent the coldest months of the year stoking the furnace. Indeed, had discomfort been experienced by Otto Cirque that winter, its cause was not *cold* but *heat*. He was methodical in attending to this heat. He took the business of fire seriously. He glided between wood stack and hearth, ensuring, as much as a man might, a constancy of temperature, an even burning rate. The palms of his hands were black with soot; his cheeks were rosy red. Apart from Bald Sherry, no one knew he was there.

But he could not remain safe and warm – and ignorant – forever. One morning, collecting wood before daybreak, Otto Cirque overheard a conversation between husband and wife that would act upon him like gelignite.

'Would you hurry up, my dear?' said the woman. 'It's brisk; I have not got my shawl on.'

'Shawls!' said the man. 'I am without my undershirt!'

Otto pushed his wheelbarrow out of sight and shrank back against a tree. A knot in the tree trunk settled neatly beneath his ribcage. It was not yet light; the man held a lantern and its flare moved across the ground as the two figures proceeded towards the wood pile.

'Had you been less tardy in your chores yesterday, there might be a fire already blazing,' said the woman, unfurling a bag and flapping it open.

'I hadn't known you must be so early.'

'Well, I must make a bright start, I don't know at what times they allow visitors . . .'

'I've said I will go in your place.'

'And what good would that do? Miss Pappy doesn't know you from a paperbag, sir! No, it is her friends she needs right now.' There was some shuffling and scooping of kindling.

'Well, a prison is no place for a woman to go on her own, unattended.'

'There are five of us going, my dear. Five of us.'

'Nevertheless, you are none of you strong —'

'I will have you take that back! Perhaps once upon a time I was not strong, but I am strong now! We are all of us strong.'

'It's a grievous, parlous thing nevertheless . . .'

'Well, it will be more grievous and parlous if things are allowed to go on as they are . . . I don't wish to see a friend at the end of a rope, sir, and I'm sure you don't either!'

'Well, I don't know what power any of us has. They'll keep her there till that Cirque fellow shows up — none of your lobbying, you women, will do anything. Now come, take up your bag and I'll load this in . . .'

For Otto, the impact of this was sudden and propulsive. He dropped immediately his barrow of wood and, as swiftly and invisibly as he had come amongst them, he left.

He made his way along the Ring Road, inhabiting only its margins, darting from tree to tree. When he came to Middle Pitch, the sun had still not broken. He was cold; those weeks stoking the still fires had robbed him of any resistance to the elements. He was also hungry. He walked and listened and looked out for smoke coming from chimney pots or other signs that householders were up and about.

He came to a halt, finally, at a front porch where an empty bird-cage hung. There was an eiderdown in a basket that might once have belonged to a dog. From his pocket he took a bent pin, and with it, deli-cately, fluidly, he picked the front door lock. It was not a complicated lock; there were only six moves. It came open easily.

In the near darkness, Mrs Po's lavender colour scheme shone faintly silver. A clock ticked. At the end of the hallway, the kitchen. The wire mesh door on the meatsafe was perfectly oiled and it did not squeak when he opened it. On a plate, pegged down with a tea towel, lay a leg of lamb with a fair amount of meat still attached and the fat white.

Otto Cirque ate; for weeks he had eaten little more than beans and stew with a bit of stringy chicken in it: the meat — he felt it immediately — gave him stamina. When he had finished, he wrapped the lamb bone in the tea towel and stowed it in his pocket. His face was shiny with grease. He stood still and listened. Nothing; from a very long way away, a dog.

He was not quite ready to move on: something held him. He ascended the stairs of the Po residence, stepping carefully on the runner, making not a sound. At the top, he opened a door and found himself in a room. Otto moved with silent steps. He looked over the rails and into a cot. Half wrapped and half unwrapped lay a child: its hair sticky, eyes shut. The child sighed and moved. It was beautiful: its crescent-shaped eyelids, its plump cheeks, its nose. It seemed to know he was there, because in its sleep it stretched its arms up. He lifted it out. Its nightdress slipped against its body so he was frightened it might slide out of his arms and onto the floor. But it clung with small soft muscles against him and opened its grey eyes. It did not cry. It smiled. It put its hand on his face. It smelled of milk and honey. He put his arms about it and its little head cradled in his neck. He stood still in the morning light.

In the well-appointed nursery with its folded blankets and wooden toys, the sun came suddenly into full bloom. Otto Cirque's face was damp. The baby was asleep against his neck. He lowered it gently back into its cot. He was cold now, without the warmth of the baby against him; he went slowly back down the stairs.

Otto Cirque removed one other article from the Po house that morning. It was a purely practical theft: a full-length cashmere coat with carabouche buttons and fur-trimmed cuffs and collar. Otto took it up from the sofa on which it had been carefully laid and held it to his nose: it smelled like nothing, an absolutely blank-smelling coat. Despite being designed for a lady's figure, it fit him well. It made him warm immediately; he felt his muscles relax.

It was not till some hours, and several miles, later that Otto realised he had acquired more than a warm coat. Reaching into its right-side pocket, he discovered something soft and clinking. He pulled out this soft clinking thing, and knelt down in some bushes.

Any self-respecting thief would have been delighted by the discovery: it was a lady's reticule of some sort, stuffed to the brim with notes and coins. The notes were, by no means, small in denomination; the coins were not of the penny variety. Counted out, the total sum was sufficient to provide a moderate man a good income for upwards of a year. But though Otto Cirque registered this fact, in some dimly lit portion of his brain that comprehended still the function of coins and notes in the world at large, his interest lit more firmly on something else: at the bottom of the reticule, a trinket that was painfully familiar. A dull yellow stone of very odd shape. Otto recognised it immediately.

The money from the pocket had spilled out onto the ground, but Otto did not retrieve it. Without thinking, scarcely knowing what he did, he bent down and pulled the lace from his boot. He threaded it through the clasp of the trinket, knotted it twice, and tied the contraption about his neck. He tied it tight; the trinket sat firmly at his collarbone and the bootlace chafed his neck. He was warm now; he left the coat on the ground behind him.

Chapter 35

The Pitch Penitentiary

Anyone who has been the victim of a burglary will tell you it is a profoundly unpleasant experience. No matter the bricks or weatherboards you have lain and hoisted and secured to keep you in, they can no longer be relied on to keep the world out. One's doors and bolts and window glass seem suddenly flimsy. Solid objects no longer promise commensurate solidity of mind.

At seven o'clock the next morning, the unhappy discovery was made, but only by the lesser victim to the crime. Mrs Po, finding her kitchen disturbed and the lock picked on her front door, suffered very unpleasant sensations: she took up her master key, and proceeded to the sitting room, where she checked all locks, opened all drawers and cupboards, and was relieved to find everything where it should be.

It was half an hour later that the real victim roused and descended the stairs. She was late getting up. On entering the sitting room, where the household was gathered, Ivorie Hammer immediately registered the absence of her new cashmere coat.

'Did you, Mrs Po,' she asked, 'remove my coat to some other part of the house?'

'I have not touched your coat, Mrs Hammer! We have been robbed, that is what!' said Mrs Po. 'They have even raided my meatsafe,' she went on but was stopped by a horrible moaning sound coming from her houseguest.

'Oh, Mr Hammer . . . we are ruined!'

Mr Hammer must now support his wife, who had begun to collapse at the knees.

'It is only a coat!' Mrs Po protested. 'There are other coats to be had, Mrs Hammer . . . We might have been murdered in our beds!'

'You don't understand!' said Ivorie, looking not at Mrs Po but at her husband. 'It had in it my pocket, Mr Hammer! My *pocket* . . .'

The baby began to cry. Mrs Po felt suddenly nervous. She procured a glass of cordial for Mrs Hammer, but could not otherwise think of a single suitable reassurance. She took the crying baby from Mr Hammer, and patted it instead.

Ivorie Hammer was not one to nurse protractedly a state of distress. She recovered quickly and was ready to leave the house with her husband at eight o'clock. Though all sorts of sinking thoughts occurred to her on the way, she pounded the road to Inner Pitch in what one could only describe as a fury of positive action. Ernest Hammer could hardly keep up.

'Mrs Hammer,' he cried, 'the crime will not be sooner solved if you collapse of exhaustion on your way to reporting it.'

But Ivorie kept doggedly on, and Ernest did not remonstrate with her again until they reached George Duke's shop. Only then did he express his intention to accompany her.

'Unnecessary,' she said. 'I do not need your presence to bolster my authority, Mr Hammer. I am a person of considerable civic reputation, am I not?'

'I am worried,' said Ernest, 'that you might become overwrought.'

Had he thought on it all day, it is unlikely Mr Hammer could have come up with anything more guaranteed to provoke his wife.

'I am *not* overwrought, Mr Hammer,' she said. 'I am entirely calm, and entirely practical.' She glared at him. 'Has it not occurred to you that we might need, in future, every penny we can get?'

Thus dispatched to his bread-winning duties, Ernest called to his wife to come by afterwards and let him know the result, but he did not think she heard, swallowed up by the bustle of the morning.

The Pitch Penitentiary was an old blue-stone building, damp and moss-covered and thoroughly punitive. In the middle of the road, a cabby had stopped his horses to smoke a pipe. Ivorie, unintimidated, ascended the penitentiary steps. There was a shallow walkway at the top, rendered shallower by the presence of several large doors. To her surprise, the largest of these, though heavy – a weighty sandwich of lead and wood – was unresistant. She pushed; it opened.

She stepped from a hallway into a large, rather dank office, occupied by a uniformed man at a desk. It was the Senior Sergeant. He was wearing his jacket with great rectitude, and was obviously much given over to his official capacity, but when he saw that his intruder was Mrs Hammer, something almost grateful occurred in his face. Certain lines that had become, in weeks past, more definitively etched, relaxed. He held out his hand.

'Mrs Hammer,' he said. She sat down and told him at once what had happened.

The Senior Sergeant was very attentive. With great gentleness and tact, he asked Ivorie to describe the item known as a 'hanging pocket'. With even greater gentleness and quite superlative tact, he asked her to estimate the sum contained therein. And with perfect intuition, he produced a large pale-green handkerchief at precisely the moment she arrived at a figure.

The interview might have proceeded like this, quite satisfactorily, but was suddenly interrupted by a surly, orange-faced gentleman, who knocked his cane hard on the door, and announced himself with a mouthful of syllables too impressive to ignore. The Senior Sergeant apologised profusely. Would Mrs Hammer wait for him? Indeed, she would, she said, she would not move a muscle. She would sit quietly in her chair, and think hard on any details she might have missed.

Ivorie did not, of course, sit quietly in her chair and think hard on details. For the second time, she was overcome by curiosity on the subject of *incarceration*. Throughout her interview with Senior Sergeant Starlight, she had observed a door behind him, a door upon which hung a large padlock. She would not normally have given undue attention to such a thing – this was, after all, a jailhouse; one could expect such things as locked doors – except that as she ran her eyes across the large padlock she saw it had been somehow wrongly attached so that the bolt remained entirely free. Three times Ivorie looked at it during her interview, and opened her mouth to mention it to the Senior Sergeant, and three times she thought better of it. Now that the Senior Sergeant had quit the room, she got up to investigate further.

Her hypothesis was correct: when she tried it, the bolt slipped easily out of its latch. How lax they are, these apparently irreproachable authorities, thought Ivorie, pushing the door open with her shoulder. She hoped they would be more assiduous when it came to the retrieval of her hanging pocket.

Behind the door lay a long grey-blue corridor containing, one could tell by the mere smell of it, little hope and very little charity. There was a great deal of rust in evidence, as well as appreciable quantities of pigeon droppings. A tap dripped, or was it a stalactite? The light was dim, and it made everything old and decrepit. If Mr Sweetley's courthouse had once seemed liberty denying, Ivorie recalled it now as a delightful little apartment indeed.

She made her way down the row. In one cell, an old man slept. In another, an impoverished gentleman in a tatty waistcoat held a book up close to his face. A chisel-toothed man smiled at her as she passed and wished her 'good fortune', doffing an invisible hat. Ivorie walked determinedly on. When she came to the end of the row, she did not at first notice that the last cell contained an occupant. Indeed, she prepared, somewhat disconsolately, to turn back. And then there was a murmur from behind the bars: a drowsy, familiar murmur emanating from a dark familiar shape.

It occurred to her that she'd been listening for it, or something like it, all along.

'Morag?' said Ivorie.

Her eyes shifted and jumped. Morag lay on a stretcher, with no covers except that supplied by her dress, though the dress itself could scarcely claim allegiance to any category of women's clothing – it was more like a sheath, and it wrapped her so she looked as though she were already dead.

Ivorie felt in her stomach and knees the same falling sensation that had overcome her in the tea shop. 'Morag!' she said.

Morag was not dead, but there was something distinctly wrong about her. She shifted on her stretcher bed but did not wake. The light was greyish. Ivorie leaned forwards and narrowed her eyes so she might see better.

There had never been anything consoling or hopeful or improvable in Morag's face — it was a face of such generality that it could have belonged to any man or woman at any age in history without attracting attention or opportunity to its wearer. Its wrinkles and crevices did not delineate any habitual emotion. The flesh was hard and thick. The shape was plain. The features, functional. But now it seemed to have lost even the quality of a face. Ivorie could make out no eyes, no protuberance that might count as a nose; no ridge of cheekbone or brow; no chin.

She rallied herself, and looked again. The phenomenon persisted. 'Morag,' she said again, but there was no answer.

A long time seemed to pass. Somewhere, water dripped and someone coughed. Despair, condensed into impersonal blocks of smell and sight and sound, now attached itself to Ivorie. She felt suddenly that she knew it intimately. How illusory the props with which she had fended it off!

She could not bear to look again, but she did, and the effect was the same. The light fell on Morag's sleeping face and there was no face there at all.

Ivorie felt her stomach contract. Perspiration prickled on her forehead. 'Morag!' she said, between the bars. 'Wake *up* — it is too terrible, Morag!' But Morag didn't wake, nor turn her face in such a way that the light might restore its missing features. She had gone, it seemed, or, at least, nothing of her was left that made sense.

It was the last time anybody would see Morag Pappy. Ivorie made her way back along the corridor, staggering a little, looking neither left nor right. Once on the other side of the door, she rearranged the padlock so all looked exactly as it had before. She sat down on her chair, and stared at her hands.

She was quiet when the Senior Sergeant returned, and she suddenly wanted her husband and her child very much.

Chapter 36

Duke Sherry Pty Ltd

By the time Ivorie arrived at her husband's place of employ, she was somewhat recovered, though a shiver had set up in her that would not quite abate. Nevertheless, she walked purposefully. She knocked purposefully. The door was opened by George Duke, thin as a rake, encased in purple velvet.

'Mrs Hammer, how good to see you! How exceptionally you look!'

Ivorie had only limited acquaintance with her husband's employer, but even on so narrow a basis, she could tell immediately that something was vastly altered in him. He ushered her through the doorway with swift motions and, before she was quite ready, removed her jacket and steered her down the passage.

Ivorie did not yet feel up to energetic conversation; she expressed nevertheless a polite observation regarding George Duke's improved state of health.

'Yes, yes, I am quite vigorous,' said Duke. He puffed out his chest in such a way that his head must recede several notches to counter-balance the arrangement. 'And it is all on account of your husband.'

'Indeed?' said Ivorie.

'You mean he has not told you?' said Duke. He stopped, let go of Ivorie's arm, and looked at her with astonishment. 'Your husband has cured me, Mrs Hammer! I cannot believe he would not mention it!'

Ivorie shook her head. She could not bring herself to comment sensibly. Duke, still puzzling, shook his head, too, and, walking to the end of the passage, flung open the door.

'Modesty, modesty!' he said, entering the room, shaking his index finger at Mr Hammer, who was seated therein. 'The meek shall inhabit this earth, Mr Hammer.'

'Inherit,' said Ivorie quietly, following behind.

Duke directed Ivorie to a chair and threw himself onto the box couch. He fussed with some fringing on a cushion behind his neck before leaning confidentially towards Ivorie once more. 'I admit that I sink a little at night, Mrs Hammer. I am hard to start in the morning – you will not find me up at dawn. But when, at morning tea time, I have a few mouthfuls of your husband's ardent spirits –'

'*Mrs Sherry's* Ardent Spirits,' Ernest corrected with some embarrassment. 'That is what it is called.' He came over to his wife and kissed her.

'. . . I have blood in my veins for the first time in years. I have blood ringing in my ears. Mrs Hammer, I feel I could run a marathon.'

'It is truly astonishing, Mr Duke,' said Ivorie.

Duke licked his lip. 'Your husband will take me to the site of production, won't you, Ernest? We make the excursion soon. If not today, tomorrow. If not tomorrow, well, the day after. I have such energy that I can put anything off, without fear. I can rely on being tomorrow as vigorous as I am today!' At this point, Ernest had to put out a hand to stabilise his employer, who momentarily lost his balance and nearly toppled a brass sidetable. George Duke did not notice, rising and lurching towards the luncheon table. 'But most prominent in my mind right now is luncheon!' he said, indicating Mr and Mrs Hammer should follow him.

The luncheon table was in fact not a luncheon table at all, but a loo table, upon which little loo had been recently played but many boxes and cartons had found a home, with the result that – subsequent to their removal – large clean rectilinear shapes occurred across the table surface and between them little triangles, thick with dust. Platters and forks and side plates were arranged in such a way that the triangles were neatly avoided. Ivorie observed from a distance this example of bachelor expediency and was glad that the platters had lids, which Duke now removed dramatically.

'You could not have visited at a more opportune time, Mrs Hammer. The manufacturer himself is due to arrive any minute now to discuss the possibilities. Over lunch. It is the civilised way to do business, I believe.' He propped one small buttock on the table top and began to carve frantically at the ham, not quite watching the knife, so that one was afraid for his fingers.

'I do not know that Mrs Hammer visited in expectation of luncheon,' said Ernest, looking closely at Ivorie.

'Nonsense!' said George Duke, continuing his perilous carving. 'Ah, I know your type, Ernest Hammer. You are the type of husband who will not let his wife in on a secret. Your reserve is not modesty at all.' He cut again. The knife slipped, grazing the ham bone and hitting the plate; a small chip of china flew out. 'I myself, Mrs Hammer, have never married, thus I have never understood the tendency of men to keep their wives in the dark.' He speared a slice of ham with the knife tip and transferred it to a plate. 'I have found, to the contrary, that the presence of a woman on an occasion of business is an advantage. It makes men behave better. Mr Hammer, you will let your wife stay!' He bent down towards Ivorie. 'You will stay, won't you, Mrs Hammer?'

At that moment, the front door knocker sounded. Duke plunged the carving knife into the ham, and went to answer it.

'My dear, you do not have to stay,' said Ernest. 'It is only Bald Sherry, here to discuss patents. I didn't know Duke had got a hold of him. It is bad timing indeed.'

'You did not tell me of this miracle cure,' Ivorie said wanly as though she were a convalescent in need of a miracle cure herself.

'That is because I am not convinced it *is* a cure, much less a miracle. But I don't care about that, Ivorie.' Ernest took her hand. 'What came of your journey?'

But now Ivorie fell apart completely. Everything in her went slack. She burst into tears. She flapped her hands in front of her face, she held her breath and clenched her teeth, she pressed her knuckles into her eyes – to no avail. Her composure could not be prevailed upon to return.

'Oh, my dear,' Ernest said. 'My dear, dear, Mrs Hammer.' They could hear the sound of the front door slamming shut, footsteps growing closer.

'Come,' said Ernest, assisting his wife from her chair. He led her into the back work room, and from the work room into a little porch, and from the porch to a small garden, where a gate provided emergency egress onto the lanes and alleys of Inner Pitch. 'Wait here a moment,' he said. Ivorie stood dutifully at the gate, patting at her eyes (she had retained, without meaning to, the Senior Sergeant's large pale-green handkerchief) while her husband collected their overcoats and explained their sudden departure.

We shall not follow the Hammers home; they have matters of a private nature to discuss. Imagine, however, that all things due to be said on such an occasion were said; that devoted husbands proved to be a reassurance beyond all doubt; and that wives were made stalwart again by the realisation. Morag did not evaporate from Ivorie's consciousness, but she did retreat at Ernest's insistence that everything possible would be done for her.

Let us return instead to the establishment of George Duke, where, in the Hammers' wake, a groundbreaking idea has been born.

It did not take much time for the ground between Mr Duke and Mr Sherry to be broken: it was soft, nitrogen-rich, ready for planting. The idea, once conceived, cracked through with very little resistance. Over the course of the afternoon, it became increasingly lustrous with possibility. By three o'clock Bald Sherry and George Duke figured it the loveliest thing they had ever contemplated. Though they had some small disagreement over naming it, they decided finally on Duke Sherry Pty Ltd, which, though not lyrical, was at least strong, affirmative.

Generous helpings of ardent spirits were then imbibed, smaller-than-prudent portions of ham consumed, and a discreet amount of money, referred to as the 'working capital', transferred to the person of Bald Sherry, with the promise of more upon Mr Duke's securing of investors. Thereafter, the requisite formality was swiftly ushered into being: a contract, in which each of them expressed their expectations, and to which the signature of a witness (the piano tuner from the shop opposite) was secured.

Thus came into being the first joint enterprise between Pitch and Canyon.

Once these sobrieties had been attended to, the two men got on with the vast and all-consuming business of imagining their future wealth. By half-past five, they were absolutely exhausted.

Chapter 37

The Bramah Lock

Several pages back, I am afraid I inflicted a small white lie on the reader. Very small, very white, but a lie nonetheless. Ivorie Hammer was *not* the last person to see Morag Pappy alive; one more character would have dealings, though not actual conversation, with Miss Pappy before she disappeared. That person was Otto Cirque.

His skill in the area of nuts and bolts, locks and latches, hasps and clasps and other securing contrivances, had an almost supernatural quality. He was, and always had been, a man to whom the usual forms of safekeeping did not apply. A man to whom 'keys' meant nothing. A man to whom Joseph Bramah's famous revolutionising lock, with its four hundred and ninety-four million combinations, was no obstacle at all.

But though they might seem so, Otto Cirque's lock-picking powers were not supernatural – no more than were his powers to distil good quality liquor. He could not make objects move or explode through concentration alone. To release Morag Pappy from the power of Joseph Bramah's lock required a protracted stint of labour. Eight hours to be precise. For eight hours, Otto knelt quietly in the dark beside Morag's cell, and, with his small collection of hooks and barbs and pins, worked on the famous lock. In another time, in another place, he might have had a successful career as a defuser of underwater mines.

For eight hours, Otto sustained this state of total attunement, and when finally there was a beautiful, greased crunching sound, and the lock fell open, it was as though he were released from a trance. He did not seem to know where he was or what he had been doing. He lay on his stomach on the floor.

'Otto,' said Morag.

He did not move.

'Otto,' she said. She pushed open the cell door with one hand, as though it had always been in her power to do so, and bent down beside her rescuer. 'Are you set on this?' She put her hand flat on his back.

Otto did not move. She sighed. She removed her hand. She did what he wanted. Picking him up like a small animal, she carried him inside the cell and lay him on the stretcher. His weight did not register much on the canvas. His head did not much dent the pillow. He lay panting, like a deer that has just avoided a gunman. If you looked very closely, you could see the pulse beating rapidly in his neck. Soon it would return to a normal rate and Otto Cirque would sleep, a long calm peaceful sleep.

Morag, meanwhile, waited for the morning shift change.

No one could afterwards blame Borrel Sweetley for Morag Pappy's escape. Joseph Bramah stood neatly between him and accountability – from this, he gained great relief; a second escape on his hands would have been too much to bear. Nor could you blame Robert Starlight – who was, after all, a senior sergeant and did not stoop to the performance of sentinel duty. Perhaps Ivorie Hammer might be chastised for not advising of the lackadaisical padlock arrangement she had earlier that day encountered. But she was not on the payroll of the Municipality of Inner Pitch – who was she to instruct the law enforcement agencies on security measures? In the end, of course, it was the lowly prison warden, recovering in the Inner Pitch Hospital from a blow to the head, who took the blame.

The Senior Sergeant filed a second arrest warrant on Morag Pappy, and awaited, with some apprehension, the arrival of Mr Sweetley.

'I knew it!' said Sweetley, arriving unshaven, unbreakfasted. He looked less like a superannuated gentleman these days and more like an overworked civil servant. The dark grey of jailhouse stone picked up nicely his flesh tones.

'What you lose in the pudding, you gain in the sauce,' said Borrel Sweetley. They stood outside the cell, which had last night been occupied by Morag Pappy and now, to the Senior Sergeant's great unease, contained an old man of frail appearance who, despite several vigorous attempts, could not be roused from sleep.

'Yes, yes, my plan has succeeded,' Sweetley continued, folding his arms up high across his chest. 'Morag Pappy has been precisely the decoy I hoped.'

This was the first the Senior Sergeant had heard of decoys. He looked at Sweetley not altogether gently.

'That man, Senior Sergeant,' Sweetley pointed his finger at the sleeping form, 'is the felon. The murderer. Yes, yes! He does not look like a murderer, does he?'

They both looked at him again. Otto Cirque, asleep, was very small; the bones in his head protruded. Borrel Sweetley was in a lather of excitement. Otto's presence now in the cell was an abstract example of wrongs made right, a demonstration of authority reinstated. It recuperated Sweetley's former sense of self; it redeemed him. The Senior Sergeant, however, experienced a strange headache of emotion: pity, combined with something else, something violent. Otto Cirque was so vulnerable one wanted to hurt him and protect him all at the same time.

'Justice will be served,' continued Borrel Sweetley, 'as it rightly should be. We have him, safe and sound, and can now set about finalising the evidence. Every minute particle of it.'

Soon after Mr Sweetley's departure, the Senior Sergeant sat down to consider precisely that: evidence, procured from the person of the sleeping prisoner by a subordinate officer and arranged now in a small pile before him. Several interesting articles had been removed from Otto Cirque. The Senior Sergeant took a handful of wire remnants and pins and sealed them in a brown paper package. A crumpled fabric item he took at first to be a handkerchief began, on further scrutiny, to look suspiciously like Ivorie Hammer's hanging pocket. The Senior Sergeant turned it over and over; it had a drawstring neck, a pattern of leaves and berries, a small mend. He put his hand in. It contained no money, not a coin. He felt some sympathy for Mrs Hammer.

But Mrs Hammer's hanging pocket, though incriminating, was not the hard evidence the Senior Sergeant sought. It did not establish the murders alleged by Mr Sweetley. For these, the Senior Sergeant had, as yet, no concrete proof at all. And then he turned over the last piece of evidence.

It had been coiled into a little ball and looked, at first, like a dirty, knotted bootstrap, with some kind of bauble attached. But as soon as he picked it up and began to untangle it, he saw what it was. The distinctive ear shape; the waxy yellow sheen of the stone.

Seeing it, the Senior Sergeant experienced a strange movement in the upper left region of his ribcage.

The grub that entered the Senior Sergeant's heart nearly one hundred pages ago, activated by the sight of a young woman in a bath, split open the corner of its cocoon. It was not yet a butterfly. But its brief appearance disrupted the easy bloodflow of its host. There was a sudden palpitation where there was usually reliable, measured action.

Inevitably, however, the blood settled, the steam cleared in the Senior Sergeant's mind and certain undeniable evidence reasserted itself. Upon the sparrow-coloured chest of Nelly the parlourmaid, Mrs Sherry's gris-gris came into focus. Nelly slapped her hand over her chest and dropped back into the water. But it could not be missed then, and it would not be forgotten now. It was etched into the Senior Sergeant's memory, and there was nothing he could do to erase it.

Could there, perhaps, be *two* such identical items?

The Senior Sergeant was confused. He must sit down.

Could it be that Otto Cirque and the parlourmaid were *accomplices*?

Every fibre in his being rejected such a thought.

The felon must, then, have forcibly *removed* Mrs Sherry's gris-gris from Nelly's possession, in order for it now to be found in his . . .

But this possibility, once conceived, was so awful that the Senior Sergeant's heartbeat temporarily ceased. In his stomach, his breakfast turned black and rotten. He stood, determined to take action; he sat, resolved that it was hopeless; he stood again, convinced Nelly was in desperate need of assistance; he sat, despairing: it was all too late. In this way, he conducted himself for the remainder of the day. He could not look in on the prisoner; he could not liaise further with Mr Sweetley; he wrote a brief letter, less sympathetic than it might be, to Mrs Hammer, advising her of the discovery of her hanging pocket, and spent the rest of his day by the window, weighing up the pros and cons.

In fact, he need not torment himself, because at this very moment, Nelly the parlourmaid is making her way towards him, across the difficult, treacherous topography, with a flagon of water and blistered feet. Dirt scuffs up behind her as she walks.

But she is not in danger and she is not alone. The Parathas are with her. The Parathas, however, show no caution in their progress. They are — there is no other word for it — ebullient. They are sprawling, telling jokes, doubled over. The perils of a narrow pathway do not apply to them, because right now they are the luckiest, the happiest, the *most blessed* of families. They are invulnerable. They have been singled out by good fortune. You might not believe it, but the Parathas have just won the lottery.

Part 4

Inner Pitch

Chapter 38

The sing-song list

The day the Parathas won the lottery began like any other day. Florence Paratha opened windows and let the sun in. She did not know where the various members of her family were, but the Grand Hotel contained many rooms. There was evidence, at least, that they had been up, and had eaten, and she felt grateful to them for their resolve on that matter.

It was over a year since they had been abandoned, and the Parathas had adjusted to their isolation. Indeed, Florence Paratha's enjoyment of life had been positively enhanced; she had a whole wardrobe of other women's dresses, and there was linen enough in Mrs Sherry's cupboard for everyone to have a towel and a sheet of their own. Meanwhile, in the absence of comparative examples, her children seemed the most charming and accomplished of offspring. Her husband, whom she had always loved, continued to inspire her and, all in all, she considered herself the happiest of women.

Every day, her son Julian presented her with a sack full of things appropriated from abandoned broken houses and dug up from the bottom of the canyon. There was always a novelty in that sack: yesterday, the broken portion of an equestrian's whip; the day before, a painted china basket for holding flower arrangements, only slightly chipped. Julian's excavating interests had led her decidedly to an interest of her own. Yes, Florence Paratha has, for the first time in her life, an interest.

Every afternoon, while her family attends to its independent activities, Florence probes the sack containing Julian's findings, and trawls through the broken crockery at its bottom. Bits of fine china. Cups and saucers and milk jugs. Little by little, Florence reintegrates these hopelessly broken tea sets. She sorts the pieces into piles, according to colour and pattern and size; she applies deft dobs of glue with a toothpick and the pointed end of a skewer, wiping away the excess with a piece of damp cloth. The kitchen table has become almost entirely dissociated from culinary activities.

On the table is a stack of catalogues Florence found in the hotel laundry, stashed behind the door with their pages folded in on themselves and their covers encrusted with dust and soapflakes. Having wiped them clean and flattened them, one atop the other, Florence has restored to them something of their former grace. Now she sits in her chair with one open on her lap and relishes the items illustrated therein, from the strange and ludicrous – elaborate apple corers that come apart in six pieces; raisin seeders which shuck the fruit one way, the seeds the other – to the beautifully practical – seamless, rivetless milk cans and cream cans; safety egg carriers in three sizes.

She starts out luxuriously, considering each page in detail, sipping tea, waiting for glue to dry, but increasingly she is overtaken by the rhythm of the objects themselves:

- boilers, kettles, saucepans;
- stew pans, meat pans, preserving pans;
- ewers, gridirons, coffee pots;
- round basins, deep round basins, extra-deep round basins;
- laundry scrubs, verandah scrubs, blacking daubers;
- Turk's head all-hair wall-sweepers;
- yard brooms, carpet brooms, millet brooms;
- baby combs, gents' combs, pocket combs, rake combs, dressing combs, nickel-plate brush-scrapes;
- brushes with ebonite backs, xylonite backs, satinwood and rosewood backs; whalebone and aluminium, pure-bristled and wire-bristled, soft-bristled and firm-bristled . . .

Oh, if only the late Mrs Sherry had applied more regularly to her collection of catalogues, for contained within them are the protracted visions of a lifetime of happiness. Slowly, but surely, Florence is piecing together her own collection, a little yellow with glue perhaps, but her own nevertheless. Now she sips the last of her tea, puts her catalogue away (its rhythm continuing in her head), and plunges her hand deep into the jute sack (nail brush, clothes brush, toothbrush, pet brush); she forages around amongst large pieces and small, sharp pieces and blunt (flat-bottom kettles, oblong pie dishes); and then her hand (milk pan, butterpat) fastens on something entirely un-crockerylike.

Heavy, rock-like, but too smooth to be a rock. She pulls it out (wooden bath mats, cork bath mats) and her sing-song seeps away with a faint sighing sound.

From the bottom of the jute bag, at the end of the list, Florence Paratha has retrieved a nugget of gold the size of a grown man's fist.

Chapter 39

Plans, right and wrong

Upon arriving at the bottom of the mountain range, the Paratha family was not exactly 'swept up' by former neighbours and friends. There was, however, a uniform expression of surprise on seeing them that translated fairly swiftly into the provision of food, bedding and coffee.

It was late in the day, one might have expected them to be tired, but the Parathas had a natural propensity to talk; indeed, they could not keep their good fortune to themselves – within half an hour, the fist-sized nugget had been examined by everyone. An hour later, by the camp fire, all sorts of projections were being postulated on its account; and at the expiration of three hours, with a bottle of ardent spirits open on the ground before them and the fire burning low, Bald Sherry and Thomas Paratha were cementing these projections into definite plans.

'It will be a perfect corollary,' Bald Sherry enthused, 'to an enterprise of my own, recently embarked upon.' He did not quite rub his hands, but he leaned closer to Thomas Paratha. 'Do you like what you are drinking, Mr Paratha?'

Thomas indicated in the affirmative.

'Well then,' said Bald Sherry, 'let us make a toast.' He held up his glass. 'To the Paratha family and their patronage.'

Thomas acceded to the toast. Though patronage was a concept he understood only vaguely in a utilitarian, shopkeeping way, he could tell, from the way Bald Sherry said it, that it was not something to underestimate.

'It will have to have our name, if it goes through,' he said, shyly, too embarrassed to look at Mr Sherry. 'If it gets up, I mean. If something is really made of it.'

Bald Sherry waved. 'Of course,' he said.

Thomas Paratha's eyes glowed palely in the firelight; he was not used to being central in the scheme of things; it was uncomfortable.

'Well, only if it suits,' he said. 'Only if everyone is in agreement.'

Two days later, Bald Sherry bade Thomas goodbye, locked the gold nugget in a safety box, and disappeared up the Ring Road. He did not return for a week. In those six intervening days, the Parathas suffered an acute and unrelenting anxiety. It was not until Mr Sherry reappeared that they could think clearly again, and even then, their thought processes did not immediately align with the logic of cold hard cash. There was no gold nugget in the safety box when Sherry unlocked it to show them – there were wads of greenish-brownish paper. A small shrill sound escaped Florence's mouth, and Thomas squinted intently and touched the uppermost notes delicately with the pads of his fingers. 'Well, my goodness, there is some money,' he said quietly. 'To be sure, that is a good lot of money, Mr Sherry.'

'We are rich, Thomas! We are rich!' said Florence, squeezing her husband's hand.

'We are all rich,' said Bald Sherry, 'in a manner of speaking. Thanks to your patronage.' He winked. 'You will find, Mr Paratha, at the bottom of the box, notes of purchase for items ordered under your auspices. There is much,' he lowered his eyebrows, 'to organise.' His eyebrows being by far the gravest thing about him, he repeated the gesture. 'A very great deal. A tremendous amount.'

He poured three small glasses of ardent spirits, while Thomas and Florence Paratha digested this information.

'May I take the opportunity,' he continued, 'to formalise our future association?' He stood up. 'Mrs Sherry's Ardent Spirits is pleased to lend its sponsorship to your enterprise,' he said, bowing low. Then, returning to full height, he waved his hand, dispensing with gratitude before it even had a chance to form. 'To the Paratha Family Circus,' he said and sculled his drink. The Parathas, ever unsure, promptly imitated him.

While a fortune had thus accrued to her former neighbours, Ivorie Hammer remained deep in the loss of hers.

The hanging pocket had been returned to her by registered post, accompanied by a letter from the Senior Sergeant. The culprit, she read, had been caught and detained. The hanging pocket had been found on his person; the small fortune had not. Identity was being withheld, wrote Robert Starlight, in a truncated syntax that offended her, until formal charges were laid. 'I sincerely hope,' he wrote, 'for the recovery of lost items.'

Ivorie threw the letter on the floor. She reconsidered, leaned over and picked it up, smoothed it out, re-read the last line – 'I sincerely hope' – and precisely the same urge overcame her, with the same intensity, to fling it as far away from her as possible.

In her mind's eye, her tenancy receded. She saw instead long years confined to lavender-coloured sitting rooms. She felt the dulling effect of Mr and Mrs Po's company seep into her bones. Recently, she had twice said the word *corset* when she meant *cosset*, and three times used the word *provincial* when she had meant *providential*. More and more she blamed Mr and Mrs Po, and not the lack of a dictionary, for such lapses. Meanwhile, try as she might, she could not rid herself of the apparition of Morag Pappy; she dreamt, with intensity, of her former guardian, but when she woke and tried to picture Morag's face, she could not set upon any clear picture of it – she could not remember it at all!

While Ivorie suffered thus, her husband had found not happiness perhaps, but certainly a degree of equanimity. Little by little, he and Mr Po had become friends: a friendship built on the appraisal of objects, regular hands of gin rummy, and the imbibing of small quantities of ardent spirits.

Mrs Po declared she would no longer have cards in the house. Nor would she tolerate the continued use of her kitchen table as a work station. She almost enjoyed the playacting she employed here: she was a *wife*, fed up with the domestic trespasses of a *husband* – such things were right! Mr Po smiled at her sheepishly and she gave him just the right sort of barely tolerating gaze. She also reminded them – neatly forgetting her own transgressions on this head – that in Pitch, drinking liquor was contrary to public policy. 'If you want to drink that *moonshine*,' she finished, 'you may remove yourselves *outdoors*.'

And so it was that Ernest one day found himself following Mr Po down the garden path and into that much maligned place known as the shed.

As soon as he put his foot in the doorway, he smelled it: that old smell, rank and concentrated, of failure, despondency, heavy as a horse blanket. There was a slender camp bed with blankets and pillows. There were large damp volumes: *Robinson Crusoe* and *Gulliver's Travels.* There were odds and ends, brass fixtures, bits of iron lace and pressed tin, but absolutely no sign of industry. Not even a hammer or an old saddle. Grease and dust, though, over everything.

'Mr Po,' said Mr Hammer, 'may I open a window?'

This was achieved, with some effort: the windows would rather crack their glass, it seemed, than give up the fusion of frame and sill. Ernest found a rag in his briefcase, and Mr Po watched solemnly as he cut a clean circle through the dust on a bench. Chairs were fetched. Cards were dealt, the bottle passed.

They played a two-handed variation of 500. Mr Po gripped his cards with a strange intensity. When he won, he did not speak, but produced a guttural sound that might be interpreted as laughter.

'Where, Mr Po, did you learn to play cards like that?' asked Ernest, gathering the deck towards him. 'It's lucky we don't play for money, or I'd be in the workhouse.'

Later Mr Po sat and watched Ernest re-fix a strip of walnut veneer onto a cuckoo clock. And then all work was completed, and there was nothing between them except silence.

'There is a very bad thing afoot, Mr Po,' said Ernest some minutes into this silence. 'Perhaps you have heard of it?'

Mr Po looked at the table where the deck of cards still sat. He took the top one up and turned it over. He looked at it and put it to the bottom of the stack. 'I do not much follow the newspapers,' he said.

'Well, it is yet to be made public, but the rumours abound, Mr Po. A countryman of mine, accused of terrible crimes . . .'

Mr Po flipped the next card and stood it on its end as though it might be made to hold itself up unsupported.

Ernest saw Mr Po's hand tremble, but he persisted. 'They have got him in jail, Mr Po. They look to hang him, if they can.' He lowered his voice. 'And the thing is, I do not believe he is guilty.'

Mr Po drew an ace and a seven and a king, and now his hands were really shaking.

'I know of your former occupation at the Pitch penitentiary, Mr Po,' Ernest said. 'My wife has told me.' He paused. Mr Po had become entirely still. 'I'm sorry if I cause you distress to think about a former life you would rather forget. You seem to me a most merciful man, Mr Po, a good man . . .' He stood up. He put his chair in, and then he thought better of it and took it out again and moved it around to Mr Po's side of the table. 'Mr Po,' he said again, and he put his hand on Mr Po's shoulder. He was not prepared for the transformative effect of this gesture, for at the touch of his hand, Mr Po's whole body sagged. The muscles and the spine and the bones: all softened and lightened and loosened. He seemed, indeed, to *fall*. And what he fell into was the natural, necessary shape of grief. When he began to weep, it was as though he'd found a deep rich seam that might never be exhausted.

Ernest was not destabilised by the terrible weeping of his friend. He sat quietly and kept his hand on Mr Po's shoulder.

Chapter 40

Several yards of yellow watered silk

Ernest Hammer was hereafter diverted by the increasing demands of his employer, George Duke, who now required his undivided attention on a number of tasks unrelated to the role of antiquarian and very closely bound up with that of liquor merchant.

Ernest found himself playing the role of intermediary, not just between Mr Duke and Mr Sherry (who were daily hatching furious new plans), and not just between Mr Duke and his four nervous investors (Messrs Drummond, Sprat, Munro and Lively), but also between Mr Duke and former office-bearer of Canyon, Mr Borrel Sweetley, who, as Acting Bailiff, had the ear of the Inner Pitch Council on questions of relevant proscriptive liquor regulations. The role was arduous and not to Ernest's liking, and its only compensation was that it made him privy to the general hum of opinion about Morag Pappy's strange disappearance from her jail cell and the equally strange substitute presence there of Otto Cirque. (Were they, in fact, one and the same person? Had some kind of duplicity been involved? Were bribes paid? And how was it that nobody had *seen*?) What Ernest discovered lurking behind this curiosity, to his great unease, was a stone-hard certainty about Otto's culpability. 'Must be hanged!' he heard. 'Sooner the better. Escaped once, liable to escape again.' 'An abominable creature – What is it? Six, seven murders?' 'Waste of good time and money, a trial.' 'We should never have allowed it, I said so at the time, importing such types into our society. Must hang, must hang, and will, and preferably before the year is out . . .'

These remarks, volleyed back and forth amongst the gentlemen of

Inner Pitch, created an anxiety in Ernest Hammer that would not go away, staying with him long after the men had taken their leave. In his dealings with Borrel Sweetley, however, no reassurance was to be had. Sweetley was officious to the letter on the regulatory details Ernest sought. And though Ernest once brought up the subject of Otto Cirque, Sweetley would not be drawn. He held up his hand, he shook his great head and pursed his mouth. 'We must just await trial,' he said, 'all will then come clear.' And then, after a pause in which his office and his personality struggled visibly against each other: 'I was remiss once; I shall not be so again.'

In regards to her missing fortune, Ivorie Hammer was not practising the goodly virtue of resignation. She sought practical relief from her sufferings, economic and spiritual. Action, she knew, was the cure for despair. Nothing new had come to light regarding the identity of her mother, though she could imagine her now — now that she had a name — and the image that came to her was of a soft-haired woman with a patient smile, hands clasped over her belly and wearing garb that was (strangely, unaccountably) medieval. On the morning after receiving the Senior Sergeant's letter, Ivorie left Pette in the care of Mrs Po, tucked a small box of samples under her arm, and approached the first dressmaker she came to on Mackaby Lane.

It was not the highest class establishment, but it was not the lowest either. There was giltwork on the window, and inside, a well-preserved middle-aged woman, with white hair and a trim figure, tracing patterns at a large table. Behind her, in a back room, Ivorie could hear the hum of sewing machines, the clunk of a pedal.

'Can I help you?' the dressmaker said, almost but not quite smiling; she had just rebuked her three employees in the back room, a fact that would turn out greatly to Mrs Hammer's advantage.

Within an hour, Madame Boucher, as the dressmaker was known, had ascertained that Ivorie's abilities were much greater than mere competence, and had given her a 'commission'. Ivorie was supplied with an Ebenezer Butterick pattern for a dinner dress with puffed sleeves and bustle; several yards of yellow watered silk; and two small bags of green obsidian beads to be embroidered according to an intricate pattern of anthemions, pre-sketched in dressmakers' chalk.

'How fast, do you think?' Madame Boucher said in her prim little accent.

Ivorie made an estimate; Madame Boucher narrowed her eyes, flicked something imaginary from her index finger, and nodded. 'I have ample work for you, if you do well. I need a woman of maturity to help me with my *clientele*.' She indicated the back room. 'Little girls, all three,' she hissed. 'Still sucking toffees.' Then, resuming an air of professionalism, madame sat down, propped her chin on two shiny white fists, and regarded Ivorie closely, as though calculating the waist-enhancing properties of a *crème brulee* over a *pain au chocolàt*. 'Tell me,' she said, finally, 'what do you think of a stout, elderly lady in low-necked, light-coloured silk? With a bow at back and two ruffles, hmm?'

Ivorie expressed her reservations.

'Good, good,' said madame. 'You will tell her this, how?'

Ivorie pursed her lips. 'I would praise her complexion in reference to darker tones,' she said. 'I would allude to the inelegance of excessive ruffles and bows – how distracting they are, even on a very young girl.'

'Mrs Hammer, you are a woman of tact. If my clients like you as well as I, we will do very well.' Madame Boucher stretched out her hand.

And so Ivorie began to work for Marie Boucher, the dressmaker.

For the first time, she was glad it was her dictionary, and not her sewing machine, that had fallen victim to the perils of a mountain journey.

The following day, meeting the Starlight sisters at the Mackaby Tea Rooms, Ivorie had to work hard to suppress the news of her employment, intuiting quite rightly that her friends would not approve. Fortunately, the topic of her hanging pocket intervened on her behalf. On this subject, the sisters were infinitely compassionate. They felt the loss, they said, as though it were their own. And on the associated subject – of the recently captured suspect – they felt Ivorie's every pang. Here, however, they appeared to be better informed than their friend, whose husband had not apprised her of what he knew.

'It is not to be publicly circulated . . .'

'Not yet!'

'But it seems the suspect is wanted, in the end, for rather more than *theft*, Mrs Hammer!'

They nodded.

'For murder!' said Mary.

'Ssh!' said Ann. '*Enough!*' she said. 'Mr Sweetley will make his findings known when they *are* known.'

Mary put her hand over Ivorie's. It was a gesture that, while commiserative, no longer had the power of reassurance. 'What matters is that you have faith in our brother. You must trust that he will locate the *contents* of your pocket. You must proceed with your plans as if all will be well.'

' Mary is right,' said Ann. 'In his official capacity, the Senior Sergeant is tireless . . .'

'. . . inexhaustible . . .'

'. . . comprehensive in his attentions.'

Ivorie did not mention her feelings about Robert Starlight's letter.

'Has Mr Sweetley,' Ivorie began, 'found out anything more in relation to my mother?'

Mary looked at Ann before speaking. 'If he has, Mrs Hammer, he has not shared the information with us. He has become . . . how should I say, Ann?'

'Preoccupied,' supplied Ann. 'Reserved. He does not communicate much – bound up, I hazard, in the workings of his case.'

'I am sure,' said Mary, 'that as soon as he makes headway on the subject, he will let you know. Anyway,' Mary scraped with her cake fork at a blob of cream, 'I have no doubt that your fortune will be found. That *Cirque* man must have buried it, or hidden it somewhere. He could not have spent it all –' Her hand flew suddenly to her mouth, cake fork and all. 'Oh, dear! Oh Ann. I did not mean to mention names!'

Ann looked reproachfully at her sister.

'Oh, Mrs Hammer . . .' Mary, wide-eyed, turned to Ivorie. 'You must absolutely forget what I just said!'

'It is too late now,' said Ann, fussing with her napkin. 'What's said is said, Mary.' She gave Ivorie her sternest look. 'It has not yet been made public, Mrs Hammer, but the man held for theft of your property is the very same man Mr Sweetley has sought for the last twelve months. A man named *Otto Cirque*. I know not all the ins and outs of his crimes, but I understand they are heinous. Hence the gravity of Mary's lapse, before the details have been publicly announced.' She glared again at her sister.

Indeed, Mary's lapse had produced a curious ebbing sensation in Ivorie's brain. That Otto Cirque, and the thief, and her hanging pocket might all be interrelated — it was an uncongealable set of ingredients. It made her giddy.

'And the old woman of your acquaintance is *gone*!' said Mary. 'Disappeared entirely from the cell!'

A little gust of air drew up in Ivorie's throat. 'Gone?' she said.

'Escaped!' said Mary.

'Thank heaven,' Ivorie breathed, without meaning to.

The sisters looked at each other oddly.

'I mean to say . . .' said Ivorie, and then for a moment could not speak.

'It is difficult for you,' said Mary, patting her hand. 'Let us change the subject. Ann, tell Mrs Hammer of our development.'

Having folded her napkin into a useless spear-shaped implement, Ann now shook it out and rearranged it on her knee. 'We have found you a tenancy, Mrs Hammer.'

Mary clapped her hands. 'Yes, yes. Oh, Ivorie. It is near to us, with a little garden . . .'

'It is old, Mrs Hammer, but weatherproof. And furnished.'

'There are six rooms. The landlord is a little . . .'

'He is a facetious man, I'm afraid, Mrs Hammer.'

'But willing, you see, to overlook certain difficulties.'

Ivorie regarded the sisters with some confusion.

Mary gave Ivorie's hand a squeeze. 'The landlord, it seems, might be induced to forgo the usual assurances . . .'

'In lieu of future recovery,' Ann qualified.

'He has,' Mary lowered her voice, '*pecuniary difficulties of his own*. Most fortunate!' She clapped her hands again. 'We will be neighbours!'

'Can you come on Saturday?' Ann said briskly. 'I have told him you will.'

Ivorie, still dizzy, nodded. The sisters paid the bill. The tea rooms were quit. Outside, Ivorie turned east and the others, west.

The road opened up before Ivorie. It opened up, and rolled on, and conducted her effortlessly home. All around her the pace of her machinations was gathering force, but where she was, in the eye of the storm, all was strangely calm and still.

'You reap what you sew,' she reflected. And again: 'What you sew, you reap.' She saw the neatness in the adage: the way it harmonised, so perfectly, the ideas of natural law and individual destiny. It did not matter that she misconstrued the verb – nor that, in her version, the harvest referred to bore no relation to wheat, or rice, or corn, but to several yards of yellow, watered silk. She only wished she might feel more fully, more unconditionally, at ease as beneficiary.

Chapter 41

Having once been outcasts

The Parathas, having once been outcasts, were not naturally converted by wealth to goodness. The truth is that the Parathas were materialists like the rest of us. There was no virtue in their forgiveness of the neighbours who had abandoned them: we have all heard of those who, long ostracised by their peers, accept with unseemly eagerness a late offer of membership to their club.

The people of Canyon now loved the Parathas properly, and treated them preferentially. It did not matter that Florence Paratha talked insatiably of tea sets — Rosa Minim introduced her to Eliza Chitman, who had a similar interest. It did not matter that Thomas Paratha had the quality of a one-oared boat, continually capsizing on the small rock that constituted his own dignity — Bald Sherry was looking out for him when it came to the really important rocks, the gold-impregnated ones. It did not matter that the unprepossessing Paratha girls (there were three, variously aged) did not sufficiently brush their hair or look after their hems — the women took an active interest now in correcting these small neglects. The girls could not become beautiful, but they became clean, and a sort of unhealthy vanity was even encouraged amongst them. Meanwhile, everyone agreed that Julian Paratha had become handsome.

Caught up in their newfound popularity, the Parathas did not think to enquire of Morag Pappy, whose arrest they had witnessed some months ago from the half-boarded windows of the Grand Hotel. Nor had they any idea what had become of Otto, their long-time boarder; they imagined him, if they thought of him at all, in the wild, living on small animals and edible plants.

And then, to change all that – to puncture, abruptly, their equanimity – who should come round the bend in the Ring Road one fine September morning on a clattering great thoroughbred that he did not convincingly manage but Borrel Sweetley.

The animal bolted, of its own accord, up and onto the causeway, where it described one and a half dramatic circles before its rider could prevail on it to halt. Sweetley let the reins go slack, but did not dismount. He sat a moment, perspiring, and let the horse tug at tufts of grass growing through gaps in the boards. On a flagpole above, a curious multicoloured banner swirled and dropped, dropped and swirled. It gave a sense of flourish to Sweetley's arrival. One could imagine him unfurling a scroll.

He was gratified by the speed at which the people of Canyon dropped their tools and gathered about him. All were plainly impressed by the figure he cut on horseback. It soon became clear to them, however, that Borrel Sweetley was not here for the sake of pleasantries. He did not climb out of his saddle, preserving instead a Napoleonic aloofness that was highly effective and, if it had not been for the expulsion of manure from the thoroughbred's behind, perfectly poised. He readied himself for the expiation of his moral burden. 'Friends!' he said. They gazed up at him. Someone, thinking they were stroking the horse, stroked his boot instead. 'Friends,' he repeated, 'you thought I abandoned you.'

There were dissenting murmurs.

'Come now!' said Sweetley, wagging his index finger. The horse twisted awkwardly to the right, causing him to assume an awkward posture known, in artistic circles, as the *contrapposto*. 'You did, indeed. And you had good reason, for I gave you no explanation. None at all. You might have thought me entirely vanished the last twelve months.' He snapped his fingers drily and looked pleased with himself, as though he had sustained, against all odds, a long and complex practical joke. 'But I have had your interests at heart the whole time. Your interests have been my driving force, my *raison d'etre*. And now, I am happy to tell you, my efforts have been rewarded.'

The excitement Sweetley had anticipated was somehow elusive; confusion was there in its stead. He continued to look at the crowd expectantly. They looked back, with equal expectation.

'I have good news for you, my friends. News that will put an end to old fears. That will wipe clean the slate, so to speak, and pave the way for the future. *Nemo tenetur ad impossibile* — and yet I have done it. It is over, my friends. The fugitive has been recaptured.'

There was a strange, stuporous muttering.

'In the Pitch Penitentiary, behind century-old stone, under lock and key —' he made a curt twisting motion with his finger, '—*that* is where you will now find our fugitive.' He snorted. 'Otto Cirque was cunning, he was slippery. He escaped from right under our noses. But the hand of the law has prevailed, my friends. When it comes down, it comes down! *Nolens volens! Fiat justitia!*'

There was confused silence. Those who knew Latin translated, but derived little compensation from the advantage.

'Bravo!' said Bald Sherry finally, feeling he ought to offer something concrete.

The rest of his townspeople took Mr Sherry's cue. A lacklustre applause occurred. Sweetley held up one hand to halt them. 'Let us not be premature in our celebrations. The thing is not yet over. There will be a trial, of course. In weeks ahead, there will be to-ing and fro-ing, there will be questions, and I ask you to be forthcoming in any way that you can.'

All was consolidating for Borrel Sweetley. His suspicions, like Ivorie Hammer's machinations, were gaining force. Behind him, at this very instant, yet another a caravan was progressing from Ring Road to Mountain Path. At its head was the faithful Lawrence, on a cranky over-laden packhorse. Behind Lawrence were several constables from the Senior Sergeant's command. Their horses swaggered slowly, carrying shovels and picks, food and water and camping apparatus. They were going to dig up some bones. Correction: they were going to dig up what Sweetley hoped would be the empty grave of the founder of Canyon himself: Arcadia Cirque. Sweetley wondered he had not thought to carry out this excavation earlier — but it had taken many small pennies dropping one at a time to reach the conclusion. In the archives from Canyon, he had found newspaper reports on the death of Arcadia that had slowly confirmed his suspicions; he had found playbills featuring the name of a young woman whose identity he had already begun to investigate; and he had found, what's more, the draft of a letter to none other than Morag Pappy (whose recapture, he hoped, would occur very soon).

Altogether, things were proceeding nicely. But just as Sweetley turned, satisfied with his performance, to make his way back to the comforts of Inner Pitch, he was accosted by a brown-faced young woman, strangely familiar. He recognised, with a start, the late Mrs Sherry's parlourmaid.

'Mr Sweetley,' she said, grasping the great man's boot in its stirrup. 'Take me with you. You must know someone in need of a maid. I do not want much. I will work for food and board alone.'

He looked at her, unconvinced.

'Take pity on me,' she persisted. 'Take me with you.'

He continued to look at her.

'Mr Sweetley,' Nelly positively hissed, 'I do not belong here, without a mistress.'

The words 'do not belong' were perfectly aimed darts; Mr Sweetley felt their arrival in his chest.

'Up on the back, then, miss,' he said. 'Holding on tight. It is a valiant beast. Quite the stallion. We shall see what we can do.'

And so Nelly, holding on very tightly indeed, rode home with Mr Sweetley. She did not have to look far for employment: her terms, it turned out, were quite acceptable to Mr Sweetley's own landlady. A small basement room was provided and Nelly got swiftly to work, establishing – as far as she could – her indispensability.

Chapter 42

The rich scent of blood and bone

The Parathas did not trust the law. Their imaginations could only furnish images of their forebears, clapped into the stocks and pilloried. The law had been against them from the beginning. What little they knew of its modern-day operations they imagined to be equally against them.

'They will find us *guilty by association*,' said Florence Paratha.

'No, no, my dear. They will get us on *harbouring a criminal*!' her husband replied.

'They will get us on no such thing!' said Julian. 'They will get us on *tripping on our own tongues*. And so we should say *nothing* if Sweetley brings us in as witnesses.' Julian shut his mouth and pulled his lips in tight to demonstrate. He was six feet three inches; he was the man of the house now. He looked squarely at his parents. 'It was me that hooked them Mr Otto,' he said. 'And it's sure not going to be me that hangs him.'

The Parathas were pleased to accept the wisdom of Julian's pronouncement and move on to the consideration of happier things. Tiny buds of possibility had been forming on the long-withered stems that constituted the Paratha family tree. Small nervous things, these buds stirred tentatively. They required sun. They required oxygen. They required certain warmer-than-average temperatures.

Bald Sherry intuited their presence – he knew how carefully they must be nurtured. He rallied the Parathas that evening. 'I see no reason,' he said, 'why our hopes should not come to *perfect* fruition.' He poured liberal amounts of ardent spirits. He lowered his voice. 'Mr Sweetley,' he looked around as though that great gentleman might be near, 'is all talk.

All talk, my friends. Put a pin in him and you will find he is composed of air. Otto Cirque will not hang! Of course he will not. Mr Sweetley might make his case with all the bluster in the world, but the world will see the truth of the matter.'

Thomas and Florence looked at each other, and then at Bald Sherry. Contrary to his name, Bald Sherry was a man of much hair. He shook this hair now — slightly curled, lustrous — and it seemed, to Thomas Paratha and his wife, to symbolise all the promise of the future. From the ground about them, a warm vapour rose: dung, humus. Even — if they weren't mistaken — a rich scent of blood and bone.

Can the qualities of altruism and self-interest coexist in the one personality? Sometimes, yes. In the case of Mr Sherry, his own plans and aspirations have lately become inseparable with the greater yearnings of his community.

Circumstance has made it so — it has forked and cut, tied and waxed the two destinies. Indeed, to elaborate and perhaps overextend this chapter's horticultural allusions, it seems that one ambition has been grafted so successfully to the other that they function now as a single entity.

To put it in more prosaic terms: There is no great profit to be made from a teetotalling audience. It applauds, but it holds tight all the while to its purse strings. It rides home, straight-backed on carts, looking forward to its bed and praising its economy. However, put the alcohol and the entertainment together, and see the spirits elevate and the wallets loosen! See how cares slip away and the moment reigns supreme!

This lovely piece of logic has recently been strengthened by another fact, also prosaic: the refusal of the Inner Pitch Municipal Council to countenance the licensing, in its jurisdiction, of the sale of Mrs Sherry's Ardent Spirits.

Bald Sherry does not see this turn of events as a 'blow' by any means. A by-law, as far as he understands it, is an inconsequential thing. A rack upon which one must place one's shoes, only to proceed precisely as planned, only stockinged and more quietly.

George Duke, less convinced than Sherry of the corollary between circus entertainments and alcoholic 'curatives' — he insisted on the more pharmaceutical term — has already found various surreptitious means to introduce their product to the public. Discreetly paperbagged, Mrs Sherry's Ardent Spirits is trickling through to its market. A chemist keeps a crate in a back room and takes a commission. Several doctors advocate the product to their patients. In the mornings, a small throng is visible at George Duke's rear gate. The milkman cannot get through. Nor the man who empties the privy. One hoped that neither of these persons was connected with the department of by-laws.

George Duke is not a natural breaker of laws. The nervous tension of his situation is, however, as invigorating as the product he hawks: he has never felt so alive. His fists clench. His reflexes peak. His mouth waters. He has, nevertheless, instructed his early-morning clientele carefully: there are bushes that can conceal, at a moment's notice, the contraband.

And although the efforts of Duke Sherry Pty Ltd are illegal and profit driven, although they seek to establish a dependency that might in future be exploited, the proprietors themselves are not, as a natural consequence, dishonest. There is transparency between them: they keep legible books, and are generous about one another in conversation with third parties. Even if their commercial activities are relegated, at present, to that sub-terranean place where all is mud and undercarriage, theirs is a *bona fide* partnership. It would be, if it could, law abiding.

Mr Sherry has become as honest and good as it is within his power to be. He has not siphoned off a penny of the Parathas' fortune; if Thomas Paratha or his wife ever sought to compare actual with documented proceeds they would find no discrepancy.

This, in itself, spoke volumes about the alteration in Bald Sherry. The former Bald Sherry had never let pass an opportunity to cheat his fellow man: there was water, sometimes, in the beer he served, and in the whisky, often; there was inaccurate change and spurious amendments to records of credit. He had long nurtured a utilitarian animalistic image of himself: as small, with sharp teeth and fat belly.

Now his idea of himself was changing. Little by little, Bald Sherry was beginning to see himself in a different light. It was a light that brought out his positive attributes, without throwing his negative ones irretrievably into shadow. It encouraged, indeed *required*, the coexistence of self-interest and magnanimity.

But there are niggles. He has not forgotten Otto Cirque. And as his utilitarian self gives way to one of greater fellow-feeling, he finds himself ill at ease. Certainly there is unease across the campsite on the subject, but none of his townsfolk have had as close an association with Otto Cirque as has Bald Sherry. Sometimes in the evenings, when he lays on his cot, there is a pang in his chest, a pang of pure regret, of something owed and not repaid. It is entirely new and unpleasant and it becomes confused with Sherry's feelings about his wife. These feelings are like drips coming in through holes. They interrupt his sleep; he will just be falling off, and then: *drip, drip, drip.* This is the pay-off, he realises, for giving oneself over to *feelings.* When one did not have them, one did not suffer.

He gets up, he lights his lamps, takes his pen and begins to formulate the first of many draft advertisements.

'The Paratha Family Circus,' writes Bald Sherry. 'A bold new enterprise. Modern. Visionary . . .'

In the air about him, a dozen little droplets evaporate at once.

Chapter 43

Ivorie Hammer cut

Ivorie Hammer cut. The scissors were sharp. The silk fell at her feet. Her hands, she was pleased to discover, were as able as ever. Under the table, Pette played with scraps of fabric. It occurred to Ivorie that at some distance – ten or twenty years perhaps – a daughter might make a tolerable companion. The thought made her well-inclined towards Pette, who had recently been brought to the words 'mama' and 'more', and could be seen to be developing, if not looks, personality.

In light of their intended change of residence, Ivorie's mood was positive. Mrs Po no longer had the quality of a heavy recalcitrant object. Indeed, on the brink of tipping over into the past tense, Mrs Po reverted, in Ivorie's imagination, to guardian angel.

Thus it was that when Mrs Po entered what had previously been her sitting room and had very recently become Ivorie's sewing room, Ivorie was able to reward her with a bright and beatific smile. Mrs Po accepted this smile graciously. She had come into the room with the object of taking the child for its afternoon sleep, but Pette was nowhere to be seen and she could not help but start at this: a small alarmed movement that gave Ivorie the calm advantage.

Ivorie laughed. 'She is just here, Mrs Po.' She tipped up some fabric with her foot. 'Playing!'

The child, on its knees, looked up at its mother as though at a large stuffed toy whose shape would not properly condense into meaning. 'Mama?' she said.

'Well done,' said Ivorie and, picking Pette up, abandoned for the moment her sewing and indicated that Mrs Po join her on the sofa.

'We must talk,' she said. She put the baby down and reached for Mrs Po's hand. 'I,' she said, 'can never thank you enough, Mrs Po.'

Mrs Po allowed her mouth to form into a small crescent, for the sake of good show.

'We,' said Ivorie – Pette tumbled, soundlessly, off the sofa and landed on the floor; Mrs Po picked her up – 'have grown to love your house, your garden.'

Mrs Po blinked, and stroked the back of the baby's neck.

Ivorie stopped and, gazing out the bay window, dissembled a short, private reverie, presumably concerning the flowering bushes that pressed against the window glass and the nut tree whose leaves fluttered in and out of shade. In reality, however, Ivorie was thinking of another vista entirely. The vista as spied through a fourth floor attic window from the epicentre – though *not* the best neighbourhood – of Inner Pitch.

On Saturday last, as required, she and Mr Hammer had visited their prospective tenancy. It had been a cold, grim day and neither the property nor the furnishings had been shown to great advantage. But Ivorie had dispensed immediately with all objections: the steepness of the stairwell ('How magnificent, to have a view!'), the dark ('It is so *private*. One does not feel, at every moment, illumined to all and sundry!'), the cold ('How novel we will find it,' said Ivorie, 'to be cool in summer!').

They peered into an outhouse and found it an inch deep in mud and water: 'A brass tap!' Ivorie observed. 'What a convenience!' When the landlord, at her instruction, turned that convenience on, and she found that it connected with no meaningful conduit of water, and subsequently discovered that all domestic water must be gathered from the well at lane's end: 'The exercise,' she said, 'will do me good.'

All around them the prospect of housework loomed, but Ivorie refused to see it. She did not mind that the ground floor was built up in places against flooding – the sewers, explained the landlord, could not always be relied on in this quarter – nor that the back courtyard was all paving and mud. 'I do not sit outside,' she told the landlord confidentially, 'when I can avoid it. My complexion.' He nodded, endorsing this wisdom.

Ernest Hammer reserved his opinion. There was no question that the property represented a diminishment in circumstance. As painfully as Ivorie, he had felt the loss of her savings. But he understood the complexities of their present situation: a man could not suffer his wife to live, indefinitely, in another woman's house. He must gently subside into Ivorie's wishes. He would put up with cold, darkness, narrowness. His daughter would grow and they would mark her height against the stairwell, and teach her how to get heat out of the fireplace. As they walked home that evening, he gave his assent and Ivorie kissed him and proclaimed him the best man she had ever known. Everything would smoothly proceed, she promised. She would inform Mrs Po herself.

Blinking, stroking, Mrs Po was waiting to be informed.

'The fact is,' said Ivorie, 'that Mr Hammer and I have had the good fortune to secure a *house*.' Mrs Po's face was unreadable, but Ivorie continued, proffering the most expedient explanation: 'With a spare room.'

Mrs Po continued to look blank.

'A room for Miss Pfeffersalz,' she went on.

Mrs Po's face had gone very slightly taut, like a pincushion, taking extra tension all across its surface.

'In a month's time, the lease commences,' said Ivorie. 'So I must propose my notice, Mrs Po. Regrettable as it is.' She smiled and took hold of Mrs Po's hand. '*It is time we gave you back your home!*'

Mrs Po withdrew her hand. 'And Baby Pette?' she said, not looking at her or her mother.

Ivorie laughed – a lively tinkling laugh that she immediately regretted. 'Well, she will come with us, of course.' She put her hand on Mrs Po's arm again. 'Oh, Mrs Po, we will visit!' But her landlady's arm remained inert.

Mrs Po removed Pette from her lap, stood up, and flattened the front of her skirt with her hands. She did not say anything, but walked to the roll-top desk and opened it. The top slid directly into its half-sphere resting place, and in a fraction of a second, Mrs Po had retrieved what she was after.

The medical card, dangling from its corner string, twirled clockwise and anti. Attached: a certificate of birth.

Mrs Po's eye was colourless and sharp. 'I think,' she said, 'you will find, Mrs Hammer, that there are certain legal obstacles.'

There was no comfort in triumph, Mrs Po discovered sadly. The small gaping motion she observed in Ivorie Hammer's cheek represented a painful resumption of the advantage.

Chapter 44

A prohibitory injunction

Ivorie relocated herself and Pette to the enclosed back porch. She removed pots and rakes, dusted off loose flakes of paint and brought cushions and blankets for the cane sofa. An oil lamp burned; there was an apple and a paring knife on a plate, a bottle of water, dried biscuits: the effect was ship's cabin like.

'You must go to the police, Mr Hammer!' Ivorie cried when her husband got home. '*That woman* is trying to take our child!' Ivorie held the baby in a stranglehold: pressed into bunny rugs and squashed against her chest. Ernest removed the bundle and put it on the floor where it resumed immediately the proportions and preoccupations of an infant.

Ivorie sat and recounted her story, with much elaboration and repetition, stabbing all the while at the couch cushion. 'It is too much, Mr Hammer. It is too much for me to bear!'

Ernest felt Mrs Po's audacity: it *was* outrageous, contemptible even. And yet his passions were not as inflamed as they ought, strictly speaking, to be.

'My dear,' he said. 'Let us avoid, if we can, the police.'

'Mr Hammer!' said Ivorie. She had sat all afternoon, willing him home, and now he was here, he was not saying what she wanted!

'Mrs Po is upset,' said Ernest. 'She is a sensible woman, Ivorie. But she is hurt. She thinks we abandon her. I shall speak to her.'

'Do no such thing, Mr Hammer!' said Ivorie. 'We must henceforth *dissociate* ourselves from that woman. And her husband. We must!'

And henceforth, a painful dissociation did indeed prevail. A *schism*, in fact, occurred within the household – along its female lines, at least.

Mrs Po, having long anticipated her tenants' departure, had made the requisite legal preparations some time ago. Sadly, pragmatically, she had sought out advice and made preliminary applications. A week after Ivorie's announcement, at two o'clock in the afternoon, an item known as a prohibitory injunction arrived, addressed to Mr and Mrs E. Hammer. Mr Hammer was not at home; the document was received by his wife, the delivery notice signed, the courier dismissed. Thereafter, an ominous silence. Then Mrs Po, eating in the kitchen, heard an expostulation on the other side of the wall. It ceased as abruptly as it began – muffled suddenly in a handkerchief or fist – and was replaced by the sound of heavy objects (feet in shoes) hitting the floor.

The door between kitchen and porch swung violently open. Ivorie Hammer, child in tow, took up the whole doorway. She proceeded towards her landlady, with the injunction in one hand and Pette in the other; she deposited the child on the floor, and held the injunction between finger and thumb at some distance from herself.

'I,' she said, acidly, 'am going out, Mrs Po. And as I would not wish to disobey the law, I leave the child with you. I herewith' she referred, derisively, to the injunction '– *refrain from removing the child from the premises.*' She let the piece of waxed and watermarked legal paper (which bore, one could not fail to notice, the signature of Mr Sweetley) fall from her hand. It winnowed to the floor. She did not pick it up. Nor did Mrs Po. In fact, it would remain there until later in the day when Mr Po, slipping, would retrieve it and prop it, like a Christmas card, on the table against a vase of hyacinths. Ivorie marched back across the kitchen floor and the door slammed behind her with unusual brutality, as though it had been designed, all along, not for the purposes of in- and egress, but for the guillotining of insects and fingers and former alliances between women.

There were no smug feelings in Mrs Po's breast. Having done what was necessary, she now suffered. A hot tear formed in the corner of her left eye. Her left eye only. It did not spill.

Pette, for her part, was happy to be returned to the more predictable, more reliable of her carers. True, Mrs Po was not as physically pliable as her mother and wore rather more metal and whalebone, but there were games that surpassed Ivorie's; there were feats for which she was rewarded with sweets and kisses.

Mrs Po found herself able to quell that one lone tear. It retreated, vanquished. The prospect of Pette's exceptionality – coaxed and cultivated by herself and Racine and Rosa Minim – would quench all tears that threatened in days to come. She took the child onto her lap, and squeezed it. 'Mama?' said Pette, and her grey eyes, unwavering, registered Mrs Po's pleasure.

In fact, Ivorie was not going out directly to seek reparation: she was delivering a beaded bodice to Madame Boucher. And although at this appointment her agitation spilled occasionally into her voice and gestures, she acquitted herself professionally. Madame Boucher, white-haired and pristine as a chocolate mould, said she was 'most pleased with the result' and immediately organised for Ivorie to attend one of her regular clients for a fitting. Her handshake, dry and cool, gave Ivorie confidence for the second leg of her journey.

At the Starlight home, she was taken aback by yet another new development. The door when she rang was answered not by Mrs Starlight, as was customary, but by the late Mrs Sherry's parlourmaid (whose existence, until then, Ivorie had entirely forgotten).

'Nelly!' Ivorie said. 'What are you doing here?'

But Nelly, strictly observing the protocols of her new station, merely took Mrs Hammer's coat, and led her into the parlour.

Upon Ivorie's entrance, Mary and Ann rose from the table in unison, each with an arm outstretched towards their guest.

'It seems an age since you have visited,' said Mary, drawing Ivorie to the chair beside her own.

Ann poured Ivorie a long glass of water.

'As you see, we have employed, in the interim, a serving girl,' Mary whispered.

'Mr Sweetley brought her back from the campsite,' Mary continued. 'We figure it a little work of charity.'

Ivorie nodded. She could think of nothing helpful to say on the subject of Nelly, but nor could she quite yet broach the subject of her own woes.

'Everyone doing the little they can,' Mary said. '*That* is how charity gets done.'

'*Mother*,' said Ann grimly, 'is finding the help *indispensable*.'

Nelly brought tea, curtsied. She wore an antiquated uniform, white and pale blue, in contrast to which her face seemed more scandalously brown than ever. She closed the door discreetly behind her.

'I have never seen such a complexion though,' said Ann.

Mary leaned forwards. 'It is truly ruinous. It makes me quite sorry for her.'

'It confirms, once again, our conclusions about *your origins*, Mrs Hammer.' Ann sucked hot tea into her mouth. 'Not that we need such confirmations any longer.' And the two women smiled, first at one another, and then at their friend.

'Yet more good news, Ivorie,' said Mary.

'With Mr Sweetley's help,' said Ann, 'we have discovered legal documents pertaining to your mother: *Marianne Ward*. If indeed your husband's information was correct.'

'Her name!' said Mary. 'On *three* certificates of title.'

'Three properties,' said Ann, 'in her name.'

'We have all kinds of hypotheses, Ivorie.'

Ann gave Mary a reproving look and said, 'She lists her profession as "dressmaker", Mrs Hammer. We have quizzed Mr Sweetley extensively about the situation – in case, in your present circumstances, there might have been any property still unaccounted for.'

'Still due to you . . .'

'But there was none.'

'None.'

'Which was certainly a great shame. In your present circumstance.'

'Mr Sweetley was very interested, though, in your case,' said Mary. 'In the mystery surrounding your parents. He has said he will go through the records and see what further information emerges. More *will* emerge, Ivorie, I know it: your mystery will be solved!' Mary's brightness was infectious. 'But tell us, Ivorie, how did you get on at Blennement Row? Are you taking the property?'

And so Ivorie told them the whole miserable story. A version in which she seemed more long suffering than was strictly true, and Mrs Po more malignant, and the property substantially more attractive, but a version, nevertheless, in which a basic veracity dominated. In so doing,

Ivorie cast herself yet again onto her friends' sympathy: a large awning that seemed endlessly capacious.

Mary and Ann were stricken. They had never had so unlucky a friend. Their awning was indeed capacious but it had borne up till now only the lightest of burdens.

'Oh, my dear!' said Ann. 'You must go immediately to our brother. And to Mr Sweetley. Between them, they will put this thing to rights.'

'Oh, between them they can do positively anything,' said Mary. And, to confirm the men's omnipotent influence on things of a worldly nature: 'That old woman has not turned up, you know, the one who went missing. But they have set a date for the trial of *that man*.' She nodded, and bit into a scone. 'For one month's time. I believe it will all go swiftly. Smoothly. As Mr Sweetley intends.' She swallowed. 'They are like that, Mrs Hammer. Energetic in their pursuit.'

Chapter 45

The night magistrate

Borrel Sweetley was a man obsessed. Ernest stood quietly in his office – a terrible mess of papers and memos, open books and hand-drawn diagrams – and realised Sweetley was incapable of lending his assistance to such minor issues as Mrs Po's recent transgression. Sweetley swooped and pounced and stalked, knocking over glasses of water and talking continuously. Finally, promising to do everything in his power to help, he saw Ernest out with a handshake that was so absolutely lacking in conviction that the promise shrivelled away immediately to something hopelessly insubstantial.

Ernest's application to Senior Sergeant Starlight was equally unpromising. The Senior Sergeant, seated at his desk, wore an expression so contorted and painful, so hatched and counter-hatched with premature lines that Ernest was reluctant to impose upon him. Nevertheless, he drew up a chair and outlined his predicament. The Senior Sergeant listened, and nodded, and dutifully wrote something down on paper that turned out – when Ernest opened and read it some minutes later outside the police station – to be nothing more than the name and address of a good attorney.

It was, of course, in keeping: entirely so. Appropriate. Good advice. Ernest would act on it forthwith. He found the attorney's rooms after several false starts: a building flanked by rows of identical buildings in a part of town where red brick was very much in dominance. Inside, however, Ernest was informed that there were no appointments available for several weeks with the senior attorney. Nor with the junior. There might be an unexpected vacancy in the interim, 'but nothing can be set in stone', the arthritic little clerk assured him happily. 'A vacancy cannot be relied on. The law, my friend, is always overstretched.' Ernest's name and details were transcribed onto a cancellation list, and he was sent away with a typed schedule of fees that caused him such grief that he folded it into as small a wedge as he could manage and stowed it in his deepest darkest pocket.

And as he thus disposed of one piece of information, he was recalled to another. A small crumpled paper lying in wait in the selfsame pocket and bearing, in his own writing, the address of the House of Jupon. Its appearance was propitious: Madam Slipper counted in his acquaintance as one of few people of sanity, and he wondered if she might advise him. After all, a brothel madam surely had, from time to time, need of an attorney, and a cannier species of attorney than that known to the general populace.

The House of Jupon, if you remember, was situated in a street called Goat Lane in an area known as the Bread Basin. By night, this area had none too healthful a glow; by day the symptoms of its dereliction were positively glaring. The buildings appeared to be in the process of softly tumbling down, as though they were built of biscuit and not brick. Ernest avoided a dead cat swelling in a puddle of water, and a lump of lard that, breaking up, inched its way down the gutter in fatty yellow increments. He noticed few people as he went; only several old men, sitting on stoops.

The facade of the House of Jupon was as it had been before – large and grimly ornate – but where there had been a door was now a rough wooden barricade, hastily and not very expertly put together. The hinges that had supported the original were, in one case, snapped right off, and in the other, bent and twisted out of shape. A window was also smashed, and a heavy square of cardboard had been put in its place.

He knocked on the wooden barricade. He knocked again and then called out gently.

A man across the way opened a window and observed him. 'There's no use in that,' he called down. He had a large head that took up much of the window frame and implied the existence of an even larger body beneath it. 'They're all gone.'

Ernest crossed the lane till he was beneath the window.

'Do you know what happened, sir?'

'I should say so. Having seen it all from up here at my window. Having watched it unfold, so to speak . . .'

Ernest stepped over a puddle and came closer. 'Well, if you would tell me then, sir, I would be indebted,' he called up. 'I have a friend whose wellbeing concerns me.'

At this, the large-headed man laughed and, taking a pinch of snuff from somewhere behind him, put it up his nostril. 'Of course you have,' he said. 'They are mighty good friends, those gels. Specially to an old man that can't get up stairs or down.'

Ernest waited.

'I'll tell you the story,' said the man, 'though there is not much to it and you might as easily guess it yourself. Was ten days ago now. Or just under perhaps.' He took more snuff, sneezed violently. 'It was a lively night. The house has been full, sir, ever since they got their stocks of liquor replenished. I don't mind, for they always run up a nightcap to me. I keep a lookout for the night magistrate, see. I give a whistle here if I see him coming.' He took a whistle from his pocket and illustrated with some relish. 'And the other night, I seen someone all right, so I blew away on me whistle, only they didn't hear a thing. Not a single thing. Too much customers and noise and music.' He shook his head. 'But it warn't the night magistrate, as it turn out. Don't know who it was. Looked more like a parson than a magistrate, all prinked up like he come out of a bandbox. When he bashed on the door to open up, and it didn't open up, he and his men took to it and broke it down. They weren't waiting.'

'And what then?' said Ernest.

'Well, they raided the place, of course. They don't break no door down for a warning! They took all the books away with 'em, and Madam Slipper's cashbox, and they took her in custody as a Crown witness. I know this, 'cause I heard them shout: "Open up, for you're wanted as Crown witness!"' He reached behind him and began, slowly, to fill a pipe. 'Them girls all run in a dozen directions – you got Buckley's finding your friend.'

Ernest thanked him for his information.

'That's my pleasure,' the man said, smiling now and fitting the stem of his pipe between his teeth. 'And don't you fret over your pal. You give it two weeks, three, and it will be lively as ever again. Seen it before. You can crook your elbow to it, sir!'

The man prodded the air with the end of his pipe and Ernest turned wearily for home.

Chapter 46

The collapsible child

The independent fortitude of Mrs Po and Mrs Hammer made coexistence possible and Ivorie eventually moved back into the house. The two women avoided each other in the kitchen, but sometimes came across each other in doorways. Mrs Po continued to cook; Mrs Hammer continued to eat. The baby moved between them with perfect symmetry. The prohibitory injunction grew watery and then brown against the vase of drying hyacinths.

Notes had arrived from the Starlight sisters, strong on sentiments of love and friendship, but otherwise inconclusive. Ivorie had taken it upon herself to write to Mr Sweetley: a long, fluent correspondence. She received nothing in response.

With the close of every day, her tenancy receded a little more, disintegrated a little further; bricks became dust, wallpaper curled at the edges, window glass melted. And then a letter containing hope arrived.

'Dear Mrs Hammer,' wrote Mary Starlight, 'I hope the day finds you well. If not – if you suffer as a woman of great feeling must in your position – then today you have reason to take heart! I am pleased to inform you of new developments regarding your situation. A sitting with the Inner Pitch Municipal Council is currently under consideration. The preliminaries are set in motion by our very own brother! If all proceeds as hoped, the case of your child will be heard and resolved very soon. You will hear from us when we are in possession of further information. With enduring friendship, Mary Starlight.'

So immense was the relief that Ivorie wept. Then, following relief, came a momentous exhaustion, so great, so all-consuming, that Ivorie must apply directly to bed.

But it was not an easy sleep. Whatever her body might require in the way of rest, Ivorie's mind would not allow. Image after image accosted her, faces mainly: Mrs Po's and Pette's, Mary and Ann Starlight's, Mr Sweetley's; even Otto Cirque's, a face she hardly knew, loomed up whitely like a ghost's. And then another face, devoid of features, rolling, rolling, like a great ball or drum, with no purpose and no direction, gathering speed and tumbling over and over until it was a rock and not a face at all.

When she woke, in a sweat, she was in the house alone, but it took her some minutes to work out whose house or who, for that matter, she even was.

Mrs Po met Racine Pfeffersalz and Rosa Minim halfway along the Ring Road. The two women took an arm of Mrs Po's each, and Baby Pette, who could now walk, tottered alongside the perambulator, stopping occasionally to pick up dandelions and, if she found them, ants.

'There are *such* developments down at the site,' said Rosa Minim. 'A vast delivery of lumber, only last week. And an *army* of carpenters and labourers – contracted from Pitch, paid, of course, by the Parathas. Oh, the Parathas! The wonderful, *wonderful* Parathas. And all day long, *tap, tap, tap*. It is a miracle how quick they work. Hardie's are supplying a tent, and we expect it any day now. They describe the tent – how do they describe the tent, Racine?'

Racine answered immediately: ' "A leviathan, capable of accommodating six hundred persons." '

'Six hundred persons!' Rosa Minim glowed. 'Is that not ambitious? Are we not ambitious? And Mr Sherry has ordered a new kind of lighting arrangement, that has no unpleasant odour. It is something thoroughly modern and innovative, though I can't recall . . . What is it precisely, Racine?'

'Gasaliers,' said Racine promptly, '*circular* gasaliers.'

'And an equestrian troupe have been formally invited. Thirteen horses. Seven riders. Mr Sherry has put it all in writing. In *writing*!'

Mrs Po could not help a little palpitation of the heart. She had never been to the circus; she had only once been to anything resembling theatrical entertainment, and that was a very terrible amateur play in which all the props fell down and one could not hear the actors' lines.

Arriving at the campsite, indications of progress were immediately evident. On a high wire above them, several girls practised balancing on alternate feet, pitching up their legs and twisting to face opposite directions. A boy swung himself up and over makeshift parallel bars in long swoops and rapid somersaults. Three children cartwheeled across the stage in unison while another ran behind them dancing a ribbon. The carpenters were fixing scaffolding for seating and around the stage itself, a looping string of permanent tents had been erected, from which could be heard bits of song and bits of music and children and women and men talking and arguing and laughing.

Mrs Po had never experienced anything like it. Her heart galloped and she thought briefly of herself as a young woman and her husband as a young man, and how they had loved to dance together and had once vacationed at the seaside where a Ferris wheel operated and a stall sold hot waffles and popcorn in paperbags. 'Oh lovely, lovely!' she said, and Rosa Minim squeezed her hand.

They set up picnic on a bank of grass and then, when eating was done with, Rosa said, 'Now, tell us about our little prodigy,' and chucked Pette under the chin.

'Well,' began Mrs Po, 'she has been *diagnosed as exceptional*. That's the word the doctor used. *Exceptional*. Her joints, Miss Minim, can spring right out and back again – he has seen nothing like it, he said. I myself have witnessed her perform the most unnatural contortions. For one thing, she can kiss her own elbow, Miss Minim! Bring it right up to her mouth and kiss it there on the very tip.'

'Is that not possible for anyone?' said Racine.

'It is not,' said Mrs Po. 'You try it! It is an impossibility.'

The comic spectacle then ensued of three apparently sedate old ladies on a picnic blanket raising elbows towards their mouths in an effort to kiss them. Pette, spying this, did what they unanimously failed to achieve: picked her elbow up, popped out of its socket her shoulder, and planted a wet little mouth on the point.

'See!' said Mrs Po, gathering the child into her lap and kissing her.

'Astonishing!' said Rosa Minim.

Mrs Po took a breath. 'Miss Pfeffersalz has told me that you are establishing a school, Miss Minim, that will foster the physical arts, gymnastics and suchlike . . . is that right?'

'Oh, yes, she must come to me, she must! The school is already operational – in a manner of speaking.' Rosa considered for some moments. 'The child needs lots of vigorous outdoor play! Swing sets and monkey bars. Ropes and hoops. Keep her active, Mrs Po. Activity: that is the main tenet of my philosophy. The children here, they know their ABCs, but they also know dancing, and how to execute a perfect somersault. Soon we will put them on horses, won't we, Racine!'

'She is very young,' said Racine. 'What does Mrs Hammer think of it all?'

Here Mrs Po must sidle towards the issue carefully. 'Mrs Hammer has so much on her mind at present,' she said.

'Indeed,' said Rosa. 'But she is a forwards-thinking woman! She always has been. She will be a great proponent of the cause . . .'

'She has much on her mind,' said Mrs Po. 'She is looking for a house, for one thing.'

'A house!' said Rosa Minim as though this were a mysterious project indeed. 'I must say,' she continued, 'the thought of *walls* and *roofs* strikes me these days as awfully confining. I was once so proud of my little cottage in Canyon, so horrified to see it burnt and broken apart – but now! Well, all is so changed. I am quite the advocate of a gypsy lifestyle.'

Mrs Po looked at Racine. 'And you, Miss Pfeffersalz?'

Racine snorted. 'I have got on a horse for the first time in twenty years!'

Rosa nodded emphatically several times; then, unaccountably, her face fell. 'We did hope,' she said, 'that Mrs Hammer would come back and live amongst us again. But it seems not . . .' She sighed. 'No, it seems not.'

'No, indeed,' said Mrs Po, 'I think she has not that intention.'

'But of course,' continued Rosa, 'I imagine Mrs Hammer has been quite overcome by events, Morag for instance . . . and now that poor old man.'

Mrs Po was quiet for a moment. 'You think Mr Sweetley's prisoner innocent, then?'

'Well, one never *knows* such things. One cannot look into the heart of another individual and see what is hidden there. But one *feels* for him terribly. One cannot *imagine* him being capable of such things. And Miss Pfeffersalz – you knew him personally when he was a young man. Didn't you, Racine?'

Racine had taken on an air of unusual gravity. 'The kindest man,' she said. 'A kind shy man who wouldn't hurt a flea.'

'There!' said Rosa. 'But it is all out of our hands now, entirely out of our hands. Mr Sweetley comes and goes looking for answers, but none of us know anything. We must just trust him. He is bona fide, Mr Sweetley, is he not?'

There was no answer to this, and thereafter the three ladies became silent and preoccupied for some time; with the result that Pette, unobserved, was able to freely consume the dregs of their unfinished teacups, as well as a small red beetle from the top of the picnic hamper and a large volume of dirt.

Chapter 47

The collapsible bustle

Borrel Sweetley is discovering the facts; the facts are discovering Borrel Sweetley. They no longer constitute a speculative narrative: they are in the process of crystallising into the truth. Yes, Mr Sweetley is *bona fide*.

In the evidence confiscated from the House of Jupon he had stumbled upon a name he had encountered several times already: in archival material from Canyon; in the titles office of Pitch; in the enquiries of the Starlight sisters regarding Ivorie Hammer. He had stumbled also on the name of *Morag Pappy* (this discovery being particularly delicious). He did not understand how it all fitted. But he soon would. The missing piece in the puzzle was just waiting for him to find it, and it happened like this:

The previous day, Lawrence and his party returned from their most recent fact-finding mission to Canyon — a fortnight overdue, but a return nevertheless. Now Sweetley awaited, with only a hint of impatience, his manservant's arrival in his office. On his desk: the books and ledgers removed from the establishment of Madam Slipper; a series of narrow paper page-markers he cut himself; and a quill dipped in red ink with which he might mark, and underscore, and circle.

He was, to be honest, not thinking about his case, but about his *lovelife*. Though unmoved by the hovering, half-clad women encountered in his raid on the House of Jupon, other more refined examples of femininity had begun to recapture his interest. Lately, for instance, when Miss Mary Starlight passed by him at the dinner table, he found his left hand creeping out from under the tablecloth towards her bustle, as though entirely of its own accord. That same ungovernable left hand, reaching out, pressed down on the bustle and was surprised to find it fold neatly in on itself, with almost no resistance, and then spring back into place again. He could not help but think it encouraging.

He paused, for a moment, to recall the precise sensation of Mary Starlight's collapsible bustle, then Lawrence was at the door, with a new autocratic knock. He did not wait for admission, but entered forthwith.

'Back, are we?' said Borrel Sweetley, forgetting bustles and busying himself with his red quill.

'Yes, sir,' said Lawrence, saluting. 'Discovered what you wanted.' He turned back to the doorway, and pulled into the room a large bundle of books held together by a strap.

'Aah,' said Borrel Sweetley, but did not show any extraordinary interest in Lawrence's booty. He did not direct the books to be untied, placed on the table, explained in any way. 'And the other artefacts?'

Lawrence looked confidentially at his employer and went to shut the door.

'You was right, Mr Sweetley, about that grave.' Lawrence sat down uninvited and Sweetley absorbed the audacity without remark. 'We went, and it was easy, finding that p'ticular headstone. Biggest in the graveyard, with all its fancy carving. But the coffin were dug in real deep, Mr Sweetley. Had to work a couple of days. Earth like rock out there.'

Sweetley nodded.

'But you were right. When we cranked the thing open, there wasn't nothing in it. Not a single particle o' bone. Disappeared. If they were ever there at all.' He leaned closer, and winked – an objectionable, familiar wink that Sweetley studiously ignored. 'Whole town empty, otherwise,' Lawrence continued. 'Dead and gone. Like a ghost town. Just a few dogs. Don't see no sign of the Paratha family. Don't see no sign of human life. Windows all smashed up in the hotel . . .'

'Yes, yes,' Sweetley said. 'And what of the *other* remains, Lawrence, that I asked you to retrieve?'

Here Lawrence came a little apart. 'Well, it's the damnedest thing,' he said, looking at his hands. 'We found that palm tree, exact spot. Your cross was still there, Mr Sweetley, what you put together when you said your words over Mrs Sherry. Solid as a rock.' He looked up from the scrutiny of his fingernails. 'But it's the damnedest thing. We went to that place, that exact spot. And we dug and we dug. We dug beneath the cross. And we dug around the cross. And we even spread out a good ten yards of the cross just to be sure. And we dug real deep too. There just wasn't nothing there, Mr Sweetley.' Lawrence put out his empty hands. 'Not a single bit of evidence. Not a single artefact of bone or clothing. Nothing.'

Borrel Sweetley felt a weight gather beneath his ribs. '*Mr* Lawrence,' he said. 'Come, come.'

'It's the truth,' said Lawrence. 'I swear to you. You can ask the other men. We couldn't of been more thorough.' Lawrence paused before proffering his hypothesis. 'I reckon it were dogs,' he said.

'Dogs?' said Mr Sweetley.

'Packs o' yellow dogs out there. Reckon they dug her up pretty soon after we put her in.'

'And is it your belief, Mr Lawrence, that these dogs made such a feast of Mrs Sherry that not a single *shred* of her remained. Not a rib bone, Lawrence? Not a bit of old lace?'

'Reckon they dragged her away,' said Lawrence. 'To their den.'

Borrel Sweetley was disgusted. With Lawrence. With himself. With the recalcitrance of Mrs Sherry's remains. He dismissed his servant sharply, and Lawrence went, relieved, having said his piece – and said it, he thought, pretty well.

But Borrel Sweetley continued to be disgusted. He had hoped that the disinterred remains of Mrs Sherry would – with the help of John Thaddeus, palaeoanthropologist, as expert witness – establish an indisputable link between cause of death and the evidence confiscated from Otto Cirque. He toyed with this evidence now, passing the gris-gris from hand to hand like a talisman; having taken it from the Senior Sergeant's evidence box, he had since transferred it from its original dirty bootlace to a leather string – 'in the service of recreation of the crime', he explained to Starlight. He passed the gris-gris back and forth between his hands and comforted himself with the triumph of Arcadia Cirque's empty grave, which drove another bolt home, circumstantially at least, in his case, though it did not – and here he fretted – provide motive.

He had only a matter of weeks to finalise his evidence. Quietly, he dragged towards his desk the stack of books Lawrence had deposited with him, and unbuckled the strap containing them. 'Accounts', said the first, 'of Arcadia Cirque', and the year, stamped baldly on the calf-skin in black. He turned a page or two and then, in some exasperation, flipped forwards to the middle. Several sheets of paper flew out and he gathered them and prepared to stuff them back into the book: a bill for paraffin and rope; a note of recommendation for a hostler; an invoice from a manufacturer of rope; and a torn fragment of writing. 'My dear brother Otto', he saw, and sat straight upright. It was the draft of a let-ter; there were crossings out and corrections. The hand was aristocratic, with high flourishes and low swooping tails. He smoothed it on his desk and read:

'My dear brother Otto. You are a good fellow, but you must abstain from harassing me about Marianne Ward. What is she to you? Think on that, brother. Indeed, if you continue to accost me in this way . . .'

And then the letter stopped, torn in half, by its writer presumably.

Borrel Sweetley felt his heart stop. He sat a long time with this precious piece of evidence before him and his heartbeat in utter and complete abeyance. Here it was then: the thing that had eluded him so long, the cornerstone of the whole story, the link, the buttress, the fruit. He had found *motive*.

Chapter 48

Friends with the hangman

It had become the custom of Mr Po and Mr Hammer to play cards and drink brandy in Mr Po's shed of a Saturday afternoon. This they were doing when Mr Po said an odd thing that caught Mr Hammer's attention.

He had just beaten Ernest in three consecutive games of piquet, as was the usual way of things, and he put his head down and laughed in his gruff way. 'Three hangings and you're a free man, Ernest,' he said, gathering up the cards. 'I will not put you through it again. Let's play something that errs more to your strengths.'

'What did you say, Mr Po?' asked Ernest.

'Well, I will let you off, Ernest. We need not play again, for it may mean your death . . .'

'But . . . I haven't heard that saying before, James. Three hangings and you're a free man?'

'Oh, it is common enough. Amongst the penitentiary employ, at least. Of who I once was . . .'

'But what does it mean?'

'Well, there is a law here. Does it not count everywhere?'

'What law is that?'

'That a man hanged three times, but does not succeed in dying, must be pardoned. Perhaps it is not law in the books as such, but it holds much weight as custom.'

Ernest was silent for some moments.

'Did you ever, in your former employ, see such a custom borne out?'

'I did once,' said Mr Po. He was shuffling now. 'Only the once. A

264

condemned man got up on the boards and three times they dropped him and three times it failed. Last time, they thought he was dead and cut him down, but in truth he was not, and he came to on the surgeon's slab and was good as gold.'

'And they let him free?'

'They let him free, indeed, Mr Hammer. They couldn't have not. He must be innocent, see, if God would not have him three times.'

'*Was* he innocent, do you think, Mr Po?'

'Sure he was, but God had not adjudicated on the matter.'

'What do you mean?'

'Well,' Mr Po leaned closer, 'he was friends with the hangman, Ernest. Good bosom friends, like brothers.'

'Do you mean to say then, that the hangman *manufactured* his survival?'

'Means were devised, yes. Devices were attached to the prisoner's neck at first, hidden so they might not be seen. And then, second time, a faulty trapdoor. And then a wrong length of rope sawn off partways in the middle. Easy to manufacture such tricks if you know how. If you calculate the arithmetic correctly. But we all had to be a party. We were all in on it. We had to be!' He stopped shuffling. 'Hangman still owes me favours.'

'And the men were not ambivalent about this miscarriage of justice?'

'Well, we all believed the man innocent. Believed it heart and soul. He was a fine fellow. We got to know him on good terms all his time in prison. Plus, we were paid mighty well in kind, Mr Hammer. Enough liquor to keep us for months. But them were days that liquor was free flowing. Now it is dry as dry . . . It's a sore and sorrowful kind of work when not a drink to be had at day's end. Give those men a drink *now*, Mr Hammer, and they be putty in your hands.' He held up his brandy glass and became serious. 'I might seem to speak lightly of it, Mr Hammer. But I seen too many innocent men hang in my time. And once a man is hanged, there is no bringing him back. I am no believer in the death penalty, Mr Hammer.'

'Nor am I, Mr Po,' said Ernest. 'Nor am I.'

Chapter 49

The weight of undigested puddings

In the parlour, Mrs Starlight knitted. Ann sat with her finger to her lip and a large medical tract open on her lap. Mary also read: something by Ruskin that bored her immensely. Senior Sergeant Starlight sat at the table with paper and pen, but wrote nothing.

Nelly entered and, with great tact – not a clink nor a scrape – put down a platter of small round cakes and poured tea.

'Thank you, Nelly,' said Mrs Starlight, smiling up from her knitting. 'You are an absolute gem!'

Nelly curtsied and left.

'Mother,' said Ann, twisting her long white neck. 'There is no need to *flatter* the maid so.'

Mrs Starlight, who had been smiling, stopped.

'It is inappropriate,' Ann went on, returning to the open page of her medical book. *Pericarditis*, she read: *Inflammation of the pericardium, the thin sac that contains the heart.*

'Inappropriate?' said Mrs Starlight.

'Yes, Ann is right,' said Mary, a little more gently than her sister. 'It sets the wrong tone, Mother. It is too familiar . . .'

'It encourages,' said Ann, keeping her place with her finger, 'a certain licence.'

'You are too soft, Mother!'

'Too soft?' Mrs Starlight felt a little hurt at this; as though a knitting needle had been plunged directly into the very epicentre of her softness. 'But she is a pretty little thing, and very helpful to me!'

'Pretty!' said Mary hotly. 'You think her pretty, Mother?'

'Mother,' said Ann, 'you are a wit, after all!'

'Do you not, then, think her pretty?' faltered Mrs Starlight.

Mary, overcome, nearly snorted. 'In the commonest way, Mother. She is a *parlourmaid!*'

Mrs Starlight looked genuinely perplexed. 'I did not know that such a thing was . . . precluded . . . amongst parlourmaids.'

Robert Starlight put down his pen, and turned to Mrs Starlight. 'My sisters mean, Mother, that beauty is almost always reserved for the upper classes.'

'That is *not* what we meant, Robert,' said Ann. 'You are being perverse.'

'What then do *you* think of our little parlourmaid's looks, brother?' enquired Mary.

'I think,' said Robert Starlight, 'that she has a lovely fresh air of health about her.'

'Indeed,' said Mary, with the crispest of smiles. 'And so too has the rosemary bush, but that does not transform it from a little low-lying shrub. You might stuff a roasting fowl with it, but you would not include it in a bouquet.'

'Mary is entirely correct,' said Ann, 'in her choice of metaphor. Our parlourmaid has commonplace attractions that will certainly pass with youth. Her type of looks have a short season.' She kept reading — *keratitis: Inflammation of the cornea, the transparent horny structure that forms the front covering of the eyeball.*

At this, Robert Starlight expostulated inarticulately and departed the room.

'Indeed,' Mary said, and the sisters looked at one another, for a moment truly astonished. 'He is *stranger* than ever, Ann. What could he be after?'

But what Robert Starlight was after had disappeared down the stairs and to the bottom of the house, and he had not now the conviction to follow. He stood outside the parlour door, started away from it up the passage, came back, nearly re-entered the room in which his sisters and his mother sat, then didn't. Eventually, he took hold of his senses, descended the stairs to the small room where Nelly resided, and knocked on her door.

She did not answer at once; he had to knock three times before she responded, and then it was difficult to make out what she said. 'Hello?' she seemed to say, or perhaps 'Hi!' or 'Go away!'

He opened the door.

Nelly was at her dressing table, fixing her hair; or rather, surprised in the act of fixing her hair, for her brush had frozen at her fringe and a tendril of hair swung loose across her forehead. There, on the dressing table, coiled on its leather cord, lay the gris-gris, dully orange, too large to be quickly concealed.

The Senior Sergeant shut the door soundlessly behind him. 'Miss Pottle,' he said.

Miss Pottle stood on a stool; it was otherwise not possible for her to make eye contact with her own face in the mirror. The additional height served her well at this moment, for it gave her an extra foot on her four and a half feet, and caused her to be equal with the Senior Sergeant's chest and shoulders. She instinctively put her free hand over the gris-gris.

'Miss Pottle,' the Senior Sergeant said again, more gently.

'I don't know what you think,' she said in a squeak and then, recovering herself: 'I don't know what you think, sir, to come into a lady's private room like this.' She glared at him and her fist tightened over the gris-gris.

The Senior Sergeant wished he had a hat or a jacket he might remove. He put one palm into the other; it was not quite a gesture of hand-wringing or pleading, but Nelly understood it. She saw it was his way of truth-getting and, in spite of herself, softened, loosened her grip on the gris-gris, put her hairbrush down.

'Is there something you want then, sir?' she asked. She envisaged the plainness of her room from his point of view: the very few things she had about her, the lack of ornaments and colour. He must think her an impoverished soul to make do with so little. She blushed. 'My things,' she said, 'did not survive the travelling.'

He did not give a fig for *her things*. He went to her, and took her hand. 'Miss Pottle,' he said.

She looked with bewilderment around the room, as though for an undiscovered exit route, but she left her hand in his all the while and when she had stopped looking about her, she allowed her eyes to settle on him and waited for him to speak again.

'Miss Pottle,' said the Senior Sergeant, folding her hand into his. 'You must trust me. I am not your adversary.'

'I know!' she said, snatching her hand back and then regretting it. 'I know, sir. Your family has given me a home and a livelihood. How might you, any of you, be my adversary? Without you I would be . . . I know not where!'

Certain wings beat in the Senior Sergeant's heart; wings belonging to butterflies that might not rightfully exist unless –

'The gris-gris,' he said, and nodded with his head to that item, enclosed beneath Nelly's small brown hand.

She raised her eyebrows and mouthed the words *gris-gris* in a manner that struck the Senior Sergeant as entirely devoid of calculation, as though she were waking from a dream and only just remembering its content. She slowly turned her hand over to reveal said item of jewellery, inert and apparently innocuous, ugly even.

'You must know,' continued the Senior Sergeant, 'we have been seeking this.'

Nelly nodded.

'You must know, it was wanted in connection with the death of Mrs Sherry, your former employer.'

Nelly nodded again, and swallowed. When she spoke her voice was surprisingly strong and clear and she looked directly in his eyes. 'It was not murder, you know,' she said. 'It was no such thing. My mistress took her own life. I found her, in the morning. She was hanging from the curtain rail and I cut her down and laid her out as if she had not done it.'

The Senior Sergeant remained still, and Nelly dropped the gris-gris into his hand.

'I cut her down so she would not be shamed by what she did. I removed her gris-gris so it would not rouse suspicion.' She could not tell from the Senior Sergeant's face if he understood this reasoning; she did not quite understand her actions herself; she never had, though she knew they were right. 'So you may have it now, sir, and do with it what you will. If you like to arrest me, I will go willingly.'

'Nelly, Nelly,' said the Senior Sergeant. He had descended onto one knee to better examine the gris-gris in the light from Nelly's dressing table, with the result that Nelly was higher than him now, looking down from her stool like a small bronze statue.

'Nelly,' he said. He bundled the gris-gris up with its cord and gave it back to her. 'Take this trinket and hide it, or destroy it. Do what you will, but do not let it be found again. This matter is finished with, Nelly, believe me. It will go no further. You have nothing more to fear.' He clasped her hand and within it, the gris-gris, and then he was gone. Nelly stared for some time at the space where he had been. Then she fixed her hair, once and for all, and dropped the gris-gris into the cold ashes of the fireplace.

Mr Sweetley was regularly absent from the evening meal these days, but a platter was always kept aside for him and, if he was fortunate, it retained, upon his arrival, something of its original heat. Upon his return this evening, he found the household had already retired, and so ate his meal alone, in silence. It was dutiful consumption: little pleasure in the half-warm food. He was just leaning back in his chair and preparing to smoke a pipe before contemplating dessert, when the door opened and, with a little fright, Mary Starlight appeared in its frame.

'Oh, Mr Sweetley,' she said. 'I have come down for candles.'

She was still in full dress, and her bustle swung enticingly as she moved to that part of the room where candlesticks were kept. Mr Sweetley kept his hand under strict control, but when Mary returned, he could not help but reach out towards her.

'Miss Mary,' he said. 'I have something I wish to speak to you about.'

Again, I refrain from detailing the particulars of Mr Sweetley's proposal to the younger Starlight sister. There was, in his general tone, the same gallantry and eloquence he had exercised upon the elder, but his choice of words suggested a fleshier craving that seemed both to frighten and excite Miss Mary. The example of the African cheetah was invoked, in its pursuit of the gazelle. The alpha male was mentioned in reference to the family structure of the lion's pride. Through all of it, Mary's bustle remained a subliminal, quivering presence.

'Mr Sweetley...' she said, and again: 'Mr Sweetley...' Then, recovering herself, she pulled out a chair and sat resolutely upon it, hands clasped on the tabletop before her.

'Mr Sweetley,' she said, 'how can I even consider your proposal, when you do not *confide* in me.' Her pretty mouth had never been so much a plum, an apricot, a butter bean. 'Every evening, you return so fatigued, so overwhelmed, so *laden down* with worries.'

He nodded. It was true. She understood.

'And yet,' she pondered, 'you remain at all times alone with your worries. You do not unburden yourself.' She paused. 'You do not, I imagine, wish to burden *us*.'

'That is it,' said Sweetley, shaking his head in wonder at her powers of comprehension. 'That is it precisely.'

'Mr Sweetley,' said Mary, leaning towards him and grasping, with those cool hands of hers, his knuckles. Her face was calm and sure in its motive. '*You may confide in me.*'

Sweetley looked coyly up.

'All of it. All your worries. All the particulars of your worries. I might be of help, Mr Sweetley.'

Miss Mary Starlight seemed suddenly the most rational, most comforting creature on earth.

'You must remember that my father was a magistrate,' she went on. 'I have, from him, some knowledge of the law. If you confide in me, I may be able to help in some way.' She paused again, and removed her hands, looking at him with a piercing birdlike expression borrowed from her sister. 'How, for instance, does your case progress?'

'My case!' said Sweetley. 'My case progresses.' He sighed. 'It progresses all right, Miss Mary, but it does not yet *congeal* as fully as I would like.'

'Ah,' said Mary, 'that is often the problem with these things. The facts will not satisfactorily align.'

'There is some factual alignment. We have, almost certainly, the identity of the first victim — and his cause of death is expertly certified. So, too, I have a motive that will, I doubt not, convince the magistrates. But the other murder victims . . .' He looked up, in case Mary might shudder or grow white at this slip of the word *murder*. She did neither. 'They are less tangible; details remain elusive.'

Mary urged him on.

'But it is highly confidential, Miss Mary,' said Mr Sweetley, looking nervously about the room, as if in its shadows some member of the defence party lurked.

'I understand,' said Mary, disappointed. Her chair scraped the floor in preparation for departure.

Sweetley leaped to prevent this. 'But I know you will not let my confidences go beyond the room.'

'Oh, I will not.' The chair ceased to scrape. Her hand shot out again.

'The main stumbling block,' he said, 'pertains to the most recent victim —' He hesitated again, but one glance into Mary's eyes and he knew she could bear any sort of detail. 'I had wanted to disinter the body of the late Mrs Sherry, to ascertain cause of death. As it turns out, I was unable.'

Mary contemplated this. 'But did not my brother ascertain cause of death when he first began the investigation?' The question spilled, Mary knew, a little too rapidly; she mitigated the effect with a widening of the eyes.

'Indeed, he did, Miss Mary. And we have his report. But he is not a *medical officer*. I did not wish to have to rely solely on his report, diligent though it was. I had hoped to establish a stronger connection between cause of death and the purported murder weapon.'

Mary looked pained for Mr Sweetley. 'But the man you have in custody certainly committed the crimes, Mr Sweetley, of that you are sure, are you not?'

Mr Sweetley nodded. 'I hold it with absolute conviction!' he said.

'Well, he shall hang for them. He *must* hang for them. I do not doubt your powers of persuasion, Mr Sweetley.' She smiled. 'In things of a legal bent, at least.'

They sat there, in some embarrassment. Mary rolled a candlestick beneath her fingers on the tabletop, then looked up brightly. 'And what does it matter, in the end, Mr Sweetley, if you can prove two murders, or three murders or only one: the result shall be the same. A man has only a single neck, a single life.'

This struck Mr Sweetley as a truly enlightened observation. His mood improved immediately. The weight that had lain some days in his stomach relented.

'You are quite right!' he said. 'You are absolutely right, Miss Mary! It makes things simpler. Certainly it does. It makes things perfectly clear and simple —'

Mary gave a sigh of great pleasure and relief. 'I told you I might be of assistance.' She struck the candle's base squarely on the tabletop, and a plug of wax fell out of it. 'Now tell me, Mr Sweetley, of other things. The information with which my sister and I supplied you pertaining to the identity of Mrs Hammer's mother — has that borne fruit?'

'Indeed!' said Sweetley, brightening. 'It has led to some significant findings.'

'Well, then!' Mary clapped her hands. 'Let me know more, so I can enlighten my friend! Mrs Hammer suffers so, you understand.'

Now Sweetley experienced a few moments' intense discomfort. He twisted in his chair, tapped, relit, tapped again his pipe. 'It is all very . . . delicate, I'm afraid. I do not know how I should . . .'

'Poor Mrs Hammer!' said Mary. 'She is a strong, determined woman, Mr Sweetley. She is a woman who can endure anything. I have great admiration for her.'

'We all do, Miss Mary. We all have great admiration for Mrs Hammer.' Mr Sweetley's pipe had gone out; it was finished; he laid it aside regretfully. 'And it compromises our admiration so, the way things have turned out. Matters that seemed entirely unrelated have become, of a sudden, so closely interconnected . . .'

'What do you mean, Mr Sweetley?' said Mary. She continued to smile, but her voice was tight. 'Come now, do not talk riddles.'

'Well, we have begun to suspect,' said Sweetley — he did not know how to put it but bluntly, 'that Mrs Hammer's mother was *involved* in this whole tragic affair.'

If Mary had had something in her mouth, she would surely have choked on it at this. Fortunately, there was nothing but gums and teeth and a very pale pink tongue, which cleverly scuttled out of the way of unexpected emotions. 'But how?' she said. 'Oh, Mr Sweetley, how could an honest dressmaker be involved in such a thing?'

Mr Sweetley cleared his throat. 'I'm afraid that Mrs Hammer's mother was not a dressmaker.'

'Not a dressmaker?'

'Not a bit. She was a – a –'

Mary looked at him expectantly; Sweetley hardly knew how to go on, except with antiquated and obscure euphemisms.

'She was, shall we say, Miss Mary –' he cleared his throat again '– no stranger to the *ballum rancum*.'

Mary looked entirely blank.

Sweetley tried again, in a whisper, leaning forwards across the table. 'She was a Covent Garden nun, Miss Mary!'

The cloud over Mary's face did not lift.

'She was a lady of easy virtue, Miss Mary. A public commodity. A fen. A crack. A whore.'

Miss Mary's jaw had never, in its thirty-four years, dropped – now it swung open like a trapdoor, and Mr Sweetley could see every one of her little bottom teeth.

'Oh, Mr Sweetley,' she said. 'Could that be possible? Indeed, you must be wrong! You must be!'

Borrel Sweetley shrugged and shook his head. 'We have the evidence. The evidence is more and more indisputable every day. A very dangerous, a very low type of woman, Miss Mary.'

Mary Starlight was shivering, and it was not cold in the kitchen. 'Mr Sweetley,' she said, standing up from her chair, 'I am shocked. I do not know what to say, what to do. That our *friend* . . .'

Mr Sweetley put out a hand to calm her. 'I should not have spoken, Miss Mary. I have distressed you, after all. I apologise –'

'No, no,' said Mary, still shivering but not at all interested in Mr Sweetley's warming hand. 'You have done the right thing in telling me, Mr Sweetley. I am just at a loss to know . . . You must excuse me.' She pushed the chair in to the table and gathered up her candles. 'I must go directly to my sister.'

She turned towards the door, leaving Mr Sweetley face to face with that bustle, more quiversome than ever.

'And my proposal?' said Sweetley. 'Miss Mary, my proposal?'

Mary turned and looked at him for one brief moment. 'Mr Sweetley,' she said reproachfully, 'now is hardly the time.' The door closed behind her.

No, now was not the time. Sweetley stirred a bowl of flummery he had no intention of eating. He stirred; it flopped gelatinously from the spoon back into the bowl. Now was not the time. The time had come and gone, and so had the bustle. The weight of undigested puddings settled back into his stomach.

Chapter 50

A body, a book

There had been no further missives from the Starlight sisters. Ivorie had waited and hoped. She had fed her infant. She had practised patience and forebearance: qualities quite unnatural to her. She and Mrs Po had entered a stage of stalemate, with no legal reparation yet visible on the horizon. Ivorie noticed Mrs Po looking at her wanly sometimes and wondered at it. She wondered, too, at herself. Having discovered the identity of her mother, it now seemed not to mean as much as it ought; it was a fact, but after the initial elation, it had not transformed itself into flesh or meaning or anything that could be held onto. Nothing was to be properly recuperated by it. There remained simply the lock of hair and the Mary Ann doll – just as there always had been.

Her stomach had returned to something of its former flatness, but was still scored with the marks of pregnancy. On a marble-topped table, this pink variegated effect might have been pretty; on a woman's stomach, it was not. She did not care. She no longer cared about her figure. Sometimes she found herself working hunched over, entirely indifferent to good posture.

It was not, however, that she had become despondent, despite the very many legitimate reasons she had for despondency. Her indifference to such things as her figure resulted simply from her immersion in a more satisfying undertaking.

Yes, Ivorie, like Florence Paratha, has found a new interest.

It is, ironically, an interest that requires the *services* of a figure. But though this figure might appear unvarying, due to the homogenising effects of corsetry, in fact it is no such thing. It is entirely

276

unpredictable and endlessly variable. Sometimes it is less well propor-
tioned than it might be and requires tactful padding. Sometimes it has
masculine shoulders that need to be compensated for. Sometimes it
requires two or three adjustable rows of hooks and eyes; or has a flat
bosom and requires deceptive dart-work on the bodice. It keeps Ivorie
constantly busy, tweaking, tucking, altering.

And so, Ivorie was working away at her new interest – which is, as
you might have already realised, the reawakening of an old interest
born in the days she had laboured as a young woman under the tutelage
of Ava Haricot in Pitch – when, finally, the awaited missive arrived.

It was blunt and to the point: 'Meet us,' it said, 'at the Upper Springs.
By the Aphrodite Pump. We will wait till two o'clock,' and signed, without embellishment, 'The Starlight Sisters.'

Ivorie was surprised by the reluctance with which she put down her
work. She picked the threads off her front and put the lid on her box of
pins. There was a little cramp in her right calf muscle from working the
pedal. She massaged it briefly.

It was Monday; and she was free, as the care of Pette was allocated
to Mrs Po on Mondays. It was not a good walking day, however: windy,
grey-skied. The road to the springs became progressively bad. She saw
something squashed and brown ahead of her. An animal of some kind;
she prepared to avert her eyes. But on approaching, she understood it to
be nothing more than a hessian sack, rutted into place by coachwheels,
dispersing fibres into the wind. She felt curiously angry – that a bag
might dupe her and her emotions.

The springs was a grim, moist place: waterlogged trees and very little birdsong. Today, it appeared grimmer than ever: a vapour rose from
the water; the sky and the trees appeared to merge, as though a damp
sponge had been smeared across a charcoal drawing. Crossing the bridge,
her heels made a dull noise against the wood, and several young ladies
looked up to see who came.

She scanned them quickly. Despite resemblances, none of them
proved to be Mary or Ann. Ivorie wore a watch. The watch told her
it was six minutes before two. She made her way towards the Upper
Springs, and sat down on a small dry rock beside the Aphrodite Pump. A
frond of fennel blew into her face and she brushed it off. A ridge of rock

cut into one buttock; as she moved to relieve it, she noticed something small and slimy near her foot. It was a slug. She stretched the tip of her boot out towards the objectionable dollop, caught it, and flicked. It landed in a puddle with the tiniest plop, and sank. She immediately felt regretful. She looked at her watch. It was after two.

Time, unaccounted for, is a dangerous thing. It does not get travelled through in the same way as time that is spoken for. For weeks, Ivorie had kept her anxieties at bay – or, at least, separate from one another. Now they came together, and the weight and clamour of it caused a corresponding capitulation of her nervous system. A prickle of sweat began, and with it, a feeling both rising and sinking in her stomach. Her heart drummed like a rubber mallet against her ribcage. She lifted her arm to her ear and forced herself to observe the *tick, tick, tick* of moments passing.

It was five minutes after two.

None of the distractions she usually relied upon to calm herself in moments of panic would materialise. The Latin verb, *judicare*, remained resolutely unconjugated; the German *sein* had become the most impossible concoction of irregularities; the only taxing dictionary entry she could conjure was the word *alexipharmic*, the meaning of which eluded her entirely. In desperation, she excavated her memory.

Suddenly a quote arrived, fully formed, complete with punctuation marks.

Queen Anne's Lace, it went, *Be watchful when harvesting this plant, as certain noxious weeds can be mistaken for it. Look out for the delicacy of its blooms and its furred stems. Remember: the Queen Anne has hairy legs!*

It was from a book of Morag's; a book she had kept on a shelf in her dispensary, wrapped in brown paper so it did not resemble a book at all, but a bleakly wrapped present. Ivorie saw the quote as though it had existed pristinely in her head forever. She saw its arrangement on the page, the positioning of the hyphen across a line break, a faulty ligature. She had laughed and conjured a picture of Queen Anne, half lady, half arachnid.

Once harvested, the seeds of the Queen Anne can be ground and swallowed; the flowers, fresh or dried, make a palatable tea when steeped in boiling water for up to an hour.

She saw Morag, with gloves on, picking through weeds and extracting a fine frond, dappled white with tiny flowers like a wedding posy.

Ten minutes. The agitation, having built, now dropped slightly.

Apricot kernels: a lady should imbibe twelve in a twenty-four hour period to have suc-cess with the apricot kernel remedy.

She saw something pale and orange and bird-pecked beneath an out-crop of butterfly grass in the back of Morag's house. She nibbled at it and found it was still sweet.

Internal applications of Beth Root as a tea can ease labour and reduce both pain and blood loss.

Beth Root! Beth Root! She remembered it, but what did it look like? She saw it in a bottle with a label made out in her very own hand.

Avoid Pennyroyal, Wormwood and Tansy.

She smelled, in the air, the aniseed of the wormwood growing behind Morag's laundry house; its feathery leaves, its capacity for rapid growth.

Nettle soups, spinach and watercress are especially nutritious and rich in iron in a case where anaemia is suspected.

The bent back of Morag Pappy thickened; she had on the grey dress that Ivorie liked, that was, in some lights, blue; she held a small sharp scythe; she was almost indistinguishable from the vegetation.

Burning back the grasstree once a year will have a beneficial generative effect on this plant.

In a backgarden, a bonfire, a scent of oil-impregnated leaves. All the heavy things disappearing: wood melting down to ash; paperstacks withering away in tiny black and orange threads. Ivorie watched with her knees drawn up to her chin. Morag threw on a pail of brown rags that curled and transformed into leaves. A book, as heavy as a brick, burnt like a brick, but fell apart like a book.

Ivorie was calm again. It was twenty minutes after two. She began to feel the ridge of rock beneath her iliac crest again. A tiny glitter of sun travelled through a hole in the sky. It generated a kind of contradictory heat: warm-cold, or cold-warm, she was not sure which. She under-stood now that her friends were not coming. She stood up and, with as much dignity as she could muster, departed.

Sometimes, without Ivorie knowing it, Mrs Po entered the sewing room and admired her hostage's work. She put an un-tacked collar around her neck and looked at herself in the mirror. She stroked a piece of velvet and admired the way, with a few runs of the needle, the preliminary shape of a body was already present within it. Of the machine itself, she was in awe. She checked it regularly for oil, dislodged with her fingernail a piece of gritty greasy fluff. Then she sat and looked at it — the quiet little workstation beneath her east window.

She did not hear Ivorie return, but she became aware of a subtle shift in the light and looking up, saw her tenant standing motionless in the doorway. She did not know how long she had been there, but she could see at once that something was wrong.

In Mrs Po's pocket was a letter. The letter had arrived shortly after Ivorie's departure. She knew the envelope, the smell — it was from the Starlight sisters — but she had felt no temptation to seek further. Treacherous she might be, but not wholly unscrupulous.

Ivorie accepted the letter. The paper was warm from Mrs Po's hand. She sat down beside her landlady. She did not hurry with this correspondence. Her fingernail slit the horizontal seal; the letter fell out; she read; she re-enclosed; she sat. It was a chill correspondence. There was grace in it; there was form; but there was no heart. A tremor passed through her. Mrs Po, sitting beside her, felt the activity in her own skin as a kind of creeping, expanding, prickling sensation.

Having worked so hard to keep her heart inert, Mrs Po now gave up her vigilance entirely. 'Mrs Hammer!' she said, putting out her arms.

'Oh, Mrs Po!' said Ivorie, and wept on her friend's shoulder.

Mrs Po patted and stroked the arms of her friend and then, making little mewing sounds, began to cry herself. 'Oh,' she cried, 'oh, how will you ever forgive me, Mrs Hammer?' She choked and sobbed again and could not compose herself. 'What must you think of me?' she said. 'I am not what you imagine. I would never really have taken Pette from you. I am so sorry!'

'I know, I know,' said Ivorie, rocking her friend. Mrs Po was small and light; not at all the leaden object she had seemed; her shoulders were like a sparrow's.

Mrs Po mopped her eyes. 'I'm a despicable creature. You should quite rightly have nothing more to do with me.'

'Mrs Po,' said Ivorie. 'Mrs Po — it is I who have been despicable. And foolish. And wrong-footed. Only I.'

Mrs Po's smooth grey hair formed a cap around her face, and her sleeves revealed her vulnerable too-large hands. They were good hands: strong, malleable. 'Mrs Po,' said Ivorie, taking one of these hands in her own and smiling, 'you have the hands of a piano player!'

Mrs Po sobbed, and through her sobbing became calm again. And almost happy.

Chapter 51

The trial of Otto Cirque

Time passed. Not immense amounts: small increments that added up to something short of a month. In the parlour the evening prior to Otto Cirque's trial, the Starlight sisters converse.

'I do so hope we framed our feelings *eloquently* enough.'

'Oh, we were eloquent, Mary,' Ann replied, not looking up. 'We were eloquent, but we were equally frank.'

'What I mean is, that our letter was not too harsh in tone. That it was adequately polite.'

'Considering, Mary, the impoliteness shown us, it was more than adequately polite.'

'. . . For we were duped, after all.'

'Duped.'

'How close we came to unsavoury connections!'

'How close, indeed.'

Mary indicates with thumb and forefinger. 'To connections with the very lowest kind. This far.'

'We were very fortunate.'

'In the nick of time.'

'Thank *goodness* for Mr Sweetley.'

'Thank goodness.'

'Mr Sweetley is tireless.'

'Tireless!'

'Things will go well for him, I feel.'

'He will demonstrate all his powers of persuasion tomorrow, I have no doubt.' Mary pauses. 'Is it wrong for me, Ann, to look quite forward to it?'

'My dear Mary, it is not wrong at all. You are only human. You wish, like every right-thinking person, for justice to be done.'

'Yes. That is exactly it.' Mary pauses again. 'We shall sit discreetly. Towards the back. Where the nameplate of our father hangs.'

'Precisely the spot. We must arrive early to ensure it is not occupied.'

The seat the Starlight sisters considered rightfully theirs was, fortunately, quite unoccupied upon their arrival. 'Look,' whispered Mary to Ann, 'how the court fills!'

The court was indeed filling and with a diverse range of spectators: there was jostling and whistling and waving and the vague humid smell of underclothes. Rows of otherwise comfortable spectators were imposed upon to compress and make room for more. Those who could not sit, stood. Women called to each other from opposite sides of the room, and someone, treading on someone else's skirt, almost caused a riot.

Let us escape the mayhem, acquire wings and a small buzzing noise and fly to the top corner of this stern, oak-panelled room. From here, we can see, amongst the bobbing heads and hats, certain persons of our acquaintance: the two sisters, of course, in blue and grey; some rows ahead of them, a thin gentleman in pince-nez, on one side of whom sits our good friend, Mr Hammer, who, unlike the public at large, is ill-at-ease (a fact illustrated by his frequent reparation to the small brass winder on the right-hand side of his wristwatch). Next to him is his wife, and next to her, Mr and Mrs Po, in as close proximity to one another as they have been in years. Next along, a small but compact gentleman, reeking of barberry juice, sits upright, crossing and re-crossing impatiently a pair of well-shaped calves. A small-boned Oriental woman of indeterminate age is seated in the same row, quite still and with her hands folded in her lap like two pale-coloured shells. Behind her, and to the left, a woolly grey head, attached to a curiously equine body, which, if it were to unfold itself from the confinement of the narrow wooden seat, would prove to be atrociously knobble-kneed. Towards the front, a quartet of persons are stiller than most: the Parathas. One cannot tell, from this distance, the expressions on their faces.

At the prosecution's table, there is no prosecutor as yet, but a slightly bowed prosecutor's assistant, arranging and rearranging documents. On the same side of the room are a bevy of lesser officials: the clerk of court, the registrar, the mace bearer, as well as reporters from various newspapers. There is no equivalent bustle in that part of the court assigned to the defence, no defence attorney or assistant, no books, documents or ledgers. The sheer weight of books, on one side, might threaten to capsize the arrangement were this not a courtroom, but a boat.

There is a movement in the doorway, a hush amongst the gathered spectators, and the twelve magistrates of the Inner Pitch Council arrive. They sweep down the central aisle, dark of apparel and dusty of wig, and take their places at the bench. It is a peculiarity of the Pitch judicial system that these learned men – and not the ignorant commonplace members of a jury – will pronounce guilt or innocence. It is a fact that ensures Pitch's judicial processes are above error, stupidity and prejudice. These men can be trusted absolutely. The audience stands respectfully, and sits again. There is silence; Mrs Paratha coughs.

Backstage, Borrel Sweetley is all a-tremor. He cannot help but figure today as a showdown rather than a courtcase. All night he dreamt of guns being oiled; he dreamt a large sword above his head with a keen silver tip, dangling from a mere thread of cobweb. All morning he has streamed with sweat and shook with nerves. He has repaired to a bottle of ardent spirits more times than would be considered prudent in the circumstances. If he does not succeed . . . if he lets once again the criminal escape the hands of justice . . . Failure looms and is only pushed aside by the knowledge that he is more prepared for today than he has been prepared for anything in his life. He calculates how long it will take the magistrates to assume their positions, and then he rises to make his own sweeping entrance.

Unfortunately for Mr Sweetley, however, just as he wheels forwards to make his entrance, Otto Cirque, conspicuously manacled, and exceedingly – *exceedingly* – small, is led out from a side door by two guards. The entrances of the two men coincide perfectly. The crowd gasps. For a moment Borrel Sweetley wrongly interprets this as a response to himself. But the gasp has nothing to do with the impressive figure of Borrel Sweetley and everything to do with the singularly *un*impressive figure of Otto Cirque.

In past weeks, in the eyes of newspaper readers and gossips, of self-proclaimed experts and interested laymen, Mr Otto Cirque has acquired a mythical stature: he has become massive, Goliath-like, capable of every permutation of assault and degradation. He is, in every imagination, at least seven feet tall; in many instances he has a scar on his face, or a missing eye, or a scar that runs *through* a missing eye. His head, as a matter of necessity, is lantern jawed.

But Otto Cirque, it now transpires, is nowhere near seven feet tall; nor is he scarred or lantern jawed or apparently capable of inflicting damage. Standing in the docks now, Otto resembles nothing so much as a dandelion.

A ripple passes through the crowd: men look fixedly at their breast-pockets, inside which eyeglasses are kept and, further behind, hearts persist, while women look up and around, as if they have erroneously configured the arrangement of things and the little manacled man is not the suspect, but the court stenographer, stepping up to his booth. But at the expiration of perhaps a minute, a new criminal shape is arrived at – one which fits the unexpectedly diminutive Otto Cirque, and neatly certifies his guilt. 'Them small innocent-looking men,' whispers the consensus, 'is always the most brutal.'

A courtroom is, of course, a theatre, and Borrel Sweetley's is a one-man show. Once on stage, his public persona comes to the rescue and his nerves still. 'Your honours,' he begins, directing himself to both the magistrates and the assembled audience. 'Your honours,' he says, 'I will present to you today a story that is both tragic and pathetic. A story that spans one man's life, and puts a premature end to three others. A story that has been buried, your honours. A story that will not, however, rest.' Sweetley paces before the bench. The magistrates watch him cautiously. 'Throughout this hearing,' he continues, 'I will call upon your honours to use your imaginations to reconstruct events long passed, but I will also ask you to be governed, at all times, by logic. This is a case in which logic is the key. The facts, as I will outline them, intersect in such a way that no intelligent man could fail to see their connective logic.

'And the facts are these: four decades ago, Mr Otto Cirque shot and killed his brother, Arcadia, in a fit of jealousy.' There is a small outburst in the crowd at this; the central magistrate – who appears to serve as a physical template for those on either side of him – lifts his gavel warningly.

'For forty years,' Sweetley continues, 'the death of Arcadia Cirque has been presumed a suicide – a mistaken presumption that has discredited the man and tainted his legacy. I will show that Mr Cirque could not possibly have taken his own life; and I will present evidence that proves *incontrovertibly* that his brother, Otto, had both motive and opportunity to commit the murder.'

The people of Canyon – at the back, generally, of the courtroom – process Mr Sweetley's pronouncement with a curious calm.

'Let us jump the intervening span of time,' Sweetley continues. 'Old crimes do not remained buried, your honours, much as their perpetrators might wish it were so: on the twenty-first of November 19—, the forty-year-old remains of two victims were exhumed from the surrounds of the accused's residence, and Otto Cirque was taken into custody on suspicion of murder.

'On the eighth day of his detention, the accused managed to escape from the cell in which he was held.' Mr Sweetley allows a pause, and then hammers his case home: 'There are no extentuating circumstances, no alternative suspects, no conflicting versions of events. Otto Cirque is a murderer: he was a murderer forty years ago, and he remains a murderer today. Do not be deceived by his gentle looks, your honours, nor by his inability to speak – one cannot judge a book by its binding, as we all very well know.' Sweetley pauses to let the adage assume its natural status as fact.

'I call my first witness,' he says. 'Mr Ernest Hammer.'

Mr Sweetley inflicts no interrogation on his first witness. Ernest Hammer is simply allowed, with very little interruption, to tell of the morning of the twentieth November, when Julian Paratha came to him with a haversack of bones.

At the completion of Ernest's narration, Sweetley produces a large box, black-lined, marked exhibit A. The box is conveyed from attorney's desk to the magistrates' bench and then to the witness stand.

'Are these, Mr Hammer, the bones presented to you on the morning of twentieth November by Julian Paratha?'

'If they are the same that were originally put into your safekeeping, then certainly, they are the bones presented to me by Julian Paratha.'

Sweetley nods and exhibit B is produced: a box of similar dimensions, also lined in black cloth, but containing rather more devastating specimens: two human skulls, one slightly smaller than the other.

'And these,' Sweetley continues, 'were these also removed from the residence of Otto Cirque by the authorities of Canyon the following day?'

'I believe so,' says Ernest, examining the skulls. 'I recall the discrepancy in size, and this —' He fingers the shattered area of bone on the crown of the larger skull, and the stenographer is directed to note the anomaly indicated.

'Do you recall *where* these skulls were discovered, Mr Hammer?'

'Yes, in the shed, on the Paratha property.'

'But in what manner? Were they hidden away, Mr Hammer? Were they stored somewhere, in a trunk, or a box of some kind?'

Ernest is visibly uncomfortable. 'They were on a shelf.'

'Ah, on a shelf.' Sweetley stops and thinks, as if all this is new to him. 'On display, Mr Hammer? Could you say these artefacts were on *display*?'

Ernest shifts. 'You could say that.'

He is then presented with exhibit C, an old and much battered rifle and confirms that this article was also discovered, on the same day, on the same premises.

Ernest is thanked and instructed to quit the stand to make way for Mr Sweetley's second witness, also of the establishing variety: Mr Thomas Paratha.

Thomas Paratha has thus far been spared from physical scrutiny: let it be said now, for the sake of visual clarity, that he is a worn out-looking man. If his legs and arms were once burly, from the combined efforts of digging and lifting and manoeuvring heavy objects over many years, they are now considerably depleted in mass. Thomas Paratha has about him a quality of hesitation, of structural uncertainty, of form without the requisite substance.

On the witness stand, he supplies brief particulars of his tenant's habits. It is established, with less speed than might have been hoped for, that prior to his arrest Otto Cirque had resided in the shed on the

Paratha property for as long as can be remembered. But of Otto's prior experiences and occupations, Thomas Paratha can tell the prosecutor nothing.

'Nothing?' Sweetley persists.

'Well, now . . .' Thomas Paratha scratches the base of his trousers. 'There was one thing . . .'

Sweetley waits. Thomas Paratha's belt buckle jiggles.

'When I was a much younger man, he had cause once to borrow tools of mine. That's right. He borrowed them, and he brung them right back. That was it, sir.' Thomas looks relieved.

Borrel Sweetley smiles, and takes up a pen. 'How old are you, Mr Paratha?'

'I'm sixty-three years old, sir. Born in the year 18—. Thirteenth of September.'

'And how old were you, do you think, when, as a much younger man, you loaned Mr Cirque your tools?'

'Well, it were some decades ago, I reckon. It were long before I met my wife or had my children.'

'But you don't recall, at any time thereafter, your tenant *exiting* his residence? For the purposes of work, or recreation?'

'No, sir, we simply never saw him. Brought him food, left it, took away the empty plates. We forgot he was there, almost.' Thomas's brow twitches, as though he suspects there might be something wrong in this. 'Almost forgot him entirely.'

'Thank you, Mr Paratha,' says Sweetley. 'You may leave the stand.'

The next witness is not an establishing witness, though Mr Sweetley has given her cause to believe she is. In truth, she is a witness of central importance to Mr Sweetley's case, being the only surviving contemporary of Otto Cirque, and the only remaining member of the Brothers Cirque Saturnalia.

Racine Pfeffersalz climbs the witness box gingerly, not because she is in any way infirm, but because her equestrian intrepidity does not translate to the environs of a courtroom where, she suspects, the jumps are higher, the obstacles more diverse and the crowd less easy to please.

'Miss Pfeffersalz,' says Mr Sweetley.

Racine nods.

'Will you tell the court how old you are, Miss Pfeffersalz.'

'With pleasure. I am eighty-three. And a sparkling example, I believe.'

Some laughter.

'Will you tell us how you came to know Mr Arcadia Cirque.'

Racine takes a breath and blows it sharply down her nose; she repeats this several times, as though clearing her nasal passages of congestion, or her memory of dust, and begins.

Her story errs to the long winded, but the prosecution is indulgent. We hear of Racine's early prowess on horseback, and of her discovery, having won a riding competition, by Arcadia Cirque. The audience enjoys the diversion, and by and by the necessary facts are established: the year of Miss Pfeffersalz's induction into the Brothers Cirque Saturnalia, the travels committed under that banner, and the company's ultimate settling in Canyon.

'You must have known Arcadia Cirque well, then, Miss Pfeffersalz, after all that time?' Sweetley asks. He has propped himself casually against the witness stand.

'Well enough.' She squints down at him. 'I was not *in love* with him, if that's what you think, Mr Sweetley.'

Sweetley merely smiles. 'What sort of a man would you say Arcadia Cirque was?'

Racine's face draws rigidly downwards while she thinks.

'Was he a *happy* man, for instance, Miss Pfeffersalz? Was he *energetic*, *high-spirited*?'

'Yes!' she says. 'All those things. He was the most *high-spirited* man I ever knew.'

'Did you ever, in your long association with Mr Cirque, observe any signs of *un*happiness, or despondency?'

'Never,' says Racine. 'I have seen those signs in other men, but never in Mr Cirque.'

'And would you say he was popular with the ladies, Miss Pfeffersalz?'

'Indeed, he was popular, Mr Sweetley,' says Racine, with a touch of indignation. 'He could have his pick, Mr Sweetley.'

'And *did* he have his pick?'

'Well, yes. He was not unlike other men, Mr Sweetley. He liked ladies, much as yourself, no doubt, Mr Sweetley, in your youth, of course. Much as any other man.'

'Did he ever *take his pick* in such a way as to aggravate other men?'

'I don't know what you mean, Mr Sweetley.'

'What I mean is, did he ever lure a lady away from another man?'

Racine laughed. 'Oh, when he could, Mr Sweetley, if he liked her enough. A gentleman was always wise to keep his wife away from Mr Arcadia Cirque.'

'The ladies must have been shocked by his death, Miss Pfeffersalz?'

'We all were,' says Racine.

'Would you tell the court, Miss Pfeffersalz, in what manner you understood Mr Cirque to have died.'

There is some brow-wrinkling, but Racine is not coy. 'It was suicide,' she says.

'And what form did that take, Miss Pfeffersalz; what form of suicide?'

'Mr Cirque shot himself in the head,' says Racine. 'You know that, Mr Sweetley. He was found in his rooms, with the gun in his hand.'

'Do you remember Mr Cirque's brother, Otto, Miss Pfeffersalz?'

'Of course I do, Mr Sweetley, a very shy, retiring gentleman. He was always very shy, very retiring.'

'And do you know what became of him, after his brother's death, Miss Pfeffersalz?'

Racine's face produces more signs of thinking. 'I don't know that I do, Mr Sweetley. I don't believe . . . he seemed, just, to disappear . . . Anyway, I certainly did not clap my eyes on him again.'

Sweetley changes tack. He returns to his desk, makes an efficient rattling sound with papers, and extracts a small bundle.

'You have shown us today, Miss Pfeffersalz, that you possess an excellent memory.'

Racine nods, not sure how staunchly she should confirm this.

'You would, I believe, recognise Arcadia Cirque's handwriting? Even after all this time.'

'Pffft,' says Racine.

'Would you tell me then,' says Sweetley, extracting a document from his bundle and placing it before the witness, 'if this is the handwriting of Arcadia Cirque.'

Racine removes eyeglasses from her pocket. Once secured to the front of her face, she must still move back and forth to bring into focus the item Sweetley refers her to.

'Yes,' she says. 'It could be his.'

'Will you answer more definitively, please, Miss Pfeffersalz,' intervenes the chief magistrate. 'Yes or no?'

'Well, yes, then. Oh, yes . . . he had these peculiar loops – his Ss and Fs you could not tell apart. It was particularly difficult in the light of my own name. Pfeff-er-salz: three Fs and one S.'

'Would you read to us then, Miss Pfeffersalz.'

Racine applies herself to the task. 'To Messrs Peacock and Fint,' she reads. 'Fourteen Brides Court, Inner Pitch. Tuesday seventeenth February, 18—. Dear Sirs, Please include in our standard advertisement the following additional copy, to run immediately: "Introducing Miss Marianne Ward, Contortionist, a Young Lady of Exceptional Skill and Sublime Artistry, in the first public performance of her Act: the Eastern Mirror." Yours faithfully, Arcadia Cirque.'

In that quarter of the room that contains our friends, there is a stifled shriek.

Racine looks up, blinks brightly.

'Did you know this young woman?' Sweetley says, 'this *Marianne Ward*?'

'Not well,' says Racine. 'But I remember her, of course. Very young, very pretty. Don't know what ever happened to her. Do you?'

Sweetley smiles. 'Indeed, I do not. In fact, no one does, Miss Pfeffersalz. After the death of Arcadia Cirque, there is no documented evidence of her existence. She also appears to have –' Sweetley makes his arms wide, '– disappeared. Very strange, don't you think?'

Racine is unimpressed. 'Perhaps,' she says.

'I think it strange!' says Sweetley. 'I think it very strange indeed!' He ponders this strangeness a moment and then moves on, having let it sink in. 'I have another letter for your perusal, Miss Pfeffersalz,' he says. 'In the same handwriting.' He draws out this second letter and passes it to the witness. 'It is a draft,' he tells the court, 'of a letter; the original is not in our possession.'

Racine sighs audibly. 'Yes, same handwriting, Mr Sweetley. Dear Miss

Pappy —' She becomes suddenly alert at this name, as does that portion of the courtroom without seating entitlements, pressed up against the back wall. 'Dear Miss Pappy, Your company arrived safely in Canyon last night, accompanied by my brother, Mr Otto Cirque. All are comfortably established in suitable accommodation. They are an uncommonly fine party of ladies and are well-provided for by Mrs Martha Glass, the manageress of The Grand Hotel. Your humble servant, Arcadia Cirque.'

'Thank you, Miss Pfeffersalz,' says Mr Sweetley. 'You may step down now.'

But now there is a commotion in the audience; heads turn to witness a well-dressed woman, in some distress, who has stood up and is now attempting to extricate herself from the pew in which she is held captive. A smaller woman is rising to help her, gathering up the back of her skirts, which are largely responsible for her difficulty. At last, having dislodged the skirts and reached the end of the pew, the distressed woman coughs or sobs several times, and is hurried away by her friend.

Chapter 52

Mens rea

'You knew, Mr Hammer!' said Ivorie. She was no longer crying, but she shook visibly and Ernest wished he had a spot of brandy on him with which he might calm her. He sighed and sat down next to his wife.

'My *mother!*' said Ivorie. '*Morag!*'

Ernest was silent. 'I knew some of it,' he said finally. 'I knew of the connection. But I didn't know what Mr Sweetley is alleging. I did not know they had anything to do with Mr Sweetley's case.'

'You lied to me, Mr Hammer,' said Ivorie, swatting at her eyes.

'I did, my dear, I did.' Ernest looked down at his hands.

'And now Mr Sweetley insinuates my mother was a ... and Morag ... Oh, Mr Hammer, what a foolish, *proud* woman I have been. How will I ever raise up my head?'

'You shall raise it as you always have, my dear. Besides, there is no mention made of *you*. Mr Sweetley will not name you in all this if he does not have to. There is no one but you and I to even suspect the connection.'

'And the Starlight sisters!'

Ernest made a motion with his hand that disregarded them entirely. 'Will you come back inside, Ivorie, and hear the rest of the case?'

Ivorie was quiet for a moment. 'I think not,' she said. 'If Mrs Po will take me home ...'

'I'm sure she will.'

'... I think it better. But *you* must stay, Mr Hammer, and you must report to me when you return. Every little thing – I can stand it, Ernest. Every little detail. I do not want to be in the dark.'

A courtroom will not hurry. Indeed, it is the prerogative of a courtroom to do precisely the opposite. The break for lunch was thus an extended one, and the afternoon resumed in the past tense. There was yawning quiet; fatigue. Mr Sweetley, however, had not slowed his metabolism down with a large lunch. He was quite full to the brim with success. Things went well, he knew it. He *felt* it, the sensation of elation was like no other. But it would not remain for long, for he was about to encounter his first recalcitrant witness. He called Julian Paratha to the stand without hesitation, and commenced a mannered little walk before him, meant to intimidate. But Julian Paratha was not the dumb, scavenging creature of previous years. Julian Paratha was handsome now. He was also rich. These two developments had wrought such a change in his public demeanour that he remained unbowed in the face of Mr Sweetley's authority.

'Mr Otto Cirque,' Julian said, loud and clear, in answer to Mr Sweetley's first question, 'has chose not to defend himself in this matter, and I have nothing to say neither.'

The full bench, still digesting their potato, ox tongue and gravy luncheon, were too drowsy to object.

Thereafter, at every question Borrel Sweetley fired at him, Julian Paratha merely shook his head and said: 'I have nothing to add.'

Borrel Sweetley dismissed his witness with disgust, and called the next.

Professor John Thaddeus remained conspicuously oily despite copious quantities of Pears dusting powder. He insinuated himself into the witness box and looked at Sweetley with the same mixture of contempt and boredom he had displayed on their first meeting. Upon prompting, he provided his qualifications, and was presented with the black box, exhibit B, containing two skulls, of which he gave his brief analysis (male, female, time of death).

Borrel Sweetley went slowly-slowly.

'Professor Thaddeus,' he said. 'You observe the area of shattered bone in the skull of the male deceased?'

Professor Thaddeus nodded three long times. 'Yes,' he said.

'In your field, you are considered to be a man of great expertise, are you not?'

Professor Thaddeus produced three more nods of the same duration and repeated his affirmation.

'What, then, would you say has caused that particular shattering, that hole in the cranium?'

'It is entirely consistent with a gunshot wound.'

'Is it consistent with a gunshot wound inflicted,' proceeded Mr Sweetley, looking not at his witness, but at the ceiling, 'by a man upon himself?'

Professor Thaddeus shook his head very slowly. 'No,' he said.

Sweetley affected surprise. 'And why not, professor?'

'A man who wished to shoot himself would shoot here,' the professor said and put his index finger and thumb to his right temple in the shape of a gun. 'Or here.' He lowered his head and removed the gun to the side. 'A man does not shoot himself in the centre of his forehead. It is too awkward – it requires an unnatural *twisting* of the wrist and forearm. However,' he said, 'another man might shoot him so from a distance of two, three yards . . .'

'So you *can* say, Professor Thaddeus, that the position of the gunshot wound is consistent with a bullet fired *at* the deceased by a third party?'

'I can,' said Professor Thaddeus, 'and I do.'

Sweetley produced now, exhibits D and E: two guns – a small handgun and a large and antiquated rifle. These were shown to the bench and then to Professor Thaddeus, who studied them peremptorily and looked up.

'Which of these two guns, Professor Thaddeus, in your professional opinion,' said Sweetley, 'is responsible for the damage to the skull we have referred to in exhibit B?'

John Thaddeus cleared his throat. 'I am no expert in munitions, Mr Sweetley. But the latter, I believe. The bullet shattered the skull in a way consistent with the firing pattern of an older cruder rifle. A hand gun, fired at close range, might be expected to produce a much cleaner, discreet entry wound than this.'

'Thank you, professor,' said Sweetley with more warmth than he had ever entertained towards the palaeoanthropologist.

Sweetley called Lawrence now – an easy and much-rehearsed performance, in which the prosecutor's assistant demonstrated all the credentials of a highly trained monkey. The escape of Otto Cirque from the Canyon courthouse was first presented, after which Sweetley moved to more recent developments.

'You visited the Canyon cemetery, Mr Lawrence, on the thirtieth of October this year to exhume a grave under the orders of the Pitch coroner, is that right?'

'Yes, sir,' said Lawrence.

'And whose grave were you ordered to exhume?'

'The grave of Arcadia Cirque,' said Lawrence.

'And what did you find, Mr Lawrence?'

'The grave,' said Mr Lawrence, leaning slightly out of the witness box, 'was *empty*!'

All ensuing disorder was swiftly hushed. Sweetley resumed.

'Empty, Mr Lawrence? Was there no coffin?'

'Oh, there was a coffin,' said Lawrence, leaning further out of the witness box, 'but there was nothing in it.'

'Nothing?'

'Nothing.'

'And are you sure this was the grave of Mr Cirque?'

'Positive, Mr Sweetley. We read the epitaph to make certain. And there was a name-plate on the coffin itself.'

'Thank you, Mr Lawrence,' said Sweetley, with some haste, not on account of the witness's evidence being in any way specious, but because Lawrence seemed, in his eagerness, in danger of plummeting out of the witness box altogether.

After retiring momentarily to his desk, Mr Sweetley called on Madam Slipper of the House of Jupon.

From the beginning, Borrel Sweetley treated Madam Slipper with hostility. He proffered a stack of three large ledgers and dropped them before her on the witness box. 'Would you tell the court, madam, what these books contain.'

Madam Slipper registered them with a nod. 'They are the record books of my establishment.' She glanced again. 'For the years 18— to 18—.'

'And what exactly *is* your establishment?'

'It is the House of Jupon.'

Sweetley made a slightly contemptuous sound inside his nose. 'Can you *elaborate*, Madam? What business are you in? What transactions are conducted in your establishment?'

'It is a house for ladies and gentlemen.'

'A *house*?' Sweetley was enjoying himself. 'Is it a *boarding* house?' He bestowed a smile on the audience. 'Or a *bawdy* house?'

'It is a brothel, Mr Sweetley.'

There was, naturally, a murmur of disapproval, as well as some laughter. No need, however, for gavels or stern warnings. Sweetley resumed possession of the House of Jupon record books, turned to a marked page, and laid it before Madam Slipper.

'Can you read for us, madam, the name underlined here in red?'

Madam Slipper glanced. 'It is *Marianne Ward*,' she said.

'How many times does it appear, madam, on this page and the next?'

Madam Slipper's eyes moved briskly down the page; she turned; her eyes continued to move briskly. 'Twenty times,' she said.

'And in association with what?'

'With her appointments, Mr Sweetley.'

'Do you know this girl? *Did* you know this girl?'

Madam Slipper's brow did not so much as quiver. 'Miss Ward was employed by the House of Jupon. But before my time. When the House of Jupon was under proprietorship of Miss Morag Pappy.'

In those parts of the room where the name *Morag Pappy* was more than an abstract proposition, this latest revelation struck hard. Someone laughed in disbelief; another swore in objection. The gavel must be raised and loudly tapped twice.

Sweetley continued. He produced another item for Madam Slipper's perusal.

'Will you now read this letter out loud, madam, before the court.'

'It is torn,' she said. 'It is incomplete. There is no indication of who wrote it.'

Sweetley produced another letter, and held it up to the court. 'This,' he said, 'is one of the letters identified by Mrs Pfeffersalz as being in the hand of Arcadia Cirque.' He showed it briefly to the magistracy. 'Can you tell me, Madam Slipper, if it is in the same hand?'

Madam considered the two articles, and nodded. 'It appears so,' she said.

'Will you read it to us now?'

'Of course. It says: "My dear brother Otto. You are a good fellow, but you must abstain from harassing me about Marianne Ward. What is she to you? Think on that, brother. Indeed, if you continue to accost me in this way—" Madam Slipper stopped. 'It breaks off there. There is nothing more.'

Mr Sweetley nodded, a slow comprehending nod that transmitted its conclusions powerfully about the courtroom. Madam Slipper was dismissed from the stand.

And so we come, finally, to the end of the performance. The bit characters have played their parts, the supporting cast have provided their necessary support, and now it is time for the closing soliloquoy.

Sweetley wiped his mouth on his shirt sleeve. He closed books and piled them neatly; he ran his hands through his hair in a simulation of deep thought. Then he turned, suddenly, faced half towards the bench and half towards the public, and began.

'Your Honours,' he said, 'you have heard a great deal of evidence today, some of which dates back nearly half a century, and some of which is barely two years old. But Otto Cirque is the link that holds the causal chain together. He is the common denominator, without which no product can be arrived at. At every corner we turn, he is there, silent, unnoticed. Deadly.'

Heads turned towards the accused.

'Arcadia Cirque did not take his own life, gentlemen,' Sweetley continued. 'You have heard the testimony of one of his close acquaintances: Arcadia Cirque was known to be the happiest, the most optimistic of men! Not always the most morally fastidious, perhaps —' here, a short, conspiratorial laugh between men '— but the most optimistic, nevertheless. You have also heard the testimony of Professor John Thaddeus: from the patterns of the gunshot wound, it is clear that Arcadia Cirque *could not possibly* have shot himself, that the weapon responsible was much more likely to be that which was discovered on the Paratha property. Who, then, was his murderer? There is only one suspect, your honours. I submit that forty years ago, Otto Cirque, consumed by jealousy of his brother, stole into that man's apartment, and shot him.'

He paused to let this submission gain the dark bass tones of truth.

'Let me turn now to the woman who divided these men,' he said. 'A woman possessing very little in the way of moral compunctions —' another such laugh '— but deserving of life like the rest of us. Deserving of her natural course upon this earth. We can see, from the evidence, that she was the *wedge* that drove these men apart. What happened to this woman?' He looked up and about, as though someone might actually reply. 'We may never know. But *that*, gentlemen, is the *only* mystery in our case.

'All other facts point irrefutably to the one conclusion. Forty years after his death, where were the remains of Arcadia Cirque found? Not in their official resting place, your honours. They had been disinterred and reburied on the threshold of Mr Cirque's abode.' He paused. 'The woman's bones were found there also — some of them, at least. But the skulls of the two victims were displayed on a shelf in his place of residence. Yes, Otto Cirque kept upon his shelves, like another man might keep his books, his globe of the world, his paperweights and letter openers — the *skulls* of the deceased. *Like trophies, gentlemen.* Gruesome, your honours. Not the actions of an innocent man.'

Mr Sweetley walked the length of the bench, seeking eye contact with each and every magistrate. He knew he had acquit himself well. And now, with two great arms, he hoisted the keystone of his argument.

'One fact remains, gentlemen, that establishes, beyond doubt, the guilt of the accused. Forty years ago, immediately following the death of Arcadia Cirque, the accused resiled from all human contact. Otto Cirque shut himself away, from family, from friends, from the world. Why should he do such a thing? Guilt, gentlemen. Your honours, this is a man who suffers remorse. This is a man plagued with remorse. And with absolutely good reason, for he is *thoroughly guilty*. There has been no guiltier man. Mr Cirque *himself* does not contradict us!' He gestured in wonder at this human specimen who would not mobilise to his own defence. '*Mens rea*, gentlemen, *mens rea*!'

And that was that. The capital actor took his bow, and the audience, quite inappropriately, applauded.

It took only an hour for the magistrates to return with their sentence. After a few short preliminaries, '*Suspendatur per collum*,' the chief magistrate pronounced. Or, to put it in laymen's terms: 'Let him be hanged by the neck.'

Chapter 53

Modes of proposition

Mr Borrel Sweetley felt his triumph for some time. He woke bathed in it, and went to sleep with its recollection dissolving on the back of his palate like a cough lozenge. But as with all triumphs, it inevitably lost its piquancy; it became a matter of words, with very little in the way of accompanying emotions. He held onto it nevertheless.

'Miss Ann,' he says, 'Have there been any callers for me?'

'No,' says Ann. 'I thought I told you that, Mr Sweetley, when you asked some hours ago.'

'No one from Canyon?' says Mr Sweetley. He taps with his foot and his hand, then puts two fingers to his forehead. 'I had expected some congratulations from that quarter. Indeed, it grieves me . . .'

Ann does not reply.

'Miss Mary,' he says, 'Was not my *demolition* of Madam Slipper in the witness stand a moment of triumph?'

Mary opens her mouth to answer, but Ann gets there first. 'You know very well, Mr Sweetley, that we agree entirely it was.'

'It is true, Mr Sweetley,' says Mary, 'We think it very well carried out and have said so several times.'

'It was a *moment*, though, was it not?' said Sweetley. 'I believe, in fact, it was the turning point. Do you agree, Miss Ann, that it was then that the bench really formed their opinion?'

'I have concurred on that point already, Mr Sweetley,' says Ann.

'But Miss Mary Starlight,' says Mr Sweetley, '*she* has withheld her concurrence.'

'I have not!' says Miss Mary. 'I was all concurrence. I have been all concurrence this past fortnight, Mr Sweetley.'

In truth, the Starlight sisters are no longer disposed to discussion on the subject. It is a bone chewed to the marrow, and has made Mr Sweetley almost intolerable to them.

Mrs Starlight, however, is all ears. Having not been in attendance at the hearing, there is no detail too small to engage her interest, no repetition that she will not endure, no utterance of self-congratulation that appears unearned.

When Mrs Starlight's daughters retired from the table that evening, the mother remained. Mr Sweetley gave her a glass of ardent spirits and they talked long into the night. They moved from nicety to profundity, recent triumph to past triumph, fact to fiction. Or, perhaps I should say, Mr Sweetley traversed these subjects and positions: Mrs Starlight was largely content to listen.

'The maharaja arrived directly,' said Borrel Sweetley. He took several large sips of ardent spirits and made a shape with his hands to represent the prince. '"Come, Mr Sweetley," he said. "There is no one but you."'

'Oh, Mr Sweetley,' said Mrs Starlight.

'In this case, the Indians were dogged in their denials. A very proud race, the Indians, Mrs Starlight.'

'Was that,' said Mrs Starlight, with the very slightest perturbation, 'the *Hindoostanis* or the *Red* Indians?'

'Oh, the very blackest Hindoos, Mrs Starlight. From the depths of Kerala.'

'Are they *very* frightening?'

Sweetley sipped and continued. 'As I was saying, Mrs Starlight, the Hindoos were on the verge of picking up their panniers, and escaping, for good, when I requested a private engagement with them. I will not repeat now what I said to them, but . . . what do you think was the outcome? Hazard a guess, Mrs Starlight.'

Mrs Starlight shook her head hopelessly.

'*Complete* retraction of their prior statements. *Out*right confessions, from both men. Oh, it was a coup!' He was breathless for a moment, with his head on one side.

There was a glow to Mrs Starlight's cheeks, equalled only by the lustre in Mr Sweetley's eyes. It occurred to Mr Sweetley that Mrs Starlight possessed a most perfect listening attitude. It occurred to him simultaneously that her contours – rounded, slightly plump – were pleasing in a way that her daughters' were not. He pulled his chair close, and allowed, when he replaced his glass on the tabletop, his hand to gently graze her own.

And then it tumbled out: indeed, the proposal *catapulted* from his throat as though someone had just compressed his front ribs in what is now known as the Heimlich maneouvre.

Did Mrs Starlight object to this mode of proposition? Form was nothing to Mrs Starlight. She had disliked it in her patrician husband; she could not respond to it in her daughters. 'Oh, *yes*,' she said to Mr Borrel Sweetley. And covered his hand in hers. 'Yes, yes, *yes*.'

There is little more to be said except that, upstairs, a similar, if more subtle, conversation was going on.

The conversation is taking place, if you have not already guessed, between Nelly Pottle and Robert Starlight. But it is rather more private in nature than that between Mrs Starlight and Mr Sweetley; it is all soft murmurings and shy nods – in fact, one can hardly make out any distinct words. If you look closely, however, you will see that Robert Starlight has taken the small brown left hand of Nelly Pottle and slipped onto its fourth finger a ring. And as he has done this, tears have formed in Nelly's eyes, and she has thrown her arms around her suitor's neck, and he has clasped her around the waist, and they have kissed and whispered things into each other's ears – and, really, it is the most decisive moment, and the happiest, in Robert Starlight's life. His sisters are reduced to mere sticks of wax which, having never been employed for the sake of warmth, collect only dust, a certain stickiness, some grime. Nelly Pottle, however, is warm inside Robert Starlight's arms.

You must forgive the lapse, but a little romance is necessary in a work of fiction.

Chapter 54

A case for mercy

Unlike Mr Sweetley, I do not have expansive knowledge of Latin dicta. I do, however, know one phrase: a phrase framed, I believe, for legal matters other than the criminal, and not perhaps immediately pertinent to our current situation. Nevertheless, it occurs to me now and it is this: *Non omne quod licet honestum est*. Not everything that is legal is honourable. One could also, quite freely I think, state the obverse to be equally true.

Directly following Mr Cirque's sentence, a party of men gathered at George Duke's antique shop to purchase ardent spirits. Certainly, the purchase of ardent spirits was illegal, but was it dishonourable? I think not. Let us turn now to motivation, however: were these men purchasing ardent spirits to commiserate over the plight of the accused? They were not. They were purchasing it to celebrate.

It is entirely legal to celebrate the death sentence of another man. Is it honourable? I think not. I think it horribly *dis*honourable.

A petition for clemency was drafted by Mr Po and Mr Hammer; George Duke signed it, Bald Sherry signed it, even the Senior Sergeant signed it. To a one, the people of Canyon signed it. It contained three hundred and forty-one signatures in all. It was presented to the Inner Magistracy of the Pitch Municipal Authority, and it was unanimously rejected.

Ernest Hammer and James Po, upon receiving this verdict, sat down on the steep grey steps of the Pitch Penitentiary. They said nothing for some minutes. Ernest Hammer looked at the grey stones beneath him;

James Po did similarly. There were black cawing birds overhead and someone, somewhere, whistling to a dog.

'It's not over yet,' said Ernest Hammer.

'No, it is not,' said Mr Po.

'You have made enquiries of your former acquaintance, Mr Po?'

'I have spoke to them, those that remain,' said Mr Po. 'They are willing, though I must use my persuasive powers heavily.' He prodded at the stones with his fingers, as though they might move apart for him. 'They are willing, at the price we discussed.'

'Are *you* willing, Mr Po?'

'I am merely the middle man, Ernest. If you are willing, and Mr Sherry is willing . . .'

'Mr Sherry is willing. I am willing.'

'Mr Sweetley's case seemed very strong, Mr Hammer. Are you sure?'

'I cannot believe in the death penalty, Mr Po.'

'Nor I,' said Mr Po and swung himself up from the stone step and dusted off his trousers. 'Then let's go to it, Mr Hammer.'

And so, several evenings hence, a large number of crates of Mrs Sherry's Ardent Spirits was removed from the storehouse of Mr Archibald Sherry, former publican of Canyon, and distributed, under cover of night, amongst four senior attendants of the Pitch Penitentiary. Those same four attendants indulged in a party that night, and card playing, and even a little whoring at the expense of Madam Slipper (who would be a party to no man's hanging), and it felt very much like the old days. Exactly like the old days. Did they feel dishonourable? No, they did not. Indeed, they felt duly recompensed for their hard labours, and could not wait for the completion of the bargain to gain the remainder owing.

Bald Sherry, for one, slept well that evening.

Chapter 55

A determined effort

There is one more encounter that must be detailed before we get to the death scene in our story. This encounter takes place in the Mackaby Superior Tea Rooms, where the wallpaper is green and gold and has a disturbing capacity to entrap rather than entice patrons – or so Ernest Hammer thinks upon entering that establishment, his wife on his arm, and his landlord and lady bringing up the rear. He turns to maneouvre a large perambulator over an unaccommodating door stoop.

'Is it not lovely!' whispers Ivorie, tightening her grip on her husband's arm. 'Is it not genteel?'

In fact, she feels a little unequal to the place, arriving there without her former chaperones. But she is treated as she has always been treated: shown to a table and given a menu, and accorded no deviation from the norms of civility. Ernest orders ginger cake and when it arrives it is unstinting in quantity and very moist.

'One could hardly ask for better, my dear!' says Ivorie, pouring tea for him.

'It is lovely!' says Mrs Po. 'Oh Mrs Hammer, why have I not been here before?'

Pette sits up in her pram and pushes scone crumbs through the gaps in her teeth.

'Their cakes,' says Ivorie knowingly, 'are superior. It is a superior establishment.'

Mr James Po is delivered of a slice of lemon cake and proffers it in something like a salutation.

'It is so lovely to have an outing!' says Mrs Po. 'Shall we visit the dress shops afterwards, Ivorie?'

'I will take you to Madame Boucher's,' says Ivorie.

There is determined effort on this outing not to refer to certain darknesses that hover — that might, if given free rein, consume; all is undertaken in a necessary spirit of lightness. Those issues will not be suffered today. They will not! The tea rooms will not bow to such subjects. Mrs Po and Ivorie Hammer have fellow feeling on their side. It makes lightness all the easier to entertain.

But when darkness is materially present, it will have its way.

Perhaps the Starlight sisters ought not properly to be described in terms of darkness; but they are certainly concrete, ailments and fragilities aside. When they eat, what is consumed makes its physically predictable journey; their dresses rustle; their bosoms heave.

Their bosoms are heaving now, on the other side of the tea room, where they sit in an obscured corner and take their repast.

'Oh, oh!' they hear Mrs Po say. 'I believe Baby Pette has said another word!'

Four heads anticipate, above the perambulator.

'Scone,' says Pette, crumbling said article. 'Scone.'

'Oh, the love!' says Mrs Po, and Ivorie Hammer says something similar, though less emphatic.

It is at this moment that the Starlight sisters decide their situation is no longer tolerable. They rise, the two of them, Mary a little behind her sister, Ann.

'If they see us . . .?' whispers Mary.

'We shall be courteous as always.'

'It is a most delicate situation . . .'

'An inconvenience, Mary, nothing more.'

The sisters sally forth, heads held high. They are tall ladies. They cannot help but make an impression. Ivorie sees them first, and is reminded of two ships, with high fluttering sails, bearing down upon her. She is momentarily overcome by this image, but as the sisters come closer, she notices tiny flaws. Their dresses, for instance (it is the first time she has noticed) are not entirely without fault. Ann has puckers across the chest where there ought, strictly speaking, to be tautness; and Mary's waist is not as narrow as it might be made, with a little expertise. Nor are they, in this light, as youthful as they have always seemed, but as prone to the cracks and creases of spinsterhood as she herself once was. A feeling of pity comes over her – pity, at the very least, for the remediable faults of their tailoring, but mostly for their rectitude, for which there are, as she knows, no real rewards, no compensations; only this ability to sail over the heads of others.

A meeting cannot be avoided.

Ann stops alongside them.

'Mrs Hammer,' says Ann. Her voice is beautifully modulated.

'Ann,' says Ivorie. 'Mary.'

Ann's face is hawklike. She nods to the others in the party. 'You are well, I see?'

'Quite well,' says Ivorie, and is surprised to hear that she is.

'You have received our correspondence?'

'Indeed, I have.'

Ernest puts his hand over his wife's.

Ann's eyes flicker over Ivorie's guests: Mrs Po, tightly wrung, bursting with unsaid things; Mr Po in going-out attire that has not seen the open air in years; Ernest Hammer, as neutral as an oak tree in green and brown.

'It is most unfortunate that we should meet like this,' continues Ann, 'but it cannot be helped. I am sorry for it.'

'It cannot be helped,' is all Ivorie can think to utter.

The talk in the tea rooms around them is loud; one could say anything one liked without fear of being heard. 'I think it best,' says Ann Starlight, lowering her voice nevertheless, 'that we do not meet like this again.' She flattens one hand briefly between them to make a small metaphorical barrier.

Ivorie feels a surge of pain behind her ribs, but is not sure whether it is hurt or anger. Mrs Po, beside her, feels a similar pain, but suffers no such ambivalence; she gulps down two or three unkind words that threaten to escape.

'I think it best,' continues Ann, with her voice still lowered, 'if you consider an alternative place to take tea, Mrs Hammer.'

'Not come here?' says Mrs Po.

Ann turns her face slightly towards Ivorie. 'I think it uncomfortable on both sides should we meet, Mrs Hammer.'

'Oh, Ivorie!' Mary says in a sudden rush of feeling, 'we have felt so *deceived* by you!'

'Miss Starlight,' says Ernest Hammer. 'Surely we could manage between us to –'

'I think it best,' says Ann, smiling hard.

Mrs Po is indignant. 'But we shall do no such thing!' she says. 'Tell her, Mrs Hammer.'

'It's all right,' says Ivorie, putting her hand over Mrs Po's. 'There is another tea room . . . the Dalton – I have heard it very well spoken of.'

'The Dalton, yes,' says Ann in happy approbation. Having settled things, she can properly smile now. 'That is a perfect solution. Well, we must take our leave, Mrs Hammer.'

'Scone,' says Pette, all of a sudden, holding a wet white mash up to Ann Starlight and looking at her expectantly.

Ann rears slightly. 'Oh,' she says. She leans over the pram to enquire further, as though the baby is a specimen from the zoological gardens, and then straightens again to give her verdict. 'She does not take after you, Mrs Hammer. No matter. She will, perhaps, grow out of her homeliness. I have seen it before. Come now, Mary.'

But at this point, Lucinda Po has had enough. It does not take much, a subtle shifting of her foot beyond the table. She does it almost without realising.

Ann proceeds forwards. Her lovely upright form is completely assured in its step, and then, in one long elastic second, her feet go out beneath her. Her arms splay, looking for purchase. Her long neck shoots outwards. She grabs at the curtain in the window and it ricochets from its studs.

There is complete silence in the tea rooms.

'Oh, Ann!' says Mary, scuttling to her sister's side.

Half on, half off the window ledge, Ann Starlight sprawls with her dress hitched up above her ankles.

Ernest Hammer rises immediately to help, but Ann waves him away. Her mouth opens and shuts and her face is quite white. 'Well,' she says. 'Well!'

Mary supports her to standing. 'Well!' says Ann again, and then, retrieving her purse from the floor, she exits the tea rooms, limping slightly and with part of her dress hem folded in on itself. Her sister follows her. The door closes loudly behind them and the little bell trills to mark the exit.

There is quiet for a moment at the table which contains our friends.

'Are you all right, Ivorie . . .?' says Mr Hammer.

Ivorie Hammer turns to scoop a wad of food from the cheek of her daughter. 'I don't understand exactly,' she says, 'but I am fine, Mr Hammer. Absolutely fine.'

Later that evening, a minor incident occurred in the kitchen of Mr and Mrs Po. It was a small incident, worthy of little note, but meaningful to its participants, desperately meaningful. Mrs Po was putting the last of the supper things away and had just untied and removed her apron. A dark night was going on outside, but she could see from the little kitchen window a sliver of moon and some stars.

'Mrs Po . . .' said Mr Po, entering the kitchen.

'Mr Po?' said Mrs.

'You look,' he cleared his throat, 'very fine tonight.'

'Oh, Mr Po,' said Mrs.

They came slightly closer together, Mrs Po's apron still over her arm where she had folded it.

'You were very fine, Mrs Po,' said Mr Po, 'when you – *showed up* – that woman!'

'Oh, Mr Po, what a terrible person I am!'

Mr Po came close enough to take his wife's hand. 'You have spark, Mrs Po.'

'Oh, Mr Po.'

'I am so sorry, my dear.'

'I am sorry, too. I am an old woman now, Mr Po.'

'And I an old man.'

'Well, let us be grateful then,' Mrs Po allowed her husband to draw nearer, 'that, on the point of age, there is no distinction between the sexes.'

From the moonlight in the Pos' comfortable kitchen comes a certain softness. It casts over the heads of the couple; they stand there a long while, silent, and let it fall upon them.

Chapter 56

The hours before denouement

We come now to our resolution. To this end, I ask you to collapse in your imaginations several weeks and arrive at our moment of denouement.

It is the fourteenth day of December. At six o'clock, just prior to sundown, Otto Cirque will climb up a series of steps onto the gallows and feel the trapdoor come away beneath his feet.

It is now, however, two hours earlier: it is four o'clock in the afternoon. The birds utter bright little sounds, the sun is warm, and Ivorie Hammer has been several uninterrupted hours at her sewing machine. Deep in work, she does not expect a visitor and is surprised when the doorknocker raps loudly.

It is an agent from the post office. In his hands there is a large envelope, larger than that used for ordinary letters, and more bulky.

'Hello?' says Ivorie.

'I have a correspondence addressed to Mrs Hammer,' says the postal agent, and proffers the envelope. 'I am afraid it should have been delivered to you some time ago. It got lost.'

Ivorie takes the package, looks at her own name printed on the front in familiar handwriting.

'It was mislaid,' continues the postman. He wants to be exonerated of responsibility and dismissed.

Ivorie does not answer but continues to look at the envelope.

'Well, then, I trust you are satisfied?'

Ivorie nods. There is a graze of rust-coloured material on the back flap of the envelope; it looks like blood, but it might be coffee, or chocolate.

The postal agent stands up straight to take his leave and then, making small talk, turns back. 'Will you be attending today, ma'am?'

'No,' says Ivorie Hammer, 'I think not.'

'Wise,' says the postman tipping his hat. 'Undoubtedly wise.'

Something has leapt from the bottom of Ivorie's stomach into her throat. Back inside the house, she kneels on the floor and her hands sweat; she turns the envelope upside down and shakes it so the contents rattle out: a large — a *voluminous* — correspondence, folded many times and then pressed flat. The smell of dust comes up, a tiny rivulet of sand runs from a crease.

Ivorie reads. She sits very still and very quiet for several minutes after her reading is complete. Her mind cannot adequately hold the information thus imparted. From a distance, she watches her body react: it gets up, it sits down. It goes from one side of the room to the other and back again. In its hands, an altercation has set up, a dialogue of pros and cons. At the window, the sky is in its very first shades of pink. Ivorie throws on her coat, her worn, unfashionable coat, and leaves the house.

Chapter 57

Death by hanging

Death by hanging is not a pretty death. If performed expertly, it will be swift: the neck will be fractured and death will be instantaneous. If performed inexpertly, however – if calculations are ill made in regards to the height of the drop, for instance, or the weight of the candidate – death may occur through strangulation, slow and painful, rather than fracture. The late Mrs Sherry suffered the latter death; Otto Cirque hoped for the former. The gathered crowd mostly does not mind, so long as the spectacle goes ahead as planned and it does not get too cold nor dark.

There are two hundred people gathered to watch the event. They are talkative and nervous and, some of them, excited. Others are not sure they ought to have come at all, but they are here now: they might as well stay. It is not every day that such a happening occurs.

At ten minutes to six, the doors of the penitentiary are opened. They make a heavy dragging sound and there is a pause in which nothing can be seen but the mysterious dark innards of the jailhouse beyond, and then, out of the darkness, very small and very white, appears Otto Cirque. A feather, or a twig, or a tuft of dried grass: these are the things he resembles. The gallows seems suddenly a redundant and brutish piece of machinery: two fingers pinched might easily put out his life.

The crowd becomes quiet and still; it parts down the middle to make way for the prisoner and his executioner. Some of those from Pitch become mixed up with those who have come from Canyon; some of those from Canyon find themselves elbow to elbow with the good citizens of Pitch.

Otto Cirque, hands manacled behind his back, stumbles and rights himself. He does not seem frightened. A bird – surely it is a crow – has lit on the crossbeam of the gallows and remains there, stationary.

Up the steps they go, the executioner gentle with his charge.

Up goes Otto Cirque, quiet as a lamb. How many steps are there? Six, seven? The audience counts each of these little nudges towards death. The hush descends; the sun sinks lower until it is a pink ridge at the end of the sky.

Otto stands on the platform in a position marked with an X. The executioner bends to strap his legs and the condemned man is accommodating. He looks down at his feet, and when he looks up again, those at the front see his eyes are a very pale blue. He looks out with those pale blue eyes, and unease passes through the crowd, as though suddenly they realise they are gathered to do something they have not thought through; something for which, in fact, they find they have not the courage. Something that might, in some inconclusive way, change them.

There are no last words, of course – except from Mr Sweetley, who makes the ceremonial pronouncement of guilt and sentence. Otto Cirque is motionless on the boards, and then the knot is fastened around his neck. A hood is pulled over his head, the noose is tightened, and the hatch released. The hatch falls, the rope jolts, the body falls limp. It is all quite soundless and quick.

His feet, no larger than a child's, swing gently back and forth, as though rocked by the wind.

Ivorie Hammer stands alone, not having located her husband. She stands alone, clutching a recently delivered letter from which a terrible grief emanates.

But Otto Cirque is not to play the role of martyr in this narrative. For when he is taken down he is found not to be dead at all, not in the slightest. His heart beats, his breath is scarcely altered, and his neck retains completely its integrity.

How is such a thing possible? Is he simply – with his birdlike proportions – incapable of precipitating, through bodyweight alone, his own demise? Has there been a miscalculation, of rope length, of velocity? Has he an unusually muscular neck that might withstand the infringement of a tightened noose? Such things are not unheard of. The crowd is open-mouthed, and then it begans to whisper. It whispers and whispers, and its unease grows.

Otto Cirque's body is searched for death-defying contraptions; none are found. The whispering peters out. It is beginning to get dark; it is certainly edging beyond twilight. The noose is reattached to Otto's neck, the hood returned, and the process repeated. But now a new obstacle intervenes between Otto Cirque and death. The hatch, though oiled at the hinges that morning and tested, does not properly drop. When it opens, it opens only halfway, so Otto's feet hit it and bounce, and his legs buckle unexpectedly at the knees.

The crowd grows in its unease. This is not a God-fearing society, but nor is it a society willing to wrong-foot the intent of a higher being. Just in case, however, for the third and final hanging attempt, leaden weights are attached to the ankles of Otto Cirque, and also to his wrists. Borrel Sweetley, with expressions of great agitation, tests and re-tests the hinges of the hatch, calls for grease.

Ivorie Hammer can see, up at the front, the small head of Florence Paratha nodding furiously.

Quiet falls again. Devoid of contraptions, weighed down with lead, Otto Cirque is re-fastened, re-hooded, and re-hanged. The hatch falls neatly, the rope jolts — but perhaps they have attached too much in the way of leaden weights, for the rope tears. It tears all the way through the middle till it hangs from a thread, and then the thread breaks and Otto Cirque falls to the ground.

Ivorie Hammer wants her husband. She wants her husband and her baby. She wants Racine and Mrs Po and Florence Paratha. She stoops to the cobblestones and is violently sick. When she rises again, they are taking the hood off Otto Cirque and gathering him up from the ground. They have released the rope for the last time.

He is shaken but he is alive. He stands there, very small and inert, and very alive.

In Canyon, the wind goes through its usual motions: rise and lull, rise and lull. On the floor of her dispensary, Morag Pappy is bent over a hessian sack. She tips and shakes the contents of the sack onto the floor;

sand comes out as well, and grass. She bends and scrutinises her findings; they are not remarkable:

- a cluster of seedpods;
- several stones that suit the purpose of doorstops;
- four usefully shaped sticks that, were Morag a spiritualist, might be mistaken for divining rods;
- a small chunk of volcanic rock;
- a shell as perfectly coiled as a baby's ear;
- a piece of amber with a fly trapped inside;
- the pristine skeleton of a bird; and
- a well-preserved piece of snake skin.

They topple onto the floor about her, and she is just spreading them out when a pain comes into her head.

It is a warm pain, getting hotter, and curiously mindful of blood. Morag leans closer to the floor and places her ear on it. Now she can hear it, the pain. She hears it seep in large waves from one part of her head to the next, as though something very hard and tight is becoming progressively soft and free and liquid. Her eyes stay open and she doesn't move, and the blood fills her up.

It is quite comfortable, it is peaceful. In the very last moment, she has the sensation of drowning in warm salt water.

Chapter 58

Words that fall like blows

In that correspondence that smelled of dust and spilled sand on Mrs Po's sitting room floor, Ivorie read:

Foolish women can come in many shapes and sizes, my dear Ivorie. We do not see our foolishness when we are in the midst of it; we only see it when we are beyond remedying it. Again and again I have picked up my pen to tell you this story, and every time I have put it back down. I thought not to injure you nor earn your contempt, but I have done both in spite of myself.

So here is an ending to the story I have told you.

Your mother gave birth to you soon after she set out from Canyon to find me. It was very cold and there was too much blood. Otto had followed her and found her. He tried to stop the blood but could not. Out went her life and in came yours. Such is the fate of many women. Such was the fate of your dear mother.

You were the smallest creature in the world when I came upon you on the road where you were born, but your heartbeat was strong. Your lungs opened up and took breath in and out, in and out, as though you were a little engine started up that would not stop. What a strong little life you were! How I fell in love with you immediately I saw you! Your tiny limbs like coils of hair! How ravenously you sucked on the rag Otto soaked in milk.

We buried your mother. Otto dug a hole and we laid her in it. Later, much later, he came back and retrieved her. I don't know when. But when we buried her, we found a handful of tokens in her pocket. From her ears, we removed two large yellow earrings. In her bag was a child's doll. I gave you these things. We gathered you up and we turned back to Canyon.

I found a woman to nurse you, and straightaway, your arms and legs plumped up, as did your cheeks, and your little eyes opened and looked around. Otto stayed with us for a short time, but he did not recover sufficiently from the death of your mother. Some men are like that; it is not to say their hearts are soft, but rather that, when once bent, or forged, into a particular shape they cannot be remade. Such a man was Otto Cirque.

But I have enough knowledge of men to know when their thoughts become dangerous. I have seen men at the door and not let them into the house because of this intention: it can be read in the eyes and the jaw. I saw all these signs gathering in Otto, so when he put on his coat and left the house one afternoon, I laid you quietly in your cot and I followed him. You were twelve days old. I took a rifle. You always argued over that rifle, you hated it. A woman should not have a gun, you said. I replied that a woman is the only person who might properly be trusted with one.

I followed Otto to the hotel where his brother lived. He went quietly up the stairs, and I went quietly after him. I remember those stairs with their bumps and creaks. There was a window, and a painting of a dog. There was laundry on the floor. I remember these little things as I passed them; they have become much bigger than many things since.

I did not hear every word said by Arcadia Cirque. I stood back from the door and no one knew I was there, but a sound came from Otto that raised the hair on my arm. I stood well back. Arcadia said something and laughed.

When I looked again, I saw Otto heading towards his brother with a knife in his hand. Perhaps Arcadia cannot be blamed for reaching for his gun. He always kept a gun in the drawer of his writing desk, where other men keep pens and paper and letters. He brought up his gun and when the first shot fired, Otto kept on going as though a bullet was a peanut. But I saw Arcadia lift the gun again, and this time he was firmer in his aim.

There was a second shot, but it did not come from Arcadia's gun. It came from my rifle. Perhaps you were right to hate that rifle. A gun goes off and who knows how well or ill its purpose is served. I saw Arcadia slump. I left his own gun in his lap but arranged it to tell a different story; be this good or bad, it's what I did.

And that is the story I have refrained so long from telling you. You see now why I remained silent. I went home and looked after you. I could not give you up. I didn't go back to Pitch because I had you to love and look after.

And that is the whole truth, Ivorie.

Otto Cirque did not recover. Soon after, he left and I did not see him again for *many many years. Poor Otto, dear Otto. But you recovered. You grew into a little girl and now you are a woman.*

Today I sat here and remembered your small feet. I remembered your long arms and your narrow fingers. On a piece of old card, I found your writing. You wrote very nicely. You wrote the ingredients RUTIN *and* SMARTWEED *and* POMEGRAN- ATE SEEDS *and the amounts remaining of each. You crossed your legs and with a serious face you wrote these things.*

Goodbye, Ivorie Hammer. I hope these words do not fall like blows. There is a thing I know of in you, very strong, that will endure.

Morag Pappy

Chapter 59

The Paratha Family Circus

The Starlight sisters, at their mirrors, pin flowers onto their hats and pinch their cheeks for colour.

'I had hoped for rain almost, Ann,' says Mary. 'Is that very unkind of me?'

'No, my dear, it is not,' says Ann. 'The event does not seem as though it ought to be *sunny*, in the circumstances. It is not a *sunny* event.'

'Shall we stay afterwards, for the acrobatic show, or for the ceremony only?'

'I think it would be imprudent of us to stay. We would not enjoy ourselves.' A pin goes through Ann's flower and briefly scrapes her scalp. She winces.

'Would our brother not be offended?'

Ann turns to her sister. 'Mary Starlight! What place has our brother to be offended by *us*?'

'You are right of course, Ann. Absolutely right. Though I do confess to some curiosity . . .'

'Well, one must keep one's curiosity theoretical, Mary.'

'Yes, yes, Ann. After all, people we do not wish to *rub shoulders with* . . .'

'Hold yourself always at bay, Mary.'

'. . . whose pedigree is not quite . . .'

'Precisely! Shush now, Mary, I think I hear the cab arrive.'

There is an abundance of traffic – cabs and horses and people – converging on the campsite where the marriage of Robert Starlight and

Nelly Pottle is to take place. An arbour has been constructed, trailing flowers and vines, beneath which the happy couple will travel on their way to the altar. Mr Sweetley, officiating, is honoured by this happy turn of events. 'I am honoured!' he tells Mrs Starlight as she ties and re-ties his collar. 'I thought I had lost them entirely. I did, Mrs Starlight, I did. But one knows now that they mark me as they always have.' It brings a tear to his eye. Mrs Starlight dabs the tear away. He holds her hand; when no one is looking, he kisses her cheek.

The 'Wedding March' begins and Bald Sherry, publican, takes Nelly Pottle's arm. 'You look a million pounds!' he whispers in her ear. 'Mrs Sherry would have wept to see you!' 'Do I?' she says, 'Not a million, surely, Mr Sherry.' But of course, she does look a million pounds, coming down the aisle in one of Ivorie Hammer's creations, her small feet measuring small happy increments towards her beloved.

'She is like a fairy,' says Robert Starlight to Ernest Hammer. 'I can hardly breathe, Mr Hammer. She is beautiful!' Nelly Pottle's beauty has never been remarked upon before, but now the place is abuzz with the revelation. She *is* beautiful; even the meanest amongst them must grudgingly submit to the power of her green eyes and the perfection of her figure as set off by Mrs Hammer's wedding dress. Ivorie Hammer wholly agrees, and takes much succour from the part she has played in creating this glorious vision, though she remains anxious lest Mr Sherry tread on the organza veil. But the march goes off without a hitch; Nelly is delivered whole and gleaming to her suitor and Robert Starlight gathers her in to him.

The ceremony is performed as briskly as it is in the presiding officer's power to perform it; rings are exchanged, bride and groom kiss. 'Man and wife!' says Borrel Sweetley, and rice is strewn in great handfuls so it catches in everyone's hair. It comes down and down and gets lodged in ribbons, and disappears into décolletages, and collects in the laps of dowagers. There is laughing and cheering and much shaking off of errant rice. Music begins and the marriage party are led in fits and starts to their tables where food awaits, and brandy.

It is much later in the evening, when food and drink has been consumed and speeches made, both well and ill, that the entertainment commences. The stage has been cleared and newly constructed seating unveiled; wires strung up overhead and the lamps lit.

The sun goes down; the moon comes up. In the undulating waves of heat from the gasaliers, the sawdust-strewn stage resembles yellow molten glass. Mary Starlight sits forwards with her chin in her hands, and turns excitedly to her mother. The Paratha family train the lamps this way and that, and Rosa Minim, on the sidelines, steadies her performers.

The lamps dim. A horn or two set up, to be joined by a kettle drum and a homemade viola. The orchestra increases in volume and the audience recedes into darkness. Lights cast up above them, and, from nowhere, a luminous white body swings, holding fast to an invisible trapeze before dropping headlong towards the earth.

Acknowledgments

The author would like to thank the following: my readers, Johanna Preston, Angela Howard, and Sarah Ross for their helpful feedback and suggestions; the Australia Council and Arts Victoria for grants that enabled the writing of this novel; Fran Bryson, for early encouragement; Ben Sibley, for early enthusiasm; Helen Elliot, Antoni Jach and Jackie Yowell for many years' championing; Caesar Florence-Howard for character and plot suggestions; John Hunter, for his enthusiasm and for making the thing happen; Madonna Duffy for the easy end-ride; Kylie Mason for her excellent editing; Mum and Dad for the typewriter in 1978; Chris Womersley for the gris-gris; and finally, Harry Howard, without whom the Senior Sergeant would never have come to exist.